SCHOEMANSDAL

ANDRIES-OHRIGSTAD

LYDENBURG

SWAZIS

POTCHEFSTROOM

ZULUS

WINBURG

WEENEN

PIETERMARITZBURG

PORT NATAL

TEMBUS

SAHARA
SUDAN
AFRICA

```
823        Cloete
C643t         The turning wheels
```

THE
TURNING WHEELS

BY STUART CLOETE

HOUGHTON MIFFLIN COMPANY · BOSTON

The Riverside Press Cambridge

37-28-233

∩/DD

Eva Apilner

The Riverside Press

CAMBRIDGE · MASSACHUSETTS

PRINTED IN THE U.S.A.

DEDICATED
TO
E. ARNOT ROBERTSON

CHAPTER I

1

HENDRIK VAN DER BERG and Johannes van
Reenen rode slowly over the veld, the long sour
grass brushed their stirrup irons, bent beneath
their horses' bellies and sprang back as they passed. Beyond
the dry rustling of the grass and the occasional creak of their
saddlery there was no sound; they neither spoke nor looked
at each other, but rode with their reins lying loose on the
withers of their horses, turning their heads slowly from side
to side as they searched the veld for movement.

The horses stepped lightly, with cocked ears, their sleek
hides quivering with suppressed excitement.

The Boers rode at a walk to save their horses. Soon, at
any moment, they might come across a herd of zebra; when
they found them they would ride them down, galloping after
them and stabbing them with their long hunting knives.
Ammunition was too scarce to use on zebra, and they needed
fat to grease their riems[1] and to make soap.

2

Away to their left, moving parallel with them, were the
wagons. Like ships of the line, they swept over the plain.
Their disselbooms pointing to the north where there was
room to breathe and no law, save that of the white man's
gun and the Kaffir's assegai. North to the promised land.

Men rode beside the great turning wheels and women,
lying on beds of latticed hide in the tented wagons, shouted

[1] A glossary of less familiar South African words is given at the end of this book.

to them; the fathers of their sons; the sons of their fathers; their lovers, brothers, friends. Hard, sunburnt men, bearded like prophets, mounted on small entire horses that threw their heads and opened their wide red nostrils to the hot dusty wind.

The distant lowing of cattle, the bleating of sheep and goats was an unceasing murmur, broken only by the staccato cries of the drivers to their oxen and the sharp claps of their long whips; like a cloud of sound, above a cloud of dust. These noises hung suspended in the veld and fell, becoming less than a memory in a land which had seen greater things than a crawling of men, with their women, their flocks and herds, winding like a snake through the long grass, furrowing it with a spoor, which looking back, they called a road.

When a foal, or a calf, or a child was born they gave praise for the increase; and always they prayed for fillies and heifers; and one bull or stallion or man was enough for a great number of his female kind.

It was one of the many convoys that was going north into the great unknown. One of the many that coming to ranges of mountains that were impassable, dismantled their wagons, and passed them; man handling them over cliffs and gorges and rebuilt them on the other side; that finding rivers too deep to be forded, swam their beasts and floated their wagons across. One of the many that founded the Free State and went beyond it, across the 'yellow river' into the Transvaal; and beyond that again, to its northernmost limits; to the low veld, to the banks of the Crocodile and the Limpopo.

It was the seepage of a small, great-hearted people into a continent. Secure in the knowledge that they were the chosen race, certain of their capacity to endure, and forced on by the Boer necessity for space and freedom, they followed rivers to their sources, crossed the great watersheds and followed new rivers; hunting, fighting, and reading the Bible as they wandered.

It was the great trek. The logical outcome of the freeing of the slaves by the English in the middle of a harvest, so that farmers starved while their crops stood ungarnered, rotting. Of compensation paid at a flat rate, as if among slaves, like other live stock, one was not worth more than another; compensation made payable in England, at such a distance that the collection of it often cost more than the sum collected. Of the hangings at Slagtersnek and of the ravagings of the Kaffirs with which they were no longer allowed to deal after their own fashion.

It was the migration of a people, who feeling they could stand no more, were prepared to face almost inconceivable risks for an ideal which they would have been unable to describe.

Among them were some who were related to Stephanus Bothma and the others who had hung. There was also the son, Frederick Bezuidenhout, who had been shot by the British soldiers, and a cousin of Jacob de Winter who had been murdered by the Kaffirs at van Aaards Post. Many that had been children then were now men, and all had been reared to hatred. Mustering their herds, convoy after convoy had left Cape Colony, all going one way, since there was only one way to go.

They were the voortrekkers. The men, the women, and the children, who went in front.

The wagons belonged to Hendrik van der Berg and to others who were tied to him by blood, or friendship, or political opinion.

3

In the third wagon a girl sat sewing. She was very fair with large dark eyes. Her bare legs dangled over the back of the wagon above the brake handle. It was curious how often the men thought the third wagon needed braking; no incline was too slight for them to put it on. So even downhill van Reenen's span of oxen had to pull because of Sannie van Reenen's beauty and because she had chosen to sit with her feet above the brake. It was her favourite seat.

Jakalaas, the old slave, who was continually cutting new brake blocks, cursed or smiled at his thoughts, according to his mood. His young mistress was ripe and soon she would be plucked; then she would no longer sit as she sat now, a perch too risky for a pregnant woman.

'Ai, let the young missus play like a mare in season, kicking her legs,' such things did not last long and he would as soon cut brake blocks out of the soft seringa wood or marula as do anything else. Also in looking for a good tree he sometimes found honey. It was good to find honey. To follow a honey bird and eat it from the comb, to eat it, grubs and all, with the bird fluttering anxiously about him while it waited for its share.

4

Herman van der Berg, the son of Hendrik, was eighteen, already a man, and very conscious of Sannie van Reenen, with her dark eyes like a buck's and long slim legs. Whenever he passed her father's wagon, and it was often, he looked at them, dangling, or crossed, with one foot grasping the boards, the brown toes bent round the end of the heavy planks.

His place was in front, as a scout, to keep watch for hostile Kaffirs and to find the best way for the lumbering wagons that came behind him.

The bends in the old trek pad, that so many followed later, were due to Herman van der Berg. Due to his signalling the voorloopers to the right or left, away from a tree stump or an ant bear hole; and some were due to his not signalling, to the drift of tired oxen and sleepy drivers, when he fell back to talk to Sannie to tell her of the great things he would do in the future and of the things he had already done.

To everything Sannie listened, sewing, dreaming, thinking. Certainly Herman was a fine young man, a good rider, and a quick shot; but still she was not sure. Did the filly mate with the untried colt? or with the stallion, scarred by a hundred battles? So, Sannie, talking to the boy, began to think of the father.

Herman's mother was dead. She had died bearing his father a stillborn child. She had died because Hendrik van der Berg was a man, and potent. Sannie thought of the child as she had seen it. I should like to have a son like that, she thought. I would like... Ach ja, there are many things that I would like, and she shied away from her thoughts as a horse might shy at a blowing cloth. The death of Herman's mother had left Hendrik a widower, a fact of which Sannie was becoming increasingly conscious as day followed day and night followed night. Aware of herself as a filly or a heifer is aware she stretched her shoulders upwards, forcing out her breasts, to ease her back. Neither the manner of Maria van der Berg's death, nor the death itself, affected Sannie; the woman was old, worn out. Only the cause of her death, the virility of the man to whom she had owed her pregnancy, touched the girl.

Death — in God's name, death was a common enough occurrence. Death by snake-bite, by bullet or assegai, by slipping off the disselboom of a wagon and being run over, by being thrown from a horse, by blood poisoning from a cut in the hand, by a lion or a leopard. Death by violence or in childbed; she was sixteen and had seen death in all these ways. Blood, too, her own, since God had made women that way, and the blood of wounded men, left her unperturbed.

All she knew was an uneasiness. A fretful waiting for the touch that should move her. Often of late she had felt too big for her silky skin and wished she could change it, slipping out of it like a snake. Quietly, swaying as the wagon rolled, she sewed on, her thoughts poised on the point of her needle as she drew the thread of her unexpressed desires through the fabric on her knees. She was letting out her best frock again, for the third time, to ease it round her breasts, and as she sewed she talked. Lightly as women talk, feeling rather than thinking of more serious things.

'And why should I marry you, Herman? Are you the only man in the world?' she asked.

'No, I am not the only man in the world, but I am the best man for you. Who else is there? Gert Kleinhouse who squints?' he suggested contemptuously. 'Or Cornelius Brandt, or Joachim Joubert? Do you fancy any of them? Ach, it is not possible, they are small men, small of stature, of mind and heart, mie Sannie.

'Listen,' he said. 'I will match myself against any of them in shooting at a mark, in hunting, in riding; and besides, compared to me, they are poor men.' He sat erect in his saddle looking at her, waiting for her answer. His legs were hanging down on each side of his horse, he had taken his feet out of the stirrups, and they hung low, his toes almost touching the forelegs of his horse.

From under her long lashes Sannie glanced up at him, at his legs where they dangled below his horse's barrel, at his swelling powerful thighs, at the calf muscles that bulged his moleskin trousers. He was big and he would grow more, but his father was a bigger man. A more certain man. He was proven. The very lines that seared Hendrik's face were a hall-mark of his qualities, not perhaps entirely admirable, but nevertheless qualities which made for survival under conditions where survival was no mean achievement. At home, at the Cape, she would no doubt have chosen the son. The call of youth to youth was strong, but here in the wilds it was different, and the thought of Hendrik van der Berg with his grizzled beard, his savage eyes that glittered under their bushy brows, his strong teeth and great gnarled hands that could throw a bullock, bending its neck sideways till it fell, moved her as much as the direct appeal of the young man and more subtly, for her woman's urge was towards safety and it dragged against desire. She knew that Hendrik did not pass her unnoticed, that she was a factor in his life. She knew that he had taken stock of her; her breasts, her legs, and above all, of her hips. She wriggled uncomfortably on the kaross as she thought of the looks he had given her. Looks that drove into her, through the thin cotton frocks she wore, into the very centre of her being.

But if Hendrik wanted her why did he do nothing? Perhaps he was waiting, perhaps he thought her too young. It would be good to play the son against the father and let the best man win. Whichever got her would be the best, so why trouble? Without doubt she would soon belong to one of them.

'Ja, Herman,' she said, 'perhaps you are right. After all, as you say, who else is there for me to marry?'

'Then you will marry me, Sannie?'

'I did not say so, but neither did I say that I would not marry you.'

She looked up at him again.

'It is time that I was married,' she said, 'and from what you say it seems that there is no one else. I had not thought of this before, that among all these men there is only you who is rich, unmarried, and handsome.' She stared past him at the naked picannin who led Mevrou de Jong's oxen.

'Even among the older men is there no one, Herman?' she asked. 'Have you thought of them too? Because if that is so, then I have no choice. And Herman,' she added, 'would you call a man of forty-six very old?'

'Forty-six,' he echoed.

Forty-six was his father's age. Magtig, the girl could not be thinking of that. Sannie his stepmother. Sannie to bear his half brothers and sisters. He wheeled his horse savagely, dragging him up into a rear, as he swung him round.

The girl saw the chestnut's pale fawn belly darkening to black between his thighs; the white unshod hoofs menaced her; his lips were drawn back from his teeth as the heavy bit forced his jaws open and his wild unseeing eyes stared into her own.

Sannie laughed. The horse was angry, the boy was angry, and it was good.

In a minute now the seam would be finished and she would put on the frock. By the time her father and Hendrik van der Berg were back she would have changed into the wine-red taffeta that was so becomingly sprigged with small blue flowers.

5

A herd of wildebeeste and zebra were grazing in a leegte. There were thousands of them and they covered the wide open space like a great cloth which looked, as they moved slowly forward, as if it was being dragged along, folding and wrinkling as the beasts drifted over the slight undulations of the veld, forging upwards as the ground rose, sagging away loosely as they descended into the hollows.

The pearly hides of the zebra, broken by symmetrical black stripes, made them almost invisible against the background of sunburnt yellow grass. The skins of the wildebeeste were a shining metallic blue in the strong morning light. A few ostriches, with long naked legs, stalked in small family parties among them. The cocks a vivid black and white; the hens a dirty grey.

Wildbeeste calves knelt by their dams to drink, wagging their tails up and down in their excited pleasure as they butted, with blunt, hornless heads, at their mother's udders. Zebra foals played, galloping round and round, bucking and kicking. Only the older beasts looked anxious, raising their heads from the short grass every few paces to look round.

In the daytime they were safe. Death, the swift charging death of lions, came at night. On bright moonlit nights; on dark nights, it came with a terrifying roar. And their fear of the night lasted through the days that followed them. Their existence as individual beasts depended on this never-ending vigilance; and as a herd, on the fact that they could breed faster than the lions, who only killed for food, could eat them.

6

The two Boers were riding in single file along a narrow game path when Hendrik saw the herd and pulled up. The horses, backing each other like pointers, stood motionless; only their long tails moved as they whisked at the buffalo flies that bit their bellies.

Without a word the men swung apart, one going to the right and one to the left; they rode slowly towards the flanks of the herd, picking their way among the trees.

They went up-wind and the beasts grazed on.

Suddenly a wildebeeste bull gave a coughing snort. Heads went up and wide, terrified eyes stared round. Dilated nostrils searched the breeze, sniffing. Snort followed snort. Horns clashed together as the milling herd swung this way and that. Cows nuzzled at the calves, which had run to their sides, trying to push them nearer. Zebras closed in on each other and stood with twitching ears, alert, ready to run, but as yet uncertain of where the danger lay.

Hendrik's eyes were on the herd that he could see drifting through the trees, but his mind was with the third wagon of the convoy and the girl who was sitting at the back of it, swaying like a flower on its stem, as the great wheels crashed over ant heaps, cutting through them, or fell with jarred axels into a sudden hollow.

She was young certainly, but not too young. He thought of David; and of Abishag who had lain on his bosom and cherished him. The case was not a parallel. David was old. He had taken Abishag because he needed the warmth of her young body upon his own; whereas he needed Sannie be-

cause his blood was hot. He was in his full vigour; and it
was six months since his wife had died. Surely no woman
could want more than he could give her, and young as
Sannie was he was confident of his power to wear down her
youth. In ten years he would still be a strong man, and
she, after ten years of marriage and continuous child-bearing,
would be old, her slender beauty gone, sacrificed in his
service, her widened hips a tribute to his urgency and power.
He thought of his children, they needed a mother. His
eldest girl, Susanna, did what she could, but it was not
enough. Ja, certainly his children needed a mother. But
more than they needed a mother did he need a wife. A
young one, fresh and clean. Sannie, who was as ripe as an
apricot trembling on a bough.

An old wildebeeste bull that had been sleeping in the
shade of a vaal-bos sprang up under his horse's feet.

The horse, snatching at his bit, broke into a gallop, his
nose almost touching the buck's flowing tail. The herd
swung round, hesitated, and with a swirl of manes and hoofs
clattered over the parched ground in a cloud of dust.

Riding hard, with slack reins, the two men closed in on
them. In the open leegte, after their first burst of speed,
the horses were more than equal to the herd of game. The
ostriches alone, with fluffed plumes, were able to pull away.

Hendrik drew his knife. All he had to do now was to
kill, his horse would do the rest. He felt the great muscles
contracting and expanding beneath him and the shock of his
hoofs as they struck at the ground. He could see nothing
except his horse's ears in the ever-thickening cloud of dust.
He half-closed his eyes as the bite of sand and gravel stung
his cheeks. The excitement of the hunt made words, magnificent as organ music, sing in his ears above the pounding
gallop of the maddened herd. It was like the sound of an
angry sea, a rolling vibration that became a roar as he got
among them. The horse checked as he hit a zebra's rump
with his chest, rolling him over with the unexpected impact.

Gathering himself together the stallion fought his way into the herd biting and savaging the stampeding beasts. Like a spear the horse drove through the seething mass of tossing manes, curved horns, and long, white-tipped ears.

Hendrik was among them now. On his left he could see van Reenen. They shouted to each other and he began to kill. Stab after stab he gave leaning out of his saddle. One mistake, if the black horse should fall or a girth break. He laughed. If that should happen he would be finished, trodden flat by the passing of a thousand hoofs. Still laughing and killing he rode in the herd. When he could he chose the fat colts, but anything that came near him he killed, driving his long knife into the striped hides.

His hands, legs, and saddle were smeared with blood. Blood dripped from his horse's shoulders, or mixed with dust clogged into a dull, red, glutinous mud on the long hair of his mane.

All the time as he killed he thought of Sannie, the blonde Sannie van Reenen, who was sitting at the back of her father's wagon swinging her long, fine legs.

'Ach, she is young and wild,' he thought as he leant over a galloping wildebeeste to stab at the rounded flanks of a young zebra. But the wild ones were always the best. It took a man to break them. Tame women, tame horses, tame oxen, he did not like; they were no good; and he had killed enough. Reining his horse he watched the herd gallop into the bush. For a moment the dust hung in the air obscuring the trees. For a moment there was the sound of their frenzied hoof-beats and the crash of branches as they disappeared.

Looking back the plain was spotted with beasts that lay dead or struggled to rise, getting up and falling again. He counted them roughly, in pairs, his eyes taking in two at once. Two, four, six, eight, ten. They had done well, between them they had killed thirty-six; it was more than enough and already vultures on great wings were falling from the skies.

'Ja, Johannes, that was good,' he said as he met van
Reenen, 'we are still men.' Wiping his knife on his horse's
mane he sheathed it. The blowing horses excited by the
gallop and the blood that clung to them neighed shrilly and
tried to rear, their hoofs cutting at each other. Their teeth
were bared and their ears laid back, below the line of their
necks.

Giving a last look at the dead and dying zebras the two
men swung west and cantered slowly towards the wagons.
Soon they would send their Kaffirs, not to skin the dead
beasts or to use their meat, but just to cut the yellow fat,
in granulated lumps, from their entrails, and passing swiftly
from one to another, to leave the bodies, mutilated, for
the scavengers of the veld. The vultures, the jackals, the
hyenas and the ants.

CHAPTER II

I

IN THE fourth wagon Mevrou Anna de Jong sat dozing,
hunched on her great bed. It was very hot and her
vast bulk sagging, sweated acridly. From the rolls of
fat round her neck perspiration poured down her back, stain-
ing the material of her dress; from under her chin it ran in
rivers over her chest, accumulated and seeped through the
narrow channel of her heavy breasts into the creases of her
paunch, over its massive folds, on to the bulging thighs
on which it rested. Her arms, like legs of mutton, incased
in black cotton, were folded. Her head sunk forward, nodded
as the wagon rolled. Her small eyes, black, shining buttons
sunk into her cheeks, opened and closed like those of an
animal that rested, watchfully.

Sometimes she moved a hand to rub at her inflamed eyelids, or held her arms away from her sides in a vain endeavour
to get cool. Apart from this she never moved, sitting on her
bed, from outspan to outspan.

To get Tante Anna out of her wagon a number of things
were necessary. First it must be quite motionless. Then
the steps, they were lashed under its bed, had to be hooked
on and with the aid of two natives and the encouragement
of her husband she would descend, give the surrounding
country a contemptuous glance, and demanding her chair,
would sit waiting impassively till the oxen were inspanned
again.

But despite this, little that went on was unknown to her.
By various means, her own observations, the chatter of her
Kaffirs, her intuition, her wide experience of human action
and reaction, she became aware of most things.

She knew, for instance, that her husband, a small meek man, had one of her coloured maids as his mistress. She did not blame him. She had reached an age and attained a size which would, in her opinion, have made blame ridiculous, besides, there was plenty of biblical precedent to justify the use of concubines; and if Mahomet would not come to the mountain she certainly was not going to pursue so small and inadequate a Mahomet.

It was some years since the predicant at Paal had preached a sermon about false prophets. It had made a great impression on her. Moses, he had said, had caused the Red Sea to open, the waters to divide, while Mahomet had not even been able to make a mountain come towards him. And yet it was well known that mountains, when called upon properly, could skip like young sheep and the little hills dance like lambs.

Ja, that might be so, she thought, but after all, who wanted mountains to dance? And what about the farms in the valleys? She had meant to ask the predicant about those farms and what had happened to them when the mountains moved. Men, even men of God, were so unpractical. She supposed it must be a great thing to be able to make a big berg hop about, but if she had been a man — ach God — if I had been a man, she thought, I'd sooner have had a 'mooi Meisie' like that Salomi dance in front of me with nothing on. But then, if she had been a man, she would not have been a man of God.

She wondered if Jappie knew he was sharing that yellow wench of his with Andries, one of de Lange's driver boys? That would annoy him and she would tell him about it one day when she could be bothered. After the rains came, when it would be cooler, she might do it.

But in the meantime there was this affair of Herman's with her niece. It was amusing to see how blood told. Not that her sister had been very lively and she had often wondered what Johannes van Reenen had seen in her. Still,

when it came to that, you never knew what anyone saw in
anyone else. Take herself and Jappie. How she had loved
that man. How passionate his courtship of her had been.
And then afterwards, nothing. He had used himself up
courting her, but how could she have guessed that it would
be like that. One went on appearances, by what one saw.
There was, however, no doubt about Sannie's mother having been anaemic. Everyone had said so, and in proof of it,
if it required proof, she had been unable to rear her child.
She had had no milk, not even as much as a goat. Tante
Anna looked down at her figure with satisfaction as she
thought of her own lactations. Milk, why she had always
had enough for three. Like a cow I was, she thought
happily. People used to come to see me because they wouldn't
believe the stories that they heard. She had been a fine
woman in those days and a fine woman should milk well.
What else were they for, she would like to know? Ja, she
had had udders like a cow once and that was because she
had plenty of blood. Her thoughts went back to Sannie,
she was a true de Jong, showing nothing of the van Reenen
strain. In her time she had been very like her, just such a
one as Sannie, before the fires of her flesh, she was no
mincer of words, had been smothered by the layers of fat
which made her spend most of her time planning how to
avoid unnecessary movement. Ja, Sannie was right to live
while she could, while she was slim and fast like a young
buck.

Peeping between the folds of the tent that covered the
wagon Tante Anna saw Herman ride up to Sannie on his
fine red horse. A fine young man on a fine red horse. She
preferred blue horses, but this she realized was a personal
idiosyncrasy and of no particular importance. A fine young
man remained a fine young man on a horse of any kind,
or on foot even. There were not so many upstanding young
men that a girl could be fussy about the colour of the
horses they bestrode; still, she did like blue horses best.

There were reasons for it. They might be sentimental, but her family was well known for its warmth of heart.

She sat staring over the heads of her span, over their wide, black-tipped horns at the back of the wagon in front of her. How she wished she could hear them talk.

Herman was bending forward, leaning over his horse's neck. Sannie was looking down at her sewing. How wise she was. So long as a girl looked down men gave her credit for modesty. It was curious, the value men set on this girlish modesty when what they really liked was looseness. Well, when the time came, Sannie would be loose enough for any man.

Tante Anna closed her eyes and the past which was so much more interesting than the present, because one knew how things had turned out, began to move in a series of pictures through her mind. Childhood, girlhood, marriage, her numerous confinements, the children that she had been so proud of — ach, what was the good of brooding, of saying if I had not done this, or if I had done that. The Lord had given, the Lord had taken away. Taken every one of them, except Gert Kleinhouse, the son of her daughter Kattie, and Gert squinted.

It was a pretence to say that the past was interesting. It wasn't. It was dead, with its adulteries and fornications which at the time mattered so much and now meant nothing. It was dead. Dead. And soon she too would be dead what with the bad food and the jolting of the verdamt wagon. What were they trekking for? Where were they going? When, and where, would they stop?

She, Anna de Jong, was tired of it; she had no intention of spending forty years in the wilderness. Nor had she much confidence in manna which she had never tasted. Manna, indeed; what she wanted was to find a nice piece of black ground that Jappie could irrigate and where she could plant the pumpkin seeds she had in a little rawhide bag in the bottom of her wagon box. It was more than a year since she had eaten roast pumpkin. Locusts and wild honey. She had eaten both and liked neither. They might be all right for Kaffirs and prophets, but she was a good Dutch woman, a very big Dutch woman, who needed proper food. She sighed as she thought of the food she wanted and looked over the heads of her oxen again.

What was that? Herman's horse was rearing. How well the boy rode. I wonder how Sannie can hold him off, she thought. She felt her heart beating with pleasure at his horsemanship. 'Mooi mooi.' 'He is beautiful as an angel of God,' she said. To Mevrou de Jong angels were all young men, immense and fiercely proud. What would God, after all he was old, want with a pack of women. She was profoundly contemptuous of her own sex except in their relationship to men.

Had Sannie made him angry. She smiled grossly. It was good to make men angry sometimes. She had often done it; their faces flushed and the muscles stood out on their necks. Ach Ja, and then afterwards they were no longer angry. But the time came when one could not move them. Still between those two periods, between the day when a girl first angered a man in love with her and the day when she could no longer stir men to love or fury, lay the flower of a woman's life, its blossoming.

A gun went off.

In a second old Mevrou de Jong was a different woman. Her years and fat fell from her. The explosion of a gun could only mean one thing. An ambush. Kaffirs. Picking up the blunderbuss loaded with slugs that hung from its sling above her, she jumped through the curtained front of the wagon on to its bed.

'Gang links,' she shouted, 'and span out.'

Already the wagons behind were lumbering up, their beasts trotting as the voorloopers dragged at the leaders' heads, while the drivers, who had leapt out, shouted at the straining oxen as they thrashed them. All were making for the place in the laager, the hollow square they formed each night, and by day when danger threatened. A square of wagons with their disselbooms interlaced into which the best of the livestock was run.

Men and boys who had been riding idly in ones and twos round the convoy closed in at a gallop, their guns ready. Herds of cattle and horses bellowing and neighing were urged forward by mounted herdsmen and everywhere, on each wagon, stood women and girls with guns in their hands, while children still too weak to hold firearms, loaded spare guns, pouring in powder, ramming in wads and bullets as the Kaffirs advanced towards them.

2

Hendrik van der Berg and Johannes van Reenen were riding slowly westwards when they heard the first shot. They were not uneasy. Someone was shooting a buck, or perhaps a lion or leopard had attacked a beast which had drifted away from the main herds. Such things were of everyday occurrence. Then came a fusillade of shots, some single ones, another volley. 'Magtig, the Kaffirs,' Hendrik shouted as he forced his tired horse into a gallop. Van Reenen followed him. They rode with free reins, letting the horses pick their own way through the bush. Now bending down to avoid an overhanging branch, now sitting forward as they felt their horses about to jump a low shrub and back as they leapt it. Hendrik's black put his foot on a loose stone, stumbled and recovered, his rider never moved in the saddle.

Both men were thinking of Sannie, the daughter of one of them and the woman that the other had determined to make his wife. Hendrik had been about to discuss the matter with van Reenen. He had been thinking of how to begin, wondering if this desire of his to marry a girl thirty years younger than himself might not sound foolish. Johannes would not understand his urgency. He had been a widower for many years, remaining faithful to the memory of the woman who had been Sannie's mother. All men were differently made and Hendrik had never really loved his wife. He had never felt for Maria as he did for this girl.

By God, if she were hurt he would spend the rest of his life hunting Kaffirs. His hand went to the gun on his back, without slackening speed he unslung it and rode on.

The sound of firing had increased; he could hear the shouts of the Kaffirs. Their wild cries of Bullala... Bullala. Kill ... kill.

Their first rush must have failed, he thought, that terrifying charge of oiled black bodies, flashing spears and tossing plumes. The Kaffirs only charged like that once, flinging themselves against their objective, trying to sweep over it.

In a minute they would be there; once over the next rise they would see the wagons below them. Their course of action would depend on the situation; without discussion they would adjust themselves to circumstance; and secure in their strength, and certain of their capacity, they galloped on.

They should not have gone out together. As a rule one of them stayed behind, but the country had seemed safe and it was so long since they had hunted in each other's company.

As they broke through a clearing Hendrik saw a chestnut horse coming towards them. It was young Herman's. The shaft of an assegai stuck out of its shoulder and the saddle had slipped. With a curse Hendrik almost lifted his horse forward.

They had killed his son. The Kaffirs had killed his son.

3

When Sannie saw Herman's horse begin to buck, she laughed and clapped her hands. He had said he would ride against any man for her and his chance had come. Let him ride. If he could manage that mad horse he would do. He would do very well indeed. Herman, swinging away from Sannie had forgotten that the chestnut was not fully broken, the savage pull on the bit and the feel of his heels infuriated it. As its hoofs touched the ground when it came down from its rearing turn the horse propped and began to buck. Lowering its head between its knees, its long mane flying, it went up in a taut, curved arc. Bent like a bow, with its cream-coloured tail tucked into its quarters, it bounded off in a series of tremendous leaps. Again and again it went up, coming down stiff legged, jarring Herman's spine. He had been caught unawares. With his legs clinched round the bucking horse he fought, dragging at the rein to get up the stallion's head. If he did this the horse was beaten for he could buck no more.

Entranced, Sannie watched, moistening her lips with her tongue as she leant out of the wagon. It was a fine sight. It was her doing. The chestnut was twisting in the air now, trying to burst his girths, trying by every means to dislodge the weight from his back. The gun slipped out of Herman's hand and went off. Furious with himself for behaving like a fool, a man ought to be able to manage a horse and a gun, in front of Sannie, furious with her for what she had said and the way she had said it, Herman flung himself off the horse into the long wiry grass.

He heard Sannie shout 'Pas Op,' as a Kaffir carrying a shield and assegais jumped up beside him. The horse reared, pulling the reins out of his hands. Herman, drawing his knife, flung himself at the native. All round him Kaffirs sprang up shouting.

He heard shots and the hissing war-cries of the Kaffirs. A moment later the straggling line of wagons would have been ambushed, for the leading oxen of the first span were just going down into a spruit. That was where they must have hoped to catch them.

Herman's hands slipped off the greased naked body. Feeling that he could not hold him the boy threw himself down and seized his legs. They fell together in a sprawling mass, but the Kaffir, a grown man, evaded him and kneeling on his breast raised his short stabbing spear. Herman saw the wide leaf-like blade glittering above him. All round him guns were going off and people shouted. He wondered if his father and Johannes van Reenen would hear the noise or if they were too far off.

4

Sannie was almost certain she could do it. Almost but not quite. The rest of the fight raging round her meant nothing, her attention was concentrated on the two men thrashing about in the grass in front of her. She saw a warrior, the wildcat tails round his waist swinging as he ran, throw a spear at Herman's horse and hit it. She saw the horse falter and gallop on. Would those two never separate. She could not shoot till the Kaffir was clear of Herman. Her father said the gun threw high and a little to the left. How little she wondered? She did not know the gun. It was very heavy, the one he used for elephant and buffalo. His other gun, the one he had with him, she knew well. Where was her father? Where was Hendrik van der Berg? Perhaps they had been caught alone and were now lying on the veld stuck full of spears. High and to the left. She must aim at the ground to the right of the Kaffir to get him in the body. She saw him raise his spear to strike. Praying that the flint was good, that the priming was in order, Sannie raised the hammer, rested the heavy gun and fired. Why did Herman take so long to get up? Had she killed him? Was he wounded? Reloading, she waited. When he got up she would cover him. 'Shall I go, Missis?' Jakalaas asked. 'Shall I go and bring the young Baas in?' He had picked up his assegai and was about to

jump off the wagon when Herman sprang up and ran towards them. He was alive, he was her man, Sannie thought,
as she watched him.

5

Herman saw Sannie standing on her wagon with a smoking
gun in her hand. So it was Sannie who had saved his life.
She must have rested the heavy gun against the curved
wooded struts of the tent and she had not been afraid to
fire. The risk of killing him had not stopped her. He
thought of the Kaffir, who a minute ago had been kneeling
over him, his thick lips parted in a snarl, his eyes half-
closed. Suddenly he had jerked forward as if he had received a blow, his mouth had slackened into a foolish grin,
his muscles had relaxed and the spear had fallen from his
hand as he began to cough blood that looked very dark as
it ran over his chest. It had come out of his nose in a pink
foam as he fell and his twitching fingers had opened and
closed spasmodically, clutching at the grass. He was dead
and Sannie had done it. An assegai whizzed past him,
they were coming on again, another quivered in the bed of
the wagon as he put his foot on the hub and grasped the
shining iron tyre. Taking the gun Sannie handed him, he
fired. A big native with a black ostrich plume in his head
spun round, grasping at his belly. 'Load for me, Sannie,'
he said, as he put down the gun.

'That was a fine shot, Herman,' she said, smiling, and
handed him another. The smoke of the black powder drifting round the wagons increased in density, as more and
more men joined in the fight. Old men propped themselves
up to shoot, resting their guns. The women and girls were
shooting as consistently and coolly as the men, handling
firearms as they handled their domestic utensils. Herman
saw young Marais, he could not have been more than eight,
blow the head off a warrior who had reached his father's

wagon while his mother was reloading. The mounted men, who after their first charge had drawn off on to some higher ground out of range of the assegais to reload, charged again, sweeping down, firing from the saddle and swerving away to reload once more.

6

Hendrik van der Berg and Johannes van Reenen took in the situation at a glance. Their people had succeeded in holding the Kaffirs off and the mounted men a few hundred yards to their left were preparing to charge again. Unhesitatingly the two men thundered down on to the Kaffirs. Livid with rage at the death of his son, smeared with the blood of the zebras he had killed, his black horse covered with dust and foam, Hendrik galloped to within a few yards of a thick-set native, who, beating a big oxhide shield with his kerrie, was inciting his people to attack once more.

Hearing the hoof-beats of the horses, the Kaffir turned. Guiding his horse with his knees Hendrik swung away from him and fired. The heavy bullet took him in the chest. Van Reenen, at his side, shot another, and a shower of assegais followed them as they swept past.

At that moment, seeing the diversion, the mounted Boers attacked again, this time going nearer and shooting at point-blank range. There was now no question which way the fight was going, with their leaders killed and many of their best warriors either wounded or dead, the Kaffirs hurled a last shower of spears at the wagons and drew off. Herman, who had jumped down as the Boers charged, was struck by an assegai which, passing through his arm, pinned him to the wagon-side.

The mounted men wished to pursue the fleeing natives but Hendrik forbade this as once in the heavy bush the Kaffirs would have the advantage.

'No, my friends,' he said, 'we must make a strong laager now in case they come back and when it is done we will take a commando and burn these bees out of their nest.

'He that diggeth a pit shall fall into it, and it shall be as it says in the book: an eye for an eye, a tooth for a tooth, a hand for a hand, and a foot for a foot; aye, and more than that, for not one of these will we leave alive.' With these words, and thinking of Herman, he cantered down the slope.

Oh, Absalom my son. Oh, my son Absalom. In his mind Hendrik saw the burning huts and heard the cries of the wounded. Men, women and children they would kill and the word of what he had done would go out.

As he reached the wagons he saw Sannie. Her fair hair was down, her face smudged with smoke, and her eyes bright with excitement. Never, to his mind, had she looked more beautiful. A true Boer woman who would be the mother of his sons.

'Where is Herman's body?' he asked.

'His body, Hendrik? Herman is not killed — only wounded.'

'But I saw his horse.'

'He's in the wagon,' the girl said. 'I have seen to him. It is nothing, only an assegai through the flesh of his arm.'

As she spoke Herman came out. 'You are all right, father?' he said.

'Yes, I am all right.'

Sannie had bandaged the boy with strips of linen torn hurriedly from her clothes. Hendrik could see the embroidery stained with drying blood where it was fastened above the elbow.

'I thought you were killed,' Hendrik said, and turned his horse. The fight was over, but there were things to be seen to. He began to give orders.

First, how many killed and wounded?

Only one man killed. Old Jappie de Jong. A spear had severed the arteries of his neck. Two others were wounded and one girl, but none of them severely. Among their servants, the natives and coloured folk they had with them, three were killed and five wounded. The livestock were collected and counted. Six Boers went after a herd of horses that had galloped away. The others went out to finish off the wounded natives that lay, like a black belt, about the wagons. They went in pairs to do this work, one covering the other with his gun while the first killed the wounded man with a knob kerrie. A great deal of ammunition had been used and powder and shot were what they depended on, not only for their food, but for their very lives. Still, Paul Pieters' trek was behind them and Hendrik knew that he had plenty. When he came up they would buy some from him, giving cattle in exchange, and together they would go and punish the Kaffirs, for until they had been defeated it would be unsafe to go on.

In the meantime a proper laager must be made. The wagons were got on the move, wounded oxen replaced and they swung round in a circle, the front wheels of one coming to rest by the rear wheel of the one that had preceded it. By this method the disselbooms and trek gear lay outside the laager, and in moving off the oxen could be inspanned and the column march again, each wagon falling into its relative position without confusion or delay. At night the working oxen were tied to their gear and the trek chains anchored to each other. The animals, as they settled, making an extra barrier against a sudden rush of warriors. The riding horses were kept inside, tied to the wagons, and to make the laager still more secure Hendrik had the wheels lashed together with riems, and thorn-scrub was cut and dragged under the beds of the wagons.

Fortunately the grazing was good here and there was plenty of water for the livestock.

There remained the long grass round the wagons to be cleared by dragging trees round and round which would prevent the Kaffirs from creeping up unobserved, or from setting fire to it, as they had done to Carlus Retief's convoy. Also there were graves to be dug for their own people and the bodies of the dead Kaffirs to be pulled away before they began to stink, and there was the cannon to be seen to. They had brought it with them for such an eventuality. The attack by the natives had come too suddenly for it to be used, but in a fixed laager it would be invaluable, and Von Rhule, the German, must be told to deal with it. He was a soldier and understood such matters.

Hendrik remembered the dead zebras; they could not be seen to now and more would have to be killed. A few cattle had been speared and some sheep, but it might have been a great deal worse. God had saved them from a great calamity.

Hendrik gave his horse to a Kaffir, watched him off-saddle, and told him to saddle up another.

The black, finding some loose sand, pawed up the ground, rolled, shook himself and galloped off, neighing, to the troop of mares that grazed near-by. A chestnut filly with an uneven blaze and a wall eye raised her head as he came.

CHAPTER III

I

GERT BOTHA and Jan Fourie had carried Jappie to his wagon. Young Kleinhouse, his grandson, followed leading the dead man's horse.

When Hendrik got there they were standing beside the body, turning their hats in their hands. They were glad to see him for his coming would give them a chance to get away. They had brought Jappie back. They had said:

'Tante Anna, here is Jappie, we have brought him back. Ja, he is dead.' She had looked at them as they held him sagging between them. Gert held his shoulders, Jan Fourie his legs. His feet, sockless, in veldschoen, had wobbled as they stood waiting, moving uneasily.

'Dankie kerls. Ja, Baie dankie for bringing back my man, Dankie, baie dankie.'

She had stood staring at them, swaying a little, rubbing her big fat hands together as if she was washing something, and then she had told them to put him down.

'Nie, nie, not on the ground. Set him up here on his wagon.'

She held out her arms, and taking his shoulders from Gert, dragged him over the rail. She had put down a pillow under his head, and arranged a kaross of silver jackal skins under his body. Then she sat down beside him and took his head in her lap.

So they had come hundreds of miles for this. It was for this they had left the little farm that nestled so comfortably under the big rock at Paal. Anna de Jong thought of her home. Hers and Jappie's. She thought of the orchard with its Bon Chretien pears, its peaches, cling and free stone, its apricots; of the small vineyard, of the pigs and the poultry, which had been her special province. Jappie had always said she was clever with hens, making them lay more than her neighbours, and it had always been she who had the first chicks out in the spring. She thought of a big clutch she had hatched out under a turkey hen; there had been thirty of them. And of her geese, that she used to sit plucking in the small stable, and of how when she let one go it would run gaggling away with its wings spread out, as a Kaffir handed her another holding it by its neck. In six weeks or two months they were ready to pluck again with new clean down on their breasts. She had made the mattress of their marriage bed, fifty pounds it weighed, out of goose-down from the flock she had taken with her as part of her portion when she had left her father's house. . . .

Looking up, her reverie disturbed by his approach, she saw Hendrik. He was sitting very still, mounted on a sorrel horse, watching her, his bare head on a level with her own. 'I am sorry, Tante Anna,' he said.

'Ja, Hendrik, you are sorry; and why are you sorry?' she asked angrily, 'because you have lost a man of your commando. A man who was a sure shot and a fine hunter. For you, Jappie is another gun that has gone. For me, it is something else. Ja, mynheer, for you it is one thing and for me it is another,' she repeated. 'That man,' she looked down, her small dark eyes wet with tears, her mouth trembling, 'was no hero, Hendrik,' she said. 'Nie, nie, he was just a simple man. Like a child he was. More of a child to me than those children that I bore from him. And I was used to him; many years have we done in the yoke together, walking side by side. Often we have loved each other and often we have been angry, saying bitter things to each other, and now this will never be again; it is all over, and like a severed riem my life is cut.'

Her voice broke and the tears, lost in the furrows of her

cheeks, ran down on each side of her nose. She felt them
salt on her tongue as she moistened her parched lips.

Jappie was gone.

Now she would never be able to tell him about the yellow
girl's unfaithfulness. She would never be able to tell him
anything any more. She saw Gert Kleinhouse tying Jappie's
horse to a spoke of the back wheel. It was painted bright
scarlet. Jappie had painted it before they started but most
of it had worn off. His horse, a dun with a black stripe
down its back, still saddled, stood dejectedly as if wondering
why they did not let him go.

Hendrik pointed to a big tree.

'I thought over there, Tante Anna,' he said.

'Ja, Hendrik, over there is good,' she said, 'by the big
hartecoal, it is a long-lived tree.'

Her Jappie was to lie under a tree by the trek pad in the
wilderness instead of comfortably in the kirk yard with his
fathers. She thought of the little whitewashed church at
Paarl. This was the price he had paid for adventure. Surely
it was better to be alive and at home; better even to be
governed by the English rather than dead under a tree.

'Leave me now, Hendrik,' she said. 'There are things
that I must do.'

Her husband was not the first man she had laid out, nor
would he be the last. It was a woman's work. The first and
the last rites were women's. Women brought men into the
world, other women lay with them and brought in more
children, and finally, when they had died, it was women who
prepared them for the end. She stared down at her husband.
Jappie was hers as he had never been hers before. He must
be dressed in his best suit, the clotted blood must be washed
from his earth-coloured face, his beard must be combed and
other things also must be done. Woman's work, a wife's
work. The last thing she would ever do for him. She heard
a scraping sound as Jappie's dog, a big brindle boerhound,
leapt at the wagon, his claws dragging as he pulled him-

self up. Climbing on to the loaded forepart where the
heaviest stuff was loaded over the front axle, and seeing his
master lying on the kaross the dog came down to him wagging his tail, sniffed at him, licked his face and then lay
down beside him with his head between his paws. A moment
later he got up and pushed his nose into Anna's hand.

'He is gone, Wolf,' she said. 'The old Baas is no more.'

2

By the big hartecoal two Kaffirs were digging. The
ground was very hard and they were sweating. Stripped to
the waist they swung their picks in unison, lifting them,
turning their shining heads in the air with a quick twist of
the fingers and bringing them down together with a guttural
'Hah' as they expelled their breath. When they had enough
soil loose they picked up their shovels and piled it into
a bank at the side of the grave.

The groot Baas had said it must be deep.

Other boys were bringing stones from the river bed,
carrying the big water-worn boulders balanced on their heads,
they sang softly; now and then they slowed up to do a
shuffling dance step, or stopped to stamp their feet. It was
a battle song they sang. A song of victory and a lamentation
for the brave dead. A few yards away from the boys who
were digging, on the farther side of the tree, separated from
them by the thick gnarled trunk, other Kaffirs worked.
They also were digging graves for the coloured folk who had
been killed. These could lie near, but not beside, the white
man.

Their bodies lay near them, each covered by his own
blanket. Flies in swarms buzzed over them, laying their
eggs in neat rows along their eyelids or in their nostrils.
Ants, forever active, crawled over their bodies eating the
blood and clustering in serried masses at the gaping edges
of their wounds.

Overhead vultures swung in great circles, casting their shadows on the hard-baked ground or sat replete, their heads sunk between their wings, waiting till they should be hungry once again. There were many of them but there was much meat, dead zebras and dead Kaffirs, enough to last for many days.

3

Two days after they had buried Jappie, filling his grave with carefully-packed stones so that the hyenas and jackals should not dig him up, and building another pile above him to mark the place, Paul Pieters' trek came up with them. Hendrik and Herman were riding over the bare cleared space in front of the wagons when they saw three men riding towards them. All were well mounted but there was no mistaking Paul Pieters in front of his tripling grey. As he saw them Pieters raised his gun and waving it, broke into a canter. Paul Pieters was an enormous man with a great black beard, standing six foot six in his bare feet, weighing two hundred and one pounds stripped. Still under forty he had already acquired a great reputation as a leader, combining, as he did, an almost reckless courage with a tactical astuteness which made him one of the foremost and certainly the most feared of the Kaffir fighters. The young man with him was his sister's son, Zwart Piete du Plessis. He was as tall as his uncle and would one day be as strong. Behind them rode a coloured man with a flat expressionless face. He was Zwart Piete's servant, a Griqua Bastard called de Kok. Pieters looked round, his hard dark eyes taking in everything. He had heard that Hendrik van der Berg had been attacked and had hurried to catch up with him. Turning to the boy he said, 'Make note of this, Piete, the work here has been well done. It is done as I would have done it.'

'So, Hendrik,' he said, pulling up, 'you are laagered.'

'Yes, I am laagered. I was waiting for you, Paul. I need

ammunition, and I want your help to teach these Kaffirs a lesson.'

'That is good, I will help you with thirty men. Have you got good water here?' he asked suddenly, 'enough for my beasts?'

'The river is near-by,' Hendrik answered, 'and there is plenty of water.'

'Then we will make a great laager, it is time we rested, and we will hunt Kaffirs together for a month. By that time they will know the names of Hendrik van der Berg and Paul Pieters.'

He laughed thunderously. 'Ja, by that time they will certainly know our names,' he said.

'Where are your people, Paul?' Hendrik asked.

'Behind.' He jerked his thumb over his shoulder. 'Like the cow's tail, my people are always behind. Only young Piete and his skellum of a boy can keep up with me.'

'Come, then,' Hendrik said, 'let us drink coffee till they arrive.' He turned his horse and they rode to the wagons.

'Make coffee, Susanna,' he shouted, 'here is Mynheer Paul Pieters come to join us.'

They dismounted as two boys came to take their horses.

'Let him run,' Paul Pieters said, 'he will not go far and will come when I whistle.'

'But he will fight my horse, Paul,' Hendrik said.

'Then in God's name let him fight. Let them get it over quickly. It is the will of God that these things should be, and who are we to stand between God and His will? Besides,' he went on, 'it will be a good fight, your black is a fine horse.' He looked at him admiringly, as free of his saddle and bridle, Hendrik's stallion stood watching the grey.

'They are well matched,' Pieters went on, 'and mine is a fine fighter. But one day, Hendrik, one of his sons will kill him; that also is the will of God unless he kills all his sons before they kill him, which is not possible, for he has very many and will still have them when he is too old to fight, and as he grows weaker so they grow stronger and more numerous.

'Kyk daar,' he said, 'it is yours who has started it, Hendrik.'

With bared teeth the black charged down on to the grey who got up on his hind legs to meet him. Standing almost erect, their forelegs locked round each others, they wrestled, their manes flowing as they bent their thick strong necks, snake-like, fighting for each other's throats. Squealing with rage they broke away and tried to chop, front hoof countering front hoof. Swinging round suddenly the black kicked out, catching the grey full in the ribs with both his heels.

Paul's laugh rang out. 'Your horse fights like a mare,' he said.

'Shall I stop them, baas?' a Kaffir with a whip in his hand asked.

'No, no, Frantz, let them finish. It will soon be done now.'

Recovering from the blow, the grey sank his teeth into the black's shoulder. The black retaliated by seizing his elbow and throwing him. Other loose horses had galloped up and stood watching, the mares whickering excitedly, while foals snapped playfully at each other, or tried to drink. Only one old mare with a distended barrel continued to graze unmoved.

Dust rose in clouds as they fought, less seriously now, neither very keen to go on, they bickered, tossing their heads and pawing the ground. A moment later they separated and ignoring each other drifted towards the water.

'You see, Hendrik,' Paul said, 'it is finished, they have matched each other. They will be quiet together now, unless they fight over a mare in season. If that happens one of them will be killed. And I would sooner that it were yours, Hendrik,' he went on laughing.

'Ja, you would hope that; Paul and I hope that it is yours.'

'Your coffee, mynheer.' Susanna, her head scarcely reaching the great barrel of Paul's chest was handing him a cup, while from the south came the shouts of his convoy arriving.

4

With the coming of Paul's people there was a great deal to be done. The laager had to be opened to allow his wagons to join it. The circle which now consisted of one hundred and two wagons, each occupying twenty feet, locked together was seven hundred yards in circumference.

There were two openings in the circle of wagons. One to the north where they were going and one to the south whence they had come. These openings were one wagon wide and the wagons which would act as gates in the event of attack stood beside them, their axles loaded with grease ready to run, manhandled, into the gaps. On them were the trek chains which, put round their wheels, would fasten them into place.

The combined stock of the two treks made an enormous herd; the working oxen, in spans of sixteen, numbering over a thousand, and with cows, spare oxen, heifers, tollies, calves, and bulls, totalled in horned stock alone, six thousand head. They also had five hundred horses, two hundred donkeys, a thousand goats and twenty thousand sheep.

These, when out grazing, were protected by piquets of mounted men. At night they were driven into the great kraals which had been hurriedly made by dragging trees together into rough circles, their trunks pointing inwards, like the spokes of a wheel, their branches, armed with thorns, forming an impenetrable hedge.

The circle of bare ground round the wagons had to be increased to match the size of the new laager and every tree and bush was cut to a distance of three hundred yards. Livestock was driven up and down and the wiry grass tramped to powder, blew about mixed with sand and dust whenever a breeze sprang up, or curled up into the air in the dust devils which spiralled, whistling, through the bush.

The only trees which remained standing were those within the circle of the laager and the big hartekoal beneath which Jappie and the natives killed in the battle lay under their separate piles of stones. This tree was very near now, the laager having spread outwards towards it. Every day Anna de Jong went there to pray and to thank God that for a while at least she could remain near to her husband's grave. Soon she knew they would trek on and it would be left behind, a big lone tree on which lions might sharpen their claws or buck scratch ticks from their shoulders.

Every day she laid a small offering of flowers on the stones. Yellow mimosa, which was already in flower along the edge of the spruit, or branches of sweet scented wild olive with its almost invisible, greenish flowers, and invariably, as soon as she left the grave they were eaten by the goats.

By the instructions of Hendrik, a wide clearing was cut between the wagons and the spruit so that the animals going to water could be protected from a sudden raid, and a dam was thrown across it to deepen the water.

The laager was a temporary settlement of over five hundred souls, white, black, and coloured; the centre of activities which radiated to a distance of twenty miles or more.

For five or six miles round the herds grazed under the eyes of their herders and the mounted guards. Beyond them were patrols and men in pairs hunting in ever-widening circles to supply the camp with meat. Beyond them again were the picked men whom van der Berg and Paul Pieters had sent out to reconnoitre and to locate the kraal of the Kaffirs. The kraal they meant to destroy.

Protected by this screen, the people in the laager were safe, and at night, though they slept with their guns in their hands, felt reasonably secure. They had armed men on watch and the innumerable dogs which accompanied them would give the alarm if danger threatened. Besides, the Kaffirs rarely, if ever, attacked before the dawn.

Everyone was busy refitting. It was a long time since they had halted for more than a few days at a time. Women mended clothes and made new ones for themselves, their men folk and their children. They made butter, as the cows, freshening with rest and new pasture, gave more milk, and salted it down in earthenware jars. They rendered animal fat, which, mixed with soda and wood ash, they made into soap, or prepared into candles by hanging twisted threads of cotton into cartridge shaped forms and pouring the melted grease round them, leaving it till it hardened.

Everywhere Kaffirs were coming in with sleighs, roughly made out of forked trees, loaded with the game killed by the hunters. These they skinned quickly and, stripping the meat from the bones, cut it into thin slices which after being packed between layers of salt to draw out the blood, were hung up to dry. Large numbers of buffalo, wildebeeste, koodoo, roibok, eland, roan and zwart witpentz were dragged in every day by the tired oxen. Boys played with the heads, skinning them for practice. Dogs growled and fought over the bones and severed feet. Kaffirs cut such skins as they wanted into strips for riems, or breyed them to make clothes. Here and there a man trimmed down a buffalo or eland thong into a long ox whip, or cut the breyed hide of a koodoo into achter slachs or that of a duiker ram into voorslachs.

Other men were melting down pigs of leads and casting bullets, mending saddlery or making new stocks to their guns.

Some had jacked up their wagons and were repairing wheels, fitting new spokes and felloes, or shortening their tyres. Children strayed and cried, dogs fought, cats had kittens in wagons belonging to strangers. Chickens, which had travelled hundreds of miles in crates slung beneath the wagons, and had grown so accustomed to this way of life that they would run screaming after them if they got left behind at an outspan, began to lose their bedraggled look and, with reddening combs, came in to lay. In the kraals there were animals to be doctored, tied to big poles sunk into the ground, they were thrown and dealt with. Maggot-infested wounds, sore and broken horns were smeared with mixture of grease and tar, young bulls were cut, all manner of stock branded and everything got ready for the time when they would trek on.

According to their reckoning they had come eight hundred miles. Many thought this far enough and looked about for land that they might take up. The talk was all of soil, water and grazing. Men looked lovingly at the ploughs lashed to their wagons; their shears were dull with rust. Others handled the seeds they had brought with them — wheat, oats, meilies, Kaffir corn, tobacco, vegetable seeds and the stones of peaches, plums, apricots, the pips of nartjes and sweet and sour lemons. Old men were sad when they looked at them; trees took a long time growing.

5

Herman's wound did not go on well. It was not serious but it refused to heal. The cobwebs Sannie had put on when she first dressed it had stopped the bleeding, and her fomentations of herbs had prevented inflammation, but it remained obstinately open. Tante Anna de Jong who had been called in, said it was because he would persist in using it. To which Herman answered, that while he had two arms he would use them.

Sannie, looking down, nodded her head and said, 'Ja, Tante Anna, you are right, he should not use it, many times I have told him not to.'

'You,' her aunt said scathingly; 'you would never tell any man not to do anything unless it was to encourage him to do more. Ach, sis, do you think everyone does not know what he does with his arms? And who blames him?' She looked round belligerently. 'But, ach God, is not one arm enough? Can you stay on his good side and let the other heal? Surely the man who saved us can make love with one hand.' She waddled away, turned back, and shouted, 'If you will help him.'

Sannie sat down hurriedly and picked up her sewing, as Zwart Piete du Plessis and de Kok, who were just mounting to set off on another patrol, burst out laughing.

Piete swung up and sat swaying in the saddle. 'Ja, Ja,' he cried to Herman. 'Tante Anna is right. Hurry up with your love making and come hunting Kaffirs with us.'

Herman looked at them furiously as they clattered off, their horses' hoofs raising a cloud of dust. They were right. Give him a week to get well and he would be with them. He, too, would ride out with his gun over his knees, his blanket rolled, and a bag of biltong and rusks tied to his saddle. Piete, he did not mind. Piete and he had taken to each other, but to be laughed at by de Kok, a Griqua Bastard. He went towards his father's wagon where his chestnut horse was piquetted. The wound in his shoulder was healing well, far better than his own. Calling a Kaffir, he told him to strap up the horse's leg. Taking a stirrup leather, the Kaffir ran the end through the opening below the buckle, forming a slip knot which he put over his fetlock, forcing the horse's heel against his forearm, he threw the spare end over it and buckled it fast.

The young stallion, now unable to move, stood on three legs trembling, with his ears laid back, showing the whites of his eyes.

Picking up a bucket of brine that hung from a hook on the wagon, Herman began to wash out the wound. It was granulating well, and in a few days the flesh would meet.

'Hold him fast,' he said to the boy at the horse's head, and picking up a feather he moistened it and drove it into the still-open wound.

The horse shivered at the pain, his skin becoming darkly patched with sweat.

'That is good,' Herman said. 'Make loose.'

The Kaffir undid the leather, and the horse stood on four legs once more while Herman looked at him speculatively.

He would have to be broken again. Once his arm was well, he would do it. He would get Zwart Piete to help him, it would take them a day and then they would ride out together. They could say what they liked, but there was no horse that could compare with his chestnut, except perhaps his father's black or Paul's big grey. He was out of a Basuto-Arab mare, by one of the governor's imported English stallions, and though only three years old, he was strong and tough, being veld reared and had that reserve of heart that came only with good blood. Day after day, when he had reached his full strength, he would accomplish his sixty or seventy miles and always there would be more to call on, which in an emergency would take him a hundred and fifty or two hundred at a stretch, even if it killed him.

From the horse his mind switched to Sannie. They were very alike, both being beautiful, hot-tempered and difficult to manage. Both of a high courage which had to be coaxed and was not to be driven. Sannie, the elusive coquette, alluring him and then going back as he came forward. Provoking him and then repudiating the advances she had herself called forth. What did she want? What could he do to satisfy her? Herman was getting angry, unable because of his wound to do anything, he brooded, thinking backwards and forwards, covering the same ground perpetually and unable to reach any conclusion. Unquestionably she knew what was in his mind, for his words had been very open. Sometimes he thought she loved him, for she would allow certain familiarities; at others she drew away from him with cold eyes. Yes, she was playing with him, being at one moment softly tender, yielding and bending supply towards him, and at the next cruel, drawing the sharp claws of her talk across him.

He was tired of it. Let her make up her mind one way or the other. Let her choose quickly, for there were other women, and the coming spring was in his blood.

6

When Herman left her to look at his horse, Sannie stopped sewing and climbed into her wagon. Tante Anna was right — she had been a fool. Either she wanted him or she did not. Ach God, how she wanted him. This became apparent the moment she thought of losing him, of someone else having him. There were some pretty girls with Paul Pieters' convoy, and she had not counted on the coming of a number of new women. There was a tall dark girl, a cousin of Zwart Piete's, and very like him, with her bold manner and swaggering, graceful walk. She had eyes like big, blue-black grapes which she knew how to use and long slim legs. She had seen Herman talking to her yesterday and again today. That was what Tante Anna meant when she had said, 'Do you think you are the only heifer in the kraal, mie Sannie?'

That old woman saw everything; knew everything. And now, with Jappie dead, she spent much of her time at the van Reenen's wagon, Wolf, her great dog that was as big as a calf following her, putting his nose into every pot and upsetting everything.

Dragging out a box from under the bed, Sannie pulled out her sprigged taffeta and a dark-red ribbon for her hair. Tonight they were going to dance. Yes, even Tante Anna would be surprised at what she would do tonight.

Praying that it was not too late, Sannie slipped the taffeta over her head.

Surely it would not take long to get Herman back and put that dark girl into her place. Laughing angrily, she began to comb her hair — long fair hair which looked red in the firelight and white under the light of the moon.

Sannie's sense of property was outraged. Herman was hers. Had she not saved his life? Had she not pulled out the assegai that pinned him to the wagon side at the end of the battle? Loosening it from the wood and pulling the shaft right through his arm with one determined jerk. Was it her fault that it did not heal? Her fault that he would not rest it, or keep it in a sling?

Smiling softly as she thought of him, Sannie went on combing, first one side and then the other, of her hair; holding it down with one hand while her arm rose and fell with long sweeping movements. At last she tossed her head and flung her hair back over her shoulders, where it hung in a shining golden mane down her back, on to the bed on which she sat.

Poor Herman, he was unused to illness, to being crippled, restless and uneasily fretful as a colt knee-haltered for the first time. He wandered unhappily about, and she had not been kind to him. She had great power over him and had used it unmercifully while she toyed with her fancy for his father. But that she should be challenged was another thing, and that it should be a dark girl who did it only increased her resolution to force an issue, for Sannie prided herself on her golden hair and the milk-white complexion which she guarded so carefully from the sun with a mask of breyed goat skin. As she thought of him, she heard someone scratching the canvas of the wagon tent.

'Sannie, Sannie, are you there? It is I, Herman.'

'Yes, Herman,' she said. 'I am here.' She paused. 'You can come in.'

7

Hendrik van der Berg, Paul Pieters and Johannes van Reenen sat at a table, made by pegging some planks onto four posts sunk into the ground, examining the rough map they had made of the district.

Over their heads, from the side of the wagon, a piece of sail-cloth was spread, its corners tied by riems to two trees which grew conveniently near, making a lean-to that sheltered them from the direct rays of the sun.

The map was in no sense accurate, but was as Paul

Pieters said 'gut genough.' It would do. They had compiled it from the information brought back by their scouts and hunters.

One would return and say, 'Ja, Hendrik, after two miles the river curls north 'n bietjie.'

'How much?'

'Oh, not very much for two hours' ride, maybe; going slow, that is, natuurlik, then it goes east again for three days.'

Another would say, pointing to a blue line of hills on the horizon. 'You see those mountains over there, Paul. Well, it is farther than you'd think a full day's trek, for they are big mountains — very big. But we have discovered a poort through them, and on the other side lies a big plain where the veld is good and sweet.'

The story of one, was corroborated or not corroborated, by the tales of others, and the result of these reports was the map which lay in front of them. It was good enough to go on, using it not so much as a map, but as a rough guide. Springs and pans that still held water were marked on it, hills, mountains, solitary kopjes, spruits, rivers and the drifts across them, dry water courses and game paths.

The men looking at the map, wondered where the Kaffirs' kraal was. They felt certain that somewhere within a striking distance, that is within a hundred miles, there was a native town. Young du Plessis and de Kok had gone to try and find it, according to them it lay through the poort, in the plain to the north.

'Ons can niks maak they get back,' Paul said. 'Then, if they have found it we will strike.'

'Now for the men,' he went on. 'You say fifty, Hendrik?' He ran his hand through his beard. 'Yes, I think fifty will be enough. If we surprise them it will be more than enough. If we don't, a hundred would be too little. Twenty-eight of mine and thirty-two of yours, with ten spare horses and half a dozen coloured boys. Come,' he said, 'let us make the

list. Myself and you two, Zwart Piete and de Kok, he counts
as white when it comes to fighting. Magtig, what a shot
that Griqua is. Jan de Beer, le Roux, Retief, van Diglen,
van Tromp, van de Merwe, Coetze, de Villiers, van der
Bijl, Carl Schoeman, Piete Marais, van Rensberg, de Wett,
Kruger, Labuschagne, Hoffman, Hertzog, van Zeil, du Buis,
Coenraad Potgieter, Grief Ouisthuizen, Steggman, Bezuidenhout, van Boschotten, Reitz, Bothma, Botha, Smit,
Krugel Stuurman, Davel Rousseau. . . .'

So it went on, name after name being called out, some
without further comment, others with stories of their hunting or fighting exploits attached to them. Anecdotes were
told, nicknames explained, physical peculiarities described.
Men killed in earlier skirmishes or who had died were
lamented, their qualities being exaggerated and their de-
fects charitably minimised.

Sometimes they stopped talking to stuff their pipes with
the strong tobacco they carried loose in their pockets, or to
call for more coffee, but always, inexorably, the plan went
forward; the quills scratching name after name on the paper,
or making notes of the things still to be seen to. Precisely
and with infinite pains every detail was discussed.

Old Jappie de Jong was going to be well and carefully
revenged.

8

Zwart Piete and de Kok rode north at an easy canter,
sitting loosely in their saddles, riding as the Boers always
did, with long leathers and their feet well forward in the
stirrups.

As they crossed the spruit the loose round stones of the
river bed slid away from under their horses' hoofs with a
dry rattle. Passing the big group kameel doorms that were
a landmark, they turned slightly west towards the poort in
the mountains.

Tonight they would camp in a cave they had found two days ago. It was a full fifty miles away, but they would make it by sundown, in eight hours' time.

Every hour they halted and off-saddled, and allowed the horses to roll. When they came to a spring or a pan they watered them. Twice they changed horses, de Kok being much the lighter of the two, it rested Zwart Piete's bay.

After the first ten miles they rode a hundred yards apart, de Kok in front, with their guns across their knees and slowed their horses to a triple, that running camel's gait, which eased them. Tied on to the dees of their saddles was a feed of mealies for the night, as they would be unable to let the horses graze.

At intervals both men looked back to see what the country they had come through looked like when approaching it from the north. They might have to come back fast.

Vast herds of game which had never seen a mounted man raised their heads to stare at them as they rode past, or curious, trotted towards them, snorting.

As they got nearer to the mountains they rode at a walk, halting at every clump of bush to stare anxiously over the open space between them and the next piece of cover. Accustomed to working together, they moved alternately, one watching and covering the advance of the other.

The movements of the game were their best indication of safety; as long as they grazed peacefully there was no danger.

Once they both halted with raised guns as a herd of zebra broke suddenly into a gallop, and smiled with relief to see that the cause of their panic was only a charging lion who killed almost at their feet, causing their mounts to try to bolt. Calming them, the two men swung past the lion which raising its head to growl, crouched over the fallen beast.

The foothills were only a few miles away now and the kloofs, fingers of dark green vegetation that crept up the breast-like slopes of the mountains, were so clear that they could see each tree, isolated by its shadow, standing separate from its fellows. The folds of rolling downland ran up to the sharp escarpment of the berg, where range after range piled themselves into an awe-inspiring mass of solid rock.

Piete leant forward to pat his horse's arching neck. If they were caught up there his turn of speed would be of no use. In that rough ground a horse was no match for a running Kaffir, and what did they know of what was going on up there? Perhaps even now they were being watched by bright, dark eyes. If a picannin saw them it would be enough, and it would not be long before the warriors were out, slipping from bush to bush, surrounding them in a circular net flung six or seven miles wide about them.

He had nearly been caught once, and once was more than enough. His reputation as a scout was due to the excessive caution which arose from that incident. He had been ten at the time. They — he, his father and two others — had been riding quietly over the veld when from all round them Kaffirs had sprung out of the long grass, leaping high into the air, their legs plumed with bangles of monkey skin and ostrich feathers bent under them. They had charged down, jumping like dogs, hunting for game that they scent and cannot see. Nor would he ever forget the horror of that moment. The terrible feeling of something wild and utterly implacable that was closing in on them. It had been his first experience of fear.

His father, the husband of Paul Pieters' favourite sister, had seized the bridle of his horse, the sire of the bay he was now riding, and had by sheer strength swung him round. Together they had galloped straight at the nearest of the Kaffirs. His father unable to use his gun had ridden the man down and taken an assegai through the breast. His last action as the two horses thundered along side by side was to draw the knife from his belt and prick his son's horse in the quarters. The maddened beast had plunged forward. But even then a Kaffir, his kilt of tails swinging as he ran, had almost seized Piete's foot. It was only that his horse was bolting, and that he was so light, that saved him. As he lay along the stallion's neck he felt the assegais whistle past him. Of the five who had ridden out to hunt, he alone came back. He never saw his father again, though he rode back next day to guide Paul de Pieters and a commando of enraged Boers to the place where it had happened. Since then he had fought Kaffirs without ceasing, killing his first at the age of twelve.

CHAPTER IV

WHEN the others left him Hendrik van der Berg sat on, smoking and thinking. He had much to occupy him. He was worried by his son's wound and the boy's incapacity to take his convalescence quietly. There was this attack to organise; and beyond all this was his ever-present anxiety about his people, those who had chosen him to lead them through the wilderness. Their well-being was something of which he never ceased to think — their health, that of their horses and cattle, the condition of their wagons and gear were all matters of supreme import-ance on a trek where the speed of all had to be reduced to that of the slowest member of the convoy. And above all else, their spirit had to be kept up, which was why he had suggested the dance that night. Recognising as he did how largely their determination to succeed depended on their physical condition, he was at times almost glad that they had been attacked. They needed a rest badly, but had he ordered it on those grounds, it would have made them realise how tired they were. It would have given them time to think. Time to regret. He knew there were some who wished they had never left the colony; more and more would do so as time went on. Their troubles were far from over, and to meet trouble men must be strong, animals sleek and rested.

The trek pad he had opened, which starting from the Cape, ended in the wide circle of his laager, was dotted with the graves of the men, women and children who had been killed or died on the road, littered with the bones of their livestock.

Ticks were much worse here, on some beasts one could hardly lay a hand without touching one. They clung like blue peas bloated with blood, all over them. The white tick birds, a kind of small white heron, which accompanied the herds, pulled them off, and the poultry ate those on the trek oxen. Pecking them out from under their heels or jumping up with fluttering wings at those that were on their bellies. While over all the animals the rhenoster birds ran avidly searching in the more hidden places, the base of the horns, along the lips and in the ears, for the parasites that clung there. But even with all this, there remained incredible numbers of them, and with the coming of the summer there would be more. One variety, flat and very hard, beautifully marked with pale green and gold, collected in clusters on the soft parts of the animals — under the tails of the cows, on their udders and between their legs — eating great holes into them, which if not watched, became fly-blown and soon crawled with maggots.

They had lost great numbers of horses from horse sickness, of which there were two kinds — the dinne-paarde and the dikkop-sichte, the latter being the more serious of the two and almost always proving fatal. The horses which recovered were salted, they never got it again, but they lost speed and fire. No one knew the cause of it, and every day Hendrik feared to find Zwartland down with it, his head swollen, his chest heaving as he gasped for air, drowning in the mass of soapy bubbles that oozed out of his lungs. Zwartland was the best horse he had ever had.

There were cattle diseases too; notably one, where before dying, they stood with wild eyes, grinding their teeth and charged anyone who approached them; even attacking those whom they knew well. As they got worse they would fall, as if drunk, and mill round and round on their foreheads, their hind legs kicking the ground bare of grass in a well-defined circle of which their heads were the centre. When they were cut open their heart cavities were filled with a straw-coloured liquid. Having no name for it, the Boers called this new sickness heart-water.

All these things, the attack of the Kaffirs, the press of work which inevitably followed it, and the arrival of Paul Pieters with his convoy had forced Hendrik to abandon his plans for marrying Sannie van Reenen at once. The moment was inopportune, Johannes was depressed by the death of his brother-in-law and determined to avenge it. His mind being better attuned to revenge which was negative, something forced upon him by circumstance, than to any constructive action. He was a man whose desires were atrophied, one that lived in the past, and if he brought the matter up now, van Reenen, seeing no reason for haste, would be bound to shelve it till after their expedition against the Kaffirs, and people getting to hear of his project might easily lose confidence in him if they thought he was in love. That he should wish to marry they would all understand, but they would think he should have chosen one of the widowed women, whose age more nearly approached his own.

Not that he could help thinking of Sannie. Often when he lay rolled in his kaross at night listening to the bark of the jackals and the laugh of the hyenas which hung round the camp in search of offal, or was woken by the coughing roar of a lion, he would picture her as he had seen her last, walking about in the laager, talking and laughing with the other girls, or sitting in a chair by her father's wagon industriously sewing. He was perpetually conscious of her, and secure in his position as leader, it never occurred to him that he might have rivals. He had known her since her birth and, when thinking of her in relation to others, still considered her as a child. That she was not a child, but a woman, was a fact which he was forced to recognise, thrust upon him as it was by his feelings whenever he caught sight of her, or even thought about her.

All round him the lives of his people went on. Each busy

about their small affairs, they left the main issues to him. Having chosen him to lead them, they felt their responsibility at an end.

Gloomy eyed, his bearded chin sunk on his chest, Hendrik watched them, unseeing. Their activities, like those of ants, busy at a broken nest, left him unmoved. For if they left him the greater decisions, he also left them the lesser. In this lay the great strength of this nation, their capacity for decentralisation; in it also lay their weakness. For so competent were they as individuals that they hesitated to combine even when it was necessary to do so, for acknowledging no man their master, each wished to lead and declined to follow.

From the middle of the laager came the sound of the musicians tuning up. The squeak of a fiddle, the odd wails of a concertina whose holes were partially stuffed with dust, and the sweet notes of a flute.

In the wagons the women would be dressing, pulling out their best frocks and combing their hair. From near by came the sharp tap of an axe, five or six strokes, a pause, then five or six more. Old Jakalaas, having found a nice piece of kareeboom, was fashioning a yoke.

Over everything was the soft mauve light of evening, a light so beautiful that it produced a hush. In the roseate glow, things lost their perspective and seemed to creep nearer, the weather-beaten wagons on the opposite side of the laager looked as if by stretching out his hand he could touch the cracks in their sun-scorched sides. Mounted men, riding about, appeared absurdly small, so clearly were their features and the details of their clothes and gear defined.

Smoke from the cooking fires rose in thin plumed columns, and away in the distance a hunting jackal gave its slavering cry.

2

As it grew darker old Jakalaas turned the six-foot piece of rounded timber in his hands; feeling a ridge, he took it off with a quick shearing cut of his axe and put the yoke away. Tomorrow he would finish it, lashing it on to a wagon wheel and boring holes for the skeys and the iron loop which took the trek chain. The four skey holes he would make by drilling three holes for each with an auger and burning them out with a red-hot iron. The places where he would make them were already marked and the wood lying between them must, above all the rest, be smooth so as not to chafe the necks of the oxen on whom it would lie. Jakalaas loved cattle. He loved the great wide-horned red oxen which pulled his master's wagon and the cows that he milked, taking only a little from each so that the calves should have enough.

The little skelms that tried to drink, and sometimes succeeded, while he milked, pushing their wet noses into his fingers where they pulled at their mother's tits. He laughed as he thought of their surprised angry looks when he slapped their faces with his hand or the small switch he kept lying at his feet. On trek they had drunk as they liked, but now they were in a hok — a small subsidiary kraal — and were only allowed out one by one as he milked their dams. He thought of one cow whose calf had died, of how he had skinned it, and stuffing the skin with grass, used to set it down beside her while he milked. With the dummy in front of her she allowed herself to be milked dry. He thought of heifers with their first calves that fought and kicked so that it took two boys to handle them, of Roiland, the big bull, who was so quiet that the picannins could ride on his back, and so savage in anger that he had once killed a tiger as it lay crouched over a calf.

Jakalaas took snuff and squatted, dreaming happily of cattle. He had eaten, and his belly and his heart were full.

3

The back of Sannie's wagon was arranged somewhat differently to those of the other women. Being an only child and unmarried she slept alone, so instead of the great bed which usually occupied the whole covered portion of the wagon, she had a narrow bunk. It was covered by a kaross of wildcat skin whose fringe of tails touched the pelt of an enormous leopard which lay on the floor. Over the bed hung the two silver-mounted pistols her father had given her. They were kept loaded and placed so low that when in bed she could reach them by stretching out her hand. Under the bed was the coffin-like wagon box in which she kept her clothes.

Opposite to it, running along the near side of the wagon was a long shelf. It had a ledge round it to prevent things falling off when the wagon moved. It had drawers beneath it for her toilet things and those small oddments of which she was continually in need. Over the table she had a mirror fastened to the battens of the tent and resting on the wagon side. Near the mirror at the far end were two small brass-bound barrels, one for water; it had a drinking cup attached to it by a chain; and the other which was locked was filled with brandy for use in emergencies. On the other side was a small powder barrel and a receptacle for bullets; a holder for her tinder box and a vase of polished horn in which to put flowers were clamped to the wagon. Across the front and back of the rear portion of the wagon were low wooden partitions to which the canvas curtain flaps were fastened by rings to an iron bar. They could be firmly laced together through their eyelet holes or fully opened and drawn back. In the middle of the wagon was a hanging lantern on a chain, its height adjustable by a counterpoise the shape of a small sitting man.

Herman had often looked into her wagon, but had never actually been into it before. In some way it made him feel awkward and uncouth, it put him at a disadvantage. It was not that it was in any way daintily feminine. Except for the flowers, they were big pink scented lilies which he had brought her from the vlei, it might have been a man's quarters. But being near Sannie always made him feel tongue-tied and uncomfortable, as if he were too big, and now that having let him in and drawn the curtains she ignored him and went on plaiting her hair, he felt it more than usual. He was too tall to stand upright, and she had not asked him to sit beside her.

'Well,' Sannie said at last. 'What is it? Is it time to do your arm again?'

'Ek weet nie, Sannie, about my arm.' Having got here, he did not know what he wanted to say. He had been passing and had felt an impulse to scratch at the canvas of her wagon as he went by. As a rule, when he did this she told him to go away and said she would be out soon.

'I want to talk to you,' he said. How neat her fingers were as she plaited her hair, slipping the three coils one over the other. Under, over, under, over, under, he found himself thinking it was like a thick whip that she was making.

'Talk, Herman? Have you found something new to say?' She laughed up at him. 'And why don't you sit down?' She moved up a little. He sat down diffidently, wondering if the bed would bear his weight. It had been built for Sannie who was very small and light. Also, he did not quite like sitting on her bed. To sit beside her outside was one thing, to sit beside her here another.

As if she knew what he was thinking, she said, 'It's strong enough, Herman.' And turned her head towards him. 'Come,' she went on gaily. 'What is this that you are going to tell me, this new thing?'

'Ja, it is quite new.' Herman suddenly felt very bold. 'It is this. I am tired of being played with like a tolly at the end of a riem running round and round. I am a man.

I have a wagon and a span of my own, I have horses, cattle, sheep.'

'And all you need now is a wife,' she interrupted. 'Some-one to cook for you and mend your clothes. Magtig, and you call this new. Ja, and you think that I would do. You like my baboti and my rusks, you think I am good to look upon, and you would like to lie with me. You with your cattle and your horses. Am I not the only child of my father? Will I go to a man without a portion? Magtig, I thought it was something new you had to tell me, not this old story. I thought perhaps you had come to tell me you were going to marry Zwart Piete's cousin. A fine wife she would make for you. A half-wild girl who is as dark as a Kaffir and as immodest, or his sister who hunts like a man. They say she has been out fighting with her brother, dressed as a boy.'

Sannie tossed her head contemptuously.

Through the folded-back canvas of the wagon front Her-man saw the piled goods lashed fast with riems under the dusty bucksail, above them was a triangle of sky paling now to the soft green and lilac of the evening; the sun had gone, and soon it would be dark. Sannie was still playing with him. A large bat flew past, he did not like bats, re-garding them as ill-omened. Things were not going well with him. He was no longer certain of Sannie. He could not tell what was in her mind, his arm hurt him, his red horse was wounded, his new friend, Piete, away and in danger. He thought of how he would at this time be settling down for the night somewhere in the mountains, he thought of the mocking laughter of his Griqua Bastard. He thought of Stephanie, Zwart Piete's pretty cousin, and of Sara, his twin sister, who was so big and silent. A queer girl this, moody and morose, one who ignored everyone except her brother. Her face was badly pock-marked, and though usually ex-pressionless, was as sad as that of a bush monkey when she thought herself unobserved. Sannie hated these people, but

he liked them, for they were new and strange. Zwart Piete
was his friend, and Paul Pieters was a hero, one of the big
leaders of the day. But perhaps Sannie's anger was a good
sign, perhaps she hated Stephanie because she was pretty,
because he had talked to her, perhaps...

'Listen, Sannie,' he burst out. 'Next week I shall be well.
I shall ride out on commando, but before that, before I
go ——'

'Ja, Herman, and before you go?' she asked.

He hated Sannie at that moment; hated her for what she
was doing, throwing words out at him that cut like the blows
of a whip, and all the time binding him to her by the spell
of her presence, by the very pose of her body lying back on
her bed against the cushions. What had she talked about
Stephanie du Plessis for? If she could not make up her
mind soon, he would have Stephanie. Her wishes about
the matter were clear enough. His heart beating angrily,
he seized Sannie's wrist and pulled her up.

'You are right,' he said. 'I have nothing new to tell you
— nothing. There is never anything new for a man to tell
a woman. All I can say is that I love you, and that this
cannot go on. The winter is over, the trees are putting out
their flowers, already the bees are beginning to swarm, and
birds fly about courting. In the kraals the bulls are arching
their backs and the cows restless; everywhere the sap is
rising, and it is not good for a man to live alone.'

Letting go of her wrist, his arm went round her waist.
For a moment she struggled wildly pulling back her head
and pushing him away with her hands on his shoulders,
fighting furiously as he kissed her throat and neck. She felt
his forearm hard against the small of her back, she felt his
knees against her thighs, his hand on her breast. He was
forcing her back. Through the kaross she could feel the hard
edge of her bed against her calves.

4

Tante Anna sat on her chair watching the dancers, Wolf, her big dog, lying beside her. Sometimes as dancers whom he knew came near, he would wag his tail, thumping the hard-baked ground or look up with bared fangs at strangers. Neither the woman nor the dog ever took their eyes off the people dancing on the piece of cleared earth round the great fire.

Sweating freely, the musicians stood or sat with their legs dangling over the edge of the decorated wagon that served them as a bandstand, played unceasingly. Frikkie Laurentz blew madly, with puffed red cheeks, into his oboe. He had taken this opportunity to put on his father's uniform, that of the old East India Company, and very fine he looked in it. The doublet and breeches of blue kerseymere lined with Indian linen, salemporis, which was now very hard to obtain, might have been made for him. On his legs he wore knitted stockings of bright red and on his head a fine hat, very high and imposing, with its front of tiger skin. His father had been a grenadier and the hat, unsuitable for oboe playing, tipped over one ear by his exertions, marred though it did not spoil the effect. Hans Graaf had also dressed up; he wore an officer's coat of scarlet cloth braided with silver, one, which new, must have cost a hundred gulden. Tante Anna wondered where he had got it. Not from a tailor that was certain. Still, the two men gave the band a military look which was very pleasing, and what a volume of sound they produced. Ach, music was wonderful; the power of it. Even she, newly bereaved as she was, felt her feet moving to the rhythm.

Couples whirled round in one another's arms, broke up into units or linked into chains of humanity which wove in and out of each other in the warp and woof of the round dances. The clothes of the women and girls, the silks and taffetas which had been put away for months, sprang into brilliant light as they swung near the fire or disappeared, the bright colours unilluminated, fading into the darkness as they left it. The men wore clean clothes, but had not put on their best, and carried knives and powder horns in their belts. That was Hendrik's order. Round the dancers, behind the ring of sitting women, old women too stout to dance and young ones too heavy with child, who sat on chairs or squatted on karosses watching the dancing, were a ring of coloured men holding their masters' guns and their own. Every now and then as firelight sprang up it glinted on the long barrels that they held in their hands, and the wide blades of the assegais carried by the watching Kaffirs. In the event of an attack, each Boer would run to his group of natives and seizing his gun, be ready to fight.

It was unlikely that this would happen, but Tante Anna applauded the forethought which had made provision for such an eventuality. Her hard eyes softened as she watched a girl sitting next to her slip down her frock and give her child the breast. A tall native stood beside her, his assegai point driven into the ground, his kerrie in his hand. She had been left in his charge by his master when he died, and it was understood by all that he should remain beside her even among the white people. Aaasvogel they called him, because of his keen sight, and Marietje, the wife of his baas, was safe while he lived. Poor Marietje de Wett, not yet twenty and already a widow. Tante Anna sighed. She was sorry for the girl, but in a way her pass was better than her own. Soon she would go to another man, and Louis de Wett would be forgotten, and his son weaned and learning to walk, would cling to the legs of another man, clutching at his trousers with small inquiring hands.

A Kaffir threw more wood on to the big fire, a shower of sparks went up into the air and a man, one of Paul Pieters's people stepped out to sing. His name was Grietje Martinus, Tante de Jong had heard of him. They said he had a voice which would charm the birds from the trees and bring the snakes out of their hiding-places to listen. Certainly he was a fine figure of a man, tall and powerfully built, with a great red-gold beard that reached down to his belt. His wife and child were dead. The woman having died from the bite of a snake, and the child, fostered on a Kaffir woman, only surviving her for a few weeks. This was his tragedy. All that had been his was gone, only his courage and his voice remained. Slowly, to his own accompaniment on a small harp, he began to sing. His voice, a magnificent baritone, coming from deep down in his chest, increased in volume till it seemed to fill the laager and spill out into the veld beyond. He sang a love song. He followed it with a lullaby.

In the firelight Tante Anna could see tears running down his cheeks as he sang. When he finished the song he paused and broke into one of his own compositions called 'Voorwaarts,' a song of the great trek they had all made, a song of their dangers and tribulations, of border fights on the Great Fish River and of the martyrs of Slagtersnek. As the last notes died away a lion roared, another took it up, and another. Not only birds can he charm, but lions, Anna de Jong thought, and looked at the girl by her side. Marietje's baby was asleep, his head lolling back. Marietje, her breast still out, stared with wide tear-suffused eyes at the man standing alone on the bare space by the fire. He played a final chord and tucking his little harp under his arm strode off through the people into the darkness beyond. Catching Tante Anna's eye, Marietje blushed and pulled up her dress. The child woke and cried, and once again everyone began to dance.

Missing nothing, Anna searched for Sannie in her wine-red taffeta. She was not there and nor was Herman. Herman should have been there. He was wounded in the arm, and not the leg. What were they doing? She thought suddenly of the advice she had given Sannie. What a girl to choose tonight when her absence would be conspicuous. But on the other hand, when would she get another chance like this when everyone was busy making merry, with even the Kaffirs standing about watching the dancing. Ja, Sannie was a clever little piece and capable of making the most of her opportunities. She wondered what it was about her niece which made her so attractive. She was not beautiful, she was too small and slight for that, with skimpy little hips and long thin legs. But she had something, a magnetism of some kind; it showed in the way she moved and spoke. It was the quality that they had in common. Ja, under that small, calm exterior there was this other thing that men guessed at. Ach sis men. They only wanted one thing; the only thing they could get from a woman, the only thing she had to offer them. Tante Anna sniffed loudly and then smiled — well, they would get it from Sannie, she had plenty to offer. Unless the man were young and strong it would be too much.

5

'Let us go out, Sannie,' Herman said. He could hear people moving about, and at any minute one of her friends might come and look for her.

'Out? Do you mean out of the laager?' She raised herself on her elbow. She looked at his face which she could see silhouetted against blue-black sky of the night. He was her man, her lover; what he said she would do.

'Yes, out under the stars where we can talk.'

'What about the guards?'

'Tonight they will be looking inwards watching the dancing, besides, here, on this side, I am on guard.' He got up.

As they crept out of the front of the wagon a black shadow sprang up beside them. Swirling round, Herman caught the man by the throat.

'Baas, baas, it is I,' Jakalaas gasped as he felt the fingers biting into his neck.

'Let him go, you fool,' Sannie said. 'You must not

throttle my Kaffir,' she went on, laughing gently. She turned to Jakalaas who was rubbing his neck.

'Bring your assegais and come with us,' she said.

'With you, mie meisie? And where is it in the heart of the meisie to go,' he asked.

'We are going to the river. I wish to talk to the baas.'

Trembling, the old Kaffir followed them as they dropped over the side of the wagon among the oxen, who tied to their trek-gear slept, their heads curled round on to their hind legs like dogs, or lay chewing the cud, their stomachs rumbling.

Sannie spoke to them, calling them by name: Engelsman, Bloom, Gielbeck, Bosveld, Kaptein.

Blinking their big eyes they looked at her and continued to chew, their lower jaws moving sideways as they ground the cud with their molars. Bosveld threw back his head to lick his flank, his long horns glistening in the moonlight as they walked past him.

This was certainly the madness of the white people, Jakalaas thought as he followed them. That the young baas should make love to his meisie, he understood. He had foreseen it, either this baas or another. He had lain listening to them at it for a long time. But why now, when it was all over, did they want to go and talk. What was there to talk about? What they should have done, in his opinion, was to part and sleep and when they had rested to make love again. That was the normal, the sensible, thing to do.

Out here there was danger. He stared into the black bush beyond the clearing, his eyes wide with fright. Lions. Kaffirs. And worse than either, the spooks of the warriors killed in the battles. The shafts of the assegais he carried in his hand rattled together as he thought of those wild Kaffirs — their earth-bound spirits must certainly be wandering round the encampment. They would haunt it forever since their stomachs had not been ripped open to allow their souls to escape. And no doubt his meisie would leave him alone to watch from behind an ant heap while she went off to talk with the young baas. His teeth chattering with fright he clung to their heels.

A nightjar on silent wings swept over him, and he clutched Herman's shoulder.

'I'm bang, baas,' he said, 'bie bang vir die spoke. They are all around us.'

'There are no spooks,' Herman said.

No spooks, indeed, more white man's nonsense. Oh, unquestionably the white people were very great, very strong, but of some matters they knew nothing.

CHAPTER V

THE kloof towards which Zwart Piete and de Kok were riding was very like the others which indented the foothills of the mountains, except that it was larger, opening out into a wide delta of alluvial soil on the south side, and instead of ending, ran straight on in an ever-narrowing gully which cut right through the range.

Here, in the mouth of the kloof, growing in the deposit of silt carried through it by the rushing waters of the spring and summer rains from the higher lands, were the big marula trees they had been making for. Beyond them was the valley, dark and menacing now as the sun, low in the sky, was hidden by the mountains. Only a spur on their right, covered with red aloes, was brilliantly illuminated by a shaft of light which struck it diagonally from between two peaks. The red flowers in the red light stood out against the indigo shadows of the valley.

High up above them the main berg was streaked with pink where the evening light fell on the chalky droppings of the nesting vultures. Each peak, each shoulder, each rock and every tree and bush, was stained red in varying shades; pale pink below the vultures' eyrie, orange on the bare granite face of the cliffs, dull crimson on the dark evergreen scrub which grew on the mountain slopes. Every object threw purple shadows of fantastic length, and where the trees grew close together, merged into a pattern that moved almost visibly, growing, as the sun fell.

The silence was profound, movement of man and beast

arrested, even the light breeze which had been blowing ceased, and the leaves hung immobile and unrustling on the trees.

For three minutes, for perhaps five, this would last, this miracle that divided the African day from the African night.

The men, the white man and the coloured, drew rein.

From the mountains came the bark of a baboon.

The horses, impatient at the delay, and knowing that they carried meilies for their evening feed, tossed their heads, their bits jingling. A night-appie sprang from one tree to another, spreadeagling through the air and clinging to a branch, looked down at them with wide round eyes. The spell was broken.

Taking off his hat Piete wiped his forehead, and pressing their horses' flanks with their knees the two men rode on. In an hour it would be dark.

Both were thinking of their plan. It had at least the merit of absolute simplicity. They would camp in the cave, it was near now, and in the morning would climb the mountain till they could obtain an uninterrupted view of the plain beyond it.

2

Soon after Sannie and Herman had left the wagon her father came to look for her. Climbing into it he lit the lantern and glanced round. She had been here; she had been lying down. Perhaps she was not well and had gone to get some medicine from one of her friends; thinking it a pity she should miss the dancing he shrugged his shoulders and went back.

There was no accounting for girls, any girls, and Sannie more than any other. Long ago he had given up trying to understand her movements. On one thing, however, he did congratulate himself — Sannie never did anything without a reason. It was something to have a girl who knew her own mind. He would miss her a great deal when she married, and feeling that the time was not far distant when this would happen he wondered what he would do when she left him. It would be very lonely without her. He supposed that with Jappie dead Tante Anna would come and keep house for him. This was something he did not look forward to. How different Anna was from her sister. If she had lived he would never have trekked, but she hadn't lived and he had welcomed this excuse to get away from the farm which had been their home. He was not a politician, among a nation of them; he was one of the few who did not care who ruled, a man who was happy with his flocks and herds, his pastures and his cultivated fields.

3

Hendrik van der Berg had been called by Tante Anna.

Seeing him near her and knowing very well whom he was looking for she engaged him in an interminable flood of reminiscence, speculation about their destination and complaints about the increasing heat which affected her stomach, always her weakest part since the birth of her seventh child. Details of its birth, biting comments on the obstetrical methods of the women who had attended her followed. In her opinion, after the first, the seventh confinement was the most critical. She had seen it many times, and after that, the fourteenth. Seven was a number of great significance — she hoped Hendrik realised it.

Ja, my friend, she thought, if I have to tell of the birth of all my children you shall not get away. If she devoted half an hour to each, that would be cutting it down to its very minimum, she would be able to keep him for five hours.

'Sit down,' she said, and then plunged into her first confinement, which had occurred in the middle of a baking.

'Naturally, the bread was spoilt, Hendrik; there were ten loaves, that I remember very well, but it was a fine boy.'

Surely Sannie would come soon. Out of the corner of her eye she watched Stephanie du Plessis dancing with Jan Fourie. She looked bad tempered and sulky. Martinus, the man who had sung, stood near her. She heard him ask Marietje de Wett to dance. She heard Marietje say she could not because of the child.

Turning towards her Anna said, 'Go and dance, give the baby to me.'

So Martinus had seen Marietje look at him, or had felt her look and had come to her. It was good. He had lost a woman and a child, and the girl had lost a man. How easily things readjusted themselves. With what neatness, with what perfection the plan went on, circumstance making opportunity, opportunity making circumstance in a never-ending cycle of reproduction. The baby, looking very small in her enormous lap, gazed up at her and smiled. This was a good place, the big work-roughened hands that smoothed him knew what they were about.

Anna went on talking.

Hendrik, longing to get away from this garrulous old woman, went on searching the crowd for Sannie; at last he saw her dancing with Gert Kleinhouse. How beautiful she was, with her hair dishevelled and her eyes bright.

Seeing him Sannie waved her hand in greeting. Not caring what she thought Hendrik left Tante Anna. She made no effort to restrain him and as he left drew the child closer to her, peering at it, leaning over her breasts.

'Soon you will have a little brother,' she said, and smiling, gave him her finger to suck.

4

Sannie was gay, laughing and talking excitedly to everyone. Over there, her eyes strayed to the dark ring of the laager, Herman was on the watch. Tomorrow they would meet again. She thought of her wagon. She thought of the

riverside, of the little clearing surrounded by heavy thorn
scrub where he had taken her, carrying her part of the way
so that her dress should not be torn, of old Jakalaas shivering
on guard, the moonlight tipping his spears with silver as he
crouched behind a stump.

Ja, Herman was right, the spring had come. Her life, like
a bud, had opened out; warmed by the hot blood in her
veins it had blossomed tonight. Her eyes darkened, their
pupils widened at her thoughts, her lips parted. Now she
was a woman.

Hendrik asked her to dance. Suppose he knew, she
thought? Suppose Tante Anna knew?

Seeing her laugh Hendrik said, 'You are enjoying yourself, Sannie.'

'Ja, mynheer, I am enjoying myself.'

This was life, she could feel it bubbling through her,
mounting in waves as her small feet tapped impatiently at
the ground.

'Let us go on, Hendrik,' she whispered.

His grip round her waist tightened.

5

When Zwart Piete and de Kok reached the track made
by animals crossing the range and Kaffirs coming to hunt in
the wooded slopes of the downland on its southern side, they
followed it till they came to a big naboom. Here they dismounted and leaving the horses with the Griqua, Zwart
Piete went on alone, taking a game path which ran steeply
up the hillside.

The entrance of the cave was a narrow cleft between two
rocks. One great one, which overhung a small precipice,
would be hard to pass with the horses, and a smaller one
which was part of the main outcrop attached to the mountain face by a narrow saddle. The underside of the bulging
rock was ornamented by crude drawings of animals, coloured

black, red, and yellow. He had not noticed them before and
the sight of their faint outlines, scarcely visible in the dusk,
confirmed Piete's impression that the cave had at one time
been inhabited by the little hunters who were such a curse
in the south; small yellow people whose hair grew in tight
peppercorns widely separated from each other and whose
physical peculiarity, apart from their small stature, was the
abnormal development of their posteriors which ran out at
right angles from their spinal columns. He remembered
shooting one of them, a female, in very poor condition, the
skin of whose buttocks hung in loose folds over the back of
her thighs. She had evidently been on the verge of starva-
tion and had been living on her own fat just as cattle, in
bad seasons, lived on their humps.

Thinking vaguely of the bushmen he had shot at various
times Piete cut some long grass with his knife and lighting
it, went into the cave. He wished to make certain no lion
or leopard had taken the place for its lair since he and de
Kok had been there a few days ago.

Holding the torch in his left hand and his gun in his
right he went in.

It was not a pleasant situation, but it was one which he
had been in before and understood. If there was a lion or a
leopard in the cave he would see its eyes shining like green
lamps and dropping the torch, counting on it to flare up as
the whole caught fire, he would shoot between the two green
eyes. This plan was an old one and invariably successful,
for the animal, dazzled by the glare, would back away
snarling. The only danger was that of its being a female
with cubs, they always charged at once, or of there being
two beasts. In addition to this there was the possibility of
the torch going out, or the gun misfiring.

Bats in hundreds fluttered over him making the torch
flicker and throwing shadows as large as vultures on the
high walls.

Hoping there was nothing there, more particularly no lion,

for even if he killed it the noise of the shot echoing through the mountains would be heard for miles and because with a dead lion, or even the scent of a lion in the cave, it would be impossible to get the horses through the narrow opening, Piete advanced.

6

With the reins of the two horses looped over his arm, his face expressionless, de Kok waited. He had an infinite capacity for waiting imperturbably for events to shape themselves. He knew that the art of life, like the art of hunting, consisted in being able to put oneself, geographically, into the place where things were likely to happen and to wait, watching and calculating till the moment came, and then to act recklessly, risking everything.

De Kok was a gambler, inheriting the instinct from his admixture of eastern blood, that of slave craftsmen imported from Batavia. A hunter, from the blood of Hottentot and Bushmen women with whom they had been mated, a man of overwhelming ambition, this last a gift of his white male ancestors who for generations had taken his coloured female ones.

His mother had been the slave of a rich farmer called van de Winter. He had entertained a great deal and she was somewhat uncertain as to who his father was. Nor did she consider his name a matter of great moment, her memory had waned with her looks and men had come into her life with the seasons and like the seasons she remembered them better for their qualities, good, bad, or indifferent, than for their names, anyway she had called them all mynheer and was certain only of one thing — that the father of her son had been white; so long as the men who used her were white her prestige among her fellows remained unimpaired.

Her name had been Katarina Kok and she was distantly related to Adam Kok, Kaptein Adam Kok as he styled himself, the leader of the Griqua Bastards. The prefix 'de' he had added for himself in imitation of the names of some families of Boers who were descended from the Huguenots.

At the back of his mind he had a plan; it was very elastic and could be altered to suit any circumstances which arose — that they would arise he was certain. The great trek was bound to produce something. Out of the troubled waters of Kaffir fighting, settling down in a new country away from all authority, of ever-changing values, the occasion which would give him his chance was bound to occur. Till it arose he was content to wait.

Doves flying very fast on whistling wings shot over him. They were going down to the little spruit which ran down the middle of the kloof to drink before they settled for the night. Others perched in the trees nearby cooed continuously.

De Kok listened for a shot. His master was a fine hunter, but even to fine hunters things might happen.

Something moved in the bush near him; without turning his head he looked towards the sound and saw a hyena slinking away. He wondered why it was out so early — they rarely moved till after dark; perhaps Zwart Piete had disturbed it. An adult man they would never attack; wounded men, women and children, they had been known to kill, also sleeping men. Though mainly they lived on offal and marrow from the bones too big and hard for the jackals to crack. He hated hyenas, they were sexless and uncanny, hermaphrodites that fertilised themselves. As he watched it moving clumsily, its heavy shoulders out of all proportion to its scraggy quarters, Zwart Piete came back.

'Come,' he said. And taking his horse led the way up the mountainside.

7

On the fifth day after Zwart Piete and his coloured man had ridden out Paul Pieters came to Hendrik and said, 'If they are not back tomorrow I am going to look for them.'

'You are going out? What...alone?'

'No, not alone; ten men will come with me — even now they are getting ready.'

'And if you don't come back?' Hendrik asked.

'Then you are the leader of my trek too. They will be in good hands, you will lead them Hendrik.' His face lit up, 'Ja, my friend, you will lead them to Canaan, to the land flowing with milk and honey in the north, you will lead them into the promised land. The boys will become men, the old men will die, but always the story of Paul Pieters who took his commando to find Zwart Piete will go on. There will be songs about it. That is if we go,' he added.

Hendrik was much perturbed by Paul's attitude. He knew that he meant what he said, that he would take out his men and sacrifice both them and himself in a profitless revenge. Still, it was time they did something; it was getting hotter every day. Little clouds, the forerunners of the rain, appeared and disappeared; one day soon they would mass into great banks of black storm cloud and then the rains would break. Before this happened he wanted to be over the river in front of them, but that again he could not do, he dared not do, till the power of the Kaffirs was broken; for with the river in flood behind him he would be cut off, both from retreat, or from the help of those who followed.

Work in the camp had slowed down; it was too hot to continue making biltong; instead of drying, the meat went bad. Everything that could be done to the wagons was done, their weaknesses strengthened and everyone had spare yokes, skeys, strops and riems. The animals had all put on condition and the faces of the people had filled out, losing the drawn, hollow look they had worn for so long. They were rested and eager, too eager. Haste, in wild places, was foolhardy; speed, yes, but only such speed as was consistent with security.

He wondered what could have happened to Zwart Piete. One day to ride out, one day there, one day to ride back.

Three days was ample and it was now the fifth. There was the possibility of an accident, but accidents were rare with experienced men and Piete was noted for his caution. If the Kaffirs had got him he hoped to God he was dead. In his mind he saw the young man stripped, spreadeagled, his wrists and ankles tied to pegs in the ground, by a broken ant heap, with his eyelids, ears and lips cut off; or buried alive up to the neck, in such a way that he would live for days while the ants slowly ate their way into him.

8

When the sun was high and at its hottest, while the others dozed by their wagons, or slept in the shade of the trees, Sannie followed by Jakalaas, sauntered slowly out of the laager.

Like everyone else in the camp she was affected by the uncertainty of Zwart Piete's fate. The younger children alone continued to play their games unthinkingly; driving each other about with reins made of thin riems, riding the disselbooms of the wagons as if they were horses, or clasping dirty, ragged dolls, got from under the feet of their elders.

He ought to have been back yesterday, she thought. And if he was as clever as he was supposed to be, as clever as he thought himself, he would have been back.

Sannie did not like Zwart Piete nor did she like his cousin or his sister. The former because she was jealous of her good looks, the latter because she was ugly, a parody of womanhood who followed her brother everywhere. They were twins and inseparable, doing the same things and apparently even thinking the same thoughts. She was jealous of Herman's friendship with Piete and sick of the sound of his name. Herman could talk of no one else and since this morning had done nothing but fret at his inability to accompany Paul Pieters when he went to look for him.

Drifting first this way and then that Sannie walked on.

The ground in front of her began to fall, sloping towards the river. Here in the small vlei were lilies, pink ones with dark red markings; and white ones, very delicate and fragrant, beautiful flowers which did not last in water. She stooped to pick one and sitting down pulled it idly to pieces.

Along the river bank the trees were in leaf and the thorns heavy with yellow clusters of bloom. A colony of weaver birds chattered hysterically as they wove their nests with long shreds torn from the reeds. Some were already finished and hung like pears swinging on the branches over the water, others, in the initial stages, were mere hoops of grass.

With her legs drawn up and her chin on her knees Sannie sat waiting, staring in the direction of a big Kaffir-boom that stood alone, its leafless branches covered with scarlet, tulip-like flowers.

A few yards behind her, Jakalaas, his eyes half closed and his body relaxed, leant against a tree chewing tobacco. Occasionally his thick lips parted as he spat at a big lizard with a bright blue throat. The lizard's forked tongue flicked in and out of its mouth as it looked, with unwinking eyes, from the Kaffir to the blobs of dark-brown spittle on the grass beside it.

A black locust with red wings flew past him.

A beetle rolled a ball of dung painstakingly between the tussocks at his feet. An ant crawling over his toe found a small cut, bit him, and was crushed by the cracked, pinkish sole of his other foot.

From the direction of the Kaffir-boom came the call of a pheasant. It was repeated three times. Sannie got up slowly and the Kaffir squatted down to wait. He was smiling — pheasants rarely called in the heat of the day.

9

Long after Herman had left her Sannie still lay under the Kaffir-boom, dreaming, as she stared upwards at the bright scarlet flowers which sprang so surprisingly out of the bare, bulbous branches, of the future, of Herman, of marriage. Once this attack on the Kaffirs was over they would get married, but until they could do so, what was the good of telling anyone. She disliked the coarse jokes which accompanied an open courtship, the rude bucolic laughter of the men and the sly looks of the women. She watched a blue jay swoop down onto a bee. Its breast, a brilliant king-fisher blue, flashed as it turned with a flick of its forked tail. Its head was mauve, its back green, the outside of its wings, as it perched on the tree above her, turquoise and purple. Shading her eyes with her hands she stared at it entranced. Surely nowhere in the world was there such colour as this. As she looked another joined it; screaming, they swung upwards in love-play and coming back settled, sitting very near to each other.

Birds, beasts, men and women, it was all the same. There was no answer to the questions in her mind, or perhaps what she had just seen was the answer, at once the beginning and the end.

Sitting up she shook back her hair. Beside her on the grass the flowers she had picked were dead, wilted by the sun; on the way back she would pick some more.

10

Anna de Jong was puzzled. With the death of her husband her interest in Sannie had increased; the child was, after all, her niece and she had no one else except her grandson Gert to think about. And when the choice lay between thinking of a dull young man who squinted, or of a girl who was so like what she had been as a young woman, all ideas of equity faded into non-existence. Besides, she did not believe in equity and saw no reason to practise it. It was just one of the many unpractical things which men had invented and liked to talk about.

With her hands folded in her lap she sat thinking. Unquestionably Sannie and Herman were lovers, that was easy to see. When a girl attended a man's wounds he always tried to become her lover, and when, after having done nothing but follow her about like a bottle-reared lamb, he suddenly stopped speaking to her and only gave her occasional looks, it meant that he had succeeded. This also was obvious, for since he had the feast why should he bother with the crumbs which fell from the table.

Ja, so far it was in order. But why did Sannie deny the whole business. Why did she say, 'Yes, I am very fond of Herman,' and when pressed add, 'Perhaps more than fond,' and then laugh. The only thing to do was to think of what she would have done under similar conditions. Anna sighed. Herman was a very fine young man, one to take the eye of any maid, but Sannie had known him all her life. One never liked people much whom one had known all one's life. If I had been Sannie, she thought, I would have wanted someone new. I should have hoped that among the men of a passing convoy I should have found him, or that we should have come across a lone hunter, someone really romantic; but then there was the wound and the intimacy of dressing it, of feeling him dependent on her, of knowing she had saved his life, all this would weigh against her romantic hopes, and with the coming of Paul Pieters not only men, but women had accompanied him, and the attention Herman had paid to Zwart Piete's cousin Stephanie had swung the balance. All this was good and right. But then, why not marry him at once? There could only be one reason, she was not sure if she wanted to. Of course she is not sure, Tante Anna thought. I should not have been sure. That was the trouble with men, as soon as one was chosen another seemed better. And Hendrik? What about him? He wanted the girl, but naturally he could do nothing till the attack was over. He was going to lead it with Paul Pieters and men did not trust a love-sick man. Poor Sannie, she thought, the child must be very worried. Closing her eyes Tante Anna composed herself for sleep.

II

In the late afternoon Hendrik decided to look for a new drift across the river. The one they used now was all right for mounted men but he hoped, lower down, to find a place which would be better suited to the heavily-laden wagons of the convoy.

Swinging away from the camp he rode towards the river and striking it began to ride slowly up its bed.

The place he had in mind was one where the river widened and where owing to its increased width the velocity of the water would be checked and its depth reduced. In addition to this the banks must not be too steep, though they could be cut away, and the bottom must be good. If such a place existed it would be worth while to make a deviation in order to use it. It was important to find the best possible road, not only for their own wagons, but for others who were following them, and to make the communications which were bound to exist between the isolated communities they would form when they settled and the distant province from which they had come as easy as possible.

This trek pad was not merely a hunters' road cut haphazardly into the north. It was alternatively a line of advancing civilisation and line of retreat from dangers too great, or obstacles too formidable to be overcome. It was also the only link between them and those of their relations and friends who had remained behind.

His horse's feet sinking over their fetlocks into the loose sand of the dry river bed made a rustling sound like that of a woman walking swiftly in a silk dress, or rang out crisply as he walked over an outcrop of smooth flat rock.

As he passed, turtles dropped into pools with a loud splash from the banks where they had been sunning themselves and a heron rose on great wings.

The fact that there was so little water was partly due to its being spring and partly to the amount drunk at the dam higher up by the thousands of head of domestic stock that they had with them.

Instead of widening the river grew narrower and everywhere, hung on the thorn scrubs which lined the banks, he saw the rubbish left by the summer floods. Reeds, branches, even trees were wedged among them. After a storm it must run ten feet deep.

Looking down he saw a track made by a man. Dismounting to examine the footprints more closely he recognised Herman's spoor. Why had his son come here so often?

Out of curiosity he followed the track till it turned from the river bed into a mass of yellow-flowered thorns.

Throwing his reins over his horse's head so that he would stand Hendrik made his way through the narrow tunnel.

It seemed to lead to a big Kaffir-boom.

CHAPTER VI

I

THE climb up to the cave with the horses was difficult. At first they hung back dragging at the reins and then, frightened by the noise of the loose stones which, rattling down, started others, creating small avalanches of rubble, they plunged forward almost knocking the men who led them off the twisting path. Branches caught on their gear and before they could pass under the overhanging rock, while they fidgeted on the narrow ledge with the precipice below them, they had to be off-saddled.

At last, shivering and sweating, they were forced up the narrow passage of the entrance and stood snorting in the darkness of the cave; gradually, as their fears subsided, they began to nibble at the meilies de Kok spread out on a blanket in front of them and except for an occasional startled movement, as a bat passed over their heads, settled down contentedly.

With the horses seen to, the men made camp. Zwart Piete lit a fire and put on a small copper can of water to heat. De Kok going back to the naboom obliterated, as far as he could, the spoor they had left, sweeping away the hoof and footmarks with a branch as he worked his way backwards to the cave. When the water boiled Piete threw in a handful of coffee and settled the grounds by plunging a burning stick into the mixture. He then cut two steaks from the rump of roibok they had brought with them and put them on the embers to grill, while de Kok collected enough wood to keep the fire in all night.

They ate ravenously, cutting the meat and eating it with their hunting knives, sitting near each other with their guns by their sides. They were content, the first stage of their reconnaissance was over, they had reached their destination without adventure or mishap. Piete decided to take first watch, and rolling himself in his blanket, the Griqua wriggled a hole for his hip in the dust of the floor and putting his head on his saddle closed his eyes. With his gun on his knees Piete sat staring at the fire and the blackness beyond it. They passed the night like this, sleeping and watching alternately, waking each other as soon as they tired.

Once Zwart Piete, seeing the green eyes of a leopard staring at him, threw a stone in their direction. And once, it was in one of de Kok's watches, he was woken by the whimpering cry of a young baboon and the angry bark of its mother as she silenced it.

At dawn they put the bridles on their horses and led them down to water. This time they experienced no difficulty in getting them back into the cave, and having fed them, closed the entrance, building it up with loose stones. Once again de Kok swept the path clear of spoor and after a final look at their guns, water-bottles and ammunition, they set off, following the small path which led past the cave till it faded away, losing itself in a multitude of scarcely perceptible game tracks which ran in all directions. Choosing the most likely of these, one which ran almost vertically up the mountain, they fought their way through the heavy bush. Creepers, as thick and tough as ropes, hung from the trees and in the dark-shadowed depths ferns, unlike any they had ever seen, grew from between the moist cracks of the rocks.

Everywhere, at each step they made, the thorns, with which all the scrubby bushes were armed, caught at them, tearing their clothes and hands, but at last they penetrated the thick belt of vegetation which covered the lower slopes and came to a zone where big rocks, some of them as large as houses, which having become detached from the mountain face had rolled down into piled heaps.

Beyond this area lay the main berg, its peaks towering up into the pale morning sky, thousand upon thousand of feet of bare, raw rock, mountains that even a baboon could not have scaled. But at one point, against the nearest peak, the debris was massed into a bastion of great rocks among which a few trees and bushes had succeeded in taking root. Using these as precarious handholds and by helping each other the two men managed to reach a ledge where stones and earth, caught between the split bosses of granite, had formed a small grass-covered terrace. From here, when the mist which covered the plain below them rose, they would be able to see for miles.

With his back to a big boulder de Kok sat down to wait; pulling a strip of biltong from his pocket he began to cut shreds of the dried meat with his hunting knife and to eat.

This platform, he examined it critically, was going to be hot. There was no shade and the rocks which surrounded them would not only prevent any breeze which happened to spring up from reaching them, but would also radiate the heat like the walls of a dutch oven.

Ja, it was going to be hot, but they would be safe here, and it was worth enduring a few hours' discomfort if one was assured of complete security. Today he would sleep properly instead of dozing with his eyes half closed and his hand on his gun.

Tomorrow, well, tomorrow was a long way off. He put the meat away and pulled his hat over his eyes.

Zwart Piete lit his pipe and stared, leaning on the barrel of his gun, over the expanse of cloud and mist in front of him. There was no horizon, the sky clear and blue came down, merging imperceptibly, into the blanket of mist below them.

Soon, he knew, as the heat of the sun increased, it would dissipate, sinking slowly. Trees would emerge from it, standing trunkless, and if there was a village, the huts, with only the tops of their cone-like roofs visible, would appear to float, while men and beasts would move, apparently legless, through it.

All this he would be the first white man to see. For here, beyond the range, was a new world. A world into which he would soon go and from which he might never return.

Taking his pipe from his mouth he spat into the void. Behind him, his dark eyes closed, de Kok continued to chew his meat.

2

When Hendrik van der Berg came back he did not eat. Instead he got his Bible out of the wagon box where it was kept, and read it aloud to his family as they sat round him —Herman, Susanna, his daughter, Maria, another daughter, Johanna, a year younger than Maria, and Katarina, a baby of five.

He read from the Old Testament, sitting forward with the book tilted towards the flames, pausing as they died down, or reading faster to take advantage of the light as they burnt up. The firelight made the heavy brass-bound corners of the book glow as if they were red-hot, and flickering, lit his grizzled beard till blood seemed to drip from its black shadows onto his chest.

The sonorous phrases rolled from his lips as, exalted, he read verse after verse, flinging the word of God savagely into the fire at his feet.

The children sat silent staring at him. They had never seen their father like this before. Herman and Susannah looked at each other wondering if he was ill.

At last, when his voice had become hoarse, he closed the Bible and told them to go to bed.

'What is the matter, father?' Susanna asked. 'Are you sick?'

'No, my child. I am not sick. Go to bed and leave me; I have much to think about. Too much,' he added in a whisper.

Two hours later, when she looked out of the wagon, her father was still there; his position was unchanged.

Sitting with his Bible on his knees Hendrik prayed for guidance.

In his heart he had built a city. Its streets were of fine gold, its palaces had towers of ivory. And now, like the walls of Jericho at the sound of the trumpet's seventh blast, it had crumbled about him; it had fallen into ruins.

Till he had found those crumpled and forgotten flowers at the foot of the Kaffir-boom, till following his son's spoor, he had come upon Sannie's and read the signs written so plainly on the grass where they had lain together, he had not realised how much he had counted on making her his wife. Without her there was nothing, without her to renew his strength he could not go on. Unknowingly she had become the mainspring of his life; and while he had waited for her to grow, another had taken her from him.

Not only that. Not only had he lost her, but a great wrong had been done. Her innocence had been destroyed. She had been cruelly seduced. The virgin was ravished, the lily sullied. Raising his head he stared upwards at the stars, with his stiff beard jutting out from his chin, he arrogantly demanded justice from the heavens. Justice was his right. God, the all powerful, the all just, would counsel his servant. Lowering his head, he covered his eyes with his hands. His lips moved in prayer and with a sudden decisive gesture he opened the Bible, put a thick forefinger in the middle of a page, and holding the book towards the dying fire read the passage that his forefinger touched.

'And Abraham stretched forth his hand and took the knife to slay his son.'

3

In the morning Louisa, the coloured maid who had been Jappie de Jong's mistress, came to Tante Anna and stood wriggling her bare toes in front of her.

'Ja, Louisa, what is it? What do you want?'

'I want nothing, but ——'

'You want nothing, but it is still something,' Mevrou de Jong said. 'Also, to say that you want nothing is a lie. In all the world there is no one who wants nothing. Even the white people all want something. Even I want something. I want a little house and a garden where I can plant my pumpkin seeds and a dam where my geese, if I can get any, can swim, and I want to keep pigs again and to be comfortable. I want to have this verdomt trek done. Come,' she said. 'What is it? Don't stand there gaping.'

'I want nothing,' the girl repeated; 'it is only that I have something to tell the mevrou.'

'You have nothing to tell me. Do you think that, because I am fat, I am blind?' Anna de Jong looked at the girl's figure.

'Oh,' Louisa said, 'then the mevrou knew.'

'Ja, natuurlik I knew. And I knew also about de Lange's driver boy.'

'That is not true,' the girl burst out. 'It is a lie, mevrou, a story of the other maids who are jealous.'

'Then I am very pleased to hear it is a lie, but listen to me, my girl, it will be better for you if that baby, when it is born, is white or nearly white.'

'It is not true,' the girl repeated. 'Me,' she drew herself up proudly, 'me with a dirty Kaffir. Is it likely that I should do that? Does the mevrou think it possible?' she asked.

'The mevrou does not think, she knows all things to be possible,' Anna snapped, 'and the child had better be white.'

'But sometimes the children of the coloured people are

dark. That the mevrou must have seen many times. It is well known,' she went on pouting.

'Ja, that is so, and sometimes they are not dark. But when their mothers are young and pretty I have noticed that the children are always pale in colour; and since it happens that way, it is doubtless the arrangement of God, and the whipping you will get will be a great one for breaking God's law,' and she added mentally for being unfaithful to poor Jappie. Anna de Jong sniffed and rubbed her eyes with her knuckles.

'It will be white,' Louisa said, 'but that is not what I came to tell the mevrou.'

'Then what in the name of God did you want to tell me? It is as I said. You do want something.'

'It is that I am frightened.'

She looked frightened.

'The mevrou knows that I have foretold events, that I have the gift.'

'Ja, I know very well that after something has happened you tell me you dreamed of it before. Also that you dream of many things which never happen. What is it this time?'

'Last night, mevrou, I saw a great herd of cattle, they were countless, spread out over the veld as many as the pigeons on a newly sown field of wheat; and from the herd a small, milk-white heifer went off by herself and later a young, red bull went after her. They went down to a vlei, where there were red and white flowers growing, and there the young bull had the small heifer as she stood among the flowers. After that he went his way, leaving her, and a great black bull charged him, piercing him with his horns and leaving him dead, he took the little milk-white heifer. Then she gave birth to a bull calf.'

'What — at once?' Anna de Jong interrupted.

'Ja, mevrou, it was a dream,' the girl said, 'and the calf was very big and strong, and red, like the young bull that was killed.' She paused, to build up a little heap of sand between her toes, flattened it and looked up. 'That is all, mevrou. It is not like other dreams, and it has made me afraid.'

Anna de Jong was tired of Louisa's dreams. Her mother, who had been one of her father's slaves, had also had them, and the Kaffirs had been very frightened of the old woman. But then she not only had dreams, but also perhaps, because she was old, had the capacity to interpret them. Louisa's dreams were never of any real help, for only in the light of after events could their significance be understood. This one was obviously nonsense. It was the spring, and the girl had spent too long watching the cattle. What she needed was a whipping and more work, but without a house it was hard to find enough work for a maid.

'And what do you think it means, Louisa?' she asked.

'I do not know. I thought perhaps the mevrou would be able to tell me. This I think, though, that it was a very sad dream, the small red bull and the white versie were well matched, and the big black bull too old and heavy for her.'

'Ja, Louisa, that may be so, but that pot,' her mistress pointed to a big jar of baked red earth, 'is not too heavy for a strong young maid like you. Take it and fill it with water at the spruit, and see to it you go above the dam where the water is clean.'

4

On the mountaintop the heat increased rapidly as the sun climbed into the sky; as it rose, the mist sank and the higher portions of plain became visible. Kopjes stood out isolated by white clouds of vapour, like islands in a sea whose boundaries were the pinnacle on which they waited and the range of blue mountains whose serrated contours stood out on the horizon fifty miles away.

At last the mist only hung in the deepest valleys and still they could see no village, nor sign of one.

Zwart Piete was worried. Perhaps they had been wrong. Perhaps the native kraal was not here. He was just wondering where else it could be, for the country a hundred miles round had been searched, when he heard shouts and laughter coming from below them.

De Kok put his hand on his master's arm, pulling him down, and together they crawled forward and looked over the edge of the krantz.

There, a thousand feet below them, was the village; it was a big one, of several hundred beehive huts, arranged symmetrically in three circles, one inside the other.

Even now, as they watched, the cattle in great herds were being driven out of the kraals and girls and women, naked except for little leather aprons, were streaming down in a long snake-like file to fetch water from the river. They carried water-pots balanced on their heads, and many of them had small picannins tied to their backs or bigger ones poised on their hips.

The soft song they sang while they walked, swaying, to the water, came up in waves, as the husky soprano voices rose and fell.

Piete's grip on his gun tightened. He hated Kaffirs and here they were in hundreds waiting to be killed, and here were cattle in thousands, waiting to be driven off.

He saw at once how the village could be attacked, with one force on the kopje a thousand yards beyond the village; they would occupy it in the dark, and a party of sharpshooters lying where he was now, the Kaffirs would have no chance.

Caught between two fires they would be able to kill them, men, women and children. Kill them and burn their huts.

All day in the sweltering heat he lay watching them. He saw old men drinking themselves drunk on Kaffir beer under the big tree which stood in the middle of the village; watched young warriors swagger about, or sitting in the shade, clean their spears; watched the women working, stamping meilies and fetching water; he saw them eat, saw naked mothers suckling naked babies. Saw beneath him the thousand manifold activities that, together, formed the slow perfection of native communal life, the sluggish pulse that beat so strongly under the soft black skins.

Here were Kaffirs, the people who were his enemies, the people he had fought all his life. A hundred times he saw the coming battle, saw Paul Pieters sweeping down with his horsemen, his great beard and long hair flying; saw them, leaning out of their saddles, fire into the mass of charging warriors, fire and swerve away.

It would be best to charge in two parties, one firing as the other drew away to reload, and with ten men up here firing down on top of them, picked shots who could not miss, the Kaffirs would be utterly defeated, eaten up, and once again the vultures would feast and the jackals pad home in the dawn with their swollen bellies touching the ground.

At dusk they climbed down. They would not go back tomorrow. Before they returned he must investigate the kopje from which the mounted men would operate.

5

Herman, with his hat on the back of his head and his hands in his pockets strolled out of the camp. He was very happy; his arm was out of a sling and was healing rapidly now that his body was at peace. Sannie loved him, and his horse was now able to move about freely, showing no signs of lameness.

When he had gone south for about a mile he turned west, then went north again till, striking the river, he went east along its bed. He was anxious about Zwart Piete, but, nevertheless, felt certain of his safety. Piete was too slim to be caught, and when he came back they would train his horse again, and go hunting game and fighting Kaffirs together. In the meantime, Tante Anna had lent him Jappie's dun with a black stripe down its back and zebra markings on its legs. It was well trained and very tame.

It was hot with the oppressive heat of the spring. The baked ground had no moisture to give up and its cracked surface gaped, shrunken under the drought of winter. As he trudged through the heavy sand of the river bed, it was even hotter here than in the semi-open bush veld, he thought of the battle, of Jappie, of Sannie's shot which had saved his life and of his horse. He knew very well that the chestnut thought it had put him down, and that the struggle, always inevitable between a highly strung beast and its master, would have to be fought again before the horse would be safe enough to be counted on in an emergency. He had broken many horses, and it was something to look forward to.

A kingfisher flashed from one side of the river to the other, its flight a waving line of blue and orange. Some monkeys that had been drinking turned to look at him with sad black faces and flung themselves into the trees. A cloud of scarlet and black finks rose from the reed as, opposite the Kaffir-boom, he climbed the grassy slope of the river bank, gave the call of a pheasant three times and entered the narrow tunnel through the thorns.

Herman had not seen the spoor of his father's horse. It had been covered by that of game and cattle.

6

Anna de Jong had seen Herman go out. She had seen Sannie go out, and later, had watched Hendrik van der Berg, mounted on his black horse and carrying his gun, go out. That is to say, that in the space of an hour, while dozing in her wide riempie bottomed chair, she had seen one girl and two men leave the camp.

There was nothing extraordinary in this, if they had all gone one way. The girl was young, and the men strong and unattached, but it was strange that the three people who had gone out of the laager should choose the hottest time of the day to do it, and stranger still that each should go in a different direction. Sannie with her servant north, Herman south, and Hendrik west.

It looked as if each, knowing the way the others had gone, was trying to avoid them. So strong was this conviction that she was certain they would either meet by intention, or that providence would in some way stir the pie of circumstance and force them into contact.

Through half-closed eyes she looked at Louisa asleep under a tree. The girl was very beautiful and slept gracefully relaxed, stretched out like an animal, lying half-turned on her belly with her face hidden in her arms, the curve of her hip high above the point of her shoulder. No doubt she was dreaming of bulls again. It was only surprising that the heifer in her dream had been milk white. Why had it not been a golden cream, like the colour of butter in the spring when the grass was good? Like the colour of her own skin?

Sannie, Herman, Hendrik, the names kept recurring to her mind, pairing off and dividing into the various possible combinations. Two men, one woman; a woman and a man, and another man; the other man, the woman, and a man.

Ach, what did it matter? As far as she was concerned they could do what they liked, go where they liked. It was too hot to think and certainly too hot to walk unless one were mad, or in love.

Never, even in her girlhood had Anna been fond of walking. It was unnatural to walk. Why, if men were to walk, had God provided horses to carry them and oxen to draw their wagons? Ja, she thought, that was certainly a good point; and of the three Hendrik was the only one who apparently realised this, he at least had ridden. A hard, devout man, Hendrik van der Berg. A man to be admired, followed, but not loved.

A feeling of uneasiness swept over her. Rest, real rest,

became impossible. She moved her massive buttocks, shifting her weight cautiously, as the chair groaned.

It was unbearably hot. The pale burnt-out blue of the sky was darkening to a leaden grey opacity which along the horizon was tinged by streaks of reddish purple. There was going to be a storm which might account for her feeling of discomfort and impending disaster. The calm which was spread over everything was no longer one of lethargy induced by the burning heat, but the keyed-up waiting which invariably preceded thunder.

The air was charged with latent, explosive energy. Everything seemed stretched to breaking point in this unnatural silence. Nothing outside the laager stirred, not a bird, not a lizard moved. While within it, not a dog barked, not a child cried. The heat was heavy, pregnant with stillness.

The questions which Anna de Jong had been considering so calmly and objectively a few moments before, now obtruded themselves savagely; coming out like maggots from the crevices of her mind, they began to crawl over the convolutions of her brain, banishing all possibility of sleep. There were forces at work which she could not place, events pending which she could not guess at. She felt their significance pressing at her, it was as if she was enclosed in a box whose sides kept closing in, coming nearer and nearer.

Trapped by her need for knowledge, caught in her desire for the correct interpretation of every situation, she puzzled on, but the pattern was too involved for her, there were too many alternatives, and here in the wilds there was no background of law and security, or even partial security, as a basis for reasonable deduction.

Long ago she had created a system whereby most human affairs, which were in essence much simpler than most people imagined, could be measured and their course foretold. An equation which, by means of a little manipulation, could be made to cover and explain everything, but in this case it stubbornly refused to work.

Not that she expected accuracy. Mathematics, in the sense that two apples and one apple made three apples, was, she knew when applied to adult human beings, nonsense.

But her formula allowing as it did for endless approximations and readjustments, always gave her an answer which if not absolutely accurate was near enough to the truth to satisfy her. Anna de Jong did not want a hundred per cent truth, she was content with ninety per cent. The balance, like the seasoning of food, depended on the taste of the individuals concerned. In considering the laws of human action and reaction she generously allowed for ten per cent of free will.

7

Hendrik rode with his head sunk on his chest. His eyes, deep in their sockets, blazed somberly.

God, the inscrutable, had given him guidance. Terrible guidance. All night he had prayed and thought; since midday on the previous day he had not eaten.

Nothing moved on the veld. Waves of heat rose shimmering from the ground, and the only sound was the rustle of the stiff wiry grass brushing against the legs of his horse as he walked and the scarcely perceptible thud of his unshod hooves.

In the quiet of the heat, everything slept. The ants alone, indefatigable, toiled on, moving in their string-like columns, building and carrying short lengths of grass between their jaws continuously. All life, keyed to the rhythm of that intolerable sunshine, waited panting for the cool of the evening when the beasts of the field and the birds of the air would come out to drink and eat, filling themselves hurriedly. For with the grass eaters came out the flesh eaters; and with the insects, came the birds that preyed upon them.

As he got farther from camp, Hendrik sat more erect and stared about him. Nothing in that world of grass and trees

was without significance for Hendrik van der Berg. It was
his business to read the flight of the birds and the spoor of
beasts as other men read the words of a book, putting the
signs he saw together easily, constructing them like words
into sentences and paragraphs. By these he governed his
actions, destroying and escaping destruction.

As he rode past a clump of suikerbos a duiker sprang out
and, running with its small black horns laid back, its body
compacted, made for a clump of heavy thorn scrub fifty
yards away.

The buck never reached it. Hendrik's bullet smashed its
shoulder. The shock of the concussion turned it over so that
it lay with its legs twitching and its head towards him.

Dismounting, he cut its throat, emptied it, and tying its
four legs together above its small sharp hoofs, fastened it
onto his saddle. He smiled grimly, for his plan it had been
necessary to shoot something, and at an hour when game
was not on the move, God had provided the duiker. Reloading, he turned back towards the camp and, having found
the place he sought, took cover.

The strong sunlight striking through the branches of the
trees criss-crossed the man and horse with the shadows of
their branches, spreading a black trellis over them, breaking
them up into a hundred unco-ordinated pieces, shattering
them into such invisibility that Hendrik's bluish shirt and
his horse's shining coat only added to the illusion of their
disappearance.

Sitting immobile with every faculty alert, he waited.

In half an hour, or perhaps less, it would depend on how
long he stayed dallying with Sannie, his son would pass.
The pupils of his eyes contracted and his grip on his gun
tightened. Time passed, blurred by the heat into something
almost tangible, it moved on. Hendrik's mind was filled
with pictures. His son's unsanctified love-making being distorted obscenely, visions conjured up by his own desires
tortured him. Sannie's laughter rang in his ears, he saw

her walking, talking, giving herself illicitly, lying in his son's arms, in the arms of the seducer. Sannie the pure whom he had never even kissed, but whose every gesture he knew, whose every curve by the power of his unveiling eye, was his.

He heard someone singing. It was Herman striding back, his hands in his pockets and his head held high.

Slowly, his hands firm, Hendrik raised his gun. The foresight covered Herman's chest at the base of his throat where his shirt was open. The shoulders of the back-sight came up till they were level with the top of the foresight, his finger pressed the trigger and the gun shot rang out staccato, cleaving the silence of the veld; there was a pause before the smack of the heavy bullet hitting flesh and bone came back to him. A pause, in which the boy's song hung poised on a high note in the tree tops, as he staggered, raised his hands and fell.

7

In the late afternoon the watchers on the hill to the north of the laager saw a man riding towards them from the north. He was coming very slowly and appeared to be carrying something on the saddle in front of him.

It was Zwart Piete's Griqua and what he held so carefully were a man's legs, they could see no trunk. Had the Kaffirs cut him in two? Were his master's legs all that de Kok had been able to rescue? Two men immediately galloped up to him, while a third rode for the laager with the news and led back the band of horsemen he collected. The camp, which had been waking slowly into movement, buzzed like a hive of angry bees, and gathering into groups, the people talked loudly of vengeance. Zwart Piete is dead, they cried. The Kaffirs have killed Zwart Piete.

Sannie, who after her walk had been resting in her wagon, came out in time to see Sara du Plessis run up to Herman's horse, it was the only one available, jerk a bridle into its mouth, slap on a saddle and, pulling up her skirts, spring onto its back. With a shout to her uncle, who mounted on his big grey, waited for her, she wheeled the chestnut and bucked her way out of the camp, scattering dogs, children and chickens in all directions.

The horse, enraged, tried to unseat her, but every time he bucked she hit him with a heavy sjambok. Running against the wheels of the wagons, overturning tables and chairs, the chestnut tried to scrape her off, but the girl, with her frock kilted round her waist, continued to thrash him till, giving up, he bolted after the grey and, overtaking him, the two horses thundered through the gate and, galloping neck and neck over the veld, made for the party returning with de Kok.

Sannie and her aunt joined the crowd; everyone was there, everyone except Hendrik van der Berg and his son Herman.

CHAPTER VII

I

IT SEEMED to the people waiting outside the laager that the cavalcade approaching them moved very slowly. Certainly it was right, Tante Anna thought, that the remains of a brave man should be treated with respect and not bumped about at a gallop. But these men, the Griqua and those who had ridden out to meet him, were hardly moving, and as if that was not enough, stopped every few moments to make what looked like gestures of horror, touching each other and pointing to the Bastard's burden.

At this rate it would be a long time, a quarter of an hour at least, before they arrived, so she sent Louisa to fetch her chair. Sannie, standing beside her aunt, looked round for Herman. He had told her he was coming straight back to the camp. This would upset him, and she doubted very much if any efforts of hers would now prevent him joining the punitive expedition which would go out to avenge this murder.

As the party got nearer, it became apparent that they were laughing. Slapping each other on the back and roaring with laughter to such an extent that they could hardly sit their horses.

Tante Anna, furious with impatience and unable to understand this extraordinary behaviour, banged the arms of her chair and sent Louisa running to see what had happened.

If they laughed like this, Zwart Piete could not be dead. If he was not dead, she might be able to keep Herman back. He is not strong enough to fight yet, Sannie thought, and again looked round for him. 'Magtig!' she heard someone shout. 'Magtig, what a man!' And another roar of laughter went up. Gert Kleinhouse, who was riding a little apart, was holding his stomach and the tears were running down his face.

In the middle of the group the Griqua sat his horse smiling quietly. From where they were Sannie and Tante Anna could see nothing, only the heads and shoulders of the mounted men appearing above the crowd of people on foot who pressed round them.

They saw Louisa force her way into the press and come running back. When she reached their side she was laughing so much that she could not speak.

'Oh, mevrou,' she gasped. 'Oh! Oh!'

Springing up, her mistress boxed her ears and waddled off to see for herself.

'What's all this?' she said. 'What in the name of the Almighty is it?'

The impetus of her weight carried her through the crowd to de Kok, and then, like the others, she began to laugh.

'Ja, ja,' she said; 'it is funny. It is the funniest thing I have ever seen.'

In their relief, everyone was laughing hysterically. Doubled up, Sannie clung to her aunt's arm. Oh, where is Herman? she thought. If only he could see this.

De Kok, his bare yellow legs sticking out beneath his shirt, smiled at them. With one hand he held his reins, with the other, he clung to his trousers. Tied at the bottom of both legs, they straddled his horse's shoulders stiffly. They were filled to the top with ostrich eggs from a nest he had found on his way home. Still shouting with laughter, the Boers rolled off their horses.

'Where is Hendrik van der Berg?' they asked. 'Now with de Kok to guide us we can start tomorrow. He has found the kraal,' they said. 'Where is Hendrik? Hendrik must be told.'

'I am here.'

They had not seen him come. They did not recognise his voice when he spoke.

Towering above them, they had all dismounted, on his black horse, he sat looking down at them his eyes as cold and hard as stones. At the back of his saddle was tied a duiker ram, its head hanging downwards, under the black gash of its cut throat, moving as the horse's flanks rose and fell.

In front of him, across the pummel, his arms dangling like the broken wings of a bird, was his son.

'There has been an accident,' he said. 'I have shot Herman.' He paused. 'Come to my wagon, de Kok, and give me your news.' Raising his voice, he went on, 'And tomorrow we ride out.'

De Kok was forgotten as they crowded round Hendrik. How did it happen? Why? Where? How? When?

Coldly Hendrik explained. He had been shooting. Something had moved, he had fired thinking it was a buck. The boy was dead. He had died instantly.

Overwhelmed by the tragedy and many of them crying, for Herman had been much liked, they took the body from Hendrik and carried it to the wagon.

Sannie, opening her mouth to scream, had felt her aunt's fingers on her wrist, the nails biting into her flesh.

'No, Sannie. No,' Tante Anna said.

'But he is dead, dead.'

'Ja, Sannie, he is dead, and if screams could bring your lover to life I would say scream, but they cannot, they can do nothing, no one can do anything.' And she dragged the girl away.

At that moment the storm, which had been threatening, broke with a roar of wind and an all-enveloping cloud of dust. Unnoticed in the press of passing events, the sky had fallen, covering them like an inverted leaden bowl closing them in, isolating them between its restricted horizons. The noise of the talking, the shouts and the cries were drowned in a howling gust, torn away on the dark wings of the storm. Red dust, in clouds, covered everything.

The women, their skirts pressed against them and billowing, lost in the opaque semi-darkness, pressed their hands to their eyes, while sand, particles of grit, and even small stones carried on the terrifying wind, slashed at their cheeks as they sought panic-stricken for shelter. Children cried, clutching at their mothers, as they tried to hide among their petticoats. Poultry which had gone to roost early were swept away like pheasants on unaccustomed wings. Horses which had been securely tied to the wagons smashed their riems and galloped headlong round and round.

Only the cattle stood still with their patient, high-hipped rumps turned to meet the wind.

In Tante Anna's wagon, when at last she reached it, Sannie flung herself down and, grasping the older woman's knees, gave way to paroxysm after paroxysm of dry tearless sobs.

Herman — her Herman — was dead, he had been brought back, slung like a shot buck over his father's saddle. Now they would not be married. Now life was over. Now no arms would ever hold her, no hands touch her.

Outside the storm raged, bending trees before it, or breaking them, brought them to earth with tearing, thunderous crashes. Guy ropes were whipped loose, canvas shelters hung stiffly horizontal, thrashing till they broke adrift and sailed, like kites, away. The tent of the wagon, pressed against its battens, made tight little convex squares, sails, which rocked the heavy vehicle. Rubbish of all kinds struck at it and was held there by the force of the wind, while sand and dust pouring through every crevice, piled itself in crumbling heaps.

From being dark it became light, as flash following flash illuminated everything. A wagon was struck and burst into flame, the explosion of the powder barrel it contained lost in the crash of the continuous thunder. Fortunately, before more wagons caught, the rain came down; not in drops, but in a solid mass, as if the bottom had been suddenly withdrawn from a lake.

A flood of water a foot deep swept over the veld. The Kaffirs who had been crouching beneath their master's wagons were forced to climb onto them as the water swept between the wheels.

The spruit which had been a trickling stream half an hour before was now a raging torrent whose roar could be heard above that of the storm, and then as suddenly as it had begun, the weather changed and the sun came out.

People soaked to the skin, for the canvas of the tents was incapable of withstanding such a downpour, stood white faced on the wagon beds or waded knee deep in the water, trying to rescue such as were left of their belongings.

In that hour, since Zwart Piete's servant had come back without him, Herman van der Berg had been brought in dead, a wagon had been wrecked and its occupants — the Marais family, a man, a woman and two children — killed; a vast number of sheep swept away and all possibility of attack on the Kaffirs made out of the question until the floods had subsided.

It was a disaster compared to which all the others they had passed through were as nothing, an experience which had affected everyone by the swiftness of its coming, by the piling of climax onto anti-climax, by its exposition of the awful power of their God, the God of Israel, who was a jealous God.

2

Herman's body lay on his bed. It was there that Sannie saw it, washed clean by the rain, lying surrounded by a pool of pale, pinkish water, on its canvas cover. They had not even thought of pulling a blanket over him. He had been put down and left.

A thousand conflicting ideas swept through her mind. The desire to fling herself down beside him and weep evaporated, a cold anger at death taking its place. There was nothing to weep at here. This was not the Herman she had loved; this was a stranger, a boy whose mouth hung open foolishly, whose eyes, unlit and glazed, stared vacantly upwards. No longer a young man, but dead flesh, something which must be put away before it turned rotten. The spark was gone, and nothing left to kindle that which within her had flared so easily, so recently, to meet it.

Having seen death many times, but never her own dead, she was appalled by her lack of feeling. All it meant was an end. Death did not come, that she realised suddenly was the truth of this thing; instead, life departed leaving a great vacant space in one's heart, a vacuum of thought and desire.

Herman was dead. They would bury Herman and no one but her aunt would know what he had been to her. He was already part of the past, like a flower which had bloomed and died, no longer beautiful. For a moment she thought of taking something of his. His handkerchief, a lock of his hair; and then a premonition of what was to happen came to her, a thought as swift in its passing as the flight of a bird and as certain. She needed no memento of her lover. No, rather would she remember him as he had been, passionate and strong, the young man who had taken her so angrily. A memento, she smiled sadly; she had it, and before the water dried up in the pans and grass turned yellow it would be born.

3

The next day was a sad one, more graves were dug near Jappie's, and this time they were dug quickly for the ground was soft and wet. First that of Herman, then those of the Marais with their children lying between them.

Soon, if they stayed here long enough, they would have a

cemetery, but at least this thought comforted Anna de Jong, her Jappie no longer lay alone. Sannie's self-control was perfect, she went about composed and thoughtful as if she were waiting for something. In a week now she would know.

Her only remark to her aunt was that had he been able to choose, Herman would not have chosen this place to be buried and her eyes had strayed towards the Kaffir-boom whose scarlet flowers had gone, destroyed by the storm.

Composed, dignified and withdrawn into herself Sannie moved, lost in the world of her fantasy, through the days that followed, wandering absent-mindedly through time as though it were space. Eating, talking, smiling, even laughing a little, sleeping soundly; a woman who now drew all eyes by the perfection of her youthful maturity.

4

Once the work made by the storm and flood had been dealt with the men grew uneasy and quarrelsome; they wanted to be off and have done with this place of ill omen. Every day they went down to look at the river which remained impassable. Surely soon the waters would run down and they could go. De Kok's story of the ease with which the Kaffirs could be attacked, his description of the vast herds of cattle, which, acclimatised to this hot northern area, would so swell their depleted herds, excited them. Among the Boers, as among the natives, a man's standing was inextricably tied up with the size of his herd, his importance being to a great extent measured by the number of his cattle. A man was important when he had thousands of cattle, negligible when he had none.

Few of them considered Jappie or thought of revenge; to them the coming expedition was one which would, by dealing the enemy a decisive blow, secure them from further attack and at the same time enrich them by the loot they would acquire.

Everything was ready. The men who were going with van der Berg and Paul Pieters were picked. Men in their prime, experienced hunters, fighters capable of withstanding exposure and forced marches on small rations. Their horses, having survived the trek, were as tough as their owners, true Boer horses, of Arab and Basuto strains, small, veld-reared beasts, which could forage for themselves and were well accustomed to gun-fire and war conditions.

The older men and boys were to be left in charge of the camp who, together with the women and girls, would be strong enough to hold it unless they were attacked in over-whelming numbers. In addition to them a small force of selected men who could operate mounted, independently of the laager, were also staying behind under the command of Johannes van Reenen.

5

Where the others were merely nervous and irritable, Sara du Plessis and de Kok were anxious. Twice he had tried to swim the river to get back to his master. On the first oc-casion he had nearly done it and on the second had had his horse drowned and narrowly escaped death himself.

The Bastard and his master's sister were always together staring towards the mountains and talking about Zwart Piete.

'What will he do?' Sara asked. 'How much food has he? How much ammunition?'

One thing was certain, when they did go, she was going with them and to that end had bought Herman's red colt from Hendrik. Once broken thoroughly he would be better than any of her own or her brother's beasts and all her time which was not spent on the bank of the river she devoted to the horse and soon had him under control. With his head tied to that of de Kok's horse they rode about, firing their guns, charging and wheeling. She taught him to stand quiet with the reins flung over his head, to carry a double burden and to ride down anyone she put him at. The more she saw of the horse the more she liked him and the more certain she became of her security when mounted on his back.

To Hendrik the idea of a woman going on commando was unheard of, but Paul Pieters, with whom she was going, only laughed. He was used to her and told van der Berg that he would soon forget she was a woman when he saw her fight.

6

Zwart Piete, when he sent de Kok back, had gone on towards the further range of mountains. Here was a temptation which he was unable to resist, the call of the distance, the inarticulate cry of the hills, with their ever-changing hues now light, as airy as gossamer, as transparent wood smoke; now stark and hard, their jagged peaks sharp with danger, they exercised an irresistible fascination over him and he had time to explore them — there was no need for him to return. In two days de Kok would be back and he would meet the commando when it came. De Kok could guide them as well as he.

Then came the storm. Caught in the open plain Zwart Piete shivered beside his horse with his saddle held over his head and his powder-horn securely hidden under his armpit. Now, not only would the coming of the Boers be delayed, but whether he willed it or not, his only course was to go forward for the streams between him and the cave were swollen into impassable torrents and his direction was less governed by desire than the necessity to find shelter within the restricted area which lay between the streams on his right and left.

His powder was dry — that was the one essential — and he was certainly safe from the Kaffirs at the big kraal. Without option he pressed on; he must find, within the next few days, a place where there was game, for here it had been exterminated by the natives.

If his sister and de Kok had been with him he would have been happy. He was tired of the trek, and spending all his time like a butcher killing meat for other people to eat. He wanted adventure. He wanted to see life; and it seemed to him that life was escaping him, hiding from him, among the kloofs and krantzes of the mountains in front of him.

Always, with every range he felt this, and always his heart beat faster as he climbed, ready to meet what he would see before him; and each time he was disappointed, one side of a mountain being so much like the other, the view in front so like that behind.

7

Hendrik was morose. The sympathy he received for the death of his son was unwittingly tinged with irony.

'It was a terrible thing to have happened,' they said.

'Ja, it was terrible.' But only he knew how terrible it was.

'It was doubly sad because he had no other son.' He had killed his son in order to have others by the woman his son had loved. No, he must not even think that; such thoughts must be dismissed. He had prayed, God had given him guidance, and he had punished the seducer. Like Abraham, God had demanded the sacrifice of his Isaac. Unlike Abraham, God had not saved his son. Why had he not? Why had God, the omnipotent, not caused his gun to misfire? or the boy to return a different way? Why? Because God had meant him to be punished for his sin, and he, Hendrik van der Berg, had been God's chosen instrument of vengeance.

Time after time he reread the passage he had found that night by the fire. Reread for confirmation though the words were engraved upon his mind, though they stood out as if they were cut in stone upon it.

The Lord had spoken to his servant in no uncertain voice and he had obeyed the Lord. His prayers, his thoughts, his hours of agony were past. He had come through the valley of desolation into the fair fields that stood beyond them and a great peace spread over his soul. The decision had not been his and he was without responsibility.

Once again he turned to the tenth verse of the twenty-second book of Genesis. Once again he read the words:

'And Abraham stretched forth his hand, and took the knife to slay his son.'

And why should it be wrong because it fitted in so well with his own wishes? Surely here was another manifestation of the Almighty's will; it was God's wish that Sannie should become his wife. That, fruitful, she should bear him fruit. That beautiful, her beauty should be his consolation.

Knowing what he did of the relations between her and his son he was astonished at Sannie's lack of feeling. It only added to the certainty that his action had been right. Her new composure, her new beauty, was due to relief, to freedom from the vicious bondage in which Herman had held her.

Since the death of his son the lines on his face had deepened and new ones had been added to them. His hair had become more grizzled and his eyes fiercer. Still less than ever was Hendrik van der Berg a man to be crossed in love, or spoken of lightly in anger. At the slightest opposition his fangs bared, like those of an old boar, he would turn and rend. His life, the last strong urge of his powerful virility, was at stake. The die was cast. His plough had turned the first furrow of the last field it would cultivate. The field his son had sown so carelessly, so joyously, he would rip up, tear, with strength alone, down to its very subsoil, burying Sannie's girlish memories deep under the skilled fertility of his experience. More and more, while he waited for the waters to fall, he read his Bible, turning with quick thick fingers such passages as dealt with Uriah the Hittite who was sent into the forefront of the battle, for that had been one of his plans which he had abandoned as too uncertain, skipping the story of Susanna and the elders, and concentrating only on those passages which dealt with the Almighty God's revenge, with his punishment of evil, and the distorted tortuous methods by which he achieved his inscrutable ends. More and more as he read he grew to associate himself with God. From being the instrument he became part of the thing itself, a madman who by virtue of his physical strength, temporal power, and wild religious fervour, swayed all who approached him.

8

At last the river went down and the commando assembled. In the cold grey light of the dawn, their saddles loaded with food and ammunition, they said good-bye and mounted. For a few minutes the laager seemed overfull of men and horses as they shouted to each other and sorted themselves out into groups. Bay, brown, black, chestnut, strawberry and blue roan, grey, dun, cream and piebald horses swirled about in a pattern of flowing manes and tails, a disorder which remained orderly because each man and horse was a complete unit, carrying its own supplies and capable of fighting its own battles. That they were riding out in one body in no way destroyed their undisciplined individuality; they were separate men, who for a specified purpose were co-operating under the somewhat tentative command of their own elected leaders.

A few final shouts, calls of 'Are you all ready, then voorwarts,' and they moved off raggedly. A force of fifty white men, one white girl dressed as a boy mounted on a chestnut horse, and their armed, coloured servants and spare horses.

Well equipped, angry at being delayed, led by the visionary Paul Pieters and the coldly-raging Hendrik they were going to smite the Philistines. Where before they might have been content to defeat them, they now intended to destroy and to leave nothing, not a roof on a hut, not a pot unbroken, not so much as a calf or a lamb alive. What they could not drive off they would kill, what they could not kill they would burn.

By the leaders rode de Kok, slouching in his saddle, his dark eyes missing nothing. Beside him was Sara du Plessis, who, only by a conscious effort managed not to ride on ahead. Her brother had been alone in the wilds among hostile Kaffirs for ten days. Was he safe? Was he even alive?

Nothing the Griqua could say would satisfy her. It was useless for de Kok to point out that Zwart Piete had often spent a month hunting alone, to repeat stories which she already knew of his prowess and his cunning.

Whatever de Kok said Piete was only a boy of twenty. What chance had he among those savage mountains, alive with Kaffirs, leopards, lions and snakes. In her imagination every disaster she had ever heard of overtook him. And if he was safe, how would they ever find him? Where would he be? Even the Bastard's skill at spooring would be useless after such rains as they had had. Their one hope was, that having been so much together, they would be able to guess the way his mind had worked and follow him.

The Boers rode silently, spread out in a loose diamond formation which was capable, by the mere turning of their horses, to face in any direction. No longer boastful they were occupied by their thoughts. Thoughts of the past, of their wives and children in the laager and of the future which might so quickly be shortened to the length of time it took for an assegai to fly from a black hand into their breasts. That they would all return was possible but unlikely. Some of them were certain to die up in those mountains and each hoped it would be one of the others. Yes, hoped it, even if it was his best friend.

9

Anna de Jong's indigestion was not better, but it troubled her less now that she had no time to think about it. Her flatulence being chronic was only a subject for thought and conversation when all others failed her. It remained a conversational reserve, a last line of defence, a cross she either bore with silent fortitude or when the occasion demanded it, flaunted.

Sannie was going to have a child and though this, in her opinion, was a most natural, in fact the only natural result of an adequate love affair, it would nevertheless, among others less open minded than herself, create a scandal which must, somehow, be avoided. Nor was she happy about Herman's death. Hunting accidents occurred but rarely, and never quite so opportunely. She remembered hearing the shots, one of which had killed Herman and the other the duiker ram. Hendrik was a fine shot and he was out for meat. She had made inquiries on this point and it appeared Susanna had asked him to shoot something for the pot. But why when shooting for food had he gone in the heat of the day instead of waiting till the evening when game was on the move? There were a number of whys in this matter; the pieces did not fit except in one way. The way which made it murder.

Considered calmly this was the answer; and also considered calmly, for Sannie to marry Hendrik was the most practical solution of the other problem. It was not only the solution, but it would also be his punishment, for Hendrik would get no joy of Sannie. She would sap him, break him and, in the end, leave him. The grapes would be bitter as gall in Hendrik's mouth and his strength turned to weakness in her small hands. His punishment would be that of achieving his ends and finding them nothing, of having dug a pit and fallen into it himself. Marriage, it was most reasonable of Hendrik to want to get married. It was in fact impossible for a man to farm without a wife to manage his home. But why a girl like Sannie? Why not a competent widow? A widow like herself for instance.

Anna admired Hendrik van der Berg greatly. His having

killed his son, though unquestionably wicked, was at least the decisive act of a man who seeing things as they were took a hand, twisting the tail of providence as though it were a refractory bullock to make it jump his way. She sighed deeply and began to plan Sannie's immediate future and her own, more nebulously, with Johannes van Reenen. Her brother-in-law was a dull man — it was only with an effort that one could respect him.

Still, it was a pity about Herman; he had been a fine young man, full of promise and a pleasant sight for a woman's eyes.

CHAPTER VIII

I

MANY months ago, many hundred miles to the south, there had been a big war dance as there was each autumn. In Chaka's great kraal, regiment after regiment of Zulus had danced, stamping till the reed huts shook, advancing, their thousand feet moving as one, their glistening, oiled bodies bent, their plumes waving, their spears shining.

Each regiment headed by its captains, some of them grey-headed, scarred with wounds, passed before their king. Regiments with white oxhide shields, regiments with red, with parti-coloured shields, black and white, red and white. Sometimes slipping past as silently as buck, running on their toes, at others halting to stamp and raise their weapons, the short wide blade assegais with which they charged when they had thrown their spears. On they came in a well drilled, never-ending stream, their kilts of wildcat tails flowing as they ran, the ostrich plumes in their heads dipping and swaying. Sometimes two regiments would run at each other in mimic battle, passing through one another's ranks and reforming. Foam flecked their lips as they awaited the signal of the black elephant, the black bull, before whom lions trembled and the very leaves fell from the trees in fear as he approached.

'Give us blood,' they chanted, 'give your men blood in which to dip their spears. The spears of the young men are thirsty, oh Chaka, oh black elephant.'

Among his indunas the king sat silent, watching impas-

sively. Wrapped in a kaross of leopard skin he never moved
as they charged up to him, their bloodshot eyes looking into
his own.

In his hand he held a throwing assegai with a long, thin
shaft. At last he stood up, the robe fell from him, and he
stood naked save for his loincloth of breyed skin towering
over his men. The assegai was raised, his biceps swelled;
he paused, smiled, and flung it north.

That was the signal. In whatever direction he flung, his
impis would go, taking death and destruction with them.
One year it was one way, another year it was in a different
direction, but the result remained the same, the spears of
his young men drank blood.

With a shout they were off, wheeling past him, they trotted
out to kill, regiment after regiment, under their captains
they swept by, raising their assegais in the royal salute,
their cries of 'bayete, bayete,' re-echoing in the hills. In an
hour the kraal was empty save for the seasoned veterans
who were the king's own guard; away to the north there
were some clouds of dust.

2

The Boers, guided by de Kok, reached the range before
dark, and dividing, took cover. When the moon rose they
advanced again, going straight through the kloof and de-
bouching silently through the poort, onto the plain.

Looking much bigger than they were in the moonlight
they wound in single file over the veld towards the kopje
where they would lie hidden till it was time to attack. After
some argument they had decided to wait till the sun was
well up and hot; by then the Kaffirs, having eaten, would be
dozing in the shade and more vulnerable than in the deceptive light of the dawn.

Ten men climbed to the mountain plateau where de Kok
and Zwart Piete had lain. Their instructions were not to

fire till the battle had begun. Once engaged, this fire would disconcert the natives and allow the main party to force the attack, pressing it home, as the natives swung about trying to meet the new onslaught from above.

Lying beside their horses the men dozed, talked in whispers of the coming fight, or prayed to the Lord of Hosts. Tired by their ride most of them oscillated between the wildest optimism and the most profound depression. Only the more hardened slept, those who from their wide experience of war had become fatalists, or who deeply religious had faith enough to leave all in the hands of that God who had chosen, so markedly, the Boer people for his own. The kopje on which they lay had a depression in its centre, and here, unless someone actually stumbled upon them, they could, even in broad daylight, remain unobserved.

The night passed, growing colder as the dawn approached, but at last the sun rose and the men, shivering and blowing on their numbed fingers, crept to the edge of the kopje to peer down into the plain beyond.

In two or three hours they would attack. With grim, stiffened faces, they looked at each other and drew in their belts. Their stomachs had grown small with fear.

Life was stirring in the village, columns of smoke rose, cocks which had crowed all night, challenging each other, were now silent and the lowing of the cattle, the deep throaty roar of the kraaled bulls, the sheep-like cry of calves and heavy maternal call of the cows filled the air.

The Kaffirs were moving about, singly and in groups; looking absurd, like very perfect dolls the size of ants, they went unconcernedly about their small affairs.

This was what the Boers on the kopje saw, but de Kok from the mountains saw something else. He was the first to see it.

All round the village, almost a mile from it, where the grass was long and sour, he saw a movement. At first he thought it was his imagination, that it was wind stirring the grass, and finally he realized that it was not wind— wind could not blow in three directions at once.

Closer and closer came the movement. Every moment the circle was getting smaller, drawing in, approaching the open, tramped out sweet grass which surrounded the village.

He touched the arm of the man lying next to him.

'Look,' he said, 'look.'

As he spoke the Zulus broke cover. The returning impis, depleted in numbers, but with their blood lust unappeased, were on their way south, on their way home. Going north they had killed and ravished, coming south they continued to do so.

With a wild shout they ran forward, their war plumes tossing, jumping high into the air as they ran. They swept inwards towards the village brandishing their spears, their big shields raised.

The Kaffirs, entirely unprepared, tried to fight. They formed small groups round which the oncoming wave of Zulus lapped for an instant and passed on, thrusting and stabbing. These were the horns, merely the two outer portions of the main Zulu force, sent out to envelop and to hold, while the main body, two regiments, a solid mass of warriors charged irresistibly, a black wall of men that moved silently, shoulder to shoulder, spear to spear. In half an hour it was over. Where there had been a village there was a smouldering ruin. Where there had been life there was death, and death only. Everything was dead; man, woman and child had been put to the spear and every beast was driven off.

By some chance the hill where the Boers were lying had not come between the Zulus and their quarry. By some chance, by the mercy of God, those fifty white men, the one white girl, and their coloured servants, had been spared.

Had the Zulus found them they would have been eaten up, for the Zulus were as numerous as locusts. Even their horses would not have served them, for in the rough going of the kloof they would have been run down and butchered.

Slowly, holding their hats in their hands and thanking God for his mercy, the Boers rode through the smoking ruins. Vultures were already circling down, swinging in effortless intersecting arcs, dropping lower and lower with their heads poked forward, moving from side to side on their bare ruffled necks.

Dead Kaffirs, pierced many times, lay in every position. Here was one who had died fighting, here was another, who, running away, had taken an assegai in the back. Women dead, with dead babies clasped to their breasts. Girls, young women, old women with pendulous dried-up dugs, all lay as they had been killed, singly and in heaps.

Scattered among them were a few Zulus who had been killed in battle, or who, severely wounded, had been put out of their agony by their friends. A blow with a kerrie, a belly-slash with a spear, was the end a wounded Zulu warrior craved. Most were young unringed men, but few were veterans who had fought their last battle, men of property, with wives, fat black picannins and cattle, who were now offal, men who had died as they lived, by the spear.

The feelings of the Boers were mixed. Their vengeance had gone to someone else and so had the cattle; this was a severe blow, for they had looked forward to driving home those herds. But on the other hand they had suffered no casualties and with the Kaffirs exterminated they were now safe from attack and would be able to continue their trek.

What the Zulus had done in one place they had certainly done in another and the whole area must, they were certain, have been devastated.

Leaving the ruined village they turned homewards and rode slowly through the poort, talking and laughing.

With the Kaffirs defeated, the high mountains were no longer menacing, the narrow defiles no longer places to be carefully reconnoitred in fear of ambush. One of the elements of risk which perpetually menaced them had been, by an act of God, eliminated. Only the normal dangers of nature with which they were well accustomed to cope, remained.

Canaan was now theirs for the taking when they found it.

Paul Pieters and Hendrik van der Berg, riding side by side, were discussing the trek on. They had decided to part company; since there was no further necessity for mutual protection, it would be better to graze their herds apart. Towards evening they camped and soon the buck they had shot on the way were grilling on the fires.

It was only then, as the Boers who had been riding scattered over the veld seeped in, that the absence of Sara du Plessis and de Kok was noticed.

They had given one of the coloured men a message and told him to deliver it when he off-saddled for the night. They had gone back to find Zwart Piete. For a moment Paul Pieters looked upset and talked of following them. Then he laughed. What was the good of going back? Those three, Zwart Piete, his sister and de Kok, were accustomed to each other and could not be parted. Even if Sara and de Kok were brought back by force they would go again.

One day they would turn up, till then he would look after their stock, running it with his own.

Hendrik, however, took a more serious view, feeling that a white woman should not go off alone with a Griqua. He might take advantage of his position, of their isolation.

'Ja,' Pieters said, 'he might. So might a jackal take advantage of a lioness, and if he did, my friend, what would the end be do you think? A dead jackal that is all. No, God help any man who tries to interfere with Sara. She is strong and as quick as a man with a gun or a knife.'

3

Thirty miles away Sara and de Kok sat cooking their supper in the bushman's cave.

'He will have made for the mountains,' de Kok said.

'He always goes towards the mountains, and with the rivers flooded he can only have gone one way. You will see,' he went on, 'by tomorrow we will have picked up his spoor. There are not many big trees on the plain and he will have camped near one of them. That also is his habit.' De Kok was happy. He was quite confident of finding his master and things were coming his way. He had a plan. He went over the story he would tell in his mind. He would say that the commando had been eaten up by the Zulus, that only he and Sara had escaped. Ach, how he would lie. He smiled as he thought of his skill in lying. Unfortunately Zwart Piete knew what a good liar he was, but this was a lie that his master wanted to hear, one that he would be only too ready to believe. De Kok knew that his master was tired of the trek. Tired, too, of being under his uncle's command; and as for himself, he wished to get away from the white people who, while on the march treated him as one of themselves, but who, once they settled down, would once more remember that he was only a Griqua, a Bastard. His relation Adam had founded a people, why should he not do the same? Why, once they got away could he not succeed? become a president, a leader, a king? His eyes glowed as he thought of his possible greatness. He had all the necessary assets. Already he would have been great if it had not been for his yellow skin.

He sighed, thinking of the ostrich eggs he had brought back to the laager and wished he could find another nest. Even if there was only one egg in it, one ostrich egg was equal to two dozen hens' eggs, and he felt like eggs tonight. Turning to Sara he said:

'When we find the baas let us say the impis caught the commando; that all are dead and only we escaped.'

'Why should we say that?' she asked.

'Because then we shall go on together.'

'On where, de Kok?'

'Ek weet nie, just on. Listen, mie meisie, the baas wants

to go on, that we both know, and I have made up this beautiful lie to tell him. It has taken me all day and it is the finest lie I have ever thought of.' He smiled ingratiatingly. 'What a pity it would be to waste a lie like that,' he said.

Sara sat silent. She was thinking over the Griqua's words. After all, why not? They, she and her brother, did not want to settle down. They were not farmers like the other folk. And she, too, wanted to get away. In the camp she felt the eyes of the people upon her. Some sniggered as she passed, nudging each other. Some offered her the indignity of their sympathy while others ignored her, passing her by as though she was something unnatural, unclean. That they laughed she understood, for she was different, more like a man than a girl with her great stature, her strength, and the ruggedness of her pock-marked face. And her answer to their laughter was laughter and a bitter hatred of the men who would never love her and of the girls who would know those men's love. What had gone wrong in the darkness of their mother's womb that she had been formed like this? That in all but her organs she was a man. That her strength was that of a man, and that with this she should have been given a woman's heart, and that then, on top of everything, as if it were not enough, had come her illness, the pox that had ravaged her.

'Ja,' she said, 'we tell your lie. We will go on into the mountains that Zwart Piete loves so much, and see what lies beyond them. Somewhere there is the sea. I should like to see the sea. To hear people speak of things is not like seeing them for oneself. I shall sleep now and tomorrow we will go and find him and you can try your lie. It will have to be well done, de Kok, if it is to deceive my brother.' She smiled. 'It will have to be the best lie we have ever told.'

'I will think more of it while I watch,' he said, 'and be not afraid, it will be a fine lie, a very fine one indeed.'

In the morning they rode on and before crossing the plain decided to have a last look at the village. Zwart Piete, seeing the smoke of the burning huts, might have come back. If he had been there they would see his spoor. Unpleasant as the sight had been on the previous day it was now much worse. The bodies of the dead stank of putrefaction, those without abdominal wounds were grotesquely swollen, while others, partially devoured, revoltingly disfigured, lay as they had been left by the night scavengers, which, hiding in the vicinity, would return with the dusk to continue their foul work.

The big tree in the middle of the village was covered with vultures which sat unmoved, while others already gorged to such an extent that they could not fly, waddled away, clicking their beaks, or running clumsily along the ground tried to rise, flapping their enormous mouse-grey wings.

For a few days, for a week perhaps, this would go on and then nothing would be left except the white splinters of bones and the skulls that were almost indestructible.

As they rode past a hut which was not entirely destroyed a hyena with an assegai through its body tried to crawl away. Automatically they raised their guns. A few yards farther on they saw another hyena dead, speared, and two dead jackals. Beyond them, propped against a broken wall, was a wounded Kaffir.

He was strangely ugly, very old, with a creased, wizened face. Beside him stood a sheaf of assegais and round him, perched on the blackened walls, were vultures waiting for the end.

'Shall I shoot?' de Kok asked, raising his gun.

The Kaffir's eyes met hers and Sara heard herself saying, 'No, there has been enough death here.'

Why had she said that? Never before had she spared a Kaffir.

Why did this little brown man covered in dust and blood with his twists of greasy hair falling like the tails of lizards over his face remain unmoved and unafraid when threatened? Why did he sit there with his arms folded over his chest waiting impassively, his eyes fixed so unblinkingly on her own?

'What is your name?' she asked.

'My name, white woman,' the Kaffir repeated. 'What is my name to you? I have so many names. Which shall I give you? Some of them are terrible. Once I was called The Little Flower. That was by a woman whom I loved greatly also; it was many years ago. At another time I have been called N'yala because I was so swift. Some have called me the Lion, others Tiger. Mamba I am called and Rinkals because of the venom that I can spit, but mostly I am called The Little Cloud, for I come before the storm. Behold the storm,' he said, making a gesture, 'where there was much there is now nothing. These people, dogs and sons of dogs, doubted my magic and they are gone. I breathed upon them and out of my breath came Zulus.'

'Are you not afraid?' de Kok asked. How dared he mock at them, to bandy words?

'Let me kill him, mie meisie,' he said to Sara. 'Ride on and let me kill this man.'

'Did you ask if I was afraid?' the Kaffir said. 'Or is it possible that my ears deceived me? That I, who caused these people to be destroyed and who sent for you to come to succour me should be afraid. Afraid of a woman who dresses like a man and a yellow Bastard?' he laughed. 'Destroy me,' he said, 'and you will never find the man you seek. I have seen him, I know him well, a fine young man, wild and full of ardour with hair as black as the night and eyes like the stones which burn. A young man who may do great things or ——' his voice faded away.

'Or what?' Sara asked.

'Or not do great things,' the Kaffir said. 'It is thus I have seen him.'

'Tell me more,' Sara said.

'If I were well I would tell you more, but a sick man cannot consult the dead. If, when the body is weak I send my spirit among them it might not return, the tie between my spirit and my body not being strong enough to recall it.'

'If you can do all these things how is it that you are wounded?' de Kok asked.

'That, for an ignorant Bastard, is an intelligent question and the answer lies not in the small mystery of my wound, but in the much greater one of my being alive where all else is dead. Now I have spoken enough,' he closed his eyes.

Sara dismounted and went towards him. De Kok covered her advance with his gun, pointing it at the Kaffir's breast.

The girl was mad, as mad, as reckless as her brother whose servant he was.

'Let me see your wound,' the girl said.

'There it is.' The Kaffir showed her a gash in his thigh. 'It is nothing; with good mouti it would be well in a week, but without mouti, without food, or water, it will bring death; and they,' he pointed to the vultures perched about him, 'would consume me. That,' he said, 'is their gratitude for the many I have given to them, for the killings I have caused.'

Turning to de Kok Sara said, 'Put up your gun, we will keep this man.'

'Keep him, mie meisie? What for?'

'Because I say we will keep him. Dismount and put him on your horse.'

With the Kaffir gripping its mane, with Sara riding beside him and de Kok leading the horse, they made for a group of trees by the river some four miles away. Here Sara decided to camp, while de Kok cast about for signs of his master.

The Kaffir was helped off the horse and made as comfortable as possible while Sara considered the question of his wound. As far as she could see no muscles were severed and if it could be kept clean there was no reason why it should not heal quickly. He had lost blood and must be fed, but with food and water and the flies kept away, there should be no difficulty in curing him. Leaving him propped against a tree with his spears beside him she went out to look for some herbs near the water.

Finding what she wanted, she came back and showed them to him. He nodded his head. This was good mouti. Sara rolled them in her hands, bruising them and working them, till their juices began to run out and then pointing to the wound asked him if he was ready. Setting his teeth he allowed her to dress his leg. In the distance she heard a shot. De Kok had killed something; tonight they would have fresh meat.

Before dark de Kok came back with a stien buck and said he had picked up Zwart Piete's trail. He had recognised his way of arranging the stones on which he cooked.

4

In the laager Tante Anna was talking to Sannie. Everything was very quiet and everyone subdued. The commando was not back yet and in the minds of each was the thought of how many empty saddles there would be when it returned. How many dead and how many wounded?

'A man's love is like cream, Sannie,' the old woman said. 'It ripens and then when the moment comes it must be churned before it turns bad.'

'And yet you always say the best butter is made when the cream is slightly sour, Tante Anna,' Sannie answered absent-mindedly. This trick of talking in parables was a weakness of her aunt's.

'Sour, yes, but not rotten.'

'And you think Hendrik looks sour?'

'Ja, sour as sour-lemon, mie Sannie.'

'I don't want to marry him,' Sannie burst out. 'It was his son I loved.'

'Ja, and it's his son's son you are going to bear. You are certain, Sannie?' she asked.

'Ach, ja, I am certain.'

'Then when he comes back you will marry him.' God help him, she thought.

Sannie, looking sullen, consented. She had always known it would be the one or the other, and now apparently it was to be both. But she did not want both, she wanted her lover. She wanted his arms about her, to feel him near her, desirous of her. Hendrik revolted her now. The way he had held her when they had danced came back to her. She did not want those hands on her. Coarse, old and searching, they frightened her. She realised that his attraction, when she had weighed him in her mind against his son, had been due to the resemblance between them. She had seen in Hendrik a more mature, a more certain Herman, and when her body had called to the boy her mind had gone out to the man. But it was with the body that one loved and clasped close, the wisdom of discretion faded. With Herman gone the very resemblance of the man to his son, of the living to the dead, turned her from him, distorting the traits she had loved till by their very resemblance they subtly offended her, making what had been lovely, gross, what had been fine, small. The look in his eyes was Herman's look, it was hungry, but without gaiety. The scent of his body was Herman's scent, but it was bitter and acrid, as if it had gone stale. And yet soon, to save herself and her child she must give herself to this man, deliver the body that Herman had loved to his father.

'It is not good to be a woman,' she said.

'It is very good. For women get everything both great and small. We are the fire; and men, ach, men are nothing. Flint and steel which strike useless sparks. Men are empty drums which make much noise about small things, while we are the vessels, carrying the future in our wombs.'

'Ja, Tante Anna, vessels to be filled by men,' Sannie said angrily.

'It is not their fault that they are made like that, mie Sannie. And what do they get out of it? Their potency is a burden, their lack of it, if they lose it, a reproach. Ach, sis, I am often sorry for men, now that I am no longer young, that is. Listen,' she went on, 'Hendrik is a fine man, a rich man.'

'Ja, Tante Anna, a fine old man,' Sannie said, 'and because his son's son is quickening I must hold him in my arms. But you are right, I will do it. It is the only way.' Yet in her heart she did not hate Hendrik. It was something to have a man like Hendrik van der Berg tame to her hand. A man whom all feared, trembling when he was near her with the urgency of his desire. And seeing Herman dead had cured her of Herman. He had looked so young, such a boy, such a foolish boy. Already the past was fading, it had not lasted long, and at times it almost seemed as if it had never been, as if she had dreamed of those afternoons under the Kaffir-boom and the night of the dance in her wagon.

5

Away among the mountains Zwart Piete was camping. He had shot a koodoo cow and with his horse knee-haltered, grazing near him he looked about for three flat stones on which to cook. Arranging them in a triangle he made a small pile of dry grass between them; on this he arranged twigs, dropping them lightly, pointing upwards and onto the twigs he put fragments of game dung; there was plenty of it about now that he was back among the herds. Striking the flint and steel he had in his brass tinder box, he blew up the charred rags and rotten wood it contained and lit the grass. As the fire took, he added bigger pieces of dung, and the sweet, almost invisible, smoke of the mis rose in a thin column.

He was quite content. Up here alone in these highlands he had found what he wanted; a peace, a silence, where secure from interruption he could think.

In a few days he would go back, by then the water in

the spruits would be run down, but now he would enjoy himself. It was very pleasant here, though colder at night than he liked. If only Sara and de Kok had been with him it would have been perfect. He wondered if the Boers had attacked the kraal yet. They might have with de Kok to guide them. He was sorry to have missed the battle. He was always sorry when he missed the chance of killing a Kaffir.

The stars came out, there seemed to be more of them up here. There seemed to be more of everything; it was a fine big country he had found. With so much game he need not worry about lions except for his horse. Getting up he caught him and sat holding him till the dawn. He would sleep when it grew hot.

6

Johannes van Reenen was surprised when Hendrik said he wished to marry his daughter. He would have been still more surprised if his sister-in-law had not prepared the way for this proposal by dropping ponderous hints about the possibility of his doing so.

Anna de Jong was so often right. It was, when he came to think of it, one of the reasons that he disliked her so much. Her sister had never been right about anything; she had always been gently, sweetly wrong. And now, if Hendrik did marry Sannie, which he would, Tante Anna would come and look after him. She had promised to do so. He did not doubt that she would do it most excellently well, but there were great objections to Tante Anna, very great objections. He sighed and looked after Hendrik who had just left him. A hundred reasons against Sannie's marriage occured to him now that it was too late to use them. She was too young, which she wasn't. That she looked after him and he could not spare her. That she might not be certain in her mind. That difference in age was too great. He had said none of these things and really it did not matter, for none of them were good reasons and Hendrik would have overridden them all. Also, since she was marriageable, Hendrik van der Berg was a good match. He was rich. He was a strong man who would look after her. His Sannie would be safe in his hands and yet it seemed only such a short time ago that she had been a baby pulling at his beard, and now she was a woman. Was more of a woman than even he, her father, knew.

All round him people were bustling about, packing their wagons. The loads were being relashed, riems tightened, brake-blocks readjusted. A party of Kaffirs were working at the drift trimming down the banks. Tomorrow they would break laager and move off. Once more the great wheels would turn, lumbering on their way.

CHAPTER IX

I

SINCE it was to be marriage, since no one saw any reason for delay, and Anna de Jong every reason for haste, it took place at once, the last event in that laager; took place while the Kaffirs were inspanning the oxen and chasing the last chickens to put them in their coops.

Anna de Jong wanted security for her niece, also she wished to get Sannie married while she was still stupid with grief and dulled into acceptance by her pain. Taking advantage of the girl's desire to get it over, to know the worst and end the suspense of waiting, she had hurried matters on. Sannie numb and acquiescent, her mind and body blunted, as pliable as dough in her hands, not caring how things went. Later she might change; would change certainly, for nature was not to be put down, but bending beneath the blows of life, would rise again, triumphant. If things were delayed Sannie might refuse to marry Hendrik or waiting, consent, and then give birth to a full-time child which would cause comment and much lifting of eyebrows among the women who were not to be deceived in these matters.

Thus the marriage which should have been a festival was hurried, almost furtive, during which men looked round at their wagons wondering if the loads were evenly distributed and lashed fast, while the women hoped that none of their poultry would be left, that the jars of salted butter would not be broken and that a calf born on the previous day would be strong enough to run with its mother.

'Wey ... Wey,' the drivers shouted as the oxen, clumped in spans together, raised their heads waiting for the riems to be put about their horns. Whips clapped, dogs barked, a rooster crowed.

Devoid of sentiment, Sannie's marriage was nothing, lost in the stark reality of the move, of anxieties about the livestock, of the bustle, which was only in abeyance during the ceremony; of the tragic things which had happened in this place, of the fact that here was no young man but an old one; all helped, adding their mite to the disillusion, turning romantic fantasy into practical necessity, travestying love, into the desire of a man for a woman as he had a horse or a gun, something that could be owned, the desire for an essential possession. When it was over there was no talk of it; the people did not drift away in groups; they hurried off to finish their own affairs. To see that no mistake was made.

Within an hour the wagons were moving and the first one, Hendrik van der Berg's, rumbled with locked back wheels through the drift. At the back of it, her feet over the brake handle, sat Sannie, his wife.

Behind his wagon came the others, matched span after matched span, red, black and parti-coloured, but Martinus the singer, as he had come to be called, had a span of creamy yellow oxen.

Like a snail uncoiling from its shell the wagons left the circle of the laager, faltered and streamed out as the trek chains took the strain.

To break them from the ground softened by the storm the oxen had to exert themselves, the achter-oxen almost on their knees as the drivers shouted to the voorloopers to swing their teams while sharply as pistol shots they cracked their long whips.

Once again the trek moved on, leaving their dead, their memories and the bones of the wild beasts they had killed for meat. The laager was gone, nothing of it was left except the great ring of wheel marks round the trees in its centre.

Once again the disselbooms pointed north and the great wheels turned.

At midday Paul Pieters rode up to Hendrik and said: 'This is where I leave you.'

The two men shook hands, Paul Pieters swirled his horse and cantered back to his people; the long snake of wagons broke into two, dividing, one segment going on, the other turning west, swinging away with Paul Pieters on his grey at its head. As they left they shouted and waved their arms in farewell, in greeting, in the hope of meeting again.

'Tot Geseen. Tot Geseen,' they cried, their voices growing fainter, their wagons smaller and smaller till at last nothing of the convoy was to be seen except a cloud of dust above the trees, a cloud no bigger than the hand of a child.

Paul Pieters was going to the plain which had been inhabited by the Kaffirs; he had decided it was good enough. Good soil, good grass and good water, all in fact that a reasonable man could desire, all that he could with justice ask of God. His wagons followed the spoor of the commando. They would have to clear a way through the kloof, but apart from that, there would be no difficulties. He had found what he sought; here on this plain he and his people would rest.

The going of Paul Pieters and his trek had an effect on Hendrik van der Berg's people. Paul, with his immense vitality, had in the short time he had been with them buoyed them up. His laughter, his rude fervour, his enthusiasm, had all become definite factors in their lives; without him and his followers things seemed flat and though still numerous they felt very alone and isolated after his departure. In addition to this, things no longer went so well. Day after day cattle deaths were reported by the herders. The dreaded heart water increased, gall sickness, due to the young grass wilting under the hot sun, caused many deaths. Three-day sickness, which as a rule animals recovered from if left alone, meant abandoning beasts, since there was no time to wait for them to recover. This factor of time became an overpowering one governing them, causing them to move on

almost hysterically. Voorwaarts. Voorwaarts. They passed
many promising places but none satisfied Hendrik. He knew
what the promised land would look like. It had been re-
vealed to him. Continually he described it to them, ecstatic-
ally, till at last it became as real to the others as it was to
him.

'It is below a range,' he said, 'and partly surrounded by
high hills; it is watered by many streams with big trees
growing scattered about in it. Trees where the cattle can
stand in the shade, up to their bellies in the buffle-grass.
There is a vlei surrounded by small fountains which re-
plenish the lake in its centre, and the whole is alive with
game and filled with birds whose brilliant plumage is a joy
to the eyes, whose song is a delight to the ears. There are
flowers everywhere and the humming of the honey bees as
they fly from bloom to bloom is never ending. Such is
Canaan, and it lies beyond us to the north. Voorwaarts.'

Voorwaarts, and again the oxen leaned patiently against
their yokes, and with their hocks bent under them, drew the
heavy wagons on. Whips clapped, men shouted and each
night they out-spanned ten miles, fifteen miles, nearer to
their goal. The leisurely advances of the old days were
done with. No longer could they trek comfortably, moving
only a few miles each day. In a fever of anxiety they surged
on to seek this land that Hendrik promised them. A land
flowing with milk and honey.

Of all the people, old Anna de Jong was the only one who
mistrusted Hendrik's inspiration. She had once seen a map
of Africa. It was shaped like a pear set upside down. The
Cape where they had come from was at the one end and it
seemed to her that soon they would reach the other.

'Magtig, what a country. What a size it was.'

She had many arguments of a geographical nature with
Johannes about it all, and about their position on this inverted pear of a continent. But when at last they reached
a stream which ran due north, she was certain that they

had discovered the source of the Nile. For in Africa no rivers run north, they all run from west to east or east to west. In this most of the others agreed with her, and they called the river the Nylstrom.

Ja, they were now in Egypt, and soon no doubt would find the Red Sea. Each day she questioned the coloured herders and the hunters on this point and verified their observations in the Scriptures.

Certainly the country was changing in character, it was more heavily wooded, better watered and hotter than anything she had imagined possible. Aloes as tall as trees grew out of the veld, and there were palm bushes in clumps as big as a loaded wagon.

2

Sannie, Mevrou van der Berg as she was now, continued day after day to sit at the back of the leading wagon. Oddly content, she sat staring backwards into the past, along the road she had come. Her pregnancy brought with its bodily discomfort a spiritual satisfaction in which her mind moved slowly, a thing apart, through a void tinged with expectancy. Instead of living, she was producing life. Caught in the trap, she waited patiently for that which would inevitably occur; when it had occurred she would go on, but till then she could float statically on the stream, unnoticing, unperturbed and unrepentant.

She had no fear. She was young and strong and her bones, still soft with girlish immaturity, would part freely, bending like the branches of a supple tree when her time came; and having parted, knit again. It was to that end she had been made. A vessel filled soon to overflow.

Hendrik's attentions which were frequent, she endured stoically; they were quite apart from life. Divorced from all reality, they were merely something unpleasant which occured at irregular intervals. She knew by the flame in his eyes when they were coming and armoured herself against him by sending her spirit out of her body to rest, perched like a bird, till he had done. This, though the act was the same, bore no relation to the rough tenderness of Herman. Here was no young flame leaping upwards, but a dull fire that burnt savagely as it was fanned by contact. To Hendrik she was something to be used, and he used her often, both by day and by night. But she minded as little as a cup would mind who drank from it. She was not sentient, she could no more be ruffled than china and, unlike china, she could not be broken.

3

Riding ahead of his people on his black horse, Hendrik, his hair slightly greyer, the skin over his high cheek bones stretched a little tighter, his eyes more savage, searched expectantly for that which had been promised him.

Guided by God, driven on by his vision, inspired, he was indefatigable. His reason for starting on the trek, his indignation with the British, was forgotten in this attack upon the horizon which retreated perpetually, running like a live thing from him. Voorwaarts, Voorwaarts. Distance was something to be devoured, to be destroyed, the meaningless miles which lay between him and the fruition of his dream, the land of plenty where Sannie should bring forth his seed.

Hour after hour as he rode he dreamed of his child. Sitting slackly in his saddle with his eyes veiled, he let his mind wander. Her pregnancy was the only satisfaction he got from Sannie, for though he took her often he got nothing from her and left her unassuaged. Left her crushed and gasping, but still triumphant, for if her body was his her spirit remained inviolate and apart. His strength was as nothing against the impalpable resistance of a girl so small, so fragile that he could have broken her like a twig, and against this passive acquiescence he raged, flinging the weapon of his potency upon it, striving vainly to conquer the citadel of her integrity, to make her his.

One day he would succeed, of this he was certain, for in the end weakness must succumb to power. Slowly and inevitably he would batter her down, weakening her by his renewed and unresting attacks.

God would not abandon him. God would one day, in His appointed time, give him the fullness of Sannie, and God would lead them to Canaan.

From God he demanded signs, and God gave him signs.

Once, when short of water the Boers had stood gazing at a trickle which ran out from between two rocks, he had cursed them for their lack of faith and, dismounting, rolled away one of the great stones. Water in abundance leapt forth, the very eye of the spring was exposed; held in abeyance for centuries, the water, as cold as ice, bubbled out, tumbling down the thirsty hillside.

Day by day the reverence of his folk for him increased, and daily his power grew, as unfailingly, never hesitating he led them on.

From where he was, seven or eight miles ahead of the wagons, Hendrik watched the mountains in the northwest burning. A pillar of smoke by day, a pillar of fire by night. Once more God had directed him, given him guidance. His sacrifice had been accepted, the death of his only son had pleased the Lord of hosts. This was the only interpretation of such events.

Confident of success, he led the wagons towards the fire. To him it was a signal, a sign and not a danger; to the others Hendrik van der Berg, the man who could make water gush from the arid rocks, was a prophet before whom the flames would part allowing them to pass unscathed through their fury. Unhesitatingly he led; unhesitatingly they followed, breasting the low hills, creaking and rolling down the cup-like depressions between them, always north, the fire still moving slowly towards them on their right.

Long before it reached them they would have passed on. There was no wind and the summer grass, exuding moisture, choked down the tangled, inflammable carpet of the last year's growth. There was danger, but it was negligible, till, as they reached an open valley between the mountains, a breeze sprang up. At first it came in small gusts which hurried the fire on, carrying the smoke in low, rolling clouds towards them. Then freshing, it took hold, and seizing the flames, flung them forward like a weapon.

Inexorably, its arc widening, the fire swept down hungrily, threatening to engulf them.

Halting the wagons, Hendrik shouted to the men to follow him, and rode forward to light the veld in front of them.

This was his answer to fire, more fire. The way to meet flame was with flame. Working feverishly with torches of grass in their hands, they sent a line of fire leaping and tumbling away from them down wind, a wave which devouring everything in front of it, would arrest the oncoming sea of flame, and another, burning more slowly, towards it.

From the wagons the women watched the black strip between the fires growing. Small hawks and insect-eating birds hung hovering above the smoke, diving into it for the fuddled insects which rose with singed wings from the ground, or stooped for the small animals that with burnt feet tried to escape.

Mounting their horses the Boers galloped wildly in the direction of the main fire and, turning, lit the veld again; burning it inwards to meet the slowly advancing flames of the first fire that was creeping up against the wind, trickling forward, licking at the grass with small orange-coloured tongues.

To be safe they must have a big piece of burnt grass, an island on which their wagons and their herds could stand and weather the storm which swept towards them.

Game caught between the two fires swung panic-stricken to the still-open flanks. Martinus the singer was knocked down by a running rhinoceros; his horse killed under him, he was picked up by Hendrik van der Berg.

Standing apart from the others, Sannie saw a lioness carrying one of her cubs in her mouth, galloping with great bounds away from the crackling flames. Coming to the second line of fire the lioness arched her back, brought her powerful quarters under her, sprang the oncoming wall of fire and stood twitching her tail on the burnt grass so near to the girl that she could see the singed ends of her whiskers. A coloured man shot her and, picking up the cub, about to kill it when Sannie took it from him. Spitting and snarling, she carried it back to her wagon.

It was spotted like a kitten; holding it by the scruff of its neck, away from her, staring at it as it wriggled and tried with small bared claws to reach her arm, she saw Hendrik, carrying Martinus on his saddle and followed by the others, thunder past her to bring up the cattle and horses. Their mounts, plunging and rearing, as the hair round their heels singed, were forced by their heavy bits and the blows of their riders' sjamboks, to face the hot ground which burnt their hoofs. Soon, bellowing and milling, the herds began to arrive. Cattle, horses, sheep, donkeys and goats were driven onto the burnt grass by the whips of the herders, as the fire, now roaring and screaming, swept up to them, broke at the black island on which they stood, and ran round them. Clouds of thick white smoke, their undersides reflecting the red glare of the flames which licked upwards at the trees, jumping, in a last frantic effort to destroy before they were carried on, drifted over them. Hardly able to breathe, their eyes streaming, the people waited, praying for the end, for the fire to pass.

In an hour it had gone, and Hendrik led them on, up the smoke-blackened hills where there was no grazing, and where little pillars of smoke still rose from the burning dung of beasts; a country of sharp jagged rocks, of tortured leafless trees, of dead stumps burning, charred, streaked with incandescent ash. They had been saved from a hideous death, and beyond them, beyond this dead stretch of mountain was Canaan. So Hendrik said.

Fearing nothing, his thighs clipped to his saddle, he rode up and down the line encouraging them. Soon, he told them they would arrive. That place, which had for so long been distant was now near, the day of rest at hand. The place where they should lie down in the green pastures and be led by the still waters.

Night coming, they camped in the desolation of the fire-swept foothills. In the distance they still saw the fire climbing the mountains to the east, hanging poised along their crests and disappearing into the valleys beyond them.

All round them big dead trees still burnt and would burn for days. The country was a desert, a desolation, but no one had been hurt except Martinus whose leg was broken. They had lost only the weakest and most easily spared of their stock; those animals which footsore or sick had been unable to keep up when the main herds had been galloped in.

4

For two days they laboured, penetrating deeper and deeper into the range. For two days their cattle had not eaten. If there had not been plenty of water they would not have been able to go on, nor could they have returned. It was a test of faith; their faith in their leader, and in their God. They had come to the place whence there was no going back and, therefore, with all haste, they pressed on, driving their jaded beasts to their uttermost and beyond it. More than ever now they looked to Hendrik to save their herds; Hendrik, the prophet, who was so certain of himself, so assured of his revelation that none doubted him nor thought that he might be wrong or fail.

On the third day he rode up a mountain side and, crossing its flat top, saw, instead of another range, a wide expanse of country spread out beneath him. There, three thousand feet below lay the promised land. There was the vlei, there were the trees, the herds of game, the rivers — all five of them.

The trek was over, here was their home.

Taking off his hat, he rode to the edge of the precipice and looked down. Never had he even dreamed of so rich a land. To carry such herds of game the grass must be good, to grow such trees the soil must be deep, and water, the one thing which was so scarce in Africa, was here in plenty. Not only the rivers that he had seen at first, but small springs, which, overflowing, ran down from the higher land. Water, which from its situation, could be led where they wanted it. Already he saw the furrows cut along the hillsides, the fruit trees and the crops. Where there was now game he saw cattle, where there were now no people he saw many.

Wheeling his horse, he rode back at a canter. All that they had to do now was to find a road down — no more than that, and soon ten men were in the saddle scouring the mountains, shouting to each other. By nightfall they had found a way for their starving cattle and, leaving the wagons where they were, they drove them down.

The herders gave glowing reports of the valley which, by their extravagance, perturbed Anna de Jong. Somewhere in all this there must be a catch. It was too simple. Ja, magtig, it was much too simple and much too good to be true. To set out like this in search of the promised land and then to find it; she shrugged her massive shoulders. They could say what they liked, but such things did not happen. Still, perhaps there might be somewhere down there where she could plant her pumpkins, some spot in which they would grow. Though it was late in the season to plant them this year. She wondered doubtfully if Johannes was as skilful a farmer as her poor Jappie had been. Deciding that it was unlikely, for Jappie had had a way with things; his hand on the land had been tender and coaxing.

Louisa's child had been born, a girl, and luckily for her
mother, not only very pale in colour but very like Jappie;
a butter-coloured miniature of the man whose daughter she
was. Sometimes Tante Anna loved the child, at others she
told Louisa to take it away, but she never forgot it and was,
though she would never acknowledge it, profoundly jealous
of Louisa who, walking proudly erect, her hips swaying, carried her master's bastard tied in a breyed goat-skin on her
back, its small head wobbling as she moved about her work.

Anna, the child was called. Anna, after Anna de Jong,
who was its father's wife.

5

It took them a week to find a wagon-way down to the
valley below them, and another week to prepare it. Cutting
trees, moving rocks and building up the hollows which
would otherwise have broken the backs of the wagons, with
banks of loose-packed stones. Even when completed, following the contours of the mountain, zigzagging dizzily along
its face, it was less a way down than a possible way — a way
in which disaster, instead of being certain, became only a
conceivable eventuality to the more optimistic; a probability
to the others.

Tante Anna, who, sitting in her chair at the top, had
spent much time watching the operations in progress, voiced
the general view when she said:

'Ja, we shall get down, perhaps even faster than we wish,
but we shall never get up again. Still, if it is the will of
God' — she was doubtful about God's will in this matter —
'that we must go, then go we will.'

After all, with Jappie dead, it did not matter much what
happened to her. But all the same, she was not going to
tempt Providence too far by going down in her wagon. This,
she felt, would be unfair both to Providence and to herself.
No, from the very first she had decided to ride down on

Jappie's dun-coloured horse. She eyed him speculatively. It was many years since she had ridden. The problem of mounting occupied her; its solution was the building of a ramp up which she could walk. Dismounting again at the bottom would solve itself if she ever got there. If there was no other way, she would wait until the horse lay down.

It was strange up here on the top of the world, with a blackened waste behind one and a vast green world spread out in front; a panorama of flat, rich bush veld which stretched on, apparently endless. It was, Anna thought, unnaturally green, vivid, livid, different in every way from anything she had seen before. But then, naturally, since they were now in Egypt it would be different and unhome-like. It was strange too, to be living, with most of the men away, in a community of women and children without sheep or cattle and only a few saddle horses, dogs and poultry about.

Ach, ja, if Hendrik van der Berg got them down safely he was a great man, a very great man indeed. She gave the wide sea of bush another look and closed her eyes. It was no good worrying, what happened would happen, and pricks were things for young people to kick against; she had long since learnt that by the use of one's intelligence they could be walked round. Getting the wagons down was Hendrik's business, getting herself down her own, and anyway, she would sooner go down than up, and it was God's mercy that it was down, that, at least, was something to be thankful for. She called Louisa to keep the flies off her face and settled herself for sleep.

Two days later they started on what many considered an impossible feat, that of getting the wagons, some of them carrying a load of over a ton, down a precipitous mountain side. Even with the practice acquired on their long trek, the descent taxed the ingenuity of the Boers to their uttermost.

Taking the back wheels off the wagons and fastening tree trunks under their axles, they began to skid them down, behind half-spans of oxen. With each they sent men with riems tied to the back and the top of the load. The dangers were those of the wagon running away and overriding the oxen, or of its turning over and falling into the precipice. Twice the first wagon hung balanced precariously, and was held swaying till it righted.

Slowly, carefully, always on the verge of disaster, and always avoiding it, they reached the bottom at last. Fresh oxen were inspanned, and wagon after wagon rolled away, lumbering and swaying through the long grass that brushed their hubs.

After trekking a year and a half they had arrived.

Here they would die. Here their children would be born.

CHAPTER X

I

NEXT day, leaving Sara with her Kaffir, de Kok prepared to ride off in search of his master.

'I will be back soon,' he said. 'In two days — in three days at the most — I shall have found him.' Turning to the old Kaffir who squatted at the foot of a tree staring vacantly into space, he said: 'If anything happens to her while I am away then my master and I will hunt you. Ja, we will hunt you into your own kraal and flay you alive in front of your wives.'

The old man grinned and, pausing to spit, said: 'My kraal is destroyed and my wives are dead. And how would you catch me, Bastard, since I can change my form at will or, if it pleases me better, I can change yours. That, I think, is what I will do. It only remains for me to decide into what I shall change you, a snake perhaps. Or a mole. Or would you like to be a bird, Bastard?' he asked.

'Pah.' He spat again. 'Your mistress will be safe with me. I will ring her about with strong medicine and fence her with spears.'

'Spears,' de Kok said contemptuously. 'You are not a fighting man.'

The Kaffir's eyes flashed angrily.

'Stand fast, Bastard,' he shouted, 'and you shall judge my spears.' Seizing a branch, he dragged himself up and, leaning against the tree, stooped for his assegais, one after another they passed over de Kok's head, the first taking off his hat, the ring of wildebeeste hair on the shaft of the last whipping his cheek as it drove past him.

'Before I was a doctor I was a captain,' the old Kaffir said. 'Now go, yellow dog, and search out your master, and when you find him, which will be at dusk on the second day, say to him these words, say unto him that "The Little Cloud which precedes the storm" is waiting for him. Say to him that you have an old Kaffir who was once called "Little Flower," and who has been called "Mamba" and "Rinkals" in your camp, a man who is wise and knows what lies beyond the mountains.'

'Aye, I shall tell him all these things, and no doubt my master will be pleased,' de Kok said. 'So pleased,' he added, 'that he will beat me with his sjambok for not having shot you at once.'

And this was the man of whom Sara said they would make a servant, a drawer of water, a hewer of wood. Aye, one day, no doubt, she would want to catch an elephant so that it could collect the eggs from under the hens with its trunk, or python, because, curled up, it would be cool to sit upon. Still, a tame witch-doctor might be useful. Magic when all was said and done, remained magic; something incontrovertible.

Turning his horse, de Kok rode away, and two hours later, making a wide cast, picked up his master's spoor. Before dark on the second day, just as that accursed witch-doctor had said, he found Zwart Piete camped, about to turn back.

'Ach, you skelm, so you have spoored me. I knew you would.'

'Ja, baas. It is my business to spoor, and you left many traces for me to see.'

Zwart Piete smiled affectionately at his man. 'I left them knowing you would come when the waters ran down.'

'Ja, I have come, baas, and the baas's sister has come also.'

'Sara? Where is Sara?'

'Over there' — the Griqua pointed over his shoulder — 'and she has a Kaffir,' he added sadly. 'A witch-doctor who called me a yellow dog. She says she is going to tame him. At one time I thought only the baas was mad, but now I see that it is different. She is even madder than you. Perhaps it is the sun. Does the baas think it is the sun?' he asked.

'If she says she will tame him, then she will do so. But what of the Kaffirs? And the attack? Did you guide them well?'

'That is a sad story, baas,' de Kok said. 'It makes my heart sore to speak of it; please do not question me much.' He took a dirty rag from his pocket and wiped his eyes. 'They are gone, all those fine men, and the women, and the little children. Dead, baas, killed, eaten up by the impis that passed. There is nobody left but us. No white folk, no Kaffirs, no beasts, no wagons, not even a dog is left alive. Like a fire the impis swept over them.' He rose and made a sweeping, dramatic gesture. 'Ach, how we fought, shooting till the guns were red hot in our hands. Hundreds fell, hundreds, no, not hundreds, baas, thousands. Blood ran in rivers, and the shouts; ach, God, the shouts, the blood, the cries, and now nothing is left, baas; nothing. Only your sister and I escaped by the mercy of God, and the swiftness of our horses.'

Half-closing his eyes, he looked at his master. 'What shall we do now?' he asked. 'Shall we go on? Over there' — he pointed to the east — 'there are things to be seen. Listen, baas,' he said, 'we are not ordinary people, you, I and your sister, let us go and make a kingdom; let us conquer strange peoples, take wives and cattle, hunt elephants, find gold. We are not farmers, we are hunters, fighters; our path is that of the bullet, not of the plough.'

Zwart Piete was silent. De Kok's dreams coincided so well with his own. 'Come,' he said; 'we will go and find my sister.' He got up.

'And you will shoot that Kaffir, baas,' de Kok pleaded. 'I do not like him; he says he was once called "Little Flower." Ja, he smells, but not like a flower.'

'If I do not like him I will shoot him,' Zwart Piete said. 'Now bring my horse.'

When de Kok had gone, Sara wondered if she had been wise. Perhaps he had been right, perhaps she should have let him shoot the Kaffir. She could not think why she had not let him. She hated Kaffirs as much as her brother, and had killed nearly as many as he. Was it because he was old? Or because he had lain there so bravely, impassively fighting off the vermin which waited for his end? Or was it — this was a frightening thought — that she had not been able to kill him? That he had, as he said, sent for them? She tried to think backwards to get clear in her mind the impulse which had led her to go back to the village.

With his eyes on her face, the Kaffir said: 'There is much thought in your head, white woman, and your thoughts are like two yoked oxen which being strange to each other, and untrained, pull different ways. You have thoughts of me and why you did not slay me, and you have thoughts of your brother whom that yellow Bastard calls his master.' From a little raw-hide bag he wore round his neck he took some powder and dropped a pinch of it on the fire. 'Keep still, inkoose,' he said, 'and I will go a short way into the times that are coming. Time,' he went on, 'is round, like a neck-lace, what is passed and what is to come are one.'

A haze of smoke rose from the fire, hanging suspended above it neither rising nor falling, but within an apparently solid outline, writhed round a central vortex into which Sara could not see. Holding up his hand, the old man peered into it intently.

'This is very strange,' he muttered. 'Very strange indeed. Do you have women in your race whose hair is very long and pale, the colour of honey in sunlight?' he asked.

'Yes, we have them,' Sara said.

'And they are esteemed, considered beautiful above the others?'

'Yes.'

'Then it is such a one that I see with your brother. Also, she has pale eyes like a jackal, midway between green and yellow. He has much pleasure in this woman and also because she is beautiful, much trouble with her. Beautiful women always bring trouble, it follows them as flies follow meat. The woman who first called me "Little Flower" was like that, a slim, proud woman for whom I had to pay twenty cows, as much as for two ordinary women, and then she would not work, and finally betrayed me, for which I killed her, which was a mistake. Had I not slain her I should have got my cows back and many of them had had calves. Ai,' he said, 'but when one is young and hot blooded one does these things. A young man makes no profit from his wife's adulteries. Ai, ai, wisdom is only bought with years, discretion with weakness. Yes, I see him with this woman. I see also an older woman very fine and fat, like the wife of a chief, and men in white clothes with much hair on their faces, and many people moving all one way, in long lines yoked to one another like oxen, but they draw nothing. Also, I see many teeth of elephants — great piles of them. More than that, I cannot see, but your brother is a great man among these people. Perhaps when I am stronger I shall see more, perhaps I shall dare to venture further among the dead ones.'

'But my brother is well?' she asked. 'He is safe?'

'Oh, yes, he is well. He is sitting by his fire holding his horse. His stomach is full and he is happy. This woman does not trouble him yet, he has no thoughts of her. Now be at rest, inkoose, there is no danger neither for him nor for us. When danger is near I will tell you, and we will make provision for it. The vulture who will pick our bones is not yet on the wing. I have medicine against every danger and while I am near nothing can harm you for my spirit is very strong, it is much too strong for my body. Ai, it is braver than a lion, its vision stronger than the sight of an eagle and in strength greater than that of an elephant. Also,' he went on, 'you wonder what you will say to your brother, who is a notable hunter of Kaffirs, about me.' He paused and, smiling, said: 'Say this to the baas, your brother, that I am yours as a horse or an ox would be yours, and that will be the answer to his questions.'

That was the answer. That was what she said to Zwart Piete when he came back.

'He is mine, Piete,' she said and that settled it, as it would have had he been a cow or a sheep.

For a few more days they remained camped till the Kaffir was well enough to travel, talking of their plans. Rinkals, as they called him, knew the country to the east and north.

Fortunately, since they had come to fight, Sara and de Kok had plenty of ammunition.

Zwart Piete did not believe a word of de Kok's story of the disaster, but was amused by his desire to break away from the routine of the trek, amused too, at his grandiose ideas.

Now, at least, he would be able to realise his ambition of adventuring in the unknown mountains, of travelling through new country independently; and since they were untrammelled by wagons or live stock, they would be able to go fast. There was much to be done, much to see. Somewhere up there, he looked east, were settlements of white people — Portuguese whom he was curious to meet. They were all strong, with good horses beneath them and ammunition in plenty, they should go far. Life hung in front of him, a ripening fruit, ready to be plucked.

At first their progress was slow, the wound in the old Kaffir's leg making him lame and unable to trot. But as soon as he gained in strength they were astonished by his speed and endurance as he ran beside them for hours, holding on to the stirrup leather first of one and then of another.

Stopping only to kill for food, they went on swiftly, eating up the distance, leaving the ashes of their fires many miles apart. Seeing mountain ranges, crossing them and leaving them to fade into the horizon at their backs.

2

Sannie, much to his disgust, gave her lion cub to Jakalaas to look after. It was not in his nature to like lions, he said, and had the meisie realised what would happen, he asked. Today it was as big as a cat; ja, that was so, in a few months it would be as big as a dog, then as big as a small ox. Did the meisie intend him to look after it then? It followed him about now and people laughed. But would they laugh when it was big? Would he be welcome if he was followed by a lion? Would he be able to get another wife? Socially, there were innumerable objections to this thing the meisie had put upon him, and it was not fair, she knew he liked visiting people, liked sitting by other men's fires. Truly, the little lion made his heart sore. He was only a Kaffir, and a lion was too grand a thing for an old Kaffir like himself to possess.

Hendrik also was somewhat at a loss about the cub, but realising that women in Sannie's condition had queer fancies, he gave in about it. It was a pretty little creature as, quite tame now, it rolled and played about like a kitten. No doubt when she had her baby he would be able to dispose of it; till then it occupied her, and it seemed in some queer way to recognise that it owed its life to her. Abandoning all thought of Sannie and her lion, he set himself the task of reorganising his community. They had, on arrival, laagered as was their custom, but now, having spent some days riding round the neighbourhood, were anxious to take up their farms and get back to their normal way of life.

On the move, they got on well enough with each other, but any form of closely knit communal life was contrary to their natures, their ideal being the patriarchal family unit, but even this, to please them, must be sub-divided into its integral parts, of a man, his woman and their children.

What they liked was to live apart, so far apart that they could not see each other's smoke, and then at intervals to foregather for a nachtmaal, or inspanning their oxen to go on a tour of visiting which might last months, calling on everyone they knew, going even hundreds of miles to do so. There they would talk of crops and cattle, of hunting, or sit silently together for hours smoking. Nothing was too small to be mentioned, discussed, argued about; men and women sitting apart, each dealing with those matters which fell in their own sphere.

In this way too, the young people courted, sitting in a room lit by a candle stuck in a bottle. The length of the candle a clear indication to the visiting swain as to how welcome he was, for when it went out he was expected to leave.

All this, their old culture, their way of life, they were anxious to resume, to force their lives back into its static pattern. It was as much for this as for anything else that they had left the Cape where outside influences, French and English, were creeping in, where the customs to which they clung were being modified and their ways laughed at, even by the more progressive of their own people.

Canaan as they had named the district, was not as flat as it had at first appeared to be; rather was it like a broken cup, surrounded on three sides by the almost sheer walls of the mountain they had come down, and on the other by a little jagged rankie. Still, the bottom of the cup was a large area, amply big enough to accommodate the thirty families van der Berg had with him.

It was shaped like the palm of a man's hand, the five fingers being streams which, rising below the mountains, flowed down into the vlei, and seeped out again as a single river at the lowest point between the bosses of the inside of the wrist, the fracture where the rankie was divided from the main mountain system. Apart from the five main streams there were innumerable other small fountains all round the base of the berg, and it was here that the Boers settled, in the kloofs, where, hidden from each other, they could live their secluded self-contained lives. In time of flood they would be able to reach each other by keeping on the high ground near the headwaters while at other seasons the rivers were all fordable on horseback.

The apportionment of farms was done in the usual manner. Hendrik had first pick and after him the others drew lots, and then rode off their properties.

To do this the head of each family or his representative started from where the last man had stopped and rode for two hours in each direction. As he changed his course, he would dismount to make a rough beacon and, mounting, gallop on, coming back in the end to the point he had started from.

Roughly, the farms were sixteen miles in circumference, and varied in size from ten to twenty thousand morgen. Though theoretically they were square, in actual fact they were of all shapes, natural obstacles having been avoided and changes of direction made to include springs or patches of particularly good grazing. Each man, as soon as he had chosen his farm, drew out, collected his herds and began to build his homestead.

Hendrik's nearest neighbours were, on the one side, Johannes van Reenen, with whom Tante Anna had, as he had feared, joined forces; and on the other, Martinus, the singer, who had left Paul Pieters' trek in order to court Marietje de Wett, and who after sufficient delay to satisfy even the most malicious tongues, had at last, almost maidenly in her reluctant pleasure, consented to marry him. Thus, in January of the year eighteen thirty-eight, was the settlement of Canaan begun. The homesteads all going up simultaneously round the crescent-shaped foot of the mountains; little huts, which would be replaced by bigger ones whose places would in time be taken by houses.

The silence of the low veld was broken for ever. These people had come to stay. It was broken like the shell of an egg. The sharp ring of axes sounded, the cries of drivers to their oxen and the barking of dogs. Where there had been peace there was now activity.

3

The site that Hendrik van der Berg had chosen for his house was, by accident, a beautiful one. Beauty, other than that of live stock, meant nothing to him, and in beasts the best were the most beautiful. Cows with roomy barrels, wide hips, big well-hung udders with long tits, easy to grasp; or fast horses that could carry weight and stay; or strong mules or sheep that clipped ten pounds of wool. These were Hendrik's standards — the standards of all his race who, seeking the practical, so often stumbled on sheer delight.

Here, where Hendrik outspanned near the mountain, its wall was split into a sharp kloof which was filled with the growth of a great wild fig from whose branches roots hung growing downwards, like straggling beards, to seek the soil and under the tree, shaded by it, was a deep pool of water fed by a strong spring. Further away were four tall appies-doorns, which from their size must have been hundreds of years old. Beyond them there was nothing but bush-veld, and the land dropped leaving the view open onto the tree-tops — a view as wide as a view of the sea.

Between the spring and the appies-doorns Hendrik kicked away a tussock of grass. This would be one corner, of his house. Calling his boys, he told them to scrape the place clean, and then driving four pegs into the bare earth, he outlined the walls. It was thirty feet by twelve. Along the line he laid, the Kaffirs dug holes with their crowbars, round holes very close to each other, and emptied them of earth with their fingers, going down as deep as they could reach working till they were up to their shoulders. Others cut trees of hard wood, Kaffir wach 'n bietje, suikerbos, hartekoal and tambouti, which they sunk into the holes, ramming them tight. More trees were cut for the rafters of the roof, reeds from the vlei for thatch, and earth was mixed with water, the Kaffirs turning it with their shovels and finally tramping it with bare feet till it reached the consistency of thick whipped cream.

This dagga they flung against the rough wood poles filling in the spaces between them, and finally plastering the whole, inside and out. The floor was also made of dagga and finished off with a layer of cow dung mixed with blood. These floors when dry turned black and took a fine polish.

The house had two rooms, each of which had a window that was fitted with a wooden shutter. The roof on the north side projected eight feet and covering the open stoep rested on massive poles up which creepers could be grown. In a fortnight Hendrik's house was finished, a hut not much better than a Kaffir's, but nevertheless, a home, somewhere to live while he developed his farm and quarried stone from the mountain side for the house he intended to build when he had time.

4

Tante Anna was pleased to be settled again. Now things could be done as they should be done. Lands were being made, trees planted, kraals put up as permanent structures. Here courting could be conducted on approved lines, babies born solemnly, with privacy, instead of like calves on the veld. Ja, even death lost some of its terrors when one could be planted neatly in a corner of one's own farm; planted in the soil one knew, on the land that one had served.

What she missed were her pots of preserves, and even if one made confiet what could one put it into? Not that one could make it, because they had no sugar. But if one had sugar?

Sugar, cloth for clothes, ammunition and a few tools were all that a community like theirs needed from the outside. Perhaps the Lord would provide these things. Hendrik said He would and, anyway, there was no need for the Almighty to hurry, for they had enough of everything to last some time, even sugar enough for ordinary purposes, if not for the making of the preserves she liked so much.

Salt also, they were short of, but one of the men had discovered a salt pan not twenty miles away and one could do without sugar more easily than salt. Hendrik saw the finger of God in this discovery, but Hendrik saw the finger of God in everything. If this was so the Almighty must have many hands, each furnished with a hundred prying fingers, poking, feeling, touching, disturbing, interfering. Sometimes Anna de Jong wished that God knew when to let well alone. When to let sleeping men lie.

It was now cool enough to go and visit Sannie.

She called for her cart.

The girl was not well and a little mad about her lion which would, without doubt, eat her baby when it was born. Ja, and then what would Sannie say? Many times she had told her that the lion would eat the baby, but her argument had lost force as there was as yet no child; but when there was, it would be too late. What, after all, was a baby to a lion? A mouthful. Less than a piece of confiet to her. If we only had sugar, she thought. And definitely, a house was no place to keep a lion.

As she drove slowly along the rough track between the big trees, over the long, very green grass, past flowering shrubs and creepers she smiled grimly. This was not Canaan, it was Eden. There were concealments in this voluptuous beauty, dangers which she felt were nearer than the others realised; and God, what a place for snakes, pythons, puff-adders, mambas, boomslangs, rinkals; wherever you looked there was a snake curled up, even when one went to collect eggs, there was often one of the accursed things asleep under a sitting hen.

She looked at the heavy sjambok at her side, wondering how many snakes she had killed with it already.

As the Cape cart banged and bounced down the rough track her mind turned to Sannie. The baby was very near now, it might come any time. As she got nearer she hoped that the lion cub was tied up. Her horses were much afraid of it; although it was as yet quite harmless, indeed, even amusing to watch, it smelt of lion to them.

How like a cat it was, and yet, how unlike. Its spots were fading now, and its loose skin rolled about over its shoulder blades as it moved.

Life was really very odd in the way it took people, very odd indeed. She supposed there must be sane people, people like herself somewhere, but, magtig, they were rare. Not that one could expect much of pregnant girls, they were entitled to their fancies, but when it came to lions that was too much. Why not an elephant or a kameel? It was nice to have pets, and as soon as she could, she would get one. Ja, she would have a baboon chained to a post in front of her house, on the top of the pole she would set a box in which it could sleep. Pets gave one something to watch. Young buck were nice too, and birds, a crane, or a secretary bird. She remembered one that Jappie had brought home many years ago; he had ridden after it, galloping it, till it could fly no more. A good pet it had been, killing many snakes and frightening no one.

Below her she could see some of Hendrik's Kaffirs clearing a piece of land. Hendrik had chosen his farm well. The soil looked rich and fat.

Soon there would be crops growing — wheat, barley, oats, grey peas, green peas, yellow peas, haricot beans; meilies and Kaffir corn in great waving fields. Soon the horses would tread out the grain on the threshing floors. Tante Anna laughed as she thought of Pierre du Toit who had tried to tread his grain with oxen. Ja, oxen, whose dung when they were chased round and got hot, was fluid. Many muids of good wheat he had spoilt by trying to be too slim. And though he cleaned it as best he could, his bread was not good that year. Magtig, it was not good. Meditating on the qualities of horse dung, which was hard and dry, which broke up and could be winnowed away, she drove on.

And yet, in the Book it said, 'muzzle not the ox which treadeth out the corn.' It was not a muzzle they wanted — ach, sis, no, it was a cork. She burst out laughing, but perhaps in those days they did not mind, or perhaps they did not have enough horses.

Ach, ja, it would be fine to see the horses cantering round, up to their bellies in the long golden corn again, their long tails flowing, as they were driven round and round, inside the mud wall of the grain floor.

She turned sharply towards the mountain, the bar supporting the pole of the Cape cart rose under the horses' necks as she checked them and fell again as the traces tightened.

There was Sannie sitting on the stoep. She waved her whip and shouted. Sannie got up heavily and came towards her. The lion cub was not with her. Perhaps Hendrik had killed it, or it might be tied up in the shade at the back of the house.

The native behind her sprang down and seized the horses' heads, while Jakalaas brought a box and set it down beside the cart. Hesitating a moment and consigning her body to the care of the Almighty, Anna de Jong closed her eyes and stepped out into space. Jakalaas put his hands forward and checked her, grasping at the part he took to be her waist. For a moment they swayed together, another step forward and she was down.

'How goes it, Sannie?' she asked.

'It goes well, Tante Anna; very well. Come in and drink coffee.'

Arm in arm, they went towards the house while the boys outspanned the horses.

'I have brought you a small barrel of pickled fish,' Anna said. 'Steenbraas, that should be very tasty. It is my last barrel,' she added, 'and I have saved them for this moment. Ja, mie Sannie, I thought many months ago of this. I said to myself, when a woman's time comes what is it she wants most in the world? First of all she wants to be delivered, that natuurlik, but after that what does she want? And suddenly it came to me. A still small voice said, "Fish,

Anna de Jong; that is what a woman wants. Something nice and tasty."

'Ach,' she went on, 'how I long for fish sometimes. Steenbraas, or a nice klipvish baked in the oven, or crayfish or mussel-fish. Always it is game or mutton, mutton or game. One day I think I shall kill a calf. Ja, mie Sannie, when your baby is born I will kill one to make a feast. I do not care what the folk think, for you know the saying; that if a farmer slaughters a calf, there must be something wrong either with the calf or the farmer.' She rolled about on her chair with laughter. 'But there is nothing wrong with me, mie Sannie, and it will not be a sick calf that I shall kill. Nie, nie. It will be a fine fat little bulliekie. For you must live well. Ja, magtig, you must have food. Can you make milk from the air?'

She leant forward and pinched one of Sannie's arms. 'You are too thin,' she said. 'A thin woman gives thin milk, but all the same, I think you will milk better than your mother.' She looked at the girl's breasts. 'Do they hurt you?' she asked.

'Ja, they hurt me.'

'Then that is good, you will get great pleasure from feeding your child if they hurt you. Ach, God, how my breasts used to hurt me and how I milked, people used to come from far to see how I milked. Even with my first one I could not keep it in, but then I was always a fine woman with much blood.'

The two sat silently for a while, drinking their coffee. The murmur of her aunt's chatter had comforted Sannie; her presence as she sat massively, staring into space dreaming of her own children, somehow made things easier. Nowhere in the world was there a bigger woman, or anyone who was more of a woman than Anna de Jong. Rounded till her convexities intersected, forming a ponderous mass of female matter, a thing that was all but oval, as specialised as a queen ant to her function of maternity.

'You are not afraid?' her aunt asked.

'Ja, Tante Anna, I am afraid,' Sannie said.

'It is nothing,' Anna said. 'Nie, nie, it is niks. With our people it is soon over, in two hours it will be over. In three days you will be up and laughing, remembering nothing.' She looked at the girl's face; she looked pale and unhappy, her time was near. 'Listen, Sannie, I will be with you. I will bring your baby into the world and, magtig, how we will laugh when it is over, when you have him rolled in his swaddling clothes. And it will be a boy — a fine boy, of that I am certain. I will stay with you now; I shall not go back. Your father can let a Kaffir cook his food. Then when I return, no doubt he will say he has missed me.'

'Klaas,' she called. 'Klaas, inspan at once and fetch Louisa and all the things I have prepared. Also tell her to bring the small barrel of salt pork, she knows where it is. Maak gou, jou skelm, ek is haastig, baie haastig.

'Now listen to me, mie Sannie, it is nothing. I will tell you of my children and you will see how easy it is. Why, once I delivered myself alone with only a Kaffir maid to help me — that was in one of the wars when we lived up by the Great Fish River. Jappie was on commando and all my people had run away. Ach, you would have laughed. Magtig, there I was with three guns on the bed beside me and that little tottie maid tied by her leg to a ring in the ceiling, or she too, would have gone. And always on the second or third Sunday I was able to ride to the church to have mie klienkie baptized. A very fine horse I had then, Sannie, big and strong and so safe that even riding through the mountains I could suckle my little one without fear. Ach, sis, here it is nothing, with all these people about as thick as the lice on a wild pig. In the old day on the border it was different, for there the Kaffirs were fighting men who had firearms and horses; they had with them escaped slaves who knew the ways of white folk and some white men, deserters from the ships. Ach,' she sighed, 'all this trek that you think so much of, what has

it been? Just a picnic that went on overlong. If it was not
that it had killed my Jappie I could laugh at the noise
people make of it.'

She took Sannie's hand. 'Do not fear — with your old
Tante Anna by you things will go well,' she said.

CHAPTER XI

I

HENDRIK was relieved to have Anna de Jong in the house, for among his Kaffir women he had no one he was prepared to count on, they were all young, careless and not to be trusted. Also, though he fought against knowledge, the presence of Louisa with her yellow baby gave him pleasure. The way she went about on her mistress's errands; deft and silent, flitting past him, her hips swaying as she moved, the way she took opportunities to pass near him; the way she looked at him sometimes, meaningly, and then let her long black lashes droop onto her creamy cheeks while her colour rose, mounted flushing upwards from her neck.

Still, this was not the moment for such thoughts as came into his head, and he spent much time outside. The land that Anna de Jong had seen begun, was now almost finished stumping, and the trees were being drawn off to make a fence about it. He had planned a furrow from one of his hillside springs that would irrigate it, and although it was autumn he would plant soon, for here in this part, it was so warm that with water led onto them he was assured most crops would grow. Also, a thing which pleased him greatly, he had found a place where he could make a storage dam just above the lands and would thus be able to accumulate and manage a strong head of water with a minimum of waste or effort.

The house now was such a woman's place that he was glad to be out of it. Anna, moving about in it like an elephant, her great haunches brushing the door-posts as she went from one room into the other. Sannie so patently about to become a mother, stoically waiting for her pangs, and the coloured girl more of a woman than she ought to be, all conspired to drive him out and all conspired to bring him back. That was how he spent his time, leaving the house in a fury and returning to it with curiosity, in doubt and fear.

But when Sannie's pains started, when he heard her cry out, he sent for his black horse and, taking his gun, went off to hunt. All the time as he rode, he thought of Sannie, treasuring her in his mind; Sannie the beautiful, who was being broken so that the seed of his loins should see light; Sannie, for whom this would only be the first of many such events; it was for this purpose she had been given to him, a bird snared by the hunter, a vessel now emptying, to be refilled.

Duty, the endless duty of paternity, the curse of his potency and the necessity that it should be continually proven was upon him.

A son had died, God had demanded this sacrifice and to what end? To the end that he should have many more, that his sons should be numberless and his grandsons fill the earth. Hunters, fighters, prophets, men like himself, they should be reared to fear God and to serve Him.

And as he thought, so he shot, killing, killing, killing. There was too much game here, they ate the grass he wanted for his herds. The sleek red cows, the mares, the ewes and the she-goats that were his. This country was rich, it was his and his sons, the first of whom was now being born, would enter into possession of it. Like God, he would make men in his own image, many men. He was the power and Sannie, his young wife, the instrument. Everything was as nothing to this, there was no pleasure, no joy to be obtained in life except by fulfilling the injunction — increase and multiply. This was the road to peace and to contemplation. Female things were beautiful only when swollen by their pregnancy, male only when taut and strung by the use of their powers.

It had been his misfortune to have a wife who, if not actually barren, had given him few children. A man had the right to expect a child a year. He thought of old van der Merwe, seventy years old, with his third wife nursing a baby. The number of his children, grandchildren and great-grandchildren, was eighty-three. When he said 'my family' it meant something; it meant a commando of men and boys; it meant fifty or sixty wagons, many thousands of cattle and horses and perhaps a hundred thousand sheep.

The mystery of the blood tie, of the begotten, held Hendrik spellbound.

That the child being born was his own he did not doubt nor did it matter, for were it his son's it was still his own, the projection of his own seed; the dead Herman its carrier. Continually, the increase of his race must spread, widening, deepening like a river — ach, ja, he saw it thus; gaining in size and strength as it flowed forward, a vast stream of which he was the source, the fountain head.

It was another revelation.

A herd of roibok passed him at a gallop, jumping yards high into the air as they ran. With each bound, the lyre-like horns of the rams were silhouetted against the sky. He did not fire, his desire to kill was gone, he had used it up. Satiated, he turned back. As he came near the house Louisa ran towards him. He felt his heart beat faster.

'Baas, baas, it is a boy. A fine one,' she said.

A moment later Anna de Jong waddled out.

'No, Hendrik,' she said, 'not yet, but do not worry, things have gone well. There were no complications.' Almost Anna wished there had been, so that she could have used her skill. 'He came head first,' she went on, 'as easily as a foal.'

Hendrik lit his pipe and sat down, he was once more a father and his wife was safe. Louisa passed him, brushing her leg against his thigh. He moved his chair and Louisa, laughing shrilly, tossed her head.

An hour later he saw his son very red and crumpled lying in Sannie's arms. Women, women with their paraphernalia, their looks and low laughter, their solidarity about this function which was so peculiarly their own, oppressed him, making him very conscious that he was a man. This time when Louisa pressed against him he did not move nor did she laugh.

2

Three days later Sannie was up, and Tante Anna, proud of her midwifery, had her horses inspanned to drive away. She could do no more; all that was necessary now was food, any quantity of it for the making of milk. She explained this at some length to Hendrik, told him also, how, if Sannie was not hungry, he could tempt her with the pickled fish. Gave him, in a last burst of affection, half her barrel of salt pork; said she'd be back tomorrow, and told the Kaffir to let go of the horses which plunged forward at a gallop. They were facing home.

Rocking and swaying in a cloud of dust, Anna de Jong left Hendrik's house, taking Louisa with her. Ja, things had gone well, thanks to God and to her.

'It is a fine boy, Louisa,' she said as she slowed down the horses.

'Ja, missus, it is a fine boy.' The coloured maid for once was not in conversational mood.

'The delivering of children is a woman's business,' Anna de Jong said.

'Ja, missus, who ever heard of a man delivering a child? Such a thing would not be decent.'

'I have heard of it. It is God's truth, and happens often now in Kapstad. It is one of the customs of the English.'

'Ach, sis, no, missus, that is not true.'

'Do you think I lie? Do you think I would bother to lie to a coloured slut?' her mistress shouted. 'I say it is true.

It is for such things as this, to save the purity of our women, that we have trekked. Also,' she added, 'because the land up here is better and costs nothing. Ja,' she went on, 'Kapstad, which was once a respectable town is now a Sodom and Gomorrah. Though they do say that the men who do these things put muslin over their heads.'

'But one can see through muslin,' Louisa said.

'Of course one can see through muslin. And if one couldn't, do you think a man could be trusted not to look? Men are like children, always looking and prying at things which don't concern them. Men are all the same, Louisa, they are no good, but the world would be a dull place for us without them. They are sent by God to plague us, as he has, in his wisdom, given fleas to dogs. Do you believe what I say now, Louisa?'

'Ja, mie meisie, I believe it. Certainly it would be dull without them, and how would we get babies?'

'Not that. Can you never stop thinking of men? I mean what I told you about men bringing children into the world with their heads wrapped up in muslin. Muslin.' Anna de Jong sniffed contemptuously.

'If the meisie says it is true, then it is true.' The way a child began was more interesting to Louisa now, than the way it came into the world. After all, once they were on the way they arrived, and not even an Englishman with his head wrapped up in muslin would be able to stop them. She went on thinking of Hendrik van der Berg; a few weeks ago it would have been easy with his wife like that. Now, she shrugged her shoulders and lay back in the cart, now it would not be so easy, but it might still be done.

Anna was in a hurry, she had been away a week, and in a week much could go wrong. The main thing that worried her was how Blesbok, her fat-tailed ram, had got on. No one understood him as she did, no one could fasten on the little cart — it was really a plank with two wheels — that carried his long, fat tail as securely, or as comfortably as she. And if it came off, not only would his tail get sore dragging along the ground, but he would suffer from constipation, being unable to void his dung.

Nowhere, not even at the Cape, was there a finer ram. She had thought of sending for him, but to do that would have been to put him in the way of the lion, to whom his lovely tail on its little wheels would have proved an irresistible attraction; and she had not brought him safely a thousand miles to be made a game of by a lion.

It was worries such as these which made one old. She loved her sheep and had six hundred of them left — a mixed lot of Kaffir sheep, thick-tailed, black-headed Persians, and a few real eastern long, fat tails like Blesbock. They were all, except the eastern sheep, being grazed up on the berg, where the grass was short and sweet. By now they should have got over their diarrhoea; that was the worst of sheep, if they weren't having one thing it was another, and sometimes many things together. But even if the young, tender grass scoured them at first, it did them good in the end, and she hoped Johannes had taken out the flock rams. It did not pay to allow the ewes to lamb twice in a year. This was one of the subjects on which they did not agree. On the trek, naturally, they could not be separated, but now things should be done properly, and the matings of the beasts controlled. She smiled as she thought of the fools who kept thin-tailed sheep, they would be sorry when their butter ran out, for the melting fat of a sheep's tail was a good substitute for it and even when one had butter, made a nice change if spread thickly onto slices of bread. She wondered if Sannie had any, she had forgotten to ask her. If not, she would take her some, it would help to keep up her strength. And no doubt one day people would come to her for her fat-tailed sheep, and she would sell them some young rams. The ewes she would not part with at any price.

3

Sannie's pride in her child was very great. It was the first thing that she had ever found completely satisfactory. It embodied all she was and all she had ever been; their lives, hers and her son's, were one thing. Here at last was something real which would go on, moving with her at her side, waxing as she waned, a newly lit flame that flickering now would one day burn brightly, strongly, in an altogether admirable fashion — a man, and she the mother of a man. Jakalaas's interest in the boy was unbounded. Leaving the lion tied up, he would stand staring at it for hours, or when Sannie left it, sit by its side dreaming happily while he picked the thorns out of his feet with a thin steel spike. He remembered his meisie as a child, her own child reviving his memories. Always when she went out he had accompanied her, and always she had come to him when she was unhappy, when her puppies or her lambs were ill it was he who had nursed them. He had brought her flowers and killed the snakes in her path, he had taught her the names and told her the virtues of many plants. And now in this new, strange land he would do the same for her son, guarding him from danger, showing him where birds nested and making him whips and little throwing kerries.

He looked at the sun, it was time to go to the kraal and begin the milking. As he rose, the cows came filing in, their bellies wide with grass, their flanks rounded with the water of their evening drink.

His life, like that of the white people, was falling back into its accustomed mould, solidifying and slowly resuming its shape and texture.

All over the place that they called Canaan the Boers were developing their homes, breaking land and building. There was no end to their building; they needed shops for their craftsmen, blacksmiths' shops, where the great leather bellows could be set up, carpenters' shops, store houses, chicken hocks. They had to make innumberable kraals for their stock; those for the milk cows, for the calves, for the heifers, for the tollies, for the fat oxen, for the working oxen. The ewes must be kept separate from the rams and the mules must be kept away from the horse and donkey mares whose foals they killed.

And each clompie of beasts had its own herders, black or coloured, who looked after them and were responsible for their well being.

The plough-shears tore long new furrows through the virgin soil, ploughing up rectangular acre after rectangular acre, working inwards till at last it was done. The sun glinted on the now shining mould-boards as they were lifted out at the headlands and dragged over the rough grass till they bit the soil again.

Once again the flocks and herds led out by the bulls and stallions, streamed over the land, weaving little paths over the veld which had been pathless.

The roots of the people were striking down into the fertile soil. Other children were born after Sannie's, and an old man died.

Soon the black patches of ploughland would be green, and the trek merely an incident between farming in one place and farming in another, something which those who had accomplished it would speak about with the self-conscious modesty of people who, knowing that they have performed a notable feat, make little of it.

Necessity, that of planting crops that they might eat, of making shoes that they might walk, of building furniture, beds, stools, tables and chairs that they might have more comfort, occupied their minds to the exclusion of all else, even to the greatness of their adventure.

4

Frikkie, as Sannie's baby was called, was very like its grandfather. This was almost inevitable, for Herman had resembled Hendrik. The van der Bergs were prepotent, a race who forced their physical traits onto their offspring from one generation to another, turning them out recognisably their own, even as infants. Always, there was the rather long upper lip and the eyes set slightly too close to the nose.

'Ja, Sannie,' Hendrik said, 'it is easy to see to what breed he belongs. We are a strong, well-marked race and beget others like ourselves.'

Turning the fly-leaf of his Bible, he read her the names of his ancestors. The name of Jacobus who had landed at the Cape of Good Hope in 1657, his name heading the list of the seventeen free burghers who had come from Holland with van Riebek. The name of Gerhart, his son, who had married Catalyn Harmaans of Middleburg, and by whom he begat Jacob, who had married Sibella Passman, and begotten Hendrik, who had married Hester Anna Laurentz, in 1780, whose son he was.

As she sat over her sewing listening to her husband's deep voice droning on, Sannie smiled. It was like something out of the holy book these pages of begettings, these issues of long-dead wombs, this endless repetition, this fearful egotism of men who saw themselves only thus, as fathers. She wondered how many of them were right. It was only a mother who knew the father of her child. Ach, ja, one could have many pages without much truth, much begetting and little begotten. Perhaps even those long biblical pedigrees were not quite what they appeared to be. People even in those days were still people, much the same in their thoughts and the feeling of their bodies as the people of today, both men and women; and betrayal was no new thing.

Poor Herman. Poor, poor Herman. All that was over,

but how good it had been while it lasted. She tried to remember his courtship of her, some of its more intimate parts,
but nothing came to her mind except how on one occasion
when they were lying side by side in the grass she had become
covered by small ticks, and how on another she had watched
some vultures swing in vast circles round and round in the
cloudless sky — she had watched them till her eyes ached.

No, she could remember nothing, and it was exasperating
that such feelings as she knew she had had should pass,
should be lost like the scent of a flower. Naturally she could
remember what they had done. Remember his urgency
which had so soon been equalled by her own. But of her
sensations, nothing.

Pulling down her bodice she gave her child the breast. He
drank avidly, sucking and pummelling with his small fat
hands.

Soon Hendrik would call her and the baby, full of warm
milk, would sleep. Hendrik, who was as avid for her as her
child, or as his son had been.

This was the power of women. This was God's gift to
them while they were young. She looked down at her hands
as they lay in her lap curved round the body of her child.
With a gesture of those hands or a touch she could inflame
a man as old, as experienced, as Hendrik van der Berg. Her
feelings for her husband were mixed; he satisfied the desires
that Herman had awakened but revolted her while he did it,
causing her, where she had gone forth to meet the young man,
to withdraw into herself from the old one.

Ja, there was pleasure to be found in men, the pleasure of
satisfaction and the pleasure of power; it was there in the
small hands that she was using to wipe her baby's mouth;
it was there in her capacity to give or to withhold herself.
Her power over Hendrik balanced very justly the scales of
her feelings, armouring her against the hurt of Herman's
death.

Smiling down at the child on her knee, neither content

nor discontent, but very strong in her knowledge, very secure in her detachment and as free spiritually as she was bodily tied, a mother, a widow in all but name, a wife, a girl whose mind moved secretly, flying like a bird through the night, she waited.

CHAPTER XII

I

AS ZWART PIETE, Sara and de Kok travelled they noticed the little bag that Rinkals carried round his neck getting fatter and fatter. He was collecting, as he went along, the specifics and necessities of his magic; an odd assortment of herbs, of roots and fruits, knuckle-bones, pellets of dung, feathers, pebbles, and was much amused at the white people's interest in his collection and at their incredulity when he told them of some of the diverse uses to which they could be put. 'Yes,' he said, 'the white man with his gun can make thunder and lightning,' — he had been much impressed by Zwart Piete's marksmanship — 'but can he make a barren woman have a child? Or can he send locusts onto the fields of his enemies so that they eat his substance and he starves, or can he, out of a thousand men, smell out an evil doer? Can he make rain? Or stop rain and cause droughts? All these are things I can do,' he said, 'but to do them I need certain charms, not many things, for being a great wizard I can do much with but little, but a little I must have.'

'Well, if you are such a great doctor, can you tell us what we shall find tomorrow?' Sara asked, smiling.

'Today,' Rinkals said, 'is the child of yesterday and the mother of tomorrow; tomorrow is already in her womb striving to be free.'

'Yes, tell us,' Zwart Piete said, 'we go on and on, and always there are nothing but mountains.'

'The great white lord is right, mountains,' the old man

said, 'yes, it is so, mountains. But would the great lord be
surprised if I said that after today there will be no more,
that is, no great ones?' he added. 'And that tomorrow the
baas will see great marvels, such things as he has never seen
before.'

'Ja, I should be very surprised,' Zwart Piete said.

'But if it was so, if what I said was true would the baas
give me a measure of tobacco? It is not much that I ask
for so great a marvel,' he whined. 'Why, men have given
me whole herds of cattle for doing much less than this.
Tomorrow,' he said, 'you will see beasts in such numbers as
you have never seen before.'

'Elephants?' Piete asked.

'Yes, elephants, for tomorrow, unless my spirit has deceived me, we come to the home of the elephants, the place
to which all elephants return to die.'

'So it is an elephant that lies curled in the womb of today,'
de Kok said.

'Not one but many.'

'If there are elephants you shall have tobacco,' Piete said.

'Thank you, baas. The baas is good. I will leave you
now and go see to it. The making of elephants is no light
matter.'

The prophecy came true. That is to say, that having
climbed the range next day they were confronted by no
more hills, and instead of rising the ground fell away, sloping down to an enormous lake edged with pink.

If these were flowers Zwart Piete had never seen anything
like them before and rode down the slope to see what it could
be.

Suddenly, as he got nearer, he realised that the whole lake
was bordered with flamingos, hundreds of thousands of
them standing all round its margin in a wide pink border.

As he came nearer they raised their heads which had been
sunk beneath the surface where they were feeding, turned
their long serpentine necks towards him and began to wade

out into deeper water. There seemed to be two kinds, one rather bigger and paler in colour than the other. Here and there birds, apparently decapitated, paddled about with their heads under the water, but most seemed to feed, standing on their long legs in the shallows.

As he came still nearer they rose in clouds, their heads looking oddly heavy for their sinuous necks, their long legs trailing out behind them; pale pink when they stood with their wings closed, they now flashed into red as their pinions opened; red, bordered heavily with black. The mud at his feet was covered with moulted feathers and the smell of droppings was like that of a chicken house, very foul and fishy.

They were so numerous that at times they darkened the sky, throwing great patches of shade, like the shadow of a cloud, over the water as they circled in continually changing formations. Hundreds would sweep together, wheel in an enormous flock and break up again, patterning the sky as they manoeuvred. Near him some hippopotami, which had been lying in the mud with only the curved tops of their backs, their eyes, and nostrils showing, reared up and plunged away.

'Is this not a great marvel, baas?' Rinkals asked. 'A marvel worth much tobacco. Have I not charmed away the hills, just because the baas said he was tired of them and that they made the feet of his horse sore.'

'Where are the elephants?' Zwart Piete asked. 'Birds have no ivory.'

'If the baas will come with me I will show him elephants. More elephants perhaps than he will wish to see. But the baas must bring no gun; later, if he wishes, he can hunt them, but tonight, if the baas dares we will watch only; tonight my spirit is very strong for elephants.'

Going back up the hillside away from the smell of the lake they made camp and ate. Before the moon rose Rinkals got up. 'Is the baas ready?' he asked.

Leaving his gun Zwart Piete followed the old Kaffir.

Keeping away from the water they walked along the hill-side for an hour, walked till the camp fire where the others slept was no more than a pin-prick of light in the distance, and then they went downwards towards some big trees between which the water shone silver-white. Here, in the shadow they waited, nor did they have to wait long; hardly had they settled themselves before the animals began to arrive. Not in ones and twos, not even in herds. They came in solid serried masses, they came in such numbers that they shook the muddy ground, causing it to quake. First a herd of elephants, led by a gigantic cow, came down to the water, to drink, to roll, to play. Among them the river horses moved about unperturbed, their feet, as they walked through the mud, making sucking noises as they lifted them. More and more came up out of the water, clambering clumsily on to the bank to graze, like cows, on the long grass.

A herd of buffalo came down, their horns curved black scimitars, the old ones looking almost white as the moonlight shone on their thick, hairless hides. A herd of giraffes, their necks swaying, came down, and spreading their long legs lowered their heads into the water to drink. More elephants, great bulls carrying tusks which must have weighed hundreds of pounds came down, drank and stood about, their stomachs rumbling. Some, in pairs, caressed each other with their trunks, their enormous ears, as big as tables, moving slowly to and fro. As the moon climbed into the sky, its light increasing, the great beasts were painted black against the bright indigo of the night, their tusks curving upwards milk white on either side of their hanging trunks. Rhinoceroses moved about aimlessly, their horns pointing to the stars. One, which came very near to them, carried a horn longer than a tall man, and the noise made by the beasts as they moved was like that of a tempest. The elephants trumpeted, hippopotamus bulls roared at each other, opening cavernous mouths, jackals cried and hyenas laughed.

Never in all his hunting had Zwart Piete seen anything

to equal this. Never had he dreamed that such a thing was possible and later if he spoke of it no one would believe him. 'You lie, Piete,' they would say. 'Ach, God, how you lie,' and they would shout with laughter, and almost he would be prepared to believe that he had not seen it, that he was not seeing it now, that Sara's Kaffir had bewitched him; but the dawn brought proof. As the animals had come, so they left, as swiftly and as suddenly, and apart from a river horse cow with a new-born calf the lake side was empty of all wild life. But the banks, and the ground round its edge, looked as if it had been ploughed up by madmen.

Soon, Rinkals said, there would be no spoor, for within an hour the sodden soil would resume its normal shape; this thing that they had seen happened every night and had happened since time began.

'You have been here before?' Zwart Piete said.

'Ja, baas, I have been many times.'

'Then what about your magic, you skelm,' Piete cried, laughing.

'Ja, baas, what about it?' the Kaffir said. 'It is very great, as one day you will see. Listen,' he went on, 'you are thinking of shooting these elephants for their teeth.'

'Yes,' Piete said, 'I was, but how did you know?'

'My spirit told me, my magic; but what I say is of what use is ivory without carriers? Let us go on and then one day we will return.'

'Yes,' Piete said, 'you are right. We will go back to the others and sleep. Tomorrow we will go on. When I tell de Kok of this he will say to me, "Baas, if this is true, come with me and show me the spoor." Ach,' he said, 'if even my own Griqua Bastard thinks I lie, of what good will it be to tell others?'

'No good, baas, if you want the ivory for yourself, there are men who will go as far as you to seek riches, and some might even go to prove your words lies and stay to reap the reward.'

'Where do we go now?' Piete asked.

'That way, baas,' Rinkals pointed north, 'and then later that way,' he pointed east. 'In five days,' he said, 'we will come to the country of a new race, tall fighting men who live on milk and blood and who have many cattle. They know me there and we shall make medicine.' He looked at the sky, 'It may even be that I will make some rain for them if their grass be poor.'

2

It came about as Rinkals had said; for five days after leaving the lake and the rich swamp which surrounded it they marched through highlands that were full of game. The herds, numbering thousands, almost covered the veld and were entirely unafraid; they were not wild animals but tame, easier to move among than cattle; and then they came upon the men of whom Rinkals had spoken. Tall men, naked save for their tanned oxhide cloaks, carrying long, narrow-bladed spears.

It came about as Rinkals had said because he knew the country like the palm of his hand, and they swung north instead of proceeding due east as they could easily have done, because he had a debt to collect from these men. A debt of some twenty cows which had been owing for two years.

That these people were honest and they would pay him he knew, but he said nothing of his debt to Zwart Piete, de Kok, or Sara. Instead, he told them about the habits of these men, of how they grazed their herds among the wild game, hurting nothing for the only meat they ate was that of their own beasts, and while there was much game, the lions and the wild dogs and the leopards left the cattle. He told them that sometimes they hunted the lion and the elephant for sport. Of how a brave man would creep up behind an elephant and sever his hamstrings, thus making him helpless; of how on other occasions they fired the grass round an ele-

phant and, as he stood not daring to move, filled him as full
as a porcupine with their spears. Time and again they would
do this, never letting him rest till at last he died of exhaustion
and the blood lost from a hundred wounds. It might take
weeks and the ivory, when they had got it, belonged to the
king; they got nothing from their hunting but the sport of
killing.

So they went on passing through these people, greeting
them as they came to a kraal, bidding them good-bye as
they left it, moving on in goodwill and friendliness till they
came to the home of a chief called Matiba. It was this man
who owed the cows, and here their greeting was not so gracious.

'Do you come in peace, Mamba?' the chief asked, 'Or do
you come bearing the tail of a leopard?' for such was their
custom if a man came in war.

'I come in peace, oh Chief Matiba, I come with empty
hands.'

'And who are those with you that ride quaggas without
stripes?' the chief said.

'Ah, those,' Rinkal said, lowering his voice, 'are not to
be called by name. They are spirits.'

'Spirits which, by report, eat and drink like other men,'
the chief said.

'Naturally, if a spirit takes the form of a man, it must eat
and drink, but do not fear, chief, they will not hurt you; it
was not for that that I summoned them out of the beyond.

'Then why did you summon them, wizard?'

'Only so that they should be there to help me in case of
need. They are very strong,' he went on, 'and there is a
small matter between us. Yes,' he said, 'a small matter of
twenty cows and in two years each cow should have had two
calves.'

'Very well do you know that cows do not have calves each
year, that they will not take the bull until their calves are
weaned.'

'That I know is usually the case, oh chief, but when you look carefully in your kraals and think for a while, you will see that these particular cows have had forty calves; more, that those forty calves are all weaned heifers, and more, that in two years the rings round the horns of their mothers are fewer than they were.'

'As cows grow older so do the rings round their horns increase, one ring to a year,' the chief said.

'Yes, that is so, oh black elephant, that is what occurs with ordinary cows, but look in your kraal and you will see that mine are different. That is because I am a great magician who caused your brother to die.'

'My brother died by the bite of a mamba.'

'And was it not as a mamba that you greeted me, oh lord? And listen, chief, so great a doctor am I that if I am left here with my attendant spirits much longer without food, or beer, those twenty cows will be forty and each with two heifer calves. Just to show you how great I am,' he said, 'I will perform a small wonder for you.' Going to Zwart Piete he said: 'Baas, give me your flask, we are in danger.

'Now, oh bull elephant,' he said, 'perhaps you have a small cup, a bowl, or a vessel.'

A girl brought him an iron cup and squatting on the ground he called for fire.

'Now,' he said, 'behold fire, behold a cup, behold water.' He filled the cup from the flask. 'Now I will cook the water. I will not cook it much, only a little,' he held it over the flame for a moment. 'Now,' he said, 'my spirit will burn up the water.'

The chief laughed, those gathered round him laughed, and the girl who had brought him the cup, she was the youngest of the chief's wives, laughed till her pointed breasts trembled.

'Watch, fools,' he said, and picking up a burning stick he touched the fluid. It caught alight, burning with a strong blue flame. 'Watch more,' Rinkals shouted, and he emptied it at the feet of the chief where it ran along the ground still burning, faded and died.

The chief was pale and speechless. 'You are a great man,' he said.

'Yes, I am great, and you will give me twenty young cows, each with two heifers nearly as large as herself.'

'It is a big price,' the chief said.

'You have but one river, oh black bull whose roar shakes the world, and what will your people do if I set it on fire? If I burn it up?'

'You shall have your cows, wizard, and then you will get hence. To see you makes my eyes sore and my bile to be bitter in my teeth.'

'I cannot leave you yet, oh chief, for these spirits that I have brought mounted on quaggas without stripes are fatiqued. Also my heart is sore for you about the loss of so many of your cows and I have a plan coming in my head by which you might easily regain them.'

'Let the plan not take too long, Mamba, or else go quickly, for I also have a plan coming. It is not easy to part with cattle when I have but to say the word, but to raise a hand.'

'You have but to raise a finger, chief, and your river burns. Give me beer, send me a maiden with it to a private hut for I would think and commune with the dead ones. Has she,' he pointed to the young wife, 'a sister? Hold,' he said, 'do not speak.' He stared at the girl and turned away. 'Send me her sister,' he said, 'and your river will be safe. It may even be that if things go well I will give you rain and tell the grass to grow about the bellies of your cattle so strongly that you will not see even the ears of the small calves.'

'And this depends on the maiden?' the chief asked.

'Ai, much may depend on a maiden, oh chief, if she be a maiden, but not in this case. A maiden is as nothing to a spirit, while to me, one is much like another provided she be comely and well formed. Speak no more words, chief, lest mischief be done; already I can feel the dead ones round me.'

3

Of all that the old Kaffir had said Zwart Piete, de Kok, and Sara understood nothing; looking at each other they had almost laughed when he set the brandy on fire and when he had strode off, followed by a young girl carrying a big pot of beer on her head, they had been unable to restrain.

'What an old skelm!' de Kok said. 'To take the baas's brandy and use it for frightening a chief into giving him beer and a woman was good; ja, it was very good.'

Since they were apparently going to stay here a few days they decided to make themselves comfortable. They had come fast, and had no objection to resting. The huts that they were given were new and clean and the fresh milk which was offered them with every mark of respect was a pleasant change of diet.

Sara, more even than the others, enjoyed the rest, and never had she seen her brother so gay and happy. Ever since they had been children together they had planned and talked of just such an adventure as this, but at the back of her mind there had always been the thought that it would not happen, the certainty that one of them would marry and leave the other. She smiled ironically as she thought of her marriage and the dreams she had had of it. That had been before she had been smitten by the smallpox, before she had grown as tall and as strong as her brother. Except that I have no beard, she thought, I might well be a man. And because of her appearance she had become manly, and more than manly, justifying her actions by her appearance, while all the time inside her she felt a woman, curiously soft and tender with a longing for a home, and for children clinging to her skirts.

Dismissing these thoughts scornfully did not help; they always returned. Whatever she might appear to be she was, and would remain, a woman. Behind the barrier of her looks and her bravado there lurked this spiritual weakness which drove her forth to hunt game and Kaffirs savagely and which, because she felt softly, made her harder than any man could be — quite merciless.

There were many lions about and Zwart Piete decided to shoot one and make a present of its skin to the chief. He spoke to Rinkals about this and he agreed that it would be a gesture of politeness. 'When will you go? Tomorrow?' he asked.

'Yes, tomorrow,' Piete said.

'Ja, that is good. Then I will at once go and ask the chief Matiba if he will give you permission to do this thing.'

Leaving Zwart Piete cleaning his gun Rinkals found the chief.

'Oh, chief,' he said, 'for so great a man it seems to me that your karosses are poor. It cannot be that you sleep with the beautiful one,' this was the sister of his helper, 'on a skin whose hair is worn off in places. How can a woman be proud of her hut however fresh and fragrant the cow dung on the floor if her bed be the bed of a slave?'

'What do you know of the beds I sleep in, Mamba?' the chief asked. 'Ai, and how do you know?'

'Again you call me Mamba, oh bull whose breath causes the hills to tremble, and again I say as Mamba I know much. As Mamba I can crawl in where men would be slain and see that which is forbidden, and this I say that a handsome coverlet is a guaranty of virtue, for cold maidens seek warm beds.'

'She is a new wife,' the chief grumbled, 'and I have twenty wives all calling for skins, each wanting the finest. But soon I will send out my young men and get her what she wants.'

'Ai, soon. But will soon be soon enough? I have looked into the future and have seen terrible things, and because I am your friend I am sending out the spirits I have brought with me to kill you a lion. I only hope that it will be in time,' he added. 'Your wife is ashamed of her couch, it is a mockery.' He paused and continued, 'Where are my heifers and my cows? I have the business of the lost ones to attend and the beer you sent today was less good than that of yesterday.'

4

There was a black-maned lion that Zwart Piete had seen on two occasions and which, it seemed to him, would make a fine present for the chief. He frequented a stony kopje some five miles from the village. Rinkals, when consulted, threw the bones and said that everything was propitious for the killing of this beast and that also no gift would please the chief more, black-maned lions being particularly favoured by him.

'Then you will come with us in the morning?' Zwart Piete said.

'Come with you, baas? Come where?' the old Kaffir asked.

'Come to seek this lion.'

'No, no, baas. Why should I who have lost no lions seek one?'

'You will come because I say so.'

'Ja, baas. I will come because you say so, but I have no lion magic with me. I had a very strong lion magic once. Ai, so strong that when a lion saw me it ran away crying like a woman.'

'That must have been strong medicine,' de Kok said.

'Ja, it was strong indeed, Bastard, like dogs they ran with their tufted tails between their legs.'

'Crying like women,' Piete said.

'Ja, baas, crying like women, with their tails between their legs.'

'Then be ready at dawn and come sober.'

'Sober,' Rinkals said, 'does the baas think that I drink that beer? That beer,' he said, 'is for the lost ones who come crying to me for it. Has the baas never heard the lost ones crying for beer?'

At dawn the party set out; Zwart Piete, de Kok, Sara and Rinkals, with the maiden who was the sister of the chief's wife tied to his wrist by a thin thong. She was chattering wildly.

'Why do you bring her?' Zwart Piete asked.

'She is my new medicine,' Rinkals said.

'For lions? Of what good is a maid against a lion?' de Kok asked.

'Let the Bastard but think for a moment,' the Kaffir said. 'Let him consider the ways of a lion. Would it not appear even to one as foolish as I know you to be, that a wise lion would prefer a young and tender maid to an old and shrivelled man? Is that not sense?'

'You talk of lions as if they were men.'

'I speak of lions as they are, and it is well known that the souls of the dead often go into the bodies of beasts. The spirits of brave men into lions, that of yellow Bastards into jackals.'

'And that of old doctors?' de Kok asked.

'If they be wise remain where they are. My soul is more than a thousand years old. Ja,' he said, 'and it rests comfortably in my body.' He put his hand on his stomach.

'Let the maid go,' Zwart Piete said, 'and we will begin.'

'The baas means that?'

'Ja, I mean it.'

'The baas has spoken, but if harm comes to me I shall haunt him. Ja, day and night my spook will torment the baas.' Reluctantly he let the girl go. Jumping away from him she ran, springing like a buck, running without turning her head.

Soon they found traces of the lion, a fresh-killed wildebeeste surrounded by his spoor. The horses plunged and reared as the scent rose from the long grass.

'He is near,' Zwart Piete said as they tied the heads of the horses together and turned them with their backs to a clump of palms where they thought the lion might be lying asleep.

'When he gets up,' Piete said, 'I will shoot and you,' he turned to de Kok and Sara, 'will wait; if he charges do not fire till he is on you, then shoot for his lower jaw and breast.'

'Shall we fire the grass?' de Kok asked.

'No, we will walk up to him; he is a tame lion.'

'What will I do?' Rinkals asked. 'I should like to help the baas in this matter. Can I not hold the horses?'

'My horses will stand,' Piete said, 'also it is not so long since you feared horses.'

'I fear them still but I am a brave man and having conquered my fear would be willing to stay with them.'

'You will stay with us and if you run I will shoot you and your spirit can go into a lion,' Zwart Piete said as they advanced slowly some ten paces apart.

The lion, which had been sleeping, rose and walked quietly away. De Kok, raising his voice, let out a cry; the lion turned and Piete fired. The lion roared, sprang forward and fell. 'Shoot,' Piete said, and two more heavy bullets took the twitching beast as Piete reloaded.

'Ai, ai,' Rinkals shouted running forward, 'I will have his claws.' Without hesitating he sprang on the body which, as the air was expelled from its lungs, gave out a terrifying roar. As he leaped away a lioness came out of the bush and seeing him standing beside her mate launched herself at him with an enormous bound. As she leapt the old Kaffir flung his spear and went down under her; almost as he fell Piete, who had reloaded, fired. The heavy bullet knocked the big beast sideways, penetrating her heart.

Picking himself up Rinkals returned to them.

'That, baas,' he said, 'was not well done. It is a shameful thing that the baas who kills so swiftly should allow a lioness to play with his servant as a cat would play with a mouse.'

'Play with you,' Piete said, 'I fired at once.'

'The lioness played with me,' Rinkals repeated. 'I was under her for a great space. She might have hurt me,' he added. 'This is a thing for which I will not forgive the baas.

A thing that I will not forget.' He rubbed his buttocks. 'And, baas,' he went on, 'I fell upon a stone.'

5

On the following day the cattle which were owed to Rinkals were driven in; twenty cows and forty heifers nearly as big as their mothers. Piete looked at them in astonishment. 'What is all this?' he asked. 'Whose cows are these?'

'They are mine,' Rinkals said. 'A present from the chief, a small sign of his respect.'

'And do you think we are going to carry this mark of his respect with us?'

'No, baas. The baas will see; I have a plan and even now I go with it to the chief.'

Finding Matiba in front of his hut Rinkals squatted down before him; he did not speak but stared past the chief.

At last, however, after looking at him sourly for some moments Matiba said, 'What now, Mamba? For what reason do you seek me?'

'I come to bid the great chief farewell. Also I would ask his counsel of certain matters which concern him. Some questions which so great a lawgiver will no doubt be able to answer.'

'If it is but answers to questions that you want you may have them, snake, but no more cattle.'

'How many cows is it the custom here to pay for a young wife?' he asked.

'Ten cows.'

'How many for an old wife? A widow?' he asked.

'Who wants old women?' the chief said.

'Not old, that is true, nobody wants them, but women shall I say no longer quite so young. Women in whom the sap flows less strongly.'

'Five cows.'

'And has the great bull such women?'

'I have many.'

'And he would part with them?'

'Oh, yes, I would part with them,' Matiba said, chuckling.

'Then, listen, oh wind that bends the mighty trees, oh bull elephant, I will give you back some of your cows for women.'

'If it was women, old ones, you wanted, why did you not ask for them at once and then there would have been no bad blood between us. Tell me what you want,' he said.

'This is what I want in return for the small service I once did you. I want the maiden who has attended to the spirits, they have become used to her presence among them and she pleases them greatly by her pretty ways; for her in the name of the spirits I will give ten cows, and for myself I want an old woman skilled in the making of beer, another who works well in the fields, for it is my heart to make a garden, and one who cooks better than the average, and a fourth who works in leather breying and tanning it; for these I will give ten cows and ten heifers.'

'And the heifers?' the chief asked. 'And the heifers that are over?'

'Those, because my heart is full, I will give back to the chief to keep in trust for me and for this, when I pass this way he will give me a seat by his fire, and meat for myself and those who are with me.'

'It is done, Mamba. I have spoken and there is a wall about the word of a chief. Though truly for so great a wizard you have gone a long way to achieve a small journey.'

'The king has spoken; I am indeed a great wizard and full of wisdom. But let the chief see that the women are strong, with all their teeth and still able to walk. Perhaps also as I am so great, the chief would give me one of his riding oxen, the one with twirly horns like koodoo that is milk white.'

'You shall have it, wizard. You shall have all you ask at dawn.'

'And, chief ——'

'Yes, Mamba?'

'Let the chief see to it that my cattle breed well. Let them
be marked and have special herders. Let them be spoken of
as the cattle of the Little Cloud Who Precedes the Storm.
The cattle of him who was once called Little Flower. Thus
shall my name be remembered, and the herds of all your people prosper.'

6

Zwart Piete was talking to Sara when Rinkals returned.

'Have you got rid of those cows?' he asked.

'Ja, baas, I have got rid of them, but it makes my heart
sore to think of it. They were beautiful cows.'

'Then be ready, for tomorrow we leave this place.'

'If the baas says so, it already is done. I will collect my
mat and pot. At dawn I shall be ready to guide the baas to
the country of the white men by the great water. In two
moons we will be there and the baas will see more wonders,
canoes with wings, great houses; he will also see the fathers
of his thunder-stick, they are fat and made of brass. Ai,
they have thunder and death in their bellies. All this I will
show the baas; ja, and because I am without malice I will
show him even though he let that lioness so ill-treat me.'

Next morning, having bidden good-bye to the chief, Zwart
Piete, de Kok and Sara waited for the old Kaffir.

'What has happened to your wizard, Sara?' Piete asked.

'I do not know, but I think he will come soon,' she said.

'He will come,' de Kok said. 'More, he comes, and he
comes not alone.'

They turned and saw a strange procession coming out of
the village.

The maid, the sister of the wife of the king, came first;
she was leading a milk-white ox whose horns were twirled
like the horns of koodoo. On the back of this ox sat Rinkals.
Behind him came four old women bearing burdens on their
heads, pots, karosses, and a roll of mats.

'What is this?' Zwart Piete shouted, riding up to him. 'What is all this?'

'Baas, this is nothing. The maid the spirits have grown fond of and will not part from; the ox is a present from the king who, seeing I could not walk, said that I must ride. The baas must remember that I fell upon a stone.'

'I remember; and these?' Piete indicated the old women.

'Oh, those,' Rinkals said. 'Those I bought from the king. They are the mothers of his young wives who trouble him and being skilled in the domestic arts will be a comfort to me, for daily my need of comfort grows.'

'But will they not trouble you?'

'Why should they? I do not sleep with their daughters.' He looked at them distastefully. 'I gave five beasts each for them,' he said, 'and they are pleased. They were much flattered. But had I asked I could have had them for nothing.'

'And the maiden? What did you pay for her?'

'Ten cows.'

'A great price,' Piete said, smiling.

'She is a lovely maiden, well formed and young; the lost ones are much pleased with her.'

'Truly,' Piete said, 'you are a great wizard. But tell me one thing, why only one maiden?'

'That is the proof of my wisdom, oh white man. For I am no longer young and my thoughts are now hotter than my blood — much hotter — and are young women warmed by thoughts? 'Let us ride on, baas; in two moons to the day, unless evil befall, we shall arrive at the great water.'

CHAPTER XIII

I

IN THE settlement life went on; went on, less well for the men than the beasts, for though the cattle were fat and increased there was much sickness among the people. Fever, which they already knew, was rampant, but nothing would drag them from soil so fertile or grass which suited their beasts so well. Their livestock were an integral part of the Boers; a man's herds were the man, his mind was a space in which the thoughts of his cattle moved mixed with the thoughts of his children, those who would inherit them.

At first they had lost many horses, but soon they discovered that horse sickness could be avoided by keeping their horses in kraals high up on the hillside and not allowing them to graze until the dew was off the grass. So among fat well liking beasts the people moved, dragging themselves to work in the rich lands, thinking themselves its owners when they were slaves to the ploughs they used, and the servants of their own calves and foals.

Grow, magtig, never had things grown like this before. Tante Anna's pumpkins, which she had planted so diffidently, sprang up with their great rough leaves and trumpet yellow flowers, fruiting and swelling till it took a big Kaffir to span one. Ach, God, had there been somewhere to sell their produce how rich they would all have become. But there was nowhere, and what, after all, were riches? A snare and a delusion, and was it not easier for a camel to pass through the eye of a needle than for a rich man to enter the gates of heaven?

Hendrik said that the fever would pass, that they would become hardened and immune to it, and so they did, many of them, but many died. The little cemeteries near the homesteads increased. Ja, the fat soil was fruitful also with crosses.

They were in contact with other treks now, others who had settled very near, less than a week on horseback away. It was through a man from one of these, passing in search of a wife, that Tante Anna heard of the sow.

Little by little, with much peach brandywine she drew the story from the visitor. It seemed that a man had started from the Cape with six pigs; he had died and the pigs, all but one sow, had failed to survive him. His widow did not understand pigs.

'Ja, one sow,' Tante Anna said, 'that is very sad. One sow, a pig alone; and how old is this sow?' she asked.

'She is eight months old.'

'Ja, that is very sad to think of a sow eight months old alone; neither a man nor a pig should live alone. And when were the others killed?'

'That is it, mevrou, that is what makes it so sad, for it was only the other day, the day before I left, that the last one, a little boar, was killed by a leopard.'

'And this woman who has the sow is sick, you say, and has a child that is small and neither milk in her breasts nor cows in milk. How sad life is. Ach, ja, a woman alone, a pig alone. De Fries you said her name was, did you not, mynheer? Once I knew some people called de Fries. I wonder if she is one of them?'

'Not de Fries, mevrou. Coetzee her name is.'

'Ach, ja, Coetzee,' Tante Anna said. 'How silly of me, but I am an old woman now and my memory is going. Once, mynheer, there was nothing that I could not remember. Ja, I even learnt a poem once. How did it go? It was about flowers and maidens. Perhaps you remember it?' she asked. 'You seem to me to be a very well-educated man, a remarkably learned man. I find your conversation both interesting and instructive.' Tante Anna looked down and raising her hands from her stomach gave her breasts a shake. She sighed, this stranger was not apparently susceptible to the charms of women though he said he was seeking a wife.

Calling Louisa she said, 'Send a boy for my grandson, Gert Kleinhouse, and tell him to come with all speed. You will stay to eat, mynheer. Ja, you must stay to eat.' She wondered if Sannie had finished those pickled fish and if it would be worth while to send a boy to see.

'That is a fine girl,' the stranger said as Louisa went out.

'A coloured wench,' Tante Anna said.

'A fine girl,' he repeated.

Ach, sis, it was always the same with men. Without regard for virtue, they were taken in by their eyes, led into evil ways by the superficiality of their vision, seeing goodness where there was only wantonness and closing their eyes to solid virtue. Certainly no one could call her wanton now, that at least age had done for her; Tante Anna wished that age had not done it. Ach, God, if I were young, she thought, I could have shown something to that Louisa; ach, sis, she has not half the tricks I had. A tear came into her eye as she thought of how provocative she had once been.

'You are sad,' the stranger said.

'Ja, mynheer, I am sad. It is the thought of that woman with a baby and no milk cow, and when I think of how I used to milk, of all the milk I have wasted, bottles and bottles of it,' she said.

Gert Kleinhouse did not come till the morning, and when he came the stranger had gone. Tante Anna was not the wife he sought.

'Now, Gert,' Tante Anna said, 'you will take a good milk cow, her calf and four tame oxen to Leman's trek, and there you will find a widow with no milk.'

'How shall I know her?' he asked.

'Fool, how do you know a dry cow? But her name is Coetzee. To this woman you will say that Tante Anna de

Jong has heard of her plight, and is making her a present of a cow.'

'Then what are the oxen for?'

'Are you God that you can drive a cow alone? Not that I think God could drive a cow alone.'

'And then what do I do?'

'You stay there with her.'

'How long do I stay?'

'You stay till she decides to give me a present in return. She will say to you, "What can I give this Mevrou de Jong for her kindness, two dry cows or some heifers?" and you will say no, to everything you will say no, till at last she will offer you the little sow that she has and then you will accept it and you will bring it back.'

'What? You will give a good milk cow for a little pig,' Gert said, 'truly you must be mad.'

'Listen, that little pig is not so little, soon it will have small ones for she is eight months old, and such is the nature of pigs. This is something that no one else seems to have considered. So go at once and be careful to milk the cow on the way, for she gives more than her calf can drink.'

'You are a slim old woman to take advantage of a widow like that.'

'No, Gert. I am not slim. I am kind. By doing this I perform an act of charity which God will reward, and soon we shall have the only pigs in the north country.'

'Ja, the only pigs, and what do I get for doing this, ouma.'

'You will get my thanks, Gert, and a small pig.'

'Will it be a little sow?'

'Nie, Gert, I am too slim for that, it will be a little boar, and when it is big you can eat it; and listen, each year I will give you a little boar. The sows are mine, never will I part with one of them.'

2

To drive four tame oxen, one milk cow and a calf through lion-infested country was no small thing and Gert, with two mounted Kaffirs, set out with a heavy heart. Truly it was a misfortune to have a grandmother like his, a woman so masterful that it was impossible to resist her. Even the thought of the pigs she would give him failed to comfort him. How did she know the sow would farrow? How was he to approach the widow Coetzee? He was nervous of widows — they knew too much. He doubted if he was clever enough to deal with a man-hungry widow. Ach, ja, his ouma demanded too much of him when she sent him on this journey. Still, widows were not necessarily old. He thought of Marietje de Wett who had married Martinus and smiled. A widow would be more practical than a young girl; she would see beyond his cross eyes, she would see deep into his soul, which was beautiful. Ja, ja, there were widows and widows. If it had not been for the milk cow with her swinging cabbage of an udder he would have trotted. He wondered if the widow was dark or fair and how much she weighed. Gert had a weakness for big, handsome women, deep breasted and wide hipped. There was much comfort to be found in the arms of such a woman.

Alert for danger he rode on with his Kaffirs chattering behind him, while in front of him the cattle moved slowly, stopping now and then to crop at the grass as they walked. Sleeping four times on the road he arrived at last and inquired for the widow Coetzee.

Leman's settlement was much like their own, at the same stage of development, but the land seemed less good and the stock in poorer condition. The widow, it appeared, lived alone on her farm in a depression of the hills to the north of the river.

It was here he found her, sitting on the stoep of her house with her child upon her knee, sitting as if she were awaiting him.

Even from a distance he could see that she was a beautiful woman with a flat face and a well-fleshed body suitably clad in a dress of black flannel cloth with a wide white turn-over collar and sleeves neatly buttoned at the wrist. Her skirt was heavy with flounces round the hem and almost hid her fine strong legs. He could not see the colour of her hair as it was covered by a big black linen kappie which came down over her shoulders.

There was about this woman an air of placid well-being which brought Gert's heart into his mouth and made him glad that he had thought of wearing his pale yellow bell-shaped top hat and the dark yellow corduroy trousers which went so well with his coat of blue nankeen. The hand of God was certainly in this. Unless more were to come of it than a sow for his grandmother why should he have been prompted to wear his best? To doubt the truth of this would be to doubt the goodness of a Providence which invariably did everything for the best.

Cocking his hat over his left eye and inflating his chest he rode slowly towards the widow who, after a quick embracing look, modestly lowered her eyes.

Dismounting, and with the reins over his arm, he approached her.

'My name is Gert Kleinhouse,' he said putting out his hand.

'I am Mevrou Coetzee,' the widow said.

'I have been sent to you by my grandmother, Tante Anna de Jong.'

'I have heard of Mevrou Anna de Jong,' the widow answered. 'Come inside and I will make you coffee and then you will tell me why you have come.'

'I have come to bring you a present from my grandmother; she is a very kind woman and has heard that you have a small child.'

'Ja, that is so, it is a boy.' Mevrou Coetzee held up her son.

'Also she has heard that you have no milk and that your best cows are dry.'

'Anna de Jong has long ears, but all she has heard is true. Ja, it is God's truth.'

'And therefore,' Gert went on, 'she has sent me to bring you a cow and a calf. The cow milks well,' he added, 'and her name is Bloometjie. When you call Bloometjie she comes. She is more like a dog than a cow, very tame and affectionate.'

'Ach, ja, mynheer, I know; once in the colony I had a tame cow. How beautiful she was. Black, with a yellow nose; Gielbeck she was named, but she died with her second calf. Ah, God, how I cried. You have no idea how I cried, mynheer, for I have a very tender heart.'

'One has but to look at you, mevrou, to see that you have a soft heart. Even on so short an acquaintance I would say your heart was as soft and as full of juice as a naartjie.'

'Ach, that is strange, mynheer, for that is what my husband always used to say. Ja, he would say, "Martha, your heart is like a naartjie.'

'So your name is Martha, mevrou. Truly that is a beautiful name. Martha,' Gert repeated.

Ignoring his remark Mevrou Coetzee said, 'Am I wrong in thinking that your horse is lame, mynheer?'

'My horse is not lame. He is never lame,' Gert said angrily.

'Then I was mistaken, but I thought he was going a little lame. It is no shame for a horse to go lame after days in the mountains. I thought perhaps a few days' rest would do him good.'

'Ah, a few days' rest, mevrou, that is another thing. A few days' rest for a horse in rich pasture is always good. It eases them,' he added.

'Rest is good for men folk, too. Ah men, they burn themselves up. You, mynheer, are the kind of man who burns himself up. Anyone could see that you are full of fire.'

Gert felt himself burning up and full of fire. 'Ja, mevrou, it is so and yet you are the first to have seen it. You are indeed different to other women. Most women,' he went on, 'are either foolish or ugly, and many are both.'

'Ach, mynheer, how you flatter me and how like you are to my dear Jan.'

'He must have been a fine man, mevrou,' Gert said.

'Fine, fine is no word to describe my Jan. Ah, God, what a man and how he could love. In love and anger, mynheer, he was a lion, very quick and bold, quite irresistible to a weak woman like myself, one who knows that women should submit themselves to that which God sends them. And when he looked at me out of his great blue eyes, mynheer, there was a storm in my heart. Ja, the very first day that I saw him when he drove up to my father's house with a pair of matched red horses in his cart I knew that he would not leave without me. In that first look he held me like a young pigeon in his hand. "Here," I said to myself, "is certainly the man who will be the father of my children," for even to a maid do such thoughts come no matter how delicate her mind may be, especially when she feels the eyes of a man upon her.'

'It is certainly sad that such a man should die,' Gert said.

'Ja, it is sad, and what a worker he was. Look at the furniture he made for me.' Mevrou Coetzee pointed to the enormous four-posted bedstead in the corner of the room. 'Ja, he was a very skilled man in all ways, and one who was much respected. I hope you will stay here and rest for a while, mynheer, there are many things about which I should like to consult you. It is not that there are no good straightforward men here, there are many of them, but it is not good that those among whom one lives should know too much of one's affairs. You have a fine open face, mynheer. You certainly are not a man to take advantage of a widow — that I saw at once when you rode up on your fine horse. Ja, ja, I am very quick to make up my mind about people,' Mevrou Coetzee said. 'It is a gift that I have and I am never wrong.'

'Baie dankie, mevrou. It is indeed kind of you to bid me stay some days.'

'And does mynheer care for the smoked thigh of an eland?' the widow asked.

'In all the world there is nothing I like as much as the smoked thigh of an eland,' Gert said. Crossing the room he looked at the small spinet that stood against the wall. 'You are musical,' he said.

'Ja, mynheer, I play, but not so much now that I have to do a man's work as well as my own.'

'Music is wonderful,' Gert said. 'Ja, it is wonderful. It twists one's stomach like a purge.'

'Then you too are musical, mynheer, you understand.'

'Ja, I am musical. Too musical. For, like love, music gives me a pain low in the stomach.'

'You play an instrument?' Martha Coetzee asked.

'I do not play,' Gert said, 'but I sing. I sing bass,' he added.

3

Hendrik was dissatisfied. Time, the one thing over which he had no control, was pressing upon him. If his seed was to inherit the earth he must have seed. Many men of his age were already several times grandfathers and was he not like Abraham to be the father of a multitude? To Abraham God had made the promise that his seed should be as the dust of the earth, of whom he had said, 'That if a man can number the dust of the earth, then shall thy seed also be numbered.'

His mind swung in anger from Sannie to Louisa; to other women; to all women, potential mothers of his children. One woman was much like another to him and only with difficulty could he differentiate between them, and yet his thoughts kept turning back to Louisa, who was fast becoming symbolic of all that he required of her sex, and because he resented Louisa's power, he raged furiously against Sannie:

Sannie whom he possessed, who was so acquiescent and un-responsive.

The more he took of her the less he had, and as her beauty and desirability increased, he flung himself like a hungry man onto the feast of her young womanhood. Gorging him-self he left her exhausted, unsatisfied, his thirst unslaked. Though he had got her with child again he had no pleasure from it and forced himself to work as a relief from thought, ripping up the soil with his plough as though it were an enemy, burning bush to clear it more quickly and killing game wantonly and without reason.

More and more, as days went by, the vision of the coloured girl kept coming to him, visiting him in the night as he lay beside his wife, following him about his work. He saw her everywhere; he saw her flitting among the trees, reflected in the dark water of the dam he had made, in the kraals of his cattle, in the bed of his wife. It was as if she had put a spell upon him, an enchantment.

Soon he began to see her in the flesh, for Tante Anna sent her often to Sannie with delicacies that she had concocted or with messages, and Louisa, knowing where Hendrik was, invariably managed to pass near him.

A coloured bitch was no receptacle for the seed of a van der Berg, but seed must have soil, and the soil of Louisa's body was rich. Having got this far, Hendrik ached for her, to hold her, to touch the softness of her skin. Coloured or not, she was a woman, and she was not deeply coloured. Surely the prepotency of his race would be strong enough to efface the stain, surely he was white enough for two.

'Kom, Bosveld, Rinkals, Witboi, Bles,' he shouted to his oxen as he turned them on the headland. 'Kom.' And his long whip cracked, clap after clap.

'I am too strong,' he said to himself. 'The Lord God has made me too strong. And of what good is one woman to a man like me? I am the instrument of God, and it is He who has made me as I am.' Once more as the long greasy furrows turned away from his driving plough he thought of Louisa and her hidden softness.

That day his oxen were much scarred by their master's long whip. A whip he had made himself out of kameel skin with an achter slaag of koodoo and voorslaag of blesbok. A bitter biting thing that curled wickedly about the sleek red hides of his working oxen and bit deep into them when he thought of the coloured wench; but much land was ploughed that day — nearly a morgen, which usually was the work of two days.

Ach, ja, by work one could kill desire, but was it right to kill it? To kill a gift of God?

Where before his cry had been onwards, it was now fertility. Fertility of soil, of cow and mare and ewe, of she-goat and of woman. Fertility, drawing life up from the depths of the past and pouring it out into the future, like the buckets attached to the endless chain of a deep cool well, one which, however much one drew upon it, never emptied; one in which the water level never fell.

4

To Louisa life was a simple thing; like a wheel her life revolved, turning continually, leaving a spoor of memory which grew ever fainter. Without much hope of the future, without regret for the past, she moved, enjoying the simple things. The pleasure of sunshine when it was cold, of shade when it was hot, of eating, of suckling her child, of lying with a man when her body demanded this of her. Pure in her utter lack of shame, Louisa was neither good nor bad. She was a woman. Her contempt for black people and other coloured ones grew daily as her child became paler with its increasing age. Little Anna was almost white, with light-brown hair.

Her dream of the milk-white heifer and the young red bull and the big black bull had come true. Her dreams now were of the big black bull alone. A big bull very strong and fierce, whose face was the face of Hendrik van der Berg and which, in her dreams, she led about by the ring through its nose. This dream also would come true. It would come true when Sannie was grown big with the child that was in her, when the meilies were high. It would come true among the thick green stems of the meilies when nearly ripe, their tassels hung like pale green horses' tails from the covered cobs.

Till then she would wait, working and showing herself now and then to the man she wanted. For by allowing him to see her she would warm his desire into a stronger thing, a flame that would devastate him, running like a grass fire in the winter through his veins.

Anna de Jong's blows when she was idle did not disturb her, they were without a sting, for the skin she whipped would soon be caressed by the hands of Hendrik van der Berg, the leader, the greatest man among them; one who killed to obtain the gratification of his desires, the big black bull of her dreams.

Her baby she now carried on her hip. Her body bent, springing like a bow upwards from the waist, remained as erect as ever, her stride as free but more supple and undulating in its movements, as balanced on the balls of her feet with her bare toes gripping the ground firmly, she walked proudly swinging her neat croup. She was a lovely creature and knew it. Strong, beautiful and healthy, she took admiration as her tribute, imperious and scornful of coloured men, she was subtly flattering and seductive to the white. Louisa was what her mother had been, and her mother's mother in their youth. She was the product of her own heredity and environment, perfectly adapted to the purpose to which she had been formed. Like an animal, she had been bred by man for his own pleasure, one of a breed evolved, as various kinds of cattle or varieties of dogs were evolved, the result of a care ful selection carried on for many years through many generations.

5

Anna de Jong was surprised when, at the end of a fort-night, she had received no news of her grandson. Had anything happened to him? Had he made a fool of himself? As the days passed it seemed to her that the little sow was the one thing necessary to add savour to her life, to give it solidity. Pigs were home-like animals. They were not like cows or sheep or horses which could be driven about indefinitely. A pig, more particularly a sow, was symbolic of settled occupation with its gruntings, wallowings, and swarms of squealing piglings.

Surely Gert must return soon driving the young sow in front of him. She wondered what it would be like. Black and white, she hoped, with more black than white on it, for white pigs suffered badly from sun-scald. Ach, one had to be very careful with white pigs, their skin was as delicate as a maiden's. She wondered how many tits she would have. The more tits a sow had the better, seven or eight a side was the best and six too few. For with a big litter some could never drink if their mother had only six tits, and suppose Gert had been foolish and unable to obtain the sow. If this had happened he could hardly bring back the cow and calf. After all, a present was a present. Still, it was no use worrying oneself; everything was in the hands of God and no doubt because of this, whatever happened, it would be for the best, even if it did not seem so at the time. Ach, ja, but without pigs one could not have pork, and she was very fond of pork, and because she was so fond of it there was a very warm place in her heart for pigs. Pigs, pork, roast pork, salt pork, sucking pig stuffed and cooked in a slow oven, blood pudding. What a tragedy it was that as one grew old food became so important. Once, food had meant nothing to her. Provided there had been enough of it and that it was well cooked, flavoured and of good quality she had not cared what it was she ate. But now it was different, her stomach was as delicate, as dainty as a sugar bird in its fancies, crying out for this and that as though it were a person. When one was young one had no control of one's carnal desires; when one was old none over one's appetite for food.

The more one thought about life the more difficult it was to see reason in it, to differentiate between good and evil, between joy and sorrow. Everything was so mixed, it was like a curry; too sweet, and it was sickly, too bitter and it was unpleasant. She sighed. I am a foolish old woman. These thoughts that I think are men's thoughts, both unwomanly and unpractical. Shading her eyes, she looked towards the mountain road; at any time now Gert might come back driving the tame oxen and the little sow. It was pleasant to think that the widow, Coetzee, was now at peace with a good milk cow. I am a good woman, she thought, 'casting my bread upon the waters.' She began to laugh, her body quivering. 'Ja, ja, bread,' she said aloud. 'And I have done more than that. I have cast a good milk cow with her calf at foot upon the waters.' She laughed at her thoughts till the tears came into her eyes, partly with amusement and partly with sorrow, as she thought of the pigs she had at home and the skilful way that Jappie had killed them, sticking them in the heart with his long sharp knife.

I

ZWART PIETE and his party advanced slowly, moving eastwards again and camping with their backs to the setting sun. At one kraal, the last in this part of the country, they arrived on the eve of a great lion hunt.

Rinkals's suggestion to the chief that his attendant spirits should kill this lion — it had taken a number of cattle — was refused on the grounds that it would be a pity to trouble the spirits with so small a matter, one with which his young men were so well able to deal, but on the other hand, if he could persuade the spirits to make the stream which flowed through their land to run more strongly both he and his people would be much obliged.

'Ai,' Rinkals said. 'Truly to make water run more strongly is no light matter, but as you desire it I will see what I can do, but first, before I can achieve anything I must see this stream, so send me a maiden to show me the way. If she be beautiful and fat there is little doubt that I can do what you wish, but she must be a comely maid, for of all spirits those of the water are the hardest to please. Ai,' he said, 'the water spirits are adamant unless a maid be lovely. Let her also bring beer,' he said, 'a great pot of it on her head, and come with a comb full of honey in her hand. With these three things I can charm the water gods no matter how sulky they be.'

'Will you not take your other spirits and your wives with you?' the chief asked.

'No,' Rinkals said, 'they are hunting spirits and deal only

with thunder and lightning. They have no knowledge of the water gods or the making of rain. Let them go with your young men, oh, chief, and let me go my ways with the maid. Fear not for her, her eyes shall not be dimmed with tears nor her body fade to insignificance. I will give her medicine, and power over the waters so that while she lives the stream will flow strongly and your herds prosper.'

To Zwart Piete he said: 'Baas, go with these people and watch over them while they hunt the lion after their fashion, while I go to the stream with this maiden and make medicine.'

'Do you ever make medicine without a maiden?' de Kok asked.

'Sometimes I do,' Rinkals said. 'Sometimes, when there are no maidens, but it is dull to work alone. Listen, baas,' he went on, turning to Zwart Piete, 'I know that you think we waste time, but it is well to have friends among these people, for one day we may pass this way again.'

'To sleep with their maidens is not the way to make friends, rather will it make enemies.'

'Sleep, baas. Sleep.' The old man raised his hands in horror. 'Long ago,' he said, 'I used to do these things, there was the one who called me Little Flower. I think I slept with her and then there were others — there must have been others, but I forget them. Women,' he said, 'are like leaves, they wither, they fall and are forgotten. Ai, baas,' he said, 'I am too old to think of these things and to speak of them makes my heart grow sore. So go, young man, and hunt lions in the company of the warriors, for me and such as me there is little comfort in such childish things, though once it was otherwise, and in my time many lions have fallen to my spears. Lions without number,' he added. 'But go now, baas, and leave me to meditate and by the aid of the lost ones whom I shall invoke set a spell on the running waters, and thus obtain the gratitude of these rude uncultured people.'

'Come,' Piete said, 'let us leave him.' And mounting their

horses, they joined the group of young men who were going out to hunt the lion which had killed their cattle. Spreading out in a long line, the warriors trotted over the veld. The buck which got up, they let pass unharmed, and at last, among some reeds near the river, they found the lion. Seeing them, he ran from them without looking back, slowly at first, but later in great bounds as they pressed him. At a thick bush he turned to face them, growling and lashing his tail. One of the men threw a stone at him and he ran again, and again turned. This time they surrounded him and mocked him, calling him a dog and a cow, and always coming closer till they ringed him about, and then one man bolder than the others stood out and challenged him, dancing in front of him, calling him names and threatening him with his spears.

'He will charge in a minute, baas,' de Kok said. 'Shall we shoot or run away?'

'We will do neither. Let us see their way of doing this thing, it is new to me.'

'It is new to me also, baas, and I do not like it,' the Griqua answered.

The lion had lowered himself and lay with only his tail moving jerkily watching the man who postured in front of him. Suddenly his tail went up, standing like a ramrod out of his body, and with a roar he charged. As he came, the man who had mocked him went down, covering himself with his big shield, and the others threw their spears, and so the lion who had stolen their cattle died, and the man at whom he had sprung rose up from under his ox-hide shield unharmed, not even scratched by the great claws.

That night there was much rejoicing in the village, for the lion was dead and the river, so Rinkals assured them, their servant, bound to the maiden by his spells. There remained only one thing to do. This was to go up to the eye of the river, the fountain where it rose, and bid it to flow more freely; it might even be necessary to beat it with a small switch, though this was a dangerous thing to do and would be more expensive. It was, however, for them to decide what he wanted done, perhaps what had already been done would be enough. After all, he was old and was not sure if the reward they offered would be enough to make him do this thing. To whip a spring was a great risk, and soon he would go to join the spirits among whom he had many friends. 'Ai,' he said, 'can I take the cows and maidens you would give me for doing this thing with me when I join the great ones?'

'We have offered you no cows and maidens,' they said.

'No, but you will offer and I have taken no offence that you have not done so. It is only your ignorance of the way a great wizard should be treated which has prevented you doing so, and perhaps a certain diffidence that fifty head of cattle would be too few for the work I have done. Your stream runs strongly and I will give you rain. The spirits have promised it,' he added.

'Fifty head,' they echoed, 'and how do we know that it will rain?'

'Yes, fifty head. It is very little I know, but I am old and no longer ambitious. Worldly wealth is without meaning for me, and a man rich in stock has many enemies for by his death others benefit. Go now into council and consider this matter, for I am weary with my labours. All day I have worked to master your river and I have it now, it is mine.' Opening his hand, he spat into his palm. 'It is mine,' he repeated, 'as the spittle in my hand is mine. I can add to it' — he spat again — 'or I can wipe it out, or burn it up. Ai, ai, to destroy a river is nothing to a man like me, I have done it many times when I was angry or the people with whom I dealt were mean and avaricious. As to rain. Do not fear, you will soon have it, and now I am going to make medicine with the white spirits and give them my commands. Now I could not whip the head waters of your river for a hundred head of cattle, for my spirit is troubled by your insults and your lack of faith. It will be best,' he added, 'to have the cattle here by the dawn, they should be fat and each should have eight teeth in its mouth.' Wrapping his kaross round him, he hobbled away to the fire where Zwart Piete, Sara and de Kok sat waiting for him.

'Tomorrow, baas,' he said, 'we shall have fifty head of stock.'

'What shall we do with them?' Piete asked.

'What shall we do with them? What does one do with cattle?' the old man grumbled. 'Ai, what does one do? One counts them, one talks about them, one drinks the milk of the cows, one eats the oxen, one praises the bulls. There is no end to what one can do with cattle. And what is a man without cows?' he asked. 'Who respects him? Even the maidens knowing he has no beasts for lobola, look at him boldly, laughing. And how is it that you who have the wisdom of the white men in your hands can ask me of what use are cattle? Truly, baas, to be old as I am is a sad thing. Ai, for now even the master whom I serve makes fun of me, makes me a laughing stock.'

'No, no,' Piete said. 'I think you are a great man, Rinkals.'

'Ai, the baas has spoken true words. Among doctors I am great, towering above them like an elephant among a company of rabbits. Great, I am more than great, a thousand years old I am, and the father of all magic, producing oxen, maidens, storms, and Zulus out of nothing.' He took a drink of beer from the calabash at his side and handed it to one of his women to be refilled. 'The baas has only to say the word and there is nothing that old Rinkals the wizard will not give him. Gold, the teeth of elephants, women, cattle, and now he says what shall we do with these beasts which we have not got yet. Wait, lord, wait. I will make medicine and we shall soon see what to do with them.'

Pulling the string of the bag round his neck, over his head, he emptied out its contents on the ground by the fire.

Squatting on his heels with his rat tails of hair falling over his wrinkled face, he scraped with bony fingers in the little heap, pulling out one thing after another. A knuckle bone from a vulture's wing, a dried scorpion, the shell of a river crab, a human ear smoked and shrivelled, some pebbles, a nugget of gold, two buttons. All this he did with his eyes closed, and then opening them he began to arrange them in a pattern moving them about while he gazed fixedly at the polished rock crystal that he had set in the centre. As he worked his eyes grew larger, and the sweat poured from his armpits, running down his shrivelled flanks. At last it was done, and sweeping away the objects he had been using, he sat back on his haunches.

For a moment he stared upwards at the star-pierced sky, and then leant forward, and said: 'Listen, baas. Listen to what I say. Once not long ago I foretold much to the baas's sister, and then I was not strong — I was very sick, nor had I the mouti' — he pointed to the heap — 'for strong medicine, but now,' his voice rose shrilly, 'tonight I have pierced the veil, torn down by the strength of my spells and this is what I have seen.

'Over there' — he raised a skinny hand and pointed — 'lies the great water and much good fortune. Also war and death through which we will pass unscathed, gaining titles and riches. Later, a hundred moons away, there will be a division among us and the death of one which will be balanced by the coming of another, and then I see blood and hear cries. Soon we will meet many people, very many. These I did not see clearly, but they are not enemies, yet before we reach this place we shall have to pass through a dead land, bare and inhospitable, without a living thing upon it, neither bird nor beast. Ai, for many days we shall see nothing alive, and here we shall live on the flesh and the milk of the beasts I have obtained for making rain.'

'But since there is no rain,' Piete said.

'There will be rain, baas.' Rinkals looked at the sky again. 'Does the baas think that if there would not be rain I should promise it to these people? Before dawn there will be rain, lord, the little river will run and the fifty head of cows be in our hands together with the gratitude and the fear of these people. Therefore, as I say, we will advance through this dead barren land with our cows, and later, before we pass out of it, they will bring us good fortune. These cows, I say, will be as a stepping stone that will lead us to the greatness on which the baas has set his heart. Now that I am alone, I am the father and mother of the baas. I will clasp him to the breasts of my knowledge, weaning him slowly till at last he is indeed a king in his understanding of the strange ways of men and able to read their hearts, becoming a second only to me in his wisdom and his cunning.'

'It seems to me,' Piete said, 'that before we met you I was the leader and that now it is you who lead.'

'I lead, baas? Why do you mock me? Can the old and fragile lead the young and fearless? Does the steinbok lead the lion? No, lord, it is not so. Because I offer the baas a plan ready made, like a piece of cooked meat on a platter, does it mean that I lead? It happens that I know the road we must go, as I know all roads, and my knowledge is there for the baas to use. Ai,' he went on, 'my knowledge is a great burden for me to bear, limitless, and heavy as a herd of elephants it lies like a great weight on my heart.'

2

The weather changed during the night as Rinkals had said it would, and the rain came down in torrents, flooding the village to such an extent that the chief came to the hut where the old man slept to implore him to make it stop.

'You are like a small child, oh, chief,' Rinkals said, 'or a woman. First you want and then you do not want. I offer to kill your lion, but no, you say, make us rain, and lo, I make rain,—much rain, never has there been so fine a rain, and then you disturb me in my slumbers to tell me that I have made more than you desire. Did you ask me to make a small rain?

I am a great wizard and when I make rain, I make rain. Go, chief, for I would sleep. But this I say, that the rain will cease with the coming of the sun. But unless my cows are ready tomorrow I will send such a rain that this one will be as nothing; such a rain that your beasts, exhausted with swimming, will die and float with their swollen bellies upwards, their legs as stiff as trees pointing to the clouds. Such a rain will I send that you will speak of this rain, of which you now complain, as a small shower, for where you had the calf of the water spirits, I will send a span of bulls beneath which you and your people will be flattened.'

In the morning the rain had stopped, and the cattle were there, a full fifty head, their horns shining, their hides, wet with the rain of the night, steaming as the power of the sun increased. A beautiful herd of red, black and yellow beasts. There were also some pale greyish ones with fine humps and a young cow that was red, spotted most beautifully with white upon her hinder parts.

Driving the herd before them, they advanced into the country which was, as Rinkals had said, desolate and God forgotten. An area where stunted roi-bos, vaal-bos and seringa trees grew among the tussocks of coarse grass; where patches of iron red conglomerate, sparkled metallically in the sunlight. Neither mountainous nor flat, the country undulated in waves whose frozen crests were topped with stones set jaggedly on end. An evil country which the old witch-doctor said was damned and inhabited only by the worst kind of spirits and spooks, the ones who were inimical not only to man and beast, but also to the water gods, the tree gods and the gods of the rich sweet grass. There was no life here, no movement, and even birds were scarce. In several days all they saw was one blue jay, a pair of shiny starlings, metal-green with red-jewelled eyes, and a solitary hoopoe. Of greater beasts, once they saw a troop of baboons, travelling, and once a male rhinoceros which Zwart Piete set out to hunt.

'Ach, God,' he said, 'here is something alive at last, let us see if he will attack.' As was his custom, he approached the beast up wind. If he could get to within thirty paces of it he would put a bullet into its small eye or between the chinks of its heavy armour.

Dismounted, these animals were simple enough to kill, for even if one missed they rushed forward with their heads low and their eyes closed seeking out their enemies, striving for them with their horns. All that was necessary when they did this was to step nimbly away and allow them to thunder past as they forged onwards mad with the rage that consumed them. Often Piete had done this, playing with one for hours, till with its strength exhausted it stood like an ox waiting to be slaughtered. But this beast did not charge, it ran away, tramping down the bushes and small trees which, springing up, barred the way of de Kok's galloping horse. Pursued by the cries of the hunters, the rhinoceros ran, his back rising and falling above the scrub.

'This is a verdamte land,' Piete said, as he remounted. 'A place where even the animals are bewitched. How much more of it, Rinkals? How many more days do we march through this desert, a country of nothing, I am tired of it.'

For variety they had only mirages to look at which conjured up sad thoughts of the fat lands they had left. Perpetual mirages, in which, shimmering through the haze of heat, they saw tall trees by the banks of great sheets of water and game on long stilt-like legs moving aimlessly about.

Apart from the heat they had also some anxiety about water, because there had been rain and there was water lying in the pans, but it was shallow and of an evil taste, and the horses, more fastidious than the cattle, only drank of it when their thirst became unendurable.

So they went on led by Rinkals till they came to a road of hard, tramped earth. Here the old Kaffir dismounted and stood fondling the ears of his white ox, his knees trembling as he clung to it for support.

'What is it?' Sara asked.

'Ikoosi. For some days now I have been afraid that we were lost, that I had missed my way. It is many hundreds of years since I was here,' he said, 'and the mind of an old man is like an old gourd; it no longer holds all that is put into it. Yes,' he went on, 'I was a young man when I was here last.'

'Then this must be a very old road,' Zwart Piete said, laughing. 'And where does it lead?'

'It is indeed an old road, baas. As old as the world. It is the path taken by those who hunt men. It leads from the country of the forests to the great water where the white men live. Ai,' he said, 'once I travelled this road shackled like a beast, driven on by the blows of whips. Many have died along this road, lord.

'Look,' he said, 'it will not take long to show the baas.' Leaving his ox which, lowering its head, curled a long black tongue round a wiry spike of grass, he ran forward into some bushes. A moment later he was back with a skull in his hand.

'The head of a young woman, lord,' he said, 'a woman with fine strong teeth.' He smelt it. 'And one not long dead. I shall keep this, it will make good medicine.' Going up to one of the old women who carried his things he dropped it into the pot on her head.

'Eeeh! Eeeh!' she cried in fright. 'I will not carry this thing,' she said, dropping the pot, which broke, while the skull, rolling out went bowling along the road.

'Oh, mother of warriors long since dead,' Rinkals said, 'the time is past when in the pride of your youthful beauty you could choose your burdens. Ai, even the men for whom you bore them and you will now carry what you are bidden.'

'And if I don't?' she screamed. 'If I won't?'

'Then, old woman, you will die. For who is there to suc-cour a woman when there is no pleasure to be found in her body and naught but venom in her tongue? Ai, ai, hag, politeness is very necessary to the aged and the useless, very necessary unless they be wizards of great renown.'

Going up to the skull he kicked it towards her. 'Pick it up,' he said, 'lest I curse you. Lest I send the spook of the young woman to whom it belongs to haunt you, a thing which it will do with much anger for the spooks of young women whose blood still runs are angry if they have to inhabit the body of an old crone who can do nothing but make beer and who, it seems to me, makes it worse and worse as time goes on.'

Remounting his ox, Rinkals pointed up the path. 'Lead on, white lord. This is the road to the great water. We, your servants, follow.'

CHAPTER XV

I

IT WAS some days after the finding of the skull that de Kok who had been riding on one of the flanks cantered up to his master.

'Baas, baas,' he said, 'there are men behind us, many men. I saw the light on their spears, and they are too numerous to fight.'

'Then, if we can't fight them we will meet them in friendship,' Piete said. 'Let us ride on to that small kopje and wait.'

It was from here, screened by the scrubby trees, that they watched the procession approach them. Out of the bush people defiled in an endless stream. First came a great negro carrying a standard fastened to a long pole. It was covered with black writing, characters which curled and twisted like notes of music, and drooped its ragged edges in the hot, windless air.

Behind him came some armed men, fierce-looking warriors carrying small round shields, swords and spears. Some of them Piete noticed were wounded and had dirty blood-stained rags wrapped round their heads and arms. They were followed by a string of Kaffirs, hundreds of them, yoked together by means of forked branches pegged round their necks. They were all young — women, men, girls, boys, and children — and marched in a straggling column with their heads bent. Many were emaciated and almost all had sores on their necks where the yokes had galled them.

Beside the slaves, at intervals, grave, bearded Arabs stalked majestically with their long, short-butted guns over their shoulders and heavy whips of rhinoceros hide in their hands.

At the tail of the caravan was an old, white-bearded Arab wearing a green head-cloth. A small boy led his white she-ass by its scarlet leather reins while his master sat, with his feet high in the short stirrups, reading. The old man was surrounded by a bodyguard of mixed race — Arabs, bastard Arabs and big negroes from the north carrying long spears and some with swords, a wild heterogeneous crowd of savage fighting men who moved easily and lightly about their master.

'Ai,' Rinkals said, 'those are bitter fighting men, baas, cruel as tigers, men whose hearts are salt like brak water. Ai, they are men who kill for gain and not for sport, or women.'

At the cries of his people the old chief, Hussien Zeid looked up.

His warriors had already surged forward with a swirl of rusty, red henna dyed tunics, their black cloaks flying out behind them, their weapons poised. This was their business, they were the fighters, they were not herders of human cattle. Putting a small horn to his mouth, the chief called them back and halted the caravan. The impassive Arabs unloosed their guns and the slaves, relieved from the burden of movement, lay down or stood with slack knees waiting. Already they had acquired some of the fatalism of their masters, what would be, would be, the creed of Islam, of resignation. Raising eyes dulled by misery and exhaustion, they watched Zwart Piete, de Kok and Sara riding towards them.

'Now,' Piete said, and simultaneously the three raised the muzzles of their guns and fired into the air.

'They come in peace,' the old Arab said to his grandson who stood beside him with his hand on the hilt of his jewelled dagger. 'They come in peace, Abstan,' he repeated. 'Their weapons are empty.'

From his tall horse, Piete looked down at the old Arab.

'I am Zwart Piete,' he said. 'How goes it, uncle?' he asked in Dutch.

'There is no God but God.'

'What does he say, de Kok?' Piete asked.

'That I do not know, baas. Let us send for our wizard who knows all tongues.' And he swung his horse to fetch him. But Rinkals had followed them, he was at their side, sitting calmly wrapped in his kaross of wildcat skin upon the back of his white ox.

'Did you ask if I knew the language of these people, Bastard?' he inquired. 'Did I hear you ask that or is it, that being old, my ears deceive me?'

'You heard rightly, wizard.'

'Shall I speak, inkoos?' Rinkals asked.

'Yes, speak, old snake,' de Kok said. 'Make it clear that we come in peace, but are ill folks to thwart.'

'Shall I do as the Bastard says?' Rinkals asked. 'Shall I speak to this man, baas?'

'Speak,' Piete said. 'Ask him whence he comes, and where he goes.'

'I will speak as the baas commands,' the old man said.

'Oh, lord,' he said to the chief, 'my master bids me tell you that we come in peace, and he asks whence you come, and where you go?'

'I come from near Delagoa Bay,' he said, 'and return thither with slaves. But who are these with you? This man whom you call master and the woman at his side, and whence come you and why are you here?'

'We come from the south, lord, and I am leading my master to the sea which he has a great desire to gaze upon.'

'There is nothing to be gained by looking at the sea. Like the wisdom of Allah, it is limitless and beyond understanding.'

'Nevertheless, oh, chief, it is his desire to see this wonder. He is yet young, and not like us who have seen all things and know them to be nothing.'

'You speak like a true believer,' the Arab said. 'And are those cattle yours? If so I will trade for them. I need food for my people for already I have lost many from hunger. My best hunters,' he went on, 'were killed in a battle with another caravan, and here, even if I had hunters, there is no game.' Turning the pages of his Koran, he read, '"Eat therefore of what you have acquired, that which is lawful and good; for God is good, gracious and merciful. Oh, prophet! Say unto the captives who are in your hands, if God shall know any good to be in your hearts, he will give you better than that which hath been taken from you; and he will forgive you, for God is gracious and merciful."'

The old Arab veiled his eyes and looked down.

'Oh, great chief,' Rinkals said, 'truly the words which fall from your mouth are like dewdrops glistening on a tall tree, very beautiful in the light of the morning, but dewdrops to thirsty men are not water, and if you will give better than that which hath been taken, then truly the end of all things is at hand and we be no longer men. Oh, chief, we ask not better, all that we ask is a full measure for our beasts. Without doubt, my master will trade the cattle,' Rinkals went on, 'but they are, as you see for yourself, beautiful beasts, fat and well liking. Ai,' he continued, 'such cattle are not given away. There are forty-five of them,' he added.

'What would your master take for them?'

'I think he might be persuaded to take two slaves for each,' Rinkals said, 'for he is a very generous man, though quick at times to anger.'

'Two each is too much,' the old Arab said, 'especially as I could, if I wished, have them for nothing.' He looked at his guards who stood with their swords drawn or loosened in their scabbards.

'That you will not do,' Rinkals said, 'for you have the face of a just man.'

'The face of a man is a book on which his past is written,

Kaffir; but man, being created of hastiness, his decisions if he be wise should be slow. Ponder well, dog, scratch many fleas before you answer me lightly.'

'Oh, chief, you have observed me closely to see that I am guileless and without vermin, and that my heart is pure.'

'God loveth the clean, and there is no God but God.'

'There is no God but God,' Rinkals repeated, 'and my master will take one and a half slaves for each beast, which will be sixty-seven and a half.'

'Can I cut a slave in two, fool?'

'That, as the chief says so wisely, cannot be done without much difficulty. Also, half a slave is of no use, for what are hands without legs to bear them from place to place? Or legs without hands to be put to a useful purpose. No, lord, by a slave and a half I mean a woman with a walking child.'

'A sucking child?'

'Unweaned children die easily and then one is worse off than before, because their mothers lose flesh, and pine.'

'And how do monkeys learn of women?'

'Monkeys, oh, lord, know nothing of women, but all old men were once young, and this is the more interesting as not all young ones live to become old.'

'Listen now, old man, who once was young, I will give sixty-seven slaves for these beasts, neither more nor less, and they shall be neither the best nor the worst, and they shall be chosen in this manner: Your master will pick one hundred and thirty-four slaves out of the first two hundred, they will be arranged in two parties of sixty-seven, and then I will take the first choice of the parties and he will take those that are left.'

'A very just plan, oh, chief, and one which my master will accept.'

'How do you know this since you have not spoken to him, dog?'

''Tis not necessary that I should speak to my master to

know his wishes. We have other ways. Thoughts flow like water between us, so close are we and so great his confidence in my unfailing wisdom.'

'The bargain is then sealed and we will camp now and slaughter twenty cows. Those beasts will take us some way through this desolate country, and later, no doubt, if Allah wills, we shall come upon other beasts.'

'Beasts, which your hunters being dead, you will not obtain.'

'If Allah wills it, we shall not obtain them; if he does, they will fall to the guns of my people.'

'And yet, oh, chief, my master is a great hunter. Might it not be wise to ask him if he would not come with you, since our paths are the same?'

'Ask him, Kaffir. Say that I should be pleased if he would join me.'

'Baas,' Rinkals said, 'we are going with them. They have given us slaves for the cows and want you to hunt for them. Is it in your heart to go?'

'I will go,' Piete said. 'We will accompany these people and hunt their meat. But what shall we do with the slaves?'

'Sell them, baas, and buy more guns and ammunition, also trade goods. I should like to have a gun for myself, baas, just a little one which would not bite me. Perhaps the baas would get one for me and tame it a little, so that I too, could throw thunder and smite with lightning.'

'Rinkals, you are an old skelm. But certainly I will get you a gun, and I will tame it so that it is as a dove in your hand.' And it was in this manner that Zwart Piete and his people joined the slavers, and it was here that Zwart Piete got his name of 'the Hunter.'

2

The journey with the caravan was slow. Day after day it travelled through a wilderness of desiccated thorn scrub, toiling like a wounded snake along the narrow sun-baked roads. Every day the slaves, who had marched many hundreds of miles and were much exhausted by the privations they had undergone, moved less easily and each day those who tried to give up, preferring death by the wayside to this endless march into captivity, were flogged by the Arabs, who used their heavy whips unmercifully, drawing blood at every stroke.

Even Zwart Piete and Sara, accustomed as they were to cruelties, were revolted by the inhuman behaviour of the slave drivers.

But it was less the brutality than the impassivity with which the punishment was inflicted that affected them. Girls and men would be flogged by Arabs who remained unmoved, especially were those who could go no further flogged, since these would in any case die, and their death under the whips was no loss and a salutary example to the others.

To beat a Kaffir in anger, one who had lost a cow, was one thing, to do this was another.

At night the deaths were reported and entered into a book, while the old chief, talking to his leaders would calculate the distance they had come, weighing it against that still to be covered. This piece of country was always expensive in slaves; lack of food, of water and the intolerable heat, all contributing to a loss of human life which the Arabs had come to consider as all but inevitable and seeing in it the will of Allah, they pressed forward, relentlessly and uncomplaining.

The last cow had long since been slaughtered, for the herd had been little more than a mouthful among so many, and had been employed only for the feeding of the picked slaves — girls of marriageable age and boys destined to become eunuchs — these fetching the highest prices in the market, there being an almost unlimited demand for the services of both in the harems of the north.

Old Rinkals, who had himself been a slave, told them much of the ways of the Arabs. 'To them these people are not men, women and children,' he said. 'They are wild cattle. When they are tamed they treat them well, indeed, they have a way of treating their slaves in such a way that even when given the chance to escape, they rarely take it. Just now it is as it would be with a herd, if they make no haste all will perish, and they will be left without profit for their work. No,' he went on, 'the Arabs treat their folk well and with great kindness. It is only those that I told you of — the man hunters — who are without the bowels of compassion. Their hearts being empty of all things but cruelty and courage, and of these there is no measure. In war, inkoos, they are lions unleashed. Ai, to them even the Zulus are as children, for the Zulus are without rancour, their spears are clean.'

From Rinkals, also, they got the tale of the fight. It appeared that it had arisen from a quarrel over a water hole, and had been savagely contested. Many, including the leader of the opposing caravan, had been killed. But he had sons and, according to the old witch-doctor, it was not over. 'For war with these people,' he said, 'is never over; no, not till the third and fourth generations is a vengeance abandoned. For many years these people had been rivals, in opposition to each other, bickering and fighting intermittently, but till now not seriously, only men of no account having been slain — slaves and mercenaries. It is in my heart, baas,' Rinkals said, 'that this is not done, that there will be more blood, and that these men have pleasure in our company, for I have told them how we fight. Out of my tales much may arise,' he added proudly. 'Certainly I bring good fortune wherever I go. Like the Little Flower I was once called, I bring much joy and my company is a decoration. Old as I am by magic, my bloom remains, my fragrance is unimpaired.'

'Did my ears deceive me, old one?' de Kok asked. 'Was it fragrance that you said?'

'It was fragrance, Bastard. That is the word I used.'

'I see, wizard, but to dog dung is fragrant,' de Kok said.

'A dog should know what to dog is fragrant,' Rinkals answered. 'And not being a yellow Bastard, I have no knowledge of dogs.'

It was only with difficulty that Zwart Piete and Sara silenced the two, for they hated and despised each other, and the savage country through which they were going affected them adversely, rasping them by the hardships they were forced to endure.

And so they drove on along the old slave road, following it as it wound through dwarf mimosa forests, over low hills, along the dry beds of sandy rivers. Pressing on from water to water, for with water men and women could be kept alive, and with whips while they lived, they could be driven.

3

At last, however, the hard country through which they were passing changed in character, from desert it merged gradually into plains of high grass, rich in game, through which ran slow-moving rivers that were heavy with water. A fat rich land of great timber trees and chocolate coloured earth. They had reached the edge of the wide coastal belt and here they halted while Zwart Piete, de Kok and Sara hunted.

Day after day they shot meat for the famished slaves, their skill fully justifying their names as hunters, exceeding even Rinkals' wildest boasts by the unfailing regularity and precision of their killing. Their bellies filled with the lean meat of game and the fat of hippopotomi, the slaves fleshed up, and many who were on the point of death recovered.

Hussien Zeid was more than pleased. Once again he had come in successful with a long string of slaves, once again his share from the sale of his wares would be no small one.

His one regret was that some two hundred slaves of mixed sexes, the whole of a small tribe which he had captured, had died from what could be nothing other than a nostalgia for the forests whence he had taken them, for at that time there had been plenty of food for all. But even with these and the other deaths, he was returning with well over a thousand head, a notable achievement, and one which he had taken grave risks to accomplish, for leaving the old slave routes he had struck into the heart of the country, breaking open a new and richly populated land, finding races who unaccustomed to firearms had proved easy to subdue.

All along, he had, where he could, bought slaves for beads, brass, wire and trade goods; as these, already tamed by their masters, died less freely than the wild ones, proved more docile and were less obstinate to handle. But when trading failed he had resorted to force of arms, raiding village after village, with the utmost savagery. Flinging his fighting men onto the kraals while others, trained to the purpose, seized the women, the young men and the children, tying them up like beasts till they could be shackled.

They had not much farther to go now, in a few days they would come to their destination — the fort of Don Jesus Miguel Jose D'Alvarez Ferrara — where the slaves would be loaded into the dhows that came up the river in search of such cargoes.

There was, indeed, one God only, and did it not say in the word: that if twenty of you persevere with constancy, they shall overcome two hundred; and if there be one hundred of you, they shall overcome a thousand of those who believe not. God is mighty and wise. God is gracious and merciful.

Kneeling on his mat, the old man turned his face to Mecca, all round him the other Arabs prayed, so did many of the negroes and bastards who had been brought up in the faith or led to see its manifold advantages. Alone a group of naked fighters stood leaning on their long spears showing their filed teeth in a grin of contempt for those who knelt and bowed themselves.

These men were without faith in ought but the strength of their arms, the length of their spears and the speed of their legs. Men of the N'coussie tribe, men apart, who ate the flesh of men. Unclean, but tolerated by Hussien Zeid for their incomparable war-like qualities and the speed with which they could run down fleeing men, faster than cheetahs, they sprang with spear and thong onto the defeated foe, leaping high into the air so that they could see those who crouched, hoping to lie hidden in grass.

Alone, as the sun set, these men stood and when Zwart Piete, de Kok and Sara du Plessis rode into the camp they smiled and raised their spears. These strange white men were hunters who killed meat and abased themselves to no one, they were people after their own hearts, and as they approached they clicked their tongues against the roofs of their mouths and slapped their bare thighs with pleasure.

CHAPTER XVI

I

THE meilies were high when Hendrik van der Berg took Louisa among them; the cobs full, the tassels fertilised, their green ends shrivelling to brown, their lower leaves already yellow.

The days, the weeks, the months that had passed bore their sudden fruit bitterly. The little foxes of desire so subtly nurtured by the coloured girl had grown, the tinder struck had flamed, bursting all bonds, for the vines of Hendrik's lusts had tender grapes. He took her and his heart sang as he gained relief.

The Lord had prospered his cause; blessed them that blessed him, cursed them that cursed him. The Lord had bidden him to go forth into the land of Canaan; and into the land of Canaan he had come.

Standing with his hand on his horse's neck, he watched Louisa go; she had been delivered by God into his hand, his seed would be multiplied as the stars of heaven, and as the sand which is upon the seashore, and his seed would possess the gates of his enemies. Slipping the reins over his horse's head, he mounted and rode slowly towards his new house where the stone walls were already breast high.

Hendrik's mind was filled only with an exaltation, a feeling of achievement. To him Louisa was merely a further instrument; that she gave willingly meant little to him, for what he wanted he took and who was there to gainsay his will or to thwart his righteous passion. Neither Sannie's distasteful reluctance of his advances nor Louisa's acqui-

escence meant anything to him; they as much as he were
planned by a God whose one desire was increase, the method-
ical addition of one to another; of creation, of multiplying
the weight and magnitude of that stream of life, of which
he, Hendrik van der Berg, was a part. God had given him
the strength to achieve his purpose as he had to Abraham,
and the words spoken to Abraham applied equally to himself. Had not God said to Abraham, 'And I will make thee
exceedingly fruitful and I will make nations of thee and
kings shall come out of thee?'

When half-way home he changed his direction, and turned
his horse towards the house of Martinus the singer. He
wished to talk to Martinus about some oxen which had
strayed and to ask if they had been found. It was just
possible that they had been stolen, for recently the Kaffirs
who had gone into hiding among the mountains had drifted
back and had come to trade such things as ivory, native
pots of red baked earth, karosses and gold dust for sheep
and cattle. Since it was impossible to live perpetually at
war, their demands, for they invariably wanted more than
their goods were worth, were met. But if they began to
steal stock they would have to be punished, and respect for
the might of the white man imposed like a yoke upon them.
If they stole he would crush them beneath his heel, but if
they did not steal he would live at peace with them, his
herds grazing beside their own.

But if it was the naked Kaffirs, as they called them because they wore no loin cloth, it would be something else,
for without cattle or women these men, the remnants of the
Zulu hordes, would be less simple to deal with. Hoping that
the presence of these people was no more than a rumour
and remembering the way the men of their race had overwhelmed the village he and Paul Pieters had been about to
attack, he feared for his settlement. But on reaching the
home of Martinus he found his fears to be groundless, for
the cattle were back. A bushman servant had spoored them

into a dry kloof where, having climbed a path too narrow to turn in, they had stood waiting for assistance. Martinus was overjoyed at their return, for among them were his two achter oxen, great yellow beasts with soft, long-lashed eyes, that when called upon by their master would move a loaded wagon by themselves, breaking their hearts or their trek gear before they abandoned their effort.

'Ach, ja, Hendrik,' Martinus said as he came towards him with a slight limp, the only result of his broken leg, 'I am glad that they are back. It may be foolish, the way I love them, but my oxen are like children to me and never since they were trained have they felt the whip.'

'I too am glad, Martinus,' Hendrik said. 'I am very glad and well I understand your feelings, for to us Boers our cattle are like our hands, as much part of us as our fingers, and above all other oxen but my own, I think yours the best I have ever seen.'

'Ah, my yellow oxen, like gold they are and above gold, for while I live my oxen remain, and above all my span, are Grootboi and Kaptein. Ach, ja, above them all I value my achter oxen, old, wise and faithful. Now, Oom Hendrik, come sit, and we will have coffee.'

'What, you still have coffee?' Hendrik asked.

'Nie, nie, who has coffee now? It is roasted wheat, but we call it coffee. What else is one to call it? Can I say "Come, Oom Hendrik, and sit on my stoep while Marietje prepares the roasted wheat?"' Martinus sat back laughing. 'But tobacco I have. Ja, and food in plenty, for this would be a good place to which you have brought us if it were not for the fever, and is in my heart that, like the sickness of the horses, it comes out the night airs and the dew. But what of Sannie's lion now, that it is big?' he asked.

'Ja, what of it, jong? It is big as you say, and one day I shall shoot it. Perhaps tomorrow, perhaps the next day, but my home will not be comfortable when I do this thing for Sannie loves it and is not even afraid of its hurting the child, and, magtig, Martinus, sometimes I think it is better to have tame lion about the house than an angry wife.'

'At least you cannot be jealous of the lion, Oom Hendrik.'

'Me jealous of my wife? Those words are ill spoken, Martinus.'

'A jest, Hendrik. Sannie is beautiful, and where there is honey there are bees.'

'Ja, Martinus, and where wild beasts come into a kraal they become carrion; where they sprang in they are dragged out, dead.'

Hendrik undid the reins of his horse from the stoep pole to which he had tied it and mounted.

'And the coffee?' Martinus asked.

'Another day, my friend, already I have been away too long.

'Too long. Ach, ja, everything took too long.' Raising the hand in which he held the reins he galloped along the track that led from Martinus' house to his own. He would be old before his children entered into their possession. Suddenly, for the first time in his life he saw his end approaching, felt a foreboding that perhaps things were not quite as he had thought them, that the slow stepping of the ox to which his existence was attuned was not fast enough. What had he done? What had he accomplished? Much, certainly, but not enough. His barns must be filled to overflowing, riches must be wrested from the soil over which he rode and his live stock increased to the limit of their latent fertility.

He must have children, grandchildren and great-grandchildren before he died, and the time was short. Lord God, how short the time for so great a task.

The scenery round him was rich with the fullness of autumn. Stained yellow and scarlet, blotched with dark crimson, it meant nothing to him. He saw it unseeing, rode past it unfeeling. The stark shadowed mountains with their green kloofs were a protection from the cold winds of the south-east, the coloured trees were shade for his stock, the smooth-running rivers were water — primary water for the use of human beings and cattle, secondary water for the furrows that wet the lands below them.

One with his horse he cantered on, his mind filled, his purpose — a purpose as old as the world. As primitive as the animals among which he lived, Hendrik allowed his thoughts to wander. Things must be hurried on, his powers pushed to their uttermost in his relations with Sannie, his wife, and Louisa, his concubine. Out of these two would spring great things — the sons who should inherit the earth.

2

Sannie in the time they had been in the low country had grown a little, and had changed a great deal in character. Her eyes had lost something of their questioning mockery; they now were veiled or smouldered with a dull, sullen anger that nothing could dispel. An anger against Hendrik and his way with her. Was she a mare or a heifer, she asked herself. Merely something to be bred from? He loved Frikkie and no doubt would love the child that was to come, when it came. And then, afterwards, it would all begin again, on and on, pregnancy after pregnancy until at last she died. She thought now of her contempt for the woman who had been Herman's mother, she who had died so early on in the trek. Hendrik was not a man, he was purpose disguised as a man, something entirely relentless, that saw but one road where there were many, and to whom she was a possession and not a woman.

High up on the berg she sat screened by the grey foliage of a sugar bush, staring down at the veld below her, the endless miles of low scrubby trees among which a few big ones stood towering like giants. A sea of savage country which ran on till it merged into the soft blue of the mountains sixty miles away. How calm it looked, how strangely intractable it was, the home of Kaffirs and wild beasts, a country that could be seen and traversed, but never mastered.

A butterfly fluttered past her and the young lion with a cat-like flick of its great paw brought it down and jumped upon it. A pale-yellow wing with a stripe of blue and a red eye fluttered onto the hot rock beside her.

Below her was the wooded cleft of the kloof. No breeze stirred the tree tops. The silence was oppressive, it lay like a blanket between the cliffs; a blanket of shimmering hot silence that hung heavily over the wild figs and tree-ferns which grew in its shadowed depths. Even the water that came spilling out of the rocks ran softly, thickly, without a splash as if it was mercury. Only the cries of the cicadas broke the silence, but their cry, because it was intermittent, rising to crescendo and stopping abruptly on a high note when it was reached, made the silence more apparent, emphasising it, underlining it. It was an intolerable silence, broken only by the intolerable singing of the insects, the shrill cry that some said they made with their mandibles and others by rubbing their legs against their wings.

With her eyes half-closed, she fondled the lion which lay extended beside her. As she touched his ribs and armpits where tufts of darkish hair were beginning to grow he rolled over, purring with pleasure and raised his enormous paws towards her shoulder, touching her softly on the arm with his horn-coloured claws retracted in their sheaths. With her lion Sannie was safe, even Hendrik would not come near her.

Dogs, what, after all, were dogs? Curs that could be kicked into submission, that were being perpetually chased from one place to another, the slavish servants of men. Here, under her hand, was a beast as fast in movement as a cat who loving her beyond all else, held death in its velvet pads. People said it was dangerous to have a tame lion. They said that in the end lions always turned on their masters. When he is full grown, they said, you will see. Ja, magtig, when he is full grown we shall see, she thought. That would not be for two years yet, a great space of time during which much might happen. The lion was big now, as tall as he would ever be, and his feet seemed too big for him, but he would grow into them, and the loose, tawny hide that covered his body would fill up. Wherever she went she took him with her, for if she left him alone at the house she knew that Hendrik would shoot him. Sannie laughed softly. Hendrik was jealous of her lion, of the caresses she gave him, of the way she played with him, letting him stand up and take cooked meat from between her lips. Twice already she had seen her lion kill swiftly, once it had been a baboon and once a dassie. On both occasions when he had jumped from her side the arc of his spring had been almost invisible, so fast that she had been unable to follow it, and both times she had driven him off with the twig she carried in her hand. But his prey had been dead, its back broken by the weight of his falling body, its neck bitten through at the base of the skull. It was then that she had seen his claws open to their fullest extent, as sharp as razors, with the strength of his powerful forearms behind them, she had seen the damage they could inflict.

Getting up, Sannie went slowly down the mountain path. If only something would happen. If only things were not always so much the same. Life here was very much what it had been at the Cape only more uncomfortable, more dangerous, but the danger was without spice. Boring day following boring day, with its routine of preparing meals, of listening to Hendrik reading out of the Bible, of sending his children off to the reed hut school with their armed attendants to be taught their letters by von Rhule, a man who had been a soldier; a profligate who recited whole chapters of the Bible cynically indifferent as to their spirit, pedantically accurate as to their letter. A man respected for his wide knowledge which was only wide when compared to the ignorance of those he taught. Kaptein von Rhule, a Prussian cavalryman who had fled to Africa, the land of opportunity, and had welded a place for himself among simple Boers by the power of his memory and the swiftness of his hand to strike. Sannie mistrusted this man with his cold grey eyes — a man who instead of slouching, walked erect, his legs moving as if he wore spurs on his heels, who rode his horse as if he were frozen into the saddle.

Sannie's knowledge of people, of ways and means, and of the final intricacies and vacuity of life was growing. The interminable talks she had listened to between von Rhule and her husband while she served them food, the endless discussions she had with her aunt, who now that she was married, threw reticence to the four winds and recounted her experiences without shame or prejudice, had all helped to mould her, while her contacts with Hendrik had hardened her till she sometimes wondered if she was a true Boer woman, for among the others she found nothing but a tacit admission of the superiority of man and a willing acquiescence to their demands which left her both nauseated and enraged. Surely there was more in life than this, surely there was some greater thing, and even if one could not grasp the stars, one should strive upwards towards them where they twinkled in the night blue sky. If birds sang in the trees, if even cows no longer young frisked in the pastures, and bellwethers fought mock battles, there must be something also for living people, some pleasure, some relaxation from this continual round of duty.

She got no joy from the new stone house that was going up, nor from furniture that was being made for it, nor the lands that were proving so fruitful all round it.

She pursued her way down the rocky path uneasily, thinking of Herman, casting her mind back to what had gone before she had loved Herman, of the feelings she had had. That of finding her skin too tight, of feeling unsung songs rising in her throat, of an unknown urgency pressing like a living thing upon her. She thought also of her first pregnancy and of the peace she had known then. This time she was getting nothing out of the child she bore under her heart, nothing except the excuse it afforded her to avoid the attentions her husband still tried to force upon her. As she thought of Hendrik she knew suddenly that she hated him, not hotly as one might hate for an instant the man one loved, but coldly and bitterly, so that she could think of inflicting pain upon him without a quickening of her pulse, without enjoyment, without alarm or excitement.

Her beauty was a gift that she had given to Herman, she felt that she might one day give it again; but give, it must be taken, and for every time it was taken her husband should pay a hundredfold. Not eye for eye, or tooth for tooth, but more than this, infinitely more for the uses to which he had put her; and if Hendrik were as strong as Samson, was she not as cunning as Delilah?

If Samson had long hair, and this Achilles, of whom von Rhule had spoken, a heel, there must be somewhere in her husband a point where he was vulnerable to the attack which she would one day launch upon him. Her mouth a hard red line in the magnolia whiteness of her face, her eyes expressionless as brown stones, she went into her house and picked up her child.

In an hour on the mountainside a hatred had been born, a loathing that would weigh heavily upon her till it was fulfilled. That it would be fulfilled she never doubted, for her faith in God, her confidence in the strength of her beauty, the knowledge of the hardness of her passionate heart and the strength of her supple hands was unimpaired. She, too, like Hendrik, would take what she wanted and thrust back that which she did not want. Till then she would wait, magtig, how she would wait till her moment came. Was it not said that the greatest virtue of womanhood was patience and did not even a small stream of water, in time, wear away a rock of granite by its imperceptible falling, by the strength and number of its drops which individually were as nothing, but which together, taken over a period, were as a mighty rushing stream.

Slowly, slowly, even as drops of falling water, as softly as drops of water, as surely, she would sap him, and when he was weakened, break him. At the thought of Hendrik broken, she laughed, and the lion sensing a new note in her voice growled angrily, baring his long white fangs and looking round for something at which to strike.

3

The desertion of Gert Kleinhouse had left Anna de Jong less perturbed than the loss of the sow, and the fact that the milk cow, Bloometjie, returned with many thanks, had owing to her long trek ceased to give milk and had, in addition, lost the use of a quarter.

Gert had, she told Sannie, behaved just like a man, falling down before the first woman who extended so much as a finger towards him.

'Ach, ja, mie Sannie, one day when my heart is less sore I shall make a journey to see this Martha, to see this Mevrou Coetzee, for surely she must be an ugly and bad-tempered woman or she would have done better than the cross-eyed Gert for a husband. Before I sent him, I should have thought of his Uncle Jan, for he also was a slim man, a dealer in deceit and cross-eyed like Gert. But I, too, am slim and I shall make a plan, and when I make a plan, mie Sannie, then things take place. Ja, it is almost unbelievable the things which happen when I begin to arrange matters. Indeed, sometimes I think my brain is as big as my body, but unlike my body it is nimble as a flea and capable of skipping about with great dexterity. Ach,' she sighed, 'to think that Gert Kleinhouse, whose nose I used to wipe with a lappie, has verneuked me out of a lovely little pig and has married a widow who is not as poor as they said, but rich. And then some blasphemers contend that the age of miracles is past — toch, that a rich widow should take Gert into her bed is a miracle equal to the turning of water into wine. And I have heard,' she went on, 'that she gave him her husband's watch — imagine it, Sannie — the watch of her dead husband no less, and that almost on the first day of their meeting. It was a good watch, too. A watch of gold with a golden key that they say keeps most excellent time, as indeed it should, being well made and as large as an egg. Also I hear that she gave him her husband's best waistcoat he made out of the spotted skin of a young calf, red and white most beautifully distributed, with large silver buttons. This widow is evidently a woman of no sensibility and without sentiment, for before one gives away the goods of one husband, a respectable woman waits till she has married the next. That is the custom among those who have been well brought up, and to give gifts to men before marriage is both unwomanly and immodest, while after it there is no necessity to give for they take what they want. I have no doubt that she sent also for her flocks and herds, down to the last hammel, that he might see how rich she was. Ach, ja, if it was not for my little sow I should be sorry for that Gert in the hands of a woman so unscrupulous and hard. And if the man, who passed and told me she was poor, returns he shall hear what I have to say about this matter. The verdamte kerl who lied for no reason and could not take his eyes off Louisa. A liar and a whoremonger, ach, ja, and I would tell him so to his face if he returns, which no doubt he will have too much sense to do, such men being as remarkable for their intelligence as they are for looseness of their lives, flourishing like green bay trees to the detriment of such people as ourselves.'

Anna de Jong folded her hands on her lap and surveyed them dispassionately, assuming an attitude of pious inactivity, while plans for the discomfiture of the woman Coetzee, her grandson Gert, and the stranger whose lies had led her astray passed through her mind. Those who verneuked Tante Anna in the end regretted it. Implacable, she bent circumstances to her ends, a fat old woman as dangerous as a puff adder lying swollen and still in the path of her enemies.

4

The coming of the smouse with his train of pack donkeys was an excitement to Hendrik's people and the relief of an anxiety to him. The Jew came, as such traders always came, arriving with his ragged bushmen servants out of the emptiness of the veld. To trade, he had without firearms penetrated the wilderness, suffering losses from wild beasts, propitiating natives with gifts, following his hooked nose into the depths of the country where men would need powder from the little barrels he had loaded onto the backs of his donkeys and the women materials for clothes, sewing-cotton, and needles. Above all, powder and needles they would need; for these things there were no substitutes.

Riding ahead on a gelded ass rather larger than the others he came in smiling, and within a few hours of his coming the bare ground in front of Hendrik's house was filled with the cape carts and the saddle horses of those who, having heard of his arrival, had come with all speed to obtain the pick of his produce, offering the money that they had brought with them, gold nuggets and dust and ivory in exchange for his wares.

And having bought they stayed to talk, for this man brought news. There was no one he did not know, no one whom he had not seen. He had heard that Zwart Piete du Plessis was hunting and trading in Mozambique, and also that he had become part owner of a slaving station up there, having become friends with the Portuguese who owned it; but this he did not credit as such good fortune was unlikely; and as he talked he sold.

'Ach, ja, mevrou,' he said, 'there is nowhere a material to equal this one. Just look at the soft sheen of the silk,' he said, unrolling the bolt, 'and where is the man who could resist the mevrou in such a frock; think also of how it will wear,' he added. Then, raising his hands, he asked them if they did not think it wonderful to be able to buy such things as this here in the wilderness as cheaply, or almost as cheaply, as they could do in the towns of the south. Pack after pack was undone as he chattered, interspersing his comments about the virtues and qualities of his products with anecdotes and family stories from the settlements he had passed through, selling as he talked, flattering, expostulating, and complaining that if he took such prices as they offered he would be ruined. Demanding why they did not ask him to give instead of to sell, and indeed at such prices his goods were gifts.

Quick and vivid as a bird among the phlegmatic Boers he overpowered them by his animation, for mentally he was like a man on a fast horse against men dismounted and puzzled by the speed of his manoeuvres.

In all the crowd of those pressing round him the only one with whom he feared to jest was the Prussian who, looking at him contemptuously and speaking to him in his own tongue, had called him a Jewish swine. On him the smouse fawned, offering him gifts which he took without even saying thank you, and mounting his horse rode away. Like vermin, these people penetrated everywhere; too insignificant to be killed they swelled gradually on the blood they sucked till at last they became dangerous, holding the very lives of many men in their hands, squeezing them between their fingers till the juice of their property ran out. By God, if he, Otto von Rhule, did not know the Jews then no one knew them. Hit them and they cringed; succour them, and before long they bit the hand that fed them. A people without a land, a people without the capacity for gratitude, to whom money was a god. Not something to be spent in enjoyment, but something which in their hands bred, increasing as if it was a living thing. Rix dollars in their hands multiplying as cattle did in the hands of a good husbandman, mounting up, filling bag after bag.

Fearful of taking they bought, obtaining without danger the things others had gained by the sweat of their brows and at the risk of their lives. He laughed.

These simple farmers had no understanding of the race. Trade? Why trade? when a shot or a blow would have given them all for nothing. Among other things in the front of his saddle hanging down on either side of his horse's shoulders was a piece of tawny silk shot with green. One day he would give it to Sannie. To Mevrou van der Berg, with apologies, mynheer; he swept off his hat and smiled ironically at an ox that raised its head to look at him. Hendrik van der Berg was like an ox; all these Boers were like oxen, strong, sleepy, slow and easy to manage if one knew the way of it. Farmers, who could not understand that he despised the land on which they toiled so patiently and clung only to the first thing he had learnt on joining his regiment, the necessity of being able to move freely and quickly, of mobility; at all costs he must have mobility and the freedom of swift manoeuvre.

5

Hendrik overwhelmed Sannie with gifts, thinking this the way to her heart, paying in money, in choice tiger skins, in ivory and gold, for all that she asked. Materials, crockery, tin ware, medicines such as camphor, turpentine, senna beans, buchu, harlemer oilie and jalap. Also he bought her such luxuries as cayenne pepper, vinegar, tea, coffee and brandy wine. For himself he bought nothing but powder and pigs of lead for casting into bullets.

After two days the smouse was still shrugging his high shoulders and smiling, still talking. Everything was finished; he was sold out. No, he was sorry he had nothing left — nothing, and he was ruined. Never in the course of all his travels had he met such hard, close traders, a people who were so slim. Before God he believed that they had all conspired to verneuk him. He pulled his long hair in his distress at the bad bargains he had made. Yes, certainly they had given him ivory, gold and skins, but he was far from home; much tribute would have to be paid on his return journey; but if any of them had letters that they wished delivered he would be willing to take them for a small sum, part paid down and part to be paid on delivery.

If he could have done it for nothing he would naturally have done so but he, like another, had to live; not that he could live opulently as they did, but in just a small way, as a wandering Jew who managed somehow to extract a living from a hard, inhospitable world. In the meantime, perhaps, someone would be kind enough to allow him to graze his donkeys and if they could spare him a little meat for himself and his boys he would be more than grateful.

CHAPTER XVII

I

THE smouse stayed for some days on Hendrik's farm, camping by the spring and feeding up his donkeys on the buffle-grass that grew in such profusion below the thorn trees in the vicinity. His time he spent calling from house to house telling tales, collecting letters, even writing them for the more illiterate. With the skill of his race in these matters he assessed everyone and everything with which he came in contact as he made his visits.

This place was rich, these people would be worth visiting again provided he could convince them of the fact that cattle meant nothing to him and that for his goods he must have gold in dust or nuggets, and ivory. To them gold was merely something which could be turned into livestock, for by a man's driven herds was his importance gauged and not by the amount of money he had hidden away in raw-hide bags. This idiosyncrasy of his about gold the smouse explained was due to a different racial outlook, and one of which in time, after a longer residence among them, he would no doubt become cured.

Ja, jong, time will cure you, they said, for cattle are true riches. See how they increase and multiply and can gold do that? they asked laughing.

'Ach, how right you are,' he said. 'If only gold would increase as do your herds, how wonderful that would be.'

And thus they talked, each laughing in his sleeve at the stupidity of the other. And then one day, early in the morning, the smouse turned the grey muzzles of his donkeys south.

In four months, or five months, if nothing befell him, he would reach the Cape, having paid heavy tribute all the way and still arriving rich. Africa to him was a fat cow, and if one had the skill and the courage, ready to be milked. A country peopled by a simple race who valued, above everything, their cattle, sheep and horses, all delicate animals, and scorned his small donkeys that could thrive anywhere, and lived so long that few had seen one dead.

When the country was at peace, which it would be as more men trekked, he would certainly buy wagons and come up here to trade, settling among the fools who hunted elephants instead of buying tusks.

They had come to lead a 'lekker lewe' and considered themselves happy because they were free to live a comfortless life, to hunt and to fight without let or hindrance, who were content to rest on their stoeps smoking their carved stone pipes while they waited for their cows to calve, or their heifers to be old enough to put to the bull, or for their tollies to be big enough to train. People who sat heavily awaiting the increase promised them of God, accepting both good and evil as God sent. Immovable in their faith and because of their simplicity, their lack of elasticity, very terrible, for nothing would sway or move them. Unexcitable in pleasure, implacable in anger, these folk were very interesting to Isaak Rosenstein, a problem which he lived by exploiting.

2

For a long time after his going the Jew provided a topic of conversation among the people he had left. To speak of him was a change from the eternal talk of crops, cattle and hunting among the men, and of cooking, children, and the laziness of their native servants among the women.

Besides the numerous things he had bought for Sannie, Hendrik had also bought a necklace of amber for Louisa, and more and more did he dwell upon her beauty, taking it as savagely as she gave it when they came together, thinking of it when he was away from her and turning the pages of his Bible till he found in the Song of Solomon, the song of songs, the words that fitted her. 'Black, but comely, oh daughter of Jerusalem,' he read, and yet not black, for her soft skin was a deep rich cream. It was the colour and had the texture of a magnolia flower. 'Her eyes were as doves, her hair a flock of goats, her teeth as white as ewes newly shorn and washed, her lips a thread of scarlet.'

By the dark strength of her womanhood Louisa possessed him and was content. Knowing her man she gave him no child and mocked at him, laughing, for thus he was not able to accept the challenge she flung at him so freely. Not till she was ready, not till the time was ripe, would she be brought to bed by this man. Were there not herbs that she knew of? Was there not ergot on the heads of the corn and on the fine grasses? So, laughing, she took him, and laughing she left him puzzled and perplexed, attacking him where he was weakest in the pride of his virility and binding him ever nearer by his unavailing efforts to attain his ends.

With the coming of the winter the heavy crops were garnered, and when the cattle walked their quarters wobbled and their humps were high, trembling with stored fat. Hunting for biltong began again, and the stock were turned into the reaped meilie lands to eat the leaves and stalks which fattened them still further till on many farms they could hardly walk, and when they did, moved slowly, swaying from side to side.

It was in this season that Sannie gave birth to her second child, a daughter whom she named Jacoba, a small, puny baby, very blond, with large grey eyes.

Sons, the arrows to his bow, were being denied to Hendrik van der Berg, and the paternity of Frikkie, which he had been prepared to forget had his child been a boy, became a charge upon him, a reproach.

It was at this time too that the Prussian meester began to ride Sannie's way. Von Rhule rarely encountered Hendrik, for his visits were timed by the movements of Louisa, who in order to take her devious path to meet van der Berg, had to go near his house.

Von Rhule neither loved nor respected Sannie, nor did he want her particularly. His actions were due to boredom and the fact that in courting the wife of Hendrik van der Berg he courted danger. Among these peaceful farmers he alone was a man brought up to war, and the excitements of the trade learnt in his youth left him contemptuous of the occupations of peace. That he, a Prussian horse soldier, should find himself schoolmaster to a lot of peasant children was either a tragedy, or a joke on the part of Providence, according to his mood. Drunk, he wept at his fall, sober he laughed at it, but his laughter was sour, charged with bitter irony: and because he cared not a rix dollar for Sannie she began to love him: in a life where there was so little to think of he gave her a focus for her wandering thoughts. Big, bluff and reckless, riding heavily over her objections, he possessed her.

One day, when he grew tired of her, he would ride away. He had done it before, he would do it again. In the meantime her tremulous beauty and the overcoming of her hesitations passed his time if not profitably, at least pleasantly.

If she could have seen him as he had been once, in his cuirass, booted and spurred, riding his bay charger with his men behind him, his courtship would have been less protracted. This thought often amused him for he had reason to know that the attraction of a uniform was no idle rumour, it was a proven fact. He had proved it many times, and it was his weakness for the wives of other men which had led him into this wilderness so far from the gay life that he loved, so far from his regiment, from the good food, from the wine, and the women to whom he was accustomed.

3

On the stoep of Johannes van Reenen's house Anna de Jong sat impassively waiting for the inevitable, content in the knowledge that mills of God were at work. Grinding everything into the flour out of which the bread of life was made. God might work slowly but how small the grindings, how fine the flour.

Nodding her chin into the rolls of her neck she smiled at the efficiency of Providence, at the justice of God.

Only today had the news come in that the widow Coetzee who had married her grandson had suffered some losses of stock and that a great flight of locusts had passed over her farm, resting there in such numbers that they weighted down the branches of the trees. That they had passed on meant nothing, for while they were there they would have laid their eggs, driving the long horns of their ovipositors deep into the ground, and with the spring rains the voetgangers would hatch out and climb, wingless, to the tops of the high grasses; clinging there insignificant little clumps of black on the grass heads. Ach, ja, so small and yet so strong, for soon they would grow, and changing colour, become striped with red and yellow and then they would trek, armies of them, marching like Zulus. Insatiable they would eat all that was in their path, missing nothing, sparing nothing, not even the bark of the trees, and none would stay them for not only were they as numerous, as numberless, as the grains of sand in a dry river bed, but, being sent by God were accepted as a manifestation of his displeasure which would be blasphemous to thwart.

All her plans for avenging the loss of her pig and the damage done to her milk cow, Bloometjie, were forgotten, for what was any plan of hers compared to this one of God's. A jealous God who, if he counted the hairs of a man's head and watched for the falling of every sparrow, certainly was not one to miss the spoiling of a cow's udder or the verneuking of a lonely widow out of a sow, even if as she had heard, time had proved her to be barren, a thing almost unknown among these beasts. And even in this, the barrenness of the sow, Tante Anna saw the finger of God, for if nothing was too small for him to overlook, nothing could be too great for him to perform.

She had watched with interest Hendrik's growing passion for her coloured maid and did nothing to thwart it. Long ago had she foreseen the end of Hendrik, seen whither his madness, for it was no less, would drive him. The meester's affair with Sannie amused her, for here again was another stone to her sling. By such things as these would the man who had murdered his son fall as Goliath had fallen, and in all these matters she took a hand, playing it skilfully, as she sat still with her small eyes staring out at the veld and her brain as active as a spider spinning web after web, strengthening their delicate structure by a word here and a silence there, for none knew better than Anna de Jong the great power of the things that were unspoken, the words that were not said. Like a blow, a word could not be recalled; it was irrevocable, which was why she used parables so often, for most of them could mean many things, and with meanings, as with so much else, there was safety in numbers.

And yet with all this no house was better conducted than Tante Anna's, no man better fed, or had his clothes in finer state of repair than Johannes van Reenen, and under her hand less calves died, and more motherless lambs were reared, for to all the world she was a mother, brooding heavily on the mysteries of maternity; not only did the birth of children interest her but the birth of everything, for no matter what men might say, here was a great wonder. To give things names was not to explain them, and never did she watch the birth of a calf and see the small thing lie like something dead in the bag of its afterbirth without surprise that such things should be; then, as one watched, the cow, stepping carefully, would lick it, opening it as if it were a letter

and eat it as she washed her calf into life. Almost at once the
small thing's white hoofs would turn dark and it would try
to rise, staggering on to its knees and crawling towards its
dam, endeavouring to drink from between her forelegs since
they were the nearest, and later finding the tits it would butt
into the swollen udder and would drink. When they did this
one could leave them, for all was well. Ach, ja, it was a fine
sight and a great marvel to see a small calf drink, to see it
stand swaying on its unaccustomed legs, its bloody navel
cord hanging wetly, its small muzzle smeared with the thick
sweet milk it sucked so eagerly. And why should that first
milk for a week be different, she wondered. So that menfolk
could not drink it, so that if you boiled it it curdled? Was this
not another marvel? Truly there was no end to the things
with which one could occupy one's mind as one sat alone
upon the stoep.

Ja, ja, in life there were many things and all were the
same, all different aspects of one mighty project. It was one
that a coloured hussy should wear a string of beads of amber,
beads that had cost much good money, and one that a cow
should bite the tail of her young calf, nipping it at the root,
to encourage it to drink. It was all part of the life stream
which ran its appointed course in spite of man and to despite
him, each living thing going its diverse way, accomplishing
its divine purpose, renewing itself by its reproductive func-
tions and finally, exhausted, dying, and being eaten that
other creatures might live and multiply. The longer she lived
the more clear it all became and the things which were so
obscure in one's youth when one's mind was clouded by the
hot coursing of one's blood, were now easily decipherable.
Nor did the path matter, for were it straight, or krom as the
hind leg of a dog, the end remained the same.

In this place, sitting as she sat now, placid and mountainous, Anna de Jong had meditated much, for since she
had come here many had died, wasting slowly away, even
the plentiful food being insufficient to keep their souls within

the shrunken frame of their bodies. But where many died, many were also being born, and her services were continually in demand, for she was no less expert in laying out the dead, than in bringing forth the children of men from the wombs of their mothers. Ja, there was not a farm which she had not visited in the one capacity or in the other. Not a drift that her horses did not know, and if she was old and fat her horses were young and strong and her hands on the reins as sure as those of a man. Two, four or six she drove with equal skill and facility, galloping them across the rough veld roads, calling to them by name, her whip clapping, springing them up the hills till the raw-hide harness was curded with the cream of their sweat.

Ja, like Jehu, the son of Nimshi, she drove fast and furiously for none called on Anna de Jong in vain.

Loved, feared, a force to be reckoned with, she was a power in the land of Canaan.

4

Contrary to all his expectations the lion added to old Jakalaas' stature for now men feared to cross him. A Kaffir with a tame lion at his side was no object of contempt to men who were reasonable, and wrapped in his dirty kaross he spent much time parading about with the lion slinking soundlessly at his heels.

It slept in his hut beside him and was more than a woman to him, for where many, nay, all men, had women who but he had a lion? And if it could not cook it caught him many buck. And if it could not talk, was that not a good thing? For only with new wives was satisfaction to be found in their conversation. Later one looked at them regretting the beautiful cows that had paid for them. But Sannie, his mistress, was the one that the lion really loved, purring deep in his maned throat when he picked up the scent of her spoor and bounding forward like a great dog when he saw her. Ai, to the lion Sannie was a goddess. It seemed to know every cadence of her voice, every gesture of her hands, and to interpret her every mood. When she was gay, which was seldom, it would play gambolling like a kitten, when she was sad it would lie still watching her, when angry stand beside her pushing its head under her arm so that it rested on her hip, growling thunderously.

No longer did Jakalaas have to worry about his mistress being out alone, for with the lion to defend her she was safe even from the wild Kaffirs who spoke her name with awe. And daily the lion grew, his mane was now very fine, sweeping over his shoulders, his elbow tufts were as big as the crest on the head of a crane, and his ever-moving tail-tip furnished with a fine harsh brush. Obedient as a dog, the lion was tame and eager to please, but one day, the old Kaffir thought, someone will anger him and then his anger would be a terrible thing to see, for in his pride and strength he will kill very surely. Every muscle that rippled under his yellow hide being a master of death, he held it in his four armed feet, between his great dripping jaws. He held it and knew he held it, no servant of man, the lion stayed because he wished to stay, and refrained from killing because he was without the desire to kill. Stalking past the men who moved out of his way, looking at him askance and muttering that he should be shot before he turned savage, before the urge that would make him one day seek a mate and send him mad, he followed his mistress or her servant. A living question among the Boers, one whose only answer was a bullet that they dared not fire.

5

And so within the shadow of the great berg life went on. Uninfluenced by the grandeur of their surroundings the Boers worked to build up the life to which they were accustomed, one place to them being much like another, the health of their beasts, their own freedom of movement their one criterion of happiness. Hardship provided they suffered no master, being infinitely preferable to controlled safety.

Rootless, the whole of Africa was theirs while their wheels would roll, their horses carry them and their powder horns remained full; the wide horizon the limit only of their unhurried movement. Loosely bound by the ties of kinship; religion and war their bond, they lived as their ancestors had lived, content with little, and eminently capable of wresting that little from the land which was their home, from any part of it where the water was plentiful and the grazing good. Tough and strong as their own riems, they battled with the forces of nature that pitted themselves against them, taking flood and drought, the encroachments of wild beasts and the attacks of insects as the normal lot of man, but always ready to inspan their oxen and to ride on, always watchful of their guns, always attentive to the condition of their wagons, which having carried them a thousand miles, would, if necessary, carry them farther. And, above all, were they unresting in the vigilance with which they regarded their long-horned draft oxen, counting them as men might their children, missing never a mark on their skins, a nick on their horns or a tick between their big cloven hoofs.

Lions and leopards took their stock, baboons stole their meilies, buck ate their corn, porcupines dug up their sweet potatoes, elephants trooped over their lands flattening what they did not eat, and still owing to the richness of the soil there was enough and more than enough.

The land of Canaan was a fat land, a land flowing with milk and honey; and the Kaffirs, the children of Ham, in its vicinity timid and propitiatory. The first smouse had been followed by others who satisfied their immediate wants and for the rest they were in the hands of God.

And yet the God who had led them so far was chastening them, giving with one hand and taking away with the other, piling favours and disasters upon them impartially. The scales which had at first been in their favour were tipping slowly, and to all but a few, imperceptibly, against them. For with the ease came sloth, her handmaiden, and with a surfeit the despondency of a valueless achievement. Behind them was a vast space strewn with the bones of their people and their livestock while in front of them was what? That they knew not, but unknowing feared, for many children were dying of fever and many had sore eyes which the simples at their disposal failed to cure, while complaints of the skin were more than common, and yet the crops grew and the herds prospered. But there was dissension among the folk. Quarrels about water and cattle, arguments about tools borrowed and not returned, were being daily brought Hendrik for his judgment where he sat on his stoep smoking while Sannie, stone-eyed, watched and waited, hating him actively, the recesses of her mind bitter against this man who had taken her, who had fathered the sickly Jacoba upon her.

Torn by his anxieties, his passion for Louisa and his useless and continued possession of Sannie, who refused him nothing and from whom he obtained less than nothing, Hendrik was aging fast. Consumed by his internal fires his flesh was wasting and his skin hung in dry yellow folds, loose upon him, and his eyes sunk deep in their sockets were unnaturally large and bright.

So beneath its fair exterior the fruit was rotten and the men's blood black with desires they did not understand and fears which they refused to express. For here was a rich fat land, a land where nothing that had been asked for, or prayed for, was refused them. Yet the shadows of the mountains brought them no peace, the swift running of the waters no joy, the increase of their herds no pleasure. This was not Canaan, it was Eden and the snake of disease was among them, while the temptress stood naked offering them the apple prosperity, which if things went on as they were they would leave no children to enjoy. Yet loth to leave the place they had suffered so much to obtain they remained, driving their roots deeper into the rich alluvial soil, but still, on occasion, looking with longing eyes at the wagons whose canvas tents were stored in the rafters of their houses, high up and to be out of reach of the ants.

6

So passed that year, for farmers a good year, in which the rains had been early, plentiful and continuous, and the crops borne by the fruitful soil heavy beyond all expectation. The next year was also good, though less so, for it was too wet. Still, it was better to have too much rain than too little; of too little rain and the disaster of drought those border Boers had nothing to learn, and thinking of their old homes looked with pleasure at the dripping leaves of the tropical vegetation which surrounded them, marvelling at its luxuriance.

It sometimes seemed to them that they could actually watch things grow, see the curling tendrils of the wild creepers mounting, hear the young shoots of grass rustle as they burst their way through the black carpet of the burnt-off mountains. It was only in 1840 that the menace of a too fecund nature began to impress itself upon their simple minds, that they began to look askance at the weeds in their lands, at their young fruit trees which grew and grew but did not bear, and at their sheep which were starving in the rank grass which was too wet to burn. Weakened, hundreds of sheep died of fluke and worms. Great numbers of jackals having been destroyed, the vultures and those which remained being insufficient to deal with the corpses which skinned lay everywhere and the blow-flies increased to such an extent that all the wooled sheep were struck, and men went about stinking of dung and rotten flesh from the dressing of their injuries. The ticks too were more plentiful than ever, for the burning of the veld which, if it did not eliminate them at least tended to reduce their numbers, was impossible, and much of the stock was in danger of dying of loss of blood alone, and all the good grass they ate went into nourishing the parasites they carried. Quarter evil, lamsiekte in which cows went about eating bones and animal refuse struck at them, while red water apart from killing most of the dogs caused also the death of many of the horned stock and horses and left those that recovered anaemic, with the blood vessels round their eyes a yellowish white and their gums as pale as the flesh of a bled calf.

Nature was not to be denied in the shadow of the berg and in the sheltered warmth of the low country. Her favours were distributed so evenly between the men who, with their domestic stock, inhabited it, and the parasitic life that preyed on them, that the Boers who could wrest a living from the niggardly country were hard put to it to exist in one which was over generous; and the flocks and herds which had increased so rapidly at first were decreasing as fast or faster than they multiplied, and the trees round the kraals were festooned with hides spread out to dry, and the counting of beasts, instead of being a pleasure, became an ever-increasing anxiety, for each day when they came in from the grazing, filing over the veld, there was always the fear that one or more would not be there, that something had died. And, on top of this, came the locusts, the wet season being favourable to them, and these the Boers refused to destroy since they were God-sent, a plague to chasten them. Some they killed, the winged insects which preceded the main swarms of marching young; for the Boers were fond of dried locusts to eat and they also made excellent food for poultry, but even the poultry was sadly depleted by the attacks of the tampans which, living in the crevices of the trees on which they perched, and in the cracks of their fowl houses, sucked their blood as they slept. Fleas, too, were incredibly prevalent, the ordinary ones were so numerous that sometimes they could be brushed off the moleskin trousers of the men in black handfuls, while the sand fleas clung in tight flat clusters round the combs and wattles of the chickens and on the ears of the dogs till they were maddened by irritation.

It even seemed to some of the people that the predicants, who had warned them against trekking, had been right. We were warned, they said. We were warned not to 'go awhoring after the high places of the north.' We were warned and still we came.

Some talked of leaving but none left; instead they turned their minds to hunting, reducing their acreage, allowed their heavy ploughs to rust and their lands to go back to grass. Why fight nature with ploughs while they had guns? Why bother to grow more than was necessary for their immediate use when it could not be sold?

Swiftly turning their minds round they saw a meaning in all this, the Lord God meant that they should hunt. Long ago they should have seen this; it was written in the amount of game that swarmed in the vicinity, so and instead of growing crops they hunted. God had pointed and they, his children, blind to the Lord God's gesture, had for three years ignored his finger and tried to do things which were contrary to reason and God's will.

Also they were fond of hunting, it came natural to them, and among the hunters none killed more wild beasts than Hendrik van der Berg, elephant after elephant falling to his gun, rhinoceros after rhinoceros. The first for their tusks; the second for their horns which were much in demand, being bought by the traders who sent them to China and India where, owing to the fact that if poison was poured into cups carved from them they changed colour; they were easily and profitably sold. These products they exchanged for powder and other necessities and it was in this manner, through the traders, that the rumours of Zwart Piete's activities and the favour he enjoyed among the Portuguese, coast Arabs, and natives of the interior, was confirmed.

7

With Hendrik away so much von Rhule did not neglect his opportunities; riding over nominally to give extra instruction to the younger children, the German did not confine his attentions to them but always found time to talk to their step-mother. Sometimes even accompanying her on her walks up the mountainside. The only educated man among them, he watched the slow disintegration of the Boers with interest, saw the inevitability of the end and awaited it with curiosity. Of all the various treks which had penetrated the north only a fraction would survive. These people were the tentacles of a greater movement, and their function was to seek out places suitable for colonisation, and although they did not realise it, to die in those places which were unsuitable. So, by process of slow elimination would a change take place and the law which pushed men ever farther into the unoccupied places of the earth be fulfilled.

Many had died, many more would die or be killed, while others, like Hendrik, would take coloured or even native women and by them breed bastards more suited to the conditions under which they lived; some would drift back, more would come, and in the end a levelling up would be effected. These men, women and children, and even the domestic beasts they had with them, were pawns in a game of whose existence the Boers knew nothing and whose ends were even to him who had given the matter some consideration, both meaningless and wanton. Cynical and irreligious he charmed and frightened Sannie by a cold sanity which at first she took for madness, later as blasphemy, and finally accepted as an unacknowledged bond between them. His view was Tante Anna's and was fast becoming her own, but he said things which she hardly dared to think, questioning the omnipotence of God, the sanctity of marriage and the acquisitiveness which made all men merchants, forcing them to amass property, cattle, gold and wives. Forced them, out of their fear of extinction, to breed families, and out of their vanity to build houses of stone which would remain behind them when they died, visible proofs that they had lived.

'No, no, Sannie,' he would say, taking her hand and playing with strong fingers on the tendons of her wrist; 'while we live let us live. In my life I have done many things both good and evil, and of them all I regret nothing, neither the good nor the bad. All that I regret are those things which I have not done, those times when I have sat idle, with my hands folded. And they,' he went on, referring contemptuously to the Boers, 'think that there is virtue in just sitting. They, who talk of nothing but God and cattle, cannot see that God, if he made us, made also our hands. He gave us hands to work with, to kill with, to use in making love.'

First Herman, then Hendrik, now Otto von Rhule. Ach, ja, Sannie thought, a woman had but to raise her little finger and she had a man. Nor need she even do that; she need do no more than she was doing now — by merely existing, one could obtain everything.

Life was not to be avoided, it came at one like a charging buffalo when one least expected it. She raised her eyes and looked at von Rhule, she was tired of fencing, of warding off circumstance, of retreating only to be followed. Here was a thorn which could be inserted into her husband's flank, one which if he did not discover it would not matter, remaining a source of purely personal amusement, and one which if it were discovered would precipitate the crisis for which she longed. Before God something must happen soon, she must get relief.

If life was like this, then let it be so, and who was she, Sannie van der Berg, to argue with life?

And so the will of God worked itself out in those parts. Sannie gave herself to Otto von Rhule, who wanted her because he was bored, and Louisa was eating into the spirit of Hendrik because he was the greatest among the people, the richest, one who could give her the things she wanted, and the others strove valiantly with the forces that the God they worshipped flung so cruelly against them in order to try them in the fire of disease and disaster, till only the strongest would be strong enough and they, the strong, broken; old before their time.

8

News from the other settlements came in with some regularity; there was a coming and going between them. People moved, visited each other, or passing by on their way to more distant places, thought nothing of deflecting their journey, by sixty miles or so, in order to pass the time of day with one who was no more than an acquaintance, so great was their desire to talk or even to sit silent with those who were not of their own immediate party, who did not know the names of their house servants, who could not recognise their saddle-horses by their action before their colour was apparent, who in fact did not know everything there was to be known about them.

Men came riding in to buy cattle, to look for wives; hunters came, and prospectors moving from range to range, talked of gold in the mountains. These last, the prospectors, were to the older men a menace, for if they found gold, the English that they had suffered so much to avoid, would follow them. Magtig, ja, if there was gold the red-coats would come, setting them, good free burghers, on an equality with the Kaffirs, making them buy the farms they had taken by the sweat of their brows and the strength of their hands on gun and bridle. Before God this was their country, they had paid for it with their earnings and bought it for their blood.

To all this the women listened, for among the women were the bitterest to be found. It was their children who had died, it was their men who had been killed. It was they who had, in many cases, urged the men to trek from the colony. It was the women who now called to their men, when with tight-lipped mouths they had listened to such talk for long enough, saying, 'And if the English come are you not still men? Have you not good horses under you and guns in your hands? Will our wagons not still roll? Are our oxen not strong in the yoke? Wherever we are there is always room beyond; we have come far but we can go farther; or is it that all those who were men are dead, and that we who rode out defiant and entire are to be gelded and inspanned to draw the English ploughs? That the freedom we demand for our children is a joke, an idle word, a sham? Is it for nothing we have borne your children on ox hides behind our wagons, like animals, alone on the veld?'

Massive and implacable in their hatred of those who had pressed them to whom all their ills and their ruin was due, they were contemptuous of the men who talked of coming to terms with the Roineks if they came, when so far they had not even crossed the Vaal. It was from those that the English had driven out of Natal that these tales came, those who had seen the might of England and who fearing it, spoke of compromise.

It was Tante Anna who turned many of these arguments into new channels. These people were hot and without philosophy, the men were angry, wasted with fever and drawn by anxiety, while the women were rancorous with hatred at the injuries they had suffered, and hysterical from the tea they drank continuously and without ceasing. Among them were many whose babies had died, whose swollen breasts hurt them, women who had, like Lucia Bothma, taken a bitch's pup to her breast for relief. Such women and the men they swayed, were dangerous, or would have been had they had leaders. They were using the English as something on which to vent their hatred of the things they did not understand. Just as a woman who had spilt the cream she was about to churn would slap the face of one of her children, or a man whose bull had died beat a Kaffir.

The English were many hundred miles away and were

busy negotiating with the Zulus, trying to prevent the Boer
commandos from pursuing their stolen cattle to enforce
their strange laws on a people who had not left their homes to
suffer such restraint. Meanwhile the plagues of Egypt were
smiting Canaan. Disease of man and beast inducing apathy,
encouraging the feeling that tomorrow was also a day, that
work done ill was still done well enough since it was done.
Adventure and hardship these folk could stand, it was something which they were capable of facing, gun in hand, but
could one face the bos-lice, the mosquitoes, the fleas and
other vermin with weapons? Could one send commandos
against them? And these men, already known as Voortrekkers, were not of ordinary farming stuff; their desire
was not for a static peace — they were the skimmings of
a race that was at once lethargic and passionate, boastful
and obstinate in the carrying out of their boasts. The more
she saw, the more she sat turning things over in her mind.
Tante Anna de Jong realised that her people, that she herself, were no more than the shear of a plough which would
in time be worn down by the stress of the life they led and
that in their wearing down they would achieve great things
which few of them would live to see, and with this certainty
in her mind Anna de Jong turned her thoughts to the best
method of saving what could be saved, of protecting herself
and hers. Where before she had woven plans for her own
amusement and the disconcertment of her enemies, she now
worked for a greater thing, the saving of a situation which
she alone foresaw. Of what use was it to talk to Hendrik?
To tell him to count the herds as they were now and to calculate their recent losses, to point to the faces of the people, to say that too many Kaffirs now came in to trade and
that it was no longer only women who came, but men also
who stared about with curious eyes, who must see in the
scattered farms rich booty to be had for the taking, and in
the remnants of their herds good meat for their empty pots;
men who asked for work, saying they would like to serve the

white people and who in many cases were given it, being employed to work on the lands, herd cattle, and sometimes even about the houses. Like the grey lourie that cried out, warning game of the coming of the hunter, events were throwing their shadows before them, calling to Tante Anna de Jong, warning her, and making her afraid.

CHAPTER XVIII

I

ZWART PIETE had prospered in Mozambique. The slaves obtained by Rinkals in exchange for the cattle had founded his now considerable fortune and his taste for travel combined with a hitherto unsuspected gift for trading had taken him far into the interior where his ventures had without exception proved successful.

Then there had been a war, the outcome of the battle between the two slaving caravans, in which the Boers had distinguished themselves and earned the gratitude of Don Jesus whose fort was now their headquarters and whose partner Zwart Piete had become. Slave raids, fighting, hunting and trading for ivory and gold had occupied him but these were beginning to pall and he often thought of his own people and suffered the nostalgia of an exile. He wished to hear his own tongue spoken again. He wished to see his uncle Paul Pieters and to know how his friends fared. He wished to talk of what he had done and to boast of the things he had seen as he sat quietly on the stoeps of Boer houses.

For a month Zwart Piete turned things over in his mind and then, bidding farewell to Don Jesus and his Arabs, rode west accompanied by his sister and de Kok.

Rinkals was sent to go to the country of the Masai and told to await his master there, for it was Zwart Piete's intention to return that way. Superbly mounted and with the confidence that comes with success Zwart Piete, his sister and servant rode out of the wide white gates of the fort, turning in their saddles to wave as they cantered across the open glacis that lay between the building and the slave barracks, traversed the cultivated lands and orchards and, following the river, soon came to the rolling country that divided the coast from the mountains.

This time, instead of taking the roundabout route by which they had come, Zwart Piete went back directly, trusting to his uncanny sense of direction and turning neither to the right nor the left, save once to avoid a belt of country where the flies attacked and killed any horse which entered it, he led his party homewards.

Where his going had been slow and devious, his return was swift and straight.

He had never believed de Kok's story of the Zulus and was amused to watch his servant growing more and more depressed as he approached the plain where the disaster was supposed to have occurred.

In the time that he had been away he had changed; his bearing was freer and his powerful body was leaner and stronger. His complexion, always dark, was now darker, burnt almost black by prolonged exposure. He wore his hair long and his beard spread harshly over his chest. His name now fitted him, Zwart Piete, the hunter — for he was all these things — a hard, dangerous young man, who looked out at life with a lowered forehead and half-closed eyes as if he was perpetually sighting his gun, as if life was something that challenged him, that must be mastered before it mastered him; and this was his view of life, for as he saw it, there were two kinds of men, those who took and those from whom things were taken; and so, without fear, without rancour and with a cold determined courage he grasped that which he needed between his sinewy hands. Always single purposed his mind was at once able to see the main issues and having seen them to concentrate on the lesser ones into which they were divided and taking these singly he demolished them ruthlessly.

As he rode he thought of what might have been. But for a
chance, but for a big rain which had at the time seemed so
inopportune and the lies of his Griqua and his sister, he
might have been a farmer, a counter of cattle, a follower of
the plough. Instead he was a hunter and a rich one at that,
acknowledging no master, free to move and to live, one who
had seen and done much, killed many beasts, and men, one
who had friends among the Portuguese, the Arabs, and the
wild Kaffirs.

That he was different to others was due to his blood, to
the admixture of Huguenot in his blood which would not give
him rest but sent him on, involving him till he was beyond
drawing back. Ja, he thought, and one day I shall go too far,
one day I shall take one chance too many, and come to hunter's end. By buffalo or elephant, by tiger or lion, by renoster
or a wounded buck it will happen; one day his snaphaan
would misfire, or his galloping horse fall and Zwart Piete the
hunter would hunt no more; but till that day he was alive
and called strongly to his folk by a voice whose urgency he
did not understand. So insistently had it called upon him to
fold his tents and to return that he had been unable to resist.
And as he got nearer his heart sang and his blood ran faster.
Even the horses seemed to know where they were going and
arching their necks, played with their bits and lashed out at
each other.

2

To Sara their return was something else. It was a going
back to a people who did not understand her or her ways.
She had nothing to say to the women whose customs were
so diverse from her own and she was tongue-tied among the
men, who were completely at a loss when confronted by her.
After years of freedom she would again be driven back into
herself, into the silence from which she had escaped.

Why had she not been born a man? And why, if she had

not been made a man, had she not been made a woman? Less than ever now, was she that. As sunburnt as her brother, dressed as he was, wearing only a hunting-shirt and raw-hide veldschoen she rode her chestnut horse, the one which had belonged to Herman van der Berg, sullenly.

Was Piete a fool that he did not know why he was returning? Had he lived so long among the beasts that, in following their example, he still did not realise what he did or what the end of his ride would be? She looked at him, at his heavily-haired forearm that supported the gun lying across his saddle bow and watched his strong hands on the reins.

Young Piete was now a grown man, one to be desired of women, to be sought in friendship by men, or to be feared by them in anger. Like a young bull that has been away from the herd too long he was going back to try his strength. Big in every way her brother was a man who stopped at nothing and respected nothing. To him there was no law but his will, and all Africa a place where he had been accustomed to enforce it; he was suited only to live in the wilder places where no one dared to question him or to doubt his swift decisions. Knowing him as she did Sara feared for her brother and for herself. Ach, God, how she loved this man, her twin who was part of her, sprung in the same hour from the same womb.

Life was extending its soft arms to him who had only known its hardness. Soon a woman would tame him, put a riem on his wildness, the halter of her affection over his head, the buckle of her breasts under his throat, and his ache for her, a strap about his loins. Her brother was of the kind that, wild with all others, is tame to one woman, if she be his woman. A man who would kill to take and die to protect. An incalculable factor of whom one could only be certain of one thing, only that whatever he began he would finish, one to whom his heart's desire was life itself, something about which he would accept no compromise. He would always scorn a palliative and reject bitterly the idea that one thing could be put in the place of another and be equally good. Whether he gained or lost meant little to Zwart Piete for he had never lost and failure to him was a word only. He had never known it as a fact.

All this for Piete, and what was there for her? With her woman's mind in her man's body she foresaw what would soon occur, foresaw his efforts to be kind to her, to think of her when his mind was full of another. It had not happened yet, they had so far marched through life as comrades, but it would happen and like a calf with a nail-spiked plank tied across its nostrils she would be slowly weaned from him, becoming something apart, something unheard of, a lone woman hunter.

Laughing bitterly she raised her gun and shot a steinbok that stood on an ant heap to watch them pass. It was a long shot, well over a hundred paces, and her shooting had been casual. Pulling up her horse she had raised her gun and fired.

They had meat, they were travelling, and still she shot. The death of the twitching buck had freed something in her, for in this business on which her brother rode so lightheart-edly she must help him. This was inevitable; no matter what he did she was with him, as inevitable as the death of a buck who had shown himself, while still in range, to Sara du Plessis in her present mood.

And so they rode silently, the white man, his sister and their servant, each lost in their dreams. Neither together nor apart, they rode as hunters ride, alertly, with an interval and a distance between them, through the thornless mopani scrub, its large, scented, doubled leaves brushing their knees as they skirted the bushes. Here and there the sameness of the vegetation was broken by an old baobab that reared its buttressed trunk out of the scrub, or a tall jakaals-bessie whose dark green foliage flung a heavy patch of shadow over the veld. So they rode day after day till they came to the range which bounded the far side of the plain where the

Kaffir village had been, and here seeing signs of white occupation they pushed their horses on.

It was thus that Zwart Piete who had ridden out a boy, returned a man to find Paul Pieters and his people assembled round three Kaffirs whom they had captured and were questioning.

So occupied were the Boers, that it was only when they were near and cantering rapidly towards them that they had looked up and seen them.

'So you are back,' Paul Pieters said. 'Ach, God, I knew that one day you would return, and while you have been away I have watched over your stock which has done well.'

'Ja, Oom Paul, I am back,' Zwart Piete said, laughing, 'and who are these?' He pointed to the natives who stood, their faces grey with fright, their eyes starting out of their heads.

'They are Kaffirs that we have taken and with whom we are discussing the question of some lost cattle. But they appear to know nothing of them which is the more extraordinary as we found them near the spoor that we were following. We found also the bones of a beast they had eaten, but of the others, the big clompie, we can find no trace, but soon they will speak, Piete. Ja, jong, soon they will speak loudly. Bring out that sjambok, Jan,' he shouted, 'and lay it in. Come, make them fast and let us begin.'

Profiting by the diversion of Zwart Piete's arrival the Kaffirs suddenly broke from the tame natives who were holding them and ran. From all round guns cracked, the Boers shooting from where they stood, so certain of their marksmanship were they that they did not hesitate to shoot between their friends, one man firing past the arm of the man in front of him.

Like wounded hares the Kaffirs fell, rolling over and over as the bullets struck them. All went down but one, who unwounded, because no one had fired at him, still ran with his elbows close to his sides and his head thrown back.

Zwart Piete, Sara and de Kok who were still mounted

swung their horses round and, with Paul Pieter's shout of 'get him alive, kerls, for dead he cannot talk,' in their ears, galloped after him.

Swinging away to the flanks of the running man and leaving de Kok to press him from the rear so as to keep him straight they rode to cut him off. Ahead of them galloped two Boer hounds, great rough-haired beasts that had been put at the fleeing Kaffir by their masters. In full cry they ran yelping, as they would have after a wounded buck and reaching their quarry threw him down as Piete and Sara closed in on them and de Kok came up.

Left alone the dogs would have torn the Kaffir to pieces, but obedient to the white men they allowed themselves to be called off, and with a riem round his neck and his hands tied behind him the Kaffir was led back to be thrashed and questioned.

It seemed that he was the brother of the chief, and that one of those killed was his son. They had gone back to watch for their pursuers and had been surprised. He promised the return of the beasts and to give compensation if he was allowed to go, to which the Boers, wanting back their stock, agreed, and following his instructions they sent off a native woman to arrange matters, holding him as hostage till the exchange could be effected.

That night after he had counted the beasts bearing his brand in his uncle's kraals Piete talked of what he had done, where he had been.

'And what are you going to do now?' Paul Pieters asked.

'Now,' he said. 'Now I am going to pass the time of day with my people. I am going to visit my friends and then, when I have had enough of this soft living, I shall return.'

'What, you are not going to stay and farm here like the rest of us?' his uncle said.

'I do not think that I am a farmer, Oom Paul. It is in my heart that I must always move. That I cannot wake to see the same mountains each morning, that I cannot watch the sun set over the same tree day after day. The time may come, perhaps, when I am old, that I shall want to farm, but now I have hunted too long to settle. I want my horse's neck in front of me. I want to see the world from between his ears with my snaphaan in my hand.'

'Ja, jong, I can see, I can understand. It is your father's blood that is in you which causes this desire for the movement. This curiosity was the one thing that I had against the man who was your father. It was the one thing of which I warned your mother. "He is a fine man, Augusta." I said, "a man to make a woman happy but his blood is wild and he will never grow fat. He is not as we are," I said, and that I believe is why she took him, Piete, because he was not like the others, and that is why some maid will take you. Because you are different, because you are like a wild steer that has never known a riem round its horns. You make me think of a young ox that I inspanned once. First he broke all the trek gear and then when I made him fast with stronger riems he gave a great leap upwards and burst his heart, so that the blood ran out of his nose and his eyes. That was a fine young ox, but he was not made for the wagon or the plough. Ja,' he said, 'you are like that ox, and though I am afraid you are no good, Piete, I love you for you are my sister's son, and by God, you are a man.' He held out his hand. 'Here,' he said, 'or wherever I am, you shall always have a home. Ja, and while I have horses you shall be mounted, and while I have food you shall eat. So stay with me till it is time for you to go and then if you are the man I think you, a man like your father, not all Dingaans impis would stop you.

'Ja, one day you will be gone,' his uncle said. 'One day you will hold out your hand, get up onto your horse and ride away, and when the folk ask for you, I shall say, "My nephew has gone." And when they say, "Where has he gone?" I shall say, "Ek weet nie, I do not know. How can I, since he does not know himself?"'

3

De Kok was almost hurt by the fact that his master had done nothing about the lies he had told. It almost seemed as if Zwart Piete had always known them for lies, as if what he had considered a dramatic and well-told tale had been wasted. Twice he tried to make Sara discuss the matter with him, for he wished to know how they had failed, but Sara was unapproachable and spent most of her time among the horses, breaking the colts or going for long solitary rides over the veld. As she rode, she thought of many things, but her thoughts kept returning to the future, and to her brother who, caught in the tide of time and circumstance, was drifting on, dragging her reluctantly in his wake. It was curious that she, who had nothing to look forward to, should see things so clearly, or perhaps it was because she had nothing that she saw it.

Slowly, as the days passed she watched the restlessness she had anticipated in her brother growing, saw him ride off to visit. Sometimes she went with him and saw him look at the young girls, give them a quick appraising glance as if he sought something, something which he knew he would recognise when he saw it. Watched him look at them and look away. So far, there was nothing. It was not that there were no pretty girls, young and buxom, all more than willing to take this man who came to them with such a romantic history out of the east. Many were related to him, distantly or nearly, all remembered him on the trek, and none of them could move him, to him none of them were anything.

Wider and wider became the circle of his unknowing search, farther farms were visited and farther settlements. Pushed on by an unease that he did not understand, for had anyone spoken to him of marriage he would have laughed and said his life was too hard to be shared by a woman, he continued to seek. And one day he decided to go and see how Hendrik van der Berg's people were getting on and how Hendrik, the father of his friend Herman, was living; also, he decided to go alone.

Following the track through the kloof, past the big marulas where he and de Kok had halted on their reconnaissance, past the cave with the bushman drawings, back to the site of the laager camp, past the graves of Jappie de Jong, Herman and the others by the big Hartekoal and over the drift where Hendrik's oxen had dragged his wagons, and following the spoor that was still visible after three years, he crossed the rivers and rode over the mountains till he came to the edge of the berg where it fell so steeply into the blue-green country of the low veld. It was the ledge on the edge of the krantz from which Hendrik, three years before, had looked down on Canaan — the promised land.

Here he halted, while he stared into the sea of bush below him. He had seen country like this before in his travels and had got out of it. Was Hendrik van der Berg mad to have settled here? Why, the very luxuriance of everything, the amount of water, the type of bush was all a menace to one who knew the country as he did. Long before he started down he knew what he would find. There would be much sickness here. Also, it was not a safe place, the mountains on the one side would shelter Kaffirs, while the bush on the other would harbour them. Boers were only safe in open country where they could operate mounted, this place was a death trap in more ways than one. Pushing his horse on to the very edge of the krantz, he shaded his eyes with his hand.

Ja, there was good grass down there, fine grass; but surely a man was mad who would endanger his life and that of his children for grass. And strategically, the place was a death trap; such open ground as there was being so intersected by slow-moving rivers, these Zwart Piete saw only as obstacles dividing one man from another, that if they were attacked they would be unable to go to each other's aid, except along the foot of the berg where they could be ambushed. Hendrik van der Berg had made a mistake, he did not know this kind of country or its dangers as he, who had spent the last three years hunting in it, did. Zwart Piete had suffered privation and almost died of fever in other valleys as beautiful, as fruitful, and as evil.

Thinking deeply, he turned his horse and went slowly down the steep road that had been made along the face of the mountain, and it was thus that Zwart Piete the hunter, riding the dappled grey Arab which he had bought from the Portuguese, rode into the settlement under the shadow of the horse-shoe berg.

And it was thus that Sannie who had seen him silhouetted against the sky came to meet him. Impelled by a curiosity which she attributed to the difference of his horse from those to which she was accustomed, she went towards the road. This man up on the berg was not from these parts. The Boer horses were not like this one, they neither carried their crests nor their tails in such a fashion; what she did not know she wished to see, so leaving her children, Sannie went to sit on a rock at the foot of the track. She had long since learnt to wait and sat relaxed and pensive, with her kappie held by its ribbons in her hand, leaning against the tree behind her.

Slowly the man on the horse grew bigger, appearing and disappearing behind rock outcrops and trees, swinging away from her as the path turned and back towards her as it turned again. Unconsciously she absorbed what she saw, took in the man sitting firmly in his saddle with his gun across his knees, took in the horse that stepped as if the ground was too hot for its small hoofs, that breathed as if the air was not sufficiently delicate for its wide nostrils.

But it was not till he came up to her that Zwart Piete saw her. She was a small woman and sat curled up with one foot beneath her. Nor, when her eyes met his, did she rise.

For a minute they remained thus, holding each other, neither moving nor speaking, the man as still as the woman, the stallion as static as the rock.

'What a small head your horse has got, mynheer,' Sannie said. 'Where does he come from?'

'From over there,' Zwart Piete pointed to the east. 'My name is Piete du Plessis,' he said, 'and I seek Hendrik van der Berg.' He looked at her again. 'And aren't you Sannie van Reenen?' he asked. 'Weren't you with us on the trek, and the friend of my friend Herman?'

'I was the friend of Herman, but Herman is dead,' she said; 'and I was Sannie van Reenen, but am now the wife of the man whom you seek. I am Mevrou van der Berg,' she said, getting up.

'You do not look like a wife,' Zwart Piete said.

'And what does a wife look like, mynheer?' she asked.

'I do not know, but not like you, mevrou. Before God, a wife does not look like you.'

Zwart Piete dismounted and came up to her as with her weight on one foot, Sannie tapped the other on the ground.

This man was different, he was disturbing. What had he meant when he said she did not look like a wife? What had he seen? She wished she had not come to meet him, but was he not seeking her husband? And would she not have met him inevitably whether she had come or not come? It would only have delayed their meeting.

'Hendrik will be glad to see you,' she said. 'And if you will come with me, mynheer, I will show you the way.'

'I will come,' Zwart Piete said. 'Ja, I will come.' And leaving his horse, he walked down the stony path after her.

'Your horse follows without being led,' Sannie said.

'Ja, my horse follows.'

'You trained him to follow?'

'Ja, I trained him to follow; all my horses follow, it is necessary that they should.'

'Why necessary?' she asked.

'Because they must follow and come when I call; I am a hunter,' he said.

'You are a hunter,' she said. 'A hunter of what, mynheer?'

'Of elephants, mevrou, and of other things.'

4

There was an air of fictitious prosperity about the settlement, an air of almost desperate success, of triumph and disaster running side by side. Here man had striven with his puny forces against the evil powers of nature in a land so fruitful that nature could afford to suffer man, able as it was at any time to overwhelm him. While man fought, nature waited, playing slowly against him, guarding her integrity with the weapons of disease and plague; with ticks that sucked the rich blood from the stock, with tampans, with fleas, with bugs in the houses, with wild beasts that killed his domestic animals and ate his crops, with locusts and borers and cut worms, with white ants which allowed men to build and then destroyed what they had built, eating out the heart of their woodwork so that only a crust remained.

All this and more Zwart Piete saw, and fully appreciating the efforts made by the Boers to stave off ruin, seeing the plans they had made to hold their enemies at bay, he smiled bitterly. With the tenacity of their race they were fighting a losing battle, pitting themselves individually against forces that would, in the end, have swamped them if they had been combined. Capable of phenomenal efforts these people were also capable of phenomenal acquiescence in adversity, taking the manifold blows that were rained upon them as acts of God, sent by him to chasten them; as rods which the Almighty was loth to spare from the backs of his children, as trials sent to test their faith, for this God of theirs was no benevolent deity, but a terrible and a jealous God.

The tide of their fortunes, when Zwart Piete arrived among them, was past the turn. It was ebbing. Here, lands had been abandoned, much less was under the plough, and the thorn bush was regaining that which had been stolen from it. There, water furrows were leaking and unmended, while many of the kraals were in a bad state of repair and the demeanour of the people was anxious with suppressed fears, their eyes questioning and their faces grim. They were tired, weakened by their long journey to this place, and their subsequent effort; while the country in which they had settled was fresh, and holding its hand had not troubled over much, certain by the weight of its deceptive fertility to achieve a final and irrevocable victory by elimination, by a delayed and continuous onslaught that nothing, no effort of man, could stay and one which could easily be accelerated by the piling of one small thing on to another, till its cumulative effect would blot out all that man had done in those parts, till nothing was left to show of man's passing but the crumpled heaps of stones where his houses had been. The dark-green rings of kweek grass marking the sight of his kraals and the small mounds of the graves of those who died there.

But more than all this did Zwart Piete fear the Kaffirs, of whom he saw several. They came unarmed it is true, leaving their assegais, but they came. By a slow process of infiltration they came and went, accustoming the white people to their presence; and where when the Boers had first come, a strange Kaffir was a rare sight, a number of them together was now a common one.

Secure in their imagined superiority the Boers not only allowed, but encouraged them by drawing on the local natives for an additional supply of labour, so that among the Kaffirs there were many who were half-tame, and who, having lived and worked among the Boers, had lost their fear of the white men and knew their ways.

These things Zwart Piete saw as he accompanied Sannie to her husband's stone house, for he was a hunter unable to mistake the signs however much his mind was occupied by the sight of the girl moving so gracefully in front of him. Already he knew that he wanted this woman, and refused to believe that she belonged to anyone. A woman who looked into a man's eyes as she had done was free and seeking.

Zwart Piete had found what he sought. He had seen the

woman he wanted and he was going to have her. He would have her if it meant blood, his own or that of others. He would have her at all cost. She was his woman and tacitly he knew that she acknowledged it, and that she would come when he called.

5

Otto von Rhule was angry, Hendrik was away and he had arranged to meet Sannie, yet she had gone out. There was a great deal that he did not understand about this woman, more than all he failed to see by what arts she held him off sometimes, or her purpose in so doing. Was he not a man, he asked himself? Was he not all that a man could possibly be? Tall, strong and brave? And was he less a man one day than another? Why, then, this coquetry, this drawing back, this running away from an issue which was so plain to him that it must also be apparent to her?

In this mood von Rhule watched the mountain road, for it was this way, he was told, that she had gone.

Having tied his horse to the branches of a tree he sat down on one of the ox skulls that were used as seats on the stoep and waited for her return. It was infuriating the way she kept him like this, it was even more infuriating that he tolerated it. Here he was behaving like a boy, allowing himself to be dealt with as if he knew nothing, and feeling things that he had thought it impossible to feel again; feeling that time spent away from her was wasted, feeling quite tongue-tied, and only conscious of an ache in his loins when he was with her. His previous experiences were for the first time proving no help to him, his knowledge of women of no assistance, for here was one so feminine that his rules no longer applied. A girl who worked by methods so intuitive that they were unknown to him, being based on something which came from deep down in her spirit and could not be dealt with by his devices, which, precise and invariable as the manoeuvres of a squadron, were without either imagination or elasticity. Also there was that infernal lion. Attractive women, he felt, should not keep lions, and when he came it was often at liberty. By the presence of the lion he knew her mood.

Getting up, he kicked at one of the stoep poles impatiently, bringing down a shower of fine dry mud flakes, the covering of the tunnels made by the ants that were working in the thatch; some of them very small and a dirty white in colour fell onto the ground. Extending his foot he rubbed them out.

What a country it was; and as he thought of the country he felt a sudden nostalgia for the pine woods and mountains of his home, and cursed Africa and the stupidities which had brought him here. He had been a fool, and had paid for his folly. He was being a fool now, and would pay for this, too; one always paid. And if he wanted a thing, he was ready to pay. No one had ever said of him, whatever else they might say, that Otto von Rhule did not meet his liabilities, that he was afraid to face his commitments. Looking up he saw her; she was coming now, and a man was with her — a tall young man, followed by a grey Arab that nuzzled at his back.

First came the woman, then the man, and then the horse; there seemed an understanding between the three of them, and a significance about the coming of a stranger at this juncture. Here was no Jewish trader to be browbeaten, no lone and penurious hunter; this was a man, a rival. And in all the world there was no man more capable of estimating men, as men, than von Rhule who had been bred to the trade of leading and of judging them.

As they approached he did not look at Sannie but at the man behind her, weighing and assessing him. Questioning his qualities, his appearance and his strength, for to von Rhule all men were one of several things, his inferiors to be ridden over roughshod, his equals to be left alone or faced if necessary, and his superiors in breeding, strength or intelligence, of whom he had met but few, and whom he had, so far, been wise enough to acknowledge and to leave alone.

Here was one who was certainly his equal and perhaps more than that, and as they came nearer he recognised him. It was Zwart Piete, who had come to be called the hunter, and who, from what they had heard, had in the time he had been away amassed a fortune, and established himself as a slaver, hunter and trader among the Portuguese.

And the more he saw of Zwart Piete the less von Rhule liked the look of him. He seemed overbold, overcareless, over-strong and over-young. Here was a man who acknowledged no law, whom nothing, neither fear of death, nor scruple, would arrest from going those ways which seemed good to him. With a smile on his lips and ignoring Sannie he went towards Zwart Piete.

'Do you remember me?' he asked.

'I remember you,' Piete said, 'you are Otto von Rhule, the meester. And how go the children, mynheer?' he asked. 'Can they all read and write? It is odd, is it not, mynheer, where the paths of men lead them? That while you taught the young ones their catechisms I have become a trader, a hunter of men and ivory. Ja, it is odd,' he went on, 'that I who was a boy am now a man, and that you who were a man, the only soldier among us, have become a woman, teaching children and visiting women while their husbands are away.'

'I have killed men for less than that, mynheer,' von Rhule said.

'Then what is there to prevent you killing me?' Zwart Piete asked. 'Nothing,' he went on, 'save that you dare not do it. I do not like you, von Rhule,' he said. 'I have never liked you, and in the time that I have been away I have learnt to speak my mind.'

Raising his hand von Rhule struck out, but Piete was before him, his blow taking von Rhule in the pit of the stomach. A moment later he had him by the arms and had flung him over his shoulder on to his back. Turning like a leopard, he knelt on the German with his hands at his throat, his thumbs on his windpipe and his knuckles driven into the arteries under his ears. Tense as a wild beast on its kill Piete bent over von Rhule. For all his bulk the German was a child in the hands of a man who had lived by his strength and courage for the whole of his life, one who existed by the speed and strength of his attack, and whose mind, bent on self-preservation in the face of perpetual danger, was so keyed that his body was always ready, his nerves and muscles blades that were never sheathed.

'Stop, Piete,' Sannie said. 'Stop! You are mad. Why did you do that?'

'He looked at you,' Piete said.

'And who are you to say who will look at me?' she asked.

'Who am I?' Piete said, slackening his hold. 'That certainly is a question. I do not know, Sannie, it is just that I do not like this man, and when he looked at you like that my anger flamed. I am sorry,' he said. 'I see that I have grown unused to living among civilised people and will go.'

Getting up, he whistled to his horse and vaulted into the saddle.

'And what about my husband?' Sannie asked. 'When will you see him if you go now?'

'Then you mean I am to stay, mevrou?'

'I mean that you stay,' she said, 'but first you will apologise to Mynheer von Rhule.'

'Apologies come hard to my mouth, mevrou. What I have said I have said, and what I have done I have done.'

Von Rhule sprang up and made for him as he spoke, only to be faced by the stallion's hoofs, for Piete had pulled him up into a rear, and the horse, a trained Arab charger, was accustomed to war and well prepared to face attack. Unmoved, his eyes cold, Zwart Piete drove his horse forward onto the man, forcing back and only bringing down his mount as Sannie stepped between them.

'Dismount,' she said, 'and apologise, and you,' she turned

to von Rhule, 'will accept his apology. This thing shall be as if it had never been, and then you will go.'

'Ja, you will go,' Piete said, 'and when you look at a woman learn to look differently and keep the lust from your eyes.'

'I will go now,' von Rhule said, 'for I accept neither apologies nor blows, and this thing can never be as if it had not been. In Germany,' he said to Zwart Piete, 'you would have died for this.'

'But as it is not Germany I shall not die, for you will not shoot me from behind, and dare not face me from the front. So tot seins, mynheer, tot seins.'

Still sitting on his horse Zwart Piete watched the German mount and ride away.

'That man is not good,' he said to Sannie. 'He is like a wild dog that jumps and jumps at a running buck till he can pull it down, tearing out its entrails as it runs. A wild dog that will not face a lion,' he added.

Sannie laughed. That had been apt, a bow drawn at a venture, for so far Piete knew nothing of her lion which was out with Jakalaas.

'And are you a lion, mynheer?' she asked.

'No, Sannie,' Piete said, speaking softly. 'I am no lion, but perhaps I might become one.'

There was no answer to this, and telling Piete to dismount and let his horse roll, she looked at the sun.

'My husband will soon be back,' she said, 'and till then perhaps mynheer can put up with me? I will do my best to entertain you.'

6

When Hendrik van der Berg returned he found Zwart Piete in his house waiting for him with Frikkie on his knee. He was telling the child tales of elephants and lions, telling him of how the Masai hunted them, telling him of the great waters that ran up against the sandy strand of Africa and of the forests that came down to their very edges, of the monkeys that swung in the trees, and of the small parrots that walked upside down along their branches.

But Zwart Piete as he talked to the child was watching the door out of which Sannie had gone.

He got up as Hendrik came in, putting the child down carefully.

'So, Oom Hendrik,' he said, 'I have come back and am visiting. My Uncle Paul Pieters sends greetings, and bids me tell you that things go well with him and his folk.'

'It is good to see you, Piete,' Hendrik said, holding out his hand. 'Is it true what we have heard of you?'

'That depends on what you have heard. Of me many things are said.'

'That you are successful and have joined with the Portuguese at the coast, that you are engaged in the traffic of slaves and have hunted right up to the deserts of the north, that you have friends among the wild Kaffirs?'

'These things are true,' Piete said.

'And you have left all this to come visiting?'

'Ja, I have left it. It was in my heart to see my folk again.'

'It was not in your heart to seek a woman among them by any chance?' Hendrik asked, laughing. 'You are now a man, and men do not live by bread alone.'

'Perhaps you are right, Oom Hendrik, but if it was so I did not know it till recently. I was called, and I came. I have travelled far since I saw you last,' he added. 'Ja, I have travelled very far, and seen many things.'

'You must tell me of them,' Hendrik said, 'but I do not think it is good to see too much, and since one cannot see all, it may be better to see little.'

'It may be better, but some men have never done with seeing, and I am one of those men. My Uncle Paul Pieters says it is the gift of my father, coming to me as my heritage from his blood; and my father was a fine man, he saved my life, more than that no man can do. You know the tale, Hendrik, of how he drove his knife into my horse and saved me from the Kaffirs?'

'I know it,' Hendrik said.

'And since then I have hunted Kaffirs, I and my sister, and we have killed many, very many. My father will be glad of what I have done, for he was a great hunter and fighter, one of the greatest on the border, and a friend in his boyhood of Coenraad Buys.'

'You will stay with us I hope,' Hendrik said. 'We have some pretty maids here that you should see. Maids who would be glad to take a man like you.'

'Ja, Baie Dankie, Hendrik, I will stay. My horse is already in your kraal.'

'He must go to the mountain,' Hendrik said, 'for there is much sickness here.'

'He can stay,' Zwart Piete said. 'He is salted and would fret without me, for we are not accustomed to be apart. Nie, Hendrik, my horse and my gun and my knife do not leave me.'

'And yet you say he is in the kraal?'

'Ja, he is in the kraal, but the gate is not so high.'

'What do you mean?'

'This,' Zwart Piete said, and pursing his lips he whistled. Hendrik looking towards the kraal saw the grey's head appear over the gate. 'He has heard your whistle, he is a good horse and you should go to him, Piete.'

'Why go to him when he will come to me. But he is a wise horse who looks before he leaps. Ja,' Piete cried, 'he comes.'

The horse, having looked at the gate, had run back and leapt, his hind hoofs tipping the top bar and cracking it. As he came Piete ran forward gun in hand and jumped onto his back, guiding him with his hands by leaning forward and covering his outside eye as he wished him to turn inwards, he cantered round, and finally pulling up opposite his host slipped from his back.

'So you see, Oom Hendrik, we are near, he and I. He is an eastern war horse, that I have trained to my ways. These horses are better than ours, more gentle, and yet more full of fire, and if you have any mares in season while I am here I will let him serve them. It will do him good.'

'If I have any I shall be glad, but in the meantime your horse has broken the gate of the kraal. But it was a fine thing to see, very fine,' Hendrik added, 'and the horse is a beautiful one, very hot, but with kind eyes and lips as soft as a woman's. Ja, Zwart Piete,' he went on, 'I am glad to see you and your horse, also it is good to know that the old ways are not dying out, for never have I seen a quicker thing than the coming of your horse and your mounting. Can you shoot from his back?' he asked.

'Ja, I can shoot from his back, and from over him also, for he will lie down, and he is like an otter in the water, many rivers has he taken me across holding onto his mane or tail. Not for many tusks would I part with him, for he is more than a horse, Oom Hendrik.'

CHAPTER XIX

I

ZWART PIETE'S visit to Canaan was protracted. As the days passed he became more and more aware that his first impressions had been correct, that things were not as they should have been and that in the event of an attack by the Kaffirs these people would be destroyed. Their only hope, if they had time, would be to laager in the small plain between the forks of the river. In his riding round he had looked in vain for any other place where there was room for the wagons to form up, and from which the defenders would have an adequate field of fire. More than ever his original opinion was confirmed, that the only place in which it was safe to farm in was the open country, in a plain such as his uncle had chosen. This bush veld was a death trap. But those to whom he spoke of it only laughed at him and said that he was so accustomed to wild natives that he did not understand the tame ones. These Kaffirs, they said, are mak, they are tame and they like us.

'Why should they like you?' Piete asked. 'Are you not worse than Zulus who come like a storm, destroy, and then go perhaps never to come again? Whereas you come and take their best grazing, kill the game on which they live, and expect them to love you. It does not make sense,' he added.

'And yet,' they answered, 'the Kaffirs are the children of Ham, it is their duty to serve us. Does it not say so in the Holy Word?'

'Ja, it says so,' Zwart Piete said, 'but do the Kaffirs know of this? Do they understand that they are the children of Ham?'

When he was not answered he said, 'I do not think they do. on the contrary it is in my mind that they think they are a people who have been dispossessed, and they are angry. You can see their anger in their eyes.'

'Who looks in a Kaffir's eyes?' they asked.

'A wise man looks in the eyes of all who approach him, for in the eyes of a man or a beast can be read their intentions; and it is by reading the intentions of those who oppose me that I live, and it is by neglecting to read that you will die.'

'You are mad, Piete; you have lived too long away from men,' they said.

'Ja, I have lived so long among the beasts that I know men, and these Kaffirs are like a wounded buffalo, one which while you follow comes circling round on its own spoor, so that instead of being behind it you are in front and very near to its horns.'

But no matter what he said or how seriously he spoke, he was laughed at. He was a boy, a young hunter who had been lucky. He was not a farmer except by proxy; he who allowed his uncle to handle his beasts while he travelled. He was not solid and lacked the Boer virtues of tenacity and steadfastness, trying to substitute an arrogant dash for stolid work, one, who rootless, accepted the sky for his ceiling and the veld for his hearth. A man who might be admired, but one in whom no confidence could be placed.

All thought this, except Martinus, who no longer sang, because Marietje's small son was dead, and his wife was sick; all but Martinus and Tante Anna de Jong who knew Zwart Piete to be a wise and far-seeing young man. Jakalaas also with whom he talked much believed in him, and was afraid, for Jakalaas had friends among the Kaffirs and had heard things that were not meant for his ears, and since hearing them had simulated a growing deafness, for he wished to hear more, and heard it.

'Baas,' he said to Zwart Piete, 'what you say is true.

Men come from all round and the naked Kaffirs are coming in, very many of them, for they have sent out to collect their wandering bands. They will be the blade of the attack, while the others, those who live near-by, will be the shaft. I have spoken to my master, baas, I have spoken to others, but they will not listen to me because my skin is black, while to you they will not listen because your beard is not yet grey. Is there then no wisdom in a white man till his sap is dry, or in an old one if he be a Kaffir?'

Pausing to spit, Jakalaas went on. 'Not that I care for anyone except mie meisie and old Tante Anna de Jong who has cured me twice when I was sick. She also gave me medicine for our lion when it had worms, which was kind of her and shows the greatness of her heart, for she does not care for lions, she does not understand them, baas, and is afraid.'

Again he paused, and looking up from where he sat beside his small fire, said: 'Will the baas not sit for a moment, there is something that I would ask him.'

Zwart Piete sat down, squatting like a native on his heels. 'Ask,' he said.

'The baas will not be angry whatever I say?'

'I shall not be angry,' Zwart Piete said.

'Then listen, baas; I am old and black, but all my life I have lived among the white folk, first as the servant of the mother of mie meisie, and now as her servant and that of her children. So it will be till I die. Does the baas believe this?' he asked.

'Ja, Jakalaas, I believe it, your meisie has told me of your services, and she loves you.'

'She told you that she loved me,' the old man said, putting his hand up to his eyes. 'That she loved a Kaffir man who was once a slave. Ja, baas, now almost can I believe in the white man's God, for since she was so high,' he made a movement with his hand, 'have I loved and served her, but never was it in my heart that she knew that I was more

than a dog at her feet. Ai, baas, then you must listen well
to what I tell you. I am an old Kaffir, but I have ears to
hear and eyes to see, and I know that you love mie meisie.
I know also that she loves you. Is it not true that you want
her, baas? And not as that other one whom you fought on
the first day wants her, but as a man should want a woman,
so that she is a comfort to him when he is cold, and a spear
in his hand when he is angry, so that she is a part of himself
and indistinguishable from himself when he thinks.'

For a moment Zwart Piete stared into the fire and was
silent. Then he said, 'It is true, Jakalaas. What you have
said is so. She is the heart of my life.'

'Then make haste and take her, baas, for things are about
to happen, and it is in my heart that she will come when you
call. Are you not a man and is she not a woman? Therefore
raise your voice to her, for she wonders that you have said
nothing, and her heart is sore. Ja, baas, like an old dog who
watches his mistress I know what goes on. She is not beautiful for she is too thin, and has a sharp-nosed face, like a
meerkat, but she is good and brave, also she is strong. She
will go as far as the baas, she will not grow tired nor will she
fear anything that may come about, and she hates that man.'

'Her husband?' Piete asked.

'Who else, baas? Who else is there for her to hate, and
who but you for her to love. Is she not a woman, young,
desirable and desiring? Is she to be mated forever to a man
old enough to be her father, one who has maggots in his
brain and cannot see that which is coming, one who lies
with coloured wenches in the fields? Is she to stay forever
with such a man? To stay till she is slain by the Kaffirs?
Ai, much have I seen but this I will not see, I will not wait
till meisie's geel haar is lying in a pool of her own blood
with the assegais of the Kaffirs through the whiteness of her
skin. Nie, nie, baas. If the baas will not do it, then I will
take her away myself. We will go into the mountains and
live there by hunting till the Kaffirs have made an end, and

then we will make our **way to** Baas Pieters, who is a man.'

'And what of her father?' Zwart Piete asked.

'He also is a fool and fearful of dissension. Neither I nor Mevrou de Jong can move him, and it is in my heart that since the mother of mie meisie died he does not care; it is like that with some men, they mate but once. So go inside now, baas, and take her while I keep watch. Do not talk, for with words much time is wasted, and she is ready. I who am old know her to be ripe, and the time is short if you would save her, for it will come soon. They wait only for more men to come and the rains to swell the rivers.'

2

When Zwart Piete went in Sannie was cooking, cutting up mutton into small bits which she fried first and then roasted.

The lion, lying like a great dog at her side with his head between his paws, looked up as Zwart Piete came in but did not move. There was an understanding between the man and the beast; they did not fear each other.

Sannie, her hands covered with the flour into which she was dipping the meat, looked round as Piete, acting on the old Kaffir's advice, put his arm over her shoulder and slowly raising her chin kissed her. For a moment he felt her stiffen with resistance, saw the lion get up and stand staring, his eyes flaring green in the light of the lantern. With his left hand he felt for his knife, loosening it in its sheath, but beyond this he made no move, neither increasing the strength of his grasp on the girl nor relaxing it, but holding her tensely with one hand on her chin, its palm against the softness of her throat, and the other on the hilt of his long knife, the herneuker his father had given to him. Neither lion nor man should keep him from this woman if she wanted him, but the decision was hers. Slowly he felt her relax, move inwards towards him, pressing her body against his own, and turning her face upwards offer her mouth to his. Her arms were about him and her fingers on his neck. As he kissed her he heard the lion lie down.

'You have been slow, Piete,' Sannie said, 'and I thought you were one who could go fast. I was even afraid that you would go too fast.'

'I will go fast now, delight of my heart,' he said, 'now nothing shall stay me, and you will come when I call?' he asked.

'Ja, I will come,' she said. 'From the first moment I saw you I knew that this would happen, and since then I have feared it. Feared that it would come and feared that it would not, but I fear no longer. Ja, Piete, at first I saw it as a cloud, and then came the storm, and then the flood sweeping everything away; the one following the other as though it were meant to be so, as if it had been arranged. Why,' she asked, 'should I have watched you high up on the krantz, staring down like a man of stone? Why should I have gone to meet you? Why should von Rhule have been here to make you fight for me because you were angry at his looks? Why did you leave your place and come seeking far and wide? Tell me all this if you can, heart of my heart. To me it seems like something planned by God. By a Providence that knew of my necessity.'

'Something that others will say was arranged by the devil,' Piete said, 'for you are not free, you belong ——'

'Ja, I belong to a man I hate, and from whom I have stood enough. And as to the devil, are we so clear as to what belongs to him and what to God? I have sometimes thought that much which is called God sent is the work of the evil one, and much which is called evil, good. Long ago I turned from God when I saw how Hendrik served him.'

'Then if you are sure, Sannie, I must go. I will ride at once, for in this I must see the others, my sister and de Kok, also I must have more horses, — one for you and spare horses and others to carry the packs. But what of your children? Have you thought of them?'

'Ja, I have thought of them. There is no place for them in this. My daughter Jacoba was forced upon me, and Frikkie will be safe. Tante Anna will see to him for she fears nothing.'

'Then you are sure, Sannie?'

'I am sure, Piete. I have thought much. What you say I will do, where you go I will follow.'

Again they kissed and Piete went out to find his horse.

Jakalaas sprang out of a shadow as he came. 'The baas is going?' he asked. 'I was wrong. I do not believe I was wrong,' he said.

'You were right, old one; I go to fetch my sister and my servant, also the led horses and my equipment.'

'So you are taking her, baas, and I shall be alone.'

'Ja, I am taking her, Jakalaas, and you will be alone. This is good-bye till I return,' Zwart Piete said, 'and meanwhile watch over her; she is my life.'

The old Kaffir clapped his hands together and knelt on the ground before the young man.

'While I live she is safe, baas, and while her lion lives she is safe, and there will be many dead before harm comes to her. Ride now, for your folk who will stand by you, and I will sharpen my spears, for there may be death in this business. You are matched against a strong hard man, baas, one who has already killed to obtain that which you are taking from him.'

'Killed?' Piete said. 'Who has he killed?'

'He killed his own son, the baas' friend. All is well known among the Kaffirs, but who are we to talk? No one saw it yet still we know, and Mevrou de Jong also knows and waits to strike. In her I think the baas has a strong friend, for she is a fine woman with a powerful mouti for the worms. The baas must remember this, and if he ever gets them, as may well happen, he must go to her.'

'When I have worms, I will remember,' Zwart Piete said as he sprang into the saddle.

By the morning he was back, he had covered seventy miles in seven hours and his horse was still strong, neighing and throwing his head when he came near Paul Pieters' mares.

Sara came out to meet him.

'So you are back,' she said as he threw his leg over his horse's neck and undid the girth. With the saddle on his arm he loosened the throat lash and pulled the bridle over the horse's head.

'Ja, I am back, and tomorrow we ride. Tell de Kok to prepare, also I want the spare horses and powder and lead and food and water.'

'So we ride tomorrow,' Sara said.

It had come at last, the blow she had dreaded for so long, and it was not as bad as she had thought it would be, for she was steeled to meet it. Perhaps it was true that nothing was as bad or as good as it appeared to be. Perhaps she would not find it so bad. Perhaps Piete would not find it so good.

Laughing, she said, 'And I know why we go. We are going to find the woman who put dough in your hair. You must have left hurriedly, Piete; and if she is thinking of you her baking will not be good. Ach, ja, when a man makes love at a baking, the bread is heavy because the woman's heart is light.' Putting her hand on his arm she said, 'Tell me who it is, Piete? Is it a girl that I know?'

'Ja, you know her, Sara.'

'Then who is it? And why do you look at me like that?'

'It is Sannie van Reenen.'

'But she is a wife. She is married to Hendrik van der Berg.'

'It is Sannie van Reenen. I prefer to think of her like that and she is my woman. I am going to take her. Are you with me, Sara, or do I ride alone?'

'I ride with you, Piete, and now I see why you want powder and food, there will be fighting.'

'There will be fighting. Both Hendrik van der Berg and

I are; men but if I am killed you and de Kok must take her on, that place is evil and she must not go back. If I am killed, ride on with her and let de Kok finish her husband, he will not fail, and then get to our friends among the Masai where Rinkals awaits us, and then go back to fort of Don Jesus, for after this, whatever comes of it, we have no place among our people, and even my uncle, the brother of my mother, will disown me.'

'You are mad, Piete.'

'Ja, I am mad, but it is my madness, and both you and de Kok will come only if you wish it, knowing all that there is to be known, weighing it in your mind and deciding whether this be the parting of the ways or whether we go on together.'

'It will be the parting of our ways, Piete, for she will come between us, but I will ride with you though it is not right to steal the wife of a man.'

'We have stolen many wives and sold them, Sara.'

'But they were black.'

'I sometimes wonder if there is as much difference as we think between black and white,' Piete said.

'Since when have you spoken like a missionary?' Sara asked. 'And do you think that God is colour blind, that he cannot see the difference between black and white? Truly I think we must all be mad, that such things can happen.

'And when do we leave?' she asked.

'At dawn, Sara, get the things ready with de Kok, and tell him to give grain to my horse for I am tired, I have come far, and it is a long time since I slept.'

'Ja, you have come far, Piete; you have come a very great way along a bad steep road.'

3

The significance of Zwart Piete's actions had not been lost on Anna de Jong, neither his coming, nor his staying, nor his going.

Zwart Piete had left quickly, leaving Sannie to explain his absence to her husband because he was coming back. He was not the man to take a facile refusal; had she refused him he would have stayed to press suit, and even if in the end he had left he would have done so reluctantly, looking back.

Nie, nie, it was not like that. Zwart Piete had ridden away through the night without halting because he had some plan in his head, of this she was certain.

Slowly, as she knitted, the old woman turned things over in her mind, thinking of the man who had gone and of his conversations with her. He was no fool, also he was just the man for her niece. Just the kind of man she admired herself, a man at once both bold and gentle, one who saw things clearly and faced them. He was all that a woman could desire, and more than most obtained. Fierce and intractable, he would suit Sannie, fitting like a gauntlet over the hand of her life. And was it accident that he had come riding in on a dappled grey stallion whose equal, she who knew much of horses, had never seen, and that even in this her own romance should have been duplicated? She pondered on what he had said about the natives, wondering if he was right about the danger in which they stood. Perhaps he was right, there was, after all, no reason why he should not be right. For all his youth Zwart Piete was experienced with Kaffirs, having fought them for more years than many older men, and he had spent the last three years almost exclusively among them. Curiously enough, though she had foreseen trouble, the danger had seemed most likely to come from the slow wearing down of disease and from the outside pressure of the wilds which, forcing them always into a smaller circle, restricting them and ringing them about, was reducing their numbers and their vitality by its passive weight; but when one came to think of it these natives were only another manifestation of this malignant force.

Tante Anna straightened herself in her chair and sat motionless thinking a little further, taking a wide view, and then narrowing it down from the future to the immediate present, to Sannie. Ja, she would go and see Sannie at once. She was curious to know what had happened, and even a look would suffice. If he had gone for good Sannie would be listless. If he was coming back she would be absent-minded, and perhaps irritable, giving half-hidden glances towards the road by which he would return. She would be restless and unable to settle down. Ach, ja, there was no mistaking the manner of a girl who awaited a lover. With older women it was different; they could act, they could dissimulate and play a part.

Thinking of how strangely things turned out Anna de Jong drove slowly, restraining the horses which pulled at their bits. She did not want to arrive with a clatter, she wanted to steal up and catch the girl unawares.

Now, she thought, is the moment to tell Sannie about Louisa, to set her aflame with anger and to remove her last scruple by the bitterness of the insult that her husband had put upon her. The art of life was to hold one's best cards till the moment came to play them, and then to follow one high card with another that was still higher. She laughed, ach, ja, even if one was old one could still watch life and still play a hand which lost nothing for being played silently. Ja, soon Hendrik van der Berg would have to meet his reckoning. This was the beginning.

At a walk she turned her horses towards the house. Soon things would happen here, and what happened would be largely due to her, due to her love of one individual and her hatred of another, due to her subtlety, to the quickness of her perceptions and her faculty for manoeuvring events, coordinating the hundred hidden threads of motive and weaving them into the pattern of her choosing.

Pulling up in front of the house she waited, sitting still with the reins slack in her hands and a picannin at her horses' heads till Sannie should come out. She wanted to see her face unguarded, unprepared, before she schooled it into the conventional smile of welcome.

When Sannie came Anna de Jong knew that Zwart Piete was going to return. The girl was in love, and after all how could it have been otherwise? Here was romance, here was the lone hunter, not as large as life, but larger, as big as one of his own elephants, riding in on a blue arab, like a prince in a child's tale, with such success in his bearing that he made the others round him look like beaten dogs; that made him shine brilliantly vital among men, who when he stood beside them, paled like ghosts, fading into insignificance.

Sitting with her hands folded and her fingers interlaced, Anna de Jong smiled. 'So he is coming back,' she said.

'Who is coming?' Sannie asked, glancing at the mountain road.

'Zwart Piete, the hunter. Call your Kaffirs to get me down, mie Sannie, for I would come in; I have much to tell you.'

CHAPTER XX

I

ZWART PIETE slept through the day and on into the night, and was woken by a loud thunderclap and the roar of falling rain. Instinctively he sprang up.

The rains had come, and Jakalaas had said the Kaffirs were only waiting for the rains. There was to be no further rest for him tonight, nor for his horse that he had put into a near-by kraal; the others were out running loose and could not be caught, so the grey must carry him again.

Sara who had heard him get up, asked what he was doing.

'I am going back,' he said, 'the rains have come and there is danger, also if I wait and the river is much flooded I shall be held up.'

'And what shall we do,' Sara asked, 'since our horses are not in?'

'You will follow, Sara,' Piete said, 'and if you cannot cross wait on this side, camping there till it runs down.'

'Can your horse do it?' Sara asked. 'He is small and has come far.'

'He has had all day to rest, mie Sara. Ja, he can do it, and so can I; we have done more than this, much more, and for less.'

Leaning on her elbow Sara watched her brother's preparations. Never before had she seen him so grim, so serious.

He had been right when he said this woman was everything to him. Here was a storm so severe that to make herself heard she had to shout, and he was going to ride seventy miles through it on a tired horse, and she knew that even if the river were in flood it would not stop him. By mid-day next day he would be back with Sannie van der Berg or he would be floating down to the sea in the swollen stream with the trees and the dead beasts on the flood for company, and when she and de Kok got there they would not know whether he was alive or dead, for the river would be too wide for them to be able to see the marks his horse would have made scrambling out on the other side, and besides there was no knowing where he would land, for in swimming a flooded river one went with the stream, forging slowly across it, hoping to meet no floating trees.

'If the river is in flood you will come back?' she pleaded.

'If the river is in flood I shall cross it.'

'Ja, you will cross it,' Sara said, 'because that woman has sent you mad.'

'Perhaps she has sent me mad, but do not fear, you well know how Blaukerl swims, and I also am like an otter in the water.'

'All this I know, but you are both tired, and the river will be swollen,' Sara protested.

'Yet we will go and we will come out on the far side, for I am a lucky man. Think how often I have done such things and you have never tried to stay me.'

'Why should I have stayed you, Piete,' she asked, 'when I was with you? What you did then I did also. But this time you ride alone, even de Kok you leave with me.'

'I shall not be long alone,' Zwart Piete said, 'and now good-bye.'

For the first time since they had been children he kissed her, and for the first time since her childhood Sara cried. He was going out alone to find his woman, and he had kissed her. She was no longer his comrade. It was, as she had known it would be, ended.

2

Zwart Piete did not hurry. The ground was slippery, the night dark, and he counted on the almost continuous lightning and on the intelligence of his horse to hold the road which was little more than a track; nor was he mad enough to face the flooded river in the darkness without resting his horse. If he came to the bank as the sun rose it would be time enough. Then he would off-saddle, feed his horse, and an hour later they would put their endurance to the test.

So with a light hand on his bridle, his knees gripping the horse's flanks when he stumbled and leaving his head free he rode on, talking to him and encouraging him. In the flashes he could see the horse's ears twitching as he cocked them forward to stare into the distance or back as he listened to his voice. A thousand times Zwart Piete thanked God for Blaukerl, for though a Boer horse might have done as much, he would not have done it as willingly. The Arab, he knew, would fight while his legs held him, while his lungs breathed and his bold heart beat. Here, no matter what occurred, there was energy and a courage which was incalculable.

He struck the bank of the river as the sun rose, at the exact point where he had crossed it on the previous night. Here he halted and dismounting allowed his horse to go.

The stallion rolled, nibbled a few blades of grass, and came for the grain that he could smell in the bag tied to the saddle.

While the horse ate, Zwart Piete stared at the rushing stream, making up his mind where he would enter it and what point he would make for on the other side. It was now a hundred yards wide and running over the tops of the scrub that lined its banks. This was the danger, for among the tree-tops neither he nor his horse could swim, and caught up in the thorny branches, would be drowned. But a mile downstream he remembered seeing an open piece of ground that was bare and treeless.

His only plan was therefore to get into the middle of the water course and allow himself to be carried down it till he came to this spot and then, using every effort, try to make a landing.

Accepting the danger, and without further consideration of the difficulties that lay in front of him, he began to make his preparations. These consisted in taking the powder from his horn, wrapping it in a piece of oiled hide and putting it on his head, underneath his hat. Next he fired his gun to empty it, and having done this lashed it to his saddle. He then undressed so that he stood naked save for his knife and belt, his clothes and shoes he made into a bundle which he also tied to the saddle, and then calling his horse he stood a moment fondling him, pulling his ears and talking to him. He had spoken to Sara of the things Blaukerl had done, but never had he done a thing like this. This was more than a flood, it was a raging torrent. He did not put a bit into his horse's mouth, he could guide him without, and he would swim better unhampered.

With a final pat he sprang into the saddle and rode to the water's edge. The horse faltered here, and putting down his head to sniff at the rushing, dark-brown stream, snorted and ran back.

Zwart Piete soothed him and put him at it again. Again he ran back and again Zwart Piete forced him on, talking to him and pressing him between his knees. This time the horse went forward, his muzzle bent to the water; went on over his fetlocks, over his knees, stumbled as he plunged into a hidden hole, and when he rose they were in deep water and the horse was swimming. Turning his head downstream Zwart Piete slipped from his back and dropped past him, holding onto a stirrup leather till he was able to grasp his tail.

The grey was a magnificent swimmer, very strong, one of those horses which by the strength of their strokes swim high in the water; not only his head but also his neck and part of his chest came out of it as he swam, and this was a great advantage as he could see where he was going and was able to avoid the rubbish which was sweeping down all round them.

At first things were easy for they were going with the stream, but would the horse be strong enough to gain the bank when they began to go obliquely, swimming still with the current but also across it. If he had been fresh Piete would have had absolute confidence in his horse, but in thirty hours they had done a hundred miles. At last they came to the reach that Zwart Piete was making for, and pulling himself forward, keeping well clear of the stallion's forelegs, he swung his head towards the shore. The difference was at once apparent; he could feel Blaukerl being swept sideways but still he gained, fighting his way on doggedly.

A big tree festooned with snakes swept past them, twisting and turning, it just missed the horse's head. Piete was calling to him, trying to make himself heard above the sound of the rushing waters. The horse must put out his final effort now, there were only a few yards to go. His head was lower in the water, and though he was swimming with all his strength Zwart Piete could feel it waning. Just as he was giving up, when he felt that they had played and lost, there was a slackening of the current; they were out of the main stream. It was almost with surprise that he felt the horse's hoofs gripping at the slippery bank, for he had not thought they would do it, felt him fight to get hold and hesitate as he gathered himself, with bent hocks, to climb out.

They were across; with lowered head and heaving flanks the grey, stained red by the muddy water that dripped from him, stood trying to recover himself, getting ready for more if it were demanded of him. Pulling off the saddle to leave the horse free Zwart Piete undid his clothes; he was trembling with cold, and dressed. Having done this he dried his gun, and loading it fired a trial shot, then reloading he made a fire by lighting some powder with his flint and steel, and lay down to rest.

They were across and alive. In two hours his horse would have recovered and they would go on.

3

Hendrik van der Berg was smoking on the stoep of his house when Zwart Piete returned.

'So you are back, Piete,' he said. He looked at his horse. 'And you ride the same horse; that is a hundred and forty miles he has done and he is not foundered. Magtig, that is a horse, jong,' he said, 'and you come at a good moment. I have a mare who will take him, a red mare with a wall eye and two white stockings. Can he take her, do you think?' he asked anxiously. 'Or is he too tired? I have kept her safe, because Sannie said you might return.'

'Let him rest now, Oom Hendrik, and take her tomorrow. If she only came on yesterday she will go three days. We are tired Blaukerl and I. Before God we are tired.'

'Then, why this haste?' Hendrik asked. 'Is not tomorrow also a day? And you have swum the river. To do that was to take a grave risk.'

'Ja, we have swum it,' Piete said. 'It was too full to cross by the drift, and there was no other way. Listen, Hendrik; you say why did I hurry and I will tell you: I came back because there is danger with the coming of the rains. Get your folk together and go into laager. I came to warn you again, and my people will follow me when the water is run down. My sister Sara and my servant de Kok, we three are as six in war, for it is our business. Get them into laager, I say, and then let us attack the Kaffirs and wipe them out before they are ready to fall upon you.'

'What, Piete, do you still believe in this nonsense? Do you think that the Lord has led us thus far to have us destroyed? Are you without faith?'

'I have faith in three things, Hendrik, myself, my gun and my horse.'

'That is not faith,' Hendrik said sternly, 'that is the blasphemous vanity of the young.'

'Then you will not do it?'

'No; and if I would, do you think my people would go when there is no danger?'

'There is danger,' Zwart Piete said. 'Must you see blood before you can recognise it? Where is von Rhule?' he went on, 'I do not like him, but perhaps being a soldier he will understand, and being one with you he may be able to persuade, where they would only laugh at me because I am young. There is danger here, Hendrik,' he repeated vehemently. 'I can smell it in the air.'

'The air smells good to me,' Hendrik said. 'It is rich and moist with the promise of fertility; tomorrow I shall begin to plough. I have just come from my lands and the rain has gone in deep. It will be a good season,' he said. 'A fruitful season; already my cows have begun to calve.'

'I am going on now,' Piete said, 'to see if I can make the others believe.'

'You waste your time, jong,' Hendrik said, 'but if you must go, take one of my horses; yours is tired and there is that mare.'

'My horse can go on. Both I and my horse can go on. Listen, Hendrik, soon my people and my other horses will be here, and if you wish to fight we will fight with you; if not, if you will not believe what I tell you, we will trek on.'

'Where will you go?'

'To the north that I have not yet seen, and then back to my friends at the coast. There are chiefs in the north with much ivory. I would arrange with them to trade, and then come back with porters and donkeys to fetch it.'

'Are you not afraid of them?' Hendrik asked.

'I am not afraid,' Piete said. 'I am well known, and if evil befall me they will pay a great price, for though I have enemies I have also many friends both black and white. I know the Kaffirs, Hendrik. I am not like you who think, like a kameel, that by standing still you are safely concealed. I tell you that here the Kaffirs have you in the pocket of their aprons. Why did you not stay in the open veld, which is suited to our way of fighting? Before God, Oom Hendrik, the beauty of this country and its softness has seduced you. Give me coffee, let my horse roll, and I will go on. Once more every man here will be warned; after that it is for them to decide. As soon as the Kaffirs have planted their meilies they will come, of this I am certain.'

Leaving Hendrik, Zwart Piete rode on to Martinus' place, from him he went to Tante Anna's, and from her to Jan Bothas and to the people beyond him. At each place he told them what he had heard and what he thought would happen, and except for Tante Anna, who believed that since so much had happened anything might follow, and Martinus who half believed, all laughed at him for his pains.

One more farm he tried, that of Lucas Labuschagne, and failing again turned back; he had tried to do his duty to these people, but his efforts were wasted. There remained his duty to Sannie and to himself. As soon as his sister and de Kok came he must get her out. Till then, he must stay at her side waiting for the blow to fall; if it fell before they came, they would be together. That was the important thing, to get back to her side. Hendrik, her husband, did not exist for Piete; he was a shadow, something that his mind refused to grasp.

With a last look over the spreading valley at the foot of the mountain that shadowed it and the bush that menaced it, he turned his horse and rode back.

Sannie would be waiting for him, listening for the sound of his horse's hoofs as she went about her work.

4

What Tante Anna had told Sannie about Hendrik and Louisa in no way disturbed her. It did not even surprise her, for she was beyond surprise and beyond disturbance. Her life was full; she had found her man. Herman had been something more than an incident due to time and circumstance, but her love for him had been a girlish idyll, something that was still precious and faintly fragrant, the flowering of a springtime bud; her intrigue with von Rhule had been born of boredom, a desire for power, and above all as a gesture by which she could retain her self-respect, with something more than a hope that she would bear this man a child and foist it onto her husband.

Hendrik she had never loved; her first thoughts of him, when she had weighed him against Herman, had been a feeling of pride that she so young and unimportant could influence a man so old and powerful. Her marriage to him had been because of Herman's child which was quickening within her and the thought that with him she would be safe.

But this feeling she had for Piete was different, it was something new, something that she always felt herself capable of, always hoped for and yet, now that it had come, half feared. It threatened to overwhelm her.

Here she was secure, and what had Piete to offer against security? To go with him meant leaving her children, meant a life spent on the wing as a thing pursued, for she never doubted that Hendrik would follow. There was no place for children in this new life, and there was danger, blood was likely to be spilt, and yet from the moment of seeing him, this going, this following of him had been inevitable. The swift flare of the one to the other, their reaching out, had been essential and was stronger than all else, stronger than anything she had thought possible, so that even leaving her children seemed a small thing when she was in his arms and a great one only when he left her. Where she had been a girl, she was now a woman; where she had blossomed as a bud, she now bloomed as a flower. Where she had seen life opening in front of her, it was now open, and she was caught in it, part of it, no longer passive but active and eager to go on.

No longer waiting in a dream while the stream swept past her, but riding it, borne on the crest of the flood.

Even her feeling of hate for Hendrik had passed; she felt more kindly towards him than she had ever done, for he was going to lose her. And lately her dislike of him had got less, even before the advent of Zwart Piete, for she had learnt to lie passive while he did what he would with her, to lie thinking of other things, of anything, so that till he left her she was outside her body. And since she had done this he had come to her less readily and less often, for his was an urgency that rose in resistance and sank before her deathlike acquiescence. Provided he did not come to her now, while she yearned for Piete, she felt her last thoughts of him would be kind; for he had only acted according to his nature as now she was acting according to her own, and to protect herself from this she determined to simulate illness, uncleanness, a week before its time, for now she would die rather than be touched; and soon she would be gone.

At the thought of Zwart Piete her heart sang. He had gone and he had come back, risking his life in a flooded river to come to her side. When she thought of him she felt sick, when she saw him her stomach twisted inside her. Even the spoor of his horse on the bare tramped ground in front of her house moved her, and if someone mentioned his name she looked down lest her eyes betray her. This was the thing she had dreamed of. This was the summer of love.

5

It was four days before Sara and de Kok rode in with the pack horses, and the spare horses running loose, following an old tame mare that wore a bell round her neck. All being entire they would not leave her, and she by temperament was sluggish, an old matron rendered complacent by much foal-bearing.

They had had to wait for the river, and even when it was

down had been at some trouble to cross it, for the drift was damaged and the bottom gone.

In those four days Zwart Piete's love-making had progressed, but neither he nor Sannie were anxious to allow their love for each other to rise beyond a certain point, and always, as if by mutual consent, they drew back from each other. These were not the snatched moments of an illicit and clandestine love, they would have time, they would have their whole lives in which the flower they saw opening would fruit, and in the meantime they must not betray themselves nor must they waste their energies, all must be saved for the effort they would shortly have to put forth, from which once it was begun there could be no drawing back.

Buying meilies from Hendrik, Zwart Piete filled his horses with grain, increasing the ration slowly till at last they were getting a full twelve pounds a day. Even the old mare was given grain, a thing she had not known for years, and she carried her head higher and swished at the flies that settled on her quarters with the energy of a young horse.

Three days after Sara and de Kok's arrival Piete decided that they were ready; his plans were made, and he bade Hendrik and Sannie good-bye.

'We have stayed overlong,' he said, 'but I wanted to get my horses hard and fat.'

'You have not stayed too long, Piete, and I have profited by your visit, if the mares have taken,' for another had been served.

'They will have taken,' Piete said. 'Blaukerl is certain, and if the mares are ready he never misses.'

'Then next year I shall have some nice foals. Does he get them blue like himself?'

'Ja, Hendrik, all his foals are blue. At first when they are born they are black, but later they change, getting paler and paler.'

'Then, you are really off?'

'Ja, I am off, and thank you for having allowed me to stay. Tot seins, Oom Hendrik.'

'Tot seins, Zwart Piete, and I wonder when I shall see you again?'

'Perhaps sooner than you think,' Piete said, 'for my movements are not certain.' Raising his gun he fired it in farewell; two more shots, those of Sara and de Kok, followed his, and sweeping off his wide felt hat to Sannie as he passed her, he broke into a canter.

They rode fast till it was nearly dark, and then made camp. They had come in a wide circle and were now only a few miles from Hendrik's house, the place they had left in the morning.

When they had eaten, de Kok left them. 'I am going, baas,' he said, 'but I shall be back before the dawn is grey.' On foot and carrying his gun he moved off into the trees.

Zwart Piete laughed. 'Is it a woman, do you think, Sara?' he asked, 'that he wants to have once more before we go?'

'How your mind runs on women,' Sara said.

'On a woman,' he said; 'for me there is but one, and de Kok is a man like another. I think he had a fancy for one of the coloured girls at Martinus'. Ja,' he went on, 'de Kok may be a Bastard but he is a fine man and more our friend than our servant.'

Without speaking again they rolled themselves in their blankets, and with their heads on their saddles lay staring up at the stars. The moon was high and the trees were sharp, against the luminous night blue of the sky the leaves, clean cut and solid, looked as if they were carved out of black stone.

Neither slept, both lay waiting restlessly for the dawn; the man in active longing, the woman in an agony of memory. Throwing her mind back, Sara thought of the days and nights she had spent with her brother, hunting and sleeping as they were now, side by side, happy, and in spite of danger and fatigue, content. All that was over now. Tomorrow Sannie would be with them and Sara would lie apart.

Back, and further back she flung her mind, trying to remember every facet of their association. This, she thought, is the big difference between a man and a woman; men thought forwards, the present being no more than a day which led towards the future. Men lived, somewhere in the beyond, in a dream world of what would happen, foreseeing, fighting, thinking, planning so that what they hoped for would come to pass. Whereas women looked back onto what they had had, saying such a time was good and wished to relive what they had known. This, rather than the hope for something better, something beyond, which sent men ever seeking, ever searching so that did they only find death they were content, for they had striven, and having seen the vision had followed it, abandoning all things, leaving all things for their search, was where women differed. Knowing that what they looked for was nothing, certain that it was, like the water of a mirage, a product of their own minds, men still went on. Ja, she thought, and now I know that I am even more of a woman than I thought, for I would go back and not forward. In front of me I can see nothing, it is an emptiness, a vessel overturned and broken. Because my face is pitted by the smallpox there is nothing there, and I will never be a wife, or a mother, unless I am taken because of my portion, because I am rich from our hunting. Ja, she thought, I am a fine hunter, better than all men save my brother Piete, I can train horses, I can break oxen, and teach dogs to follow a blood spoor and bay up the wounded game. All these things I can do, all these I must do; and yet I should like to bake bread for a man and bear him children, I should like to have a house and a garden where I could grow vegetables, and a dairy where I could make butter.

So she lay, keeping very still, thinking, and listening to her brother moving uneasily. How well she understood him. This woman was in his blood, she was lovely and he ached for her, his strength was a burden upon him, his thirst for her a river dammed up that rose continually and soon would burst its bonds. But had Sannie the qualities for this life?

Which was no life for a woman unless she was as she was, a woman who was not a woman.

It is a lie, she thought, clenching her teeth, it is a lie. I am a woman; before God I am a woman, and never so much as now, when I think thoughts that are not for such as I.

With the dawn came de Kok, very pleased with himself, and when he came Sara and her brother got up. Neither had slept, and they welcomed their servant, for already the shadow of Sannie was between them and talk was difficult.

6

Hendrik was drinking his coffee, dipping his rusks into it to soften them, when one of his Kaffirs came running with the news that all his horses were lame.

'Ja, baas,' the boy said, 'when I went to the kraal there was not one that walked sound, not one,' he repeated.

'What is the matter with them?' Hendrik asked, getting up. 'Do they look sick?'

'No, baas, they do not look sick, but seeing them so I did not wait to see what the matter was, but ran at once for the baas. Perhaps it is a snake,' he hazarded. 'Does the baas think it could be a snake?'

'How could a snake bite them all, fool?' Hendrik asked.

'I have seen a whole span bitten by a snake, baas. All were bitten as they passed. Ja, baas, it was a mamba; he struck at each one and each one died.'

'That may be so, but even with a full span he could only have bitten eight, one to each pair that walked on that side of the road; and eight oxen is not thirty horses. There is no snake with enough poison to bite thirty horses, and had they been bitten they would have been sick. Come, let us go up.'

When they came to the kraal Hendrik saw that the Kaffir had not lied. His horses were all lame, but their eyes were bright and their hair sleek and smooth. Going up to his black he caught him and ran his hand down his leg; below the knee there was heat and the tendons were puffy. He slid his hand onto the fetlock, over the pastern, and there in the horse's heel he felt something.

'Magtig,' he said, and drawing a long thorn from the horse's foot he held it up, 'these horses have been lamed!'

'This is devil's work,' he said, 'and someone will pay dearly for it.' Taking a riem from the boy he threw it over the neck of a chestnut mare with a wall eye and two white stockings; she too was lame, and from her foot he also drew a thorn. Whoever had done this work had done it well; the thorns had been poisoned and it would be a week before he could ride one of his horses again.

Thinking deeply he went back to the house.

'And the horses?' Sannie asked, coming out.

'Jantjie is right,' he said, 'they are lame, and it has been done by someone. They have all had poisoned thorns driven into their feet behind the pastern. By God, when I find that man he will not forget this day.'

'When you find him,' Sannie said; 'but will you find him? Is it so easy to find one Kaffir among a hundred others? One evil man among the thousands who are evil?'

'I will find him, Sannie, never fear, for what I say I will do is already done. My heart is as firm as a stone in these matters, yea, as hard as a piece of nether millstone; and when I am done with him his name shall be a byword, of that you may be certain, and for life he will bear my mark upon him.'

'Of it I am certain,' Sannie said, seeing in this the hand of her lover, and unwilling to argue further.

Let him think what he would of his horses, for soon he would have greater things to think of. Soon he would have to find an answer to his riddle and explain how another came to be ploughing with his heifer.

'And what will you do, Hendrik?' she asked. 'Will you go and borrow a horse?'

'I will not,' he said. 'For some days I shall walk till my

horses are well; and while I wait I shall watch, for surely this is the beginning and not the end. Somewhere there is a man who would do me an injury, and by waiting I shall catch him, for in the years that I have lived I have learnt patience, and that by waiting and watching all comes. In this alone do I see eye to eye with Anna de Jong, a woman to whom the Scriptures are as nothing. It has even come to me sometimes that she does not believe them as they stand, but selects only such small pieces as suit her mood, leaving that which is not in accord with her ideas. A woman should not have ideas; it was not for thoughts that they were fashioned.'

'And for what have they been fashioned, Hendrik?' Sannie asked.

'For the bearing of children,' he said. 'It was for that that you and all other women were fashioned, and all else is a blasphemy and a desecration.'

The swish of Sannie's print frock was the answer to Hendrik's remark.

Had she waited she would have said too much. Had he not other sheep that were not of this fold? Had his attentions not been enough to bear without their being shared by a coloured concubine, a harlot that swung her hips at all who passed? Was there no insult, no degradation too great for this man to put upon her? Had he forgotten that her blood was so much like his own, and had it not occurred to him that she too could be patient till the time came, and that she would one day flee from his tyranny as he and the others had fled from the English?

As she went out she put her anger from her and smiled at the forethought of the man to whom she was going. The man who had given her so casual a good-bye, who from his saddle, with his horse plunging under him as he made it dance, had said, 'Tot sein, mevrou.'

Till I see you, which would be before the sun cast a shadow to the east of the trees, before the herds having grazed and drunk lay down to rest in the heat of the day, waiting, as they chewed the cud, till it was time for them to make their slow way back to their kraals.

In two hours she would be gone. The kettle and the pot could not agree together, nor would the lamb lie another night beside the lion. It was over. She had slept at Hendrik's side long enough.

It was going to be hard to leave Jacoba and Frikkie, but things were hard, and there was no answer to this but one, either she must stay with her children or she must go; there could be no half measures. As she thought of this, the picture of the lioness springing through the fire with a cub in her mouth came to her mind. Lions were rarely born alone, and she too had made her choice, and choosing one out of her litter had abandoned the others to the flames. Still, it was not easy to leave children who were young and loved her; and if it was hard to blame Jacoba for her sire, it was also hard, seeing her, to forget who her father was or how she had been begotten. If like the lioness she could have taken one child with her. If only she could have taken Frikkie.

Torn this way and that Sannie hesitated, even now, with her word given and her lover waiting, she was uncertain of what she would do. Half angry that Zwart Piete had put this upon her and wishing that, as he left, he had swept her up onto his saddle and carried her off.

Certain that she was going, she still toyed with the idea of remaining, because only with this idea in her mind and the horror of what staying meant was she able to bring herself to go.

By the big appies doorns she could see Jakalaas sitting with the lion beside him. As he rubbed its throat she could see its lips drawn back in a snarling purr.

She must wait for Hendrik to go, he was getting ready, filling his pipe, and would soon be off. In a moment he would be gone, in a moment she would be alone, and then she would walk slowly away till she was lost among the trees. Once clear, she would go on swiftly, hurrying to the man who waited for her.

In the next hour something irrevocable would be done, she would have broken every tradition of her race, left a man she hated, loathed and despised for the one whom she loved and, branded a scarlet woman by her action, would follow him till either he or she met their appointed end. Follow him, serve him, and bear him children in love instead of in hatred, to that end had she been made, to that end had she been fashioned. And if, as Hendrik said, increase was a woman's only function, as well it might be, surely, then, to the woman lay the choice of by whom this thing was done?

CHAPTER XXI

1

THE sun was high straight overhead, so that there were no shadows on the ground save directly under the trees when Sannie came. She was composed and cool and walked up to Zwart Piete as if she did not see the others. When they met they were alone in the world.

While Sannie and Piete kissed, de Kok and Sara tightened the girths of the horses and held them ready. They were very fresh and full of corn and had stood saddled for many hours.

Without hurrying they mounted, and with Zwart Piete bringing up the rear turned the heads of their horses north towards the mountains, for tonight it was arranged that they should camp among them.

At first they went slowly, but soon broke from a walk into a slow tripple, from a slow tripple into a fast one, and then into a canter. So they rode, the ones in front looking over their horse's ears, while Piete watching Sannie's back turned round at intervals to see if they were followed.

The horses were now moving freely; they had settled down to their business, that of covering the ground, of setting distance between themselves and the place from which they had come. They were used to long treks, they were used to travelling fast, and though they sweated they remained fresh and ready. Before dark they had covered forty miles and were in the foothills of the mountains where they watered their horses and camped for a while. From now on they would ride more slowly, off saddling every hour, for with a high moon they could travel by night which would be cooler for the horses and better for the women. Tomorrow they would rest all day, hiding up in a kloof, and again push on when it was dark.

What Piete had said to Hendrik about not knowing the north was a lie, for he knew it well. To the last detail his plan was made, and each day's trek was planned; he had been over it all in his mind, seeing the road and building up the landmarks in his head, so that they stood out as if he actually saw them. He was making for the country of the Masai where Rinkals was waiting for them. That he would still be there Zwart Piete never doubted, for with plenty of beer and meat the old man would stay anywhere indefinitely, and by his magic was well able to extort such other hospitalities as he needed. That the chief might not be pleased to see him, for he had returned with the mothers of his wives in his train, had worried Zwart Piete momentarily, but even this Rinkals would get over, if not in one way then in another.

2

Once on the lands Hendrik began to work.

Fascinated by the lure of the fresh wetness of the turned furrows he went on ploughing, ribbing the moist ground; proud of his skill and the perfection of his work, he was lost in a dream of husbandry.

There were men who ploughed clumsily with crooked furrows, leaving banks of land untouched where the weeds of the previous year stood harshly, but Hendrik was not one of these, his work was meticulous and he ploughed himself; it was not in him to allocate such work as this to natives as some did.

The foot of the master was upon his soil, heavily upon it, as Hendrik walked in the furrow behind his span.

His thoughts were with the crops that would soon be growing; concerned with the beauty of increase; and the foolishness of Zwart Piete who saw danger where there was none and who had recklessly risked his life in a swollen stream for what was no more than an idea, the result of his own fevered imagination and the foolish talk of Kaffirs.

As he moved the stick by which he marked his acre of thirty paces, he thought of his horses and ran over in his mind those who had a grudge against him; there were many, for he had no light hand upon his Kaffirs. He employed many and changed them often.

If he could but catch him, that man would think before he lamed a Boer horse again, that was if he lived to think.

Pressing down on the wooden handles of his plough, gripping them as if they were the throat of an enemy, Hendrik worked, rejoicing in the strength that God had given him, in his skill, in his power, and in his capacity for righteous anger.

Once again it was spring, the winter was past, and the flowers would soon appear. The time of the singing birds was come and the voice of the turtle was heard in the land. The rain, the blessed rain that came from God, was moistening the soil, forcing growth upon the still small seeds, forcing them into bearing and obedience.

Was it likely that he or the others were going to be frightened by Zwart Piete's fantasies? A wild young man, who as a dog returned to his vomit and the fool to his folly, so did Zwart Piete go back to his thoughts of Kaffirs and the dangers of an attack by them. He had hunted too much and fought too much to have any ideas of solid safety. When he saw it he could not recognise it nor see that the time of strife was over, and that they of Canaan had beaten their swords into plough-shares and their spears into pruning hooks.

This was what mattered. He looked over the land: the land, the flocks and herds, the women who were the mothers of the children, and the houses and the barns that they had built. These were the real solid things that had height, width and depth, that were the result of prolonged effort, things which would go on. These lands his children would plough, these trees they would sit under, these waters they would drink; and a man's duty was simple, it was to create at once a heritage and progeny to use it. To breed sons who would take up the plough where it had been put down, and drive the furrow on into time that stretched infinitely forward joining the future to the infinite past, making it one from the six days of the creation to the last day when the final trumpet would sound. Strung through the ages were the beads of his race, the number of individuals who had gone to form him and the number of his descendants, those whom he had formed and those that he would still form, and those that they would form. Truly he was a man fearfully and wonderfully made, and one peculiarly adapted to this particular business. As he thought, half praying, half exultant, his mind divided between the past and the future, the ground broke in front of him, dividing and opening, coming apart as unable to resist; it took the point of his shear and fell back from the thigh of his moldboard, crumbling and turning in long greasy folds that smelt wetly, rich with promise. Always it was thus that he worked in the beginning of the season, lost in an ecstasy of righteous and God-given power, turning and working the land till he could work no more, till the light was gone and his oxen stood with their mouths gaping, with foam on their muzzles, and their eyes glazed as they leant against the yokes that were set upon their shoulders. With wet soil the going was heavy and with the coming of the spring their master gave them no respite, urging them on with voice and whip, forcing them forward with an urgency that to the oxen was meaningless, for to them the change of season was unavailing in its call, Hendrik himself having blunted the spear of their sap, leaving them only strength, the power to endure, and that never-ending patience which made them work uncomplainingly while they waited for the death which came to all, to bull and ox alike.

As the sun fell Hendrik turned his span inwards, and halting, made them back in their yokes by throwing clods of earth at their long faces till the chains from their yokes slacked and he was able to unhook his plough. Leaving it lying on its side against the next day's work, he called to his beasts which turned towards their kraal. As he walked behind them Hendrik undid his whip thong from the long stick, and rolling it put it into his pocket. It was a whip of his own making, one of the many that he had made.

His shirt was sticking to his flanks, his hair was matted and the dust streaked his face where he had touched it with his hands as he wiped the sweat from his eyes.

Soon, when he had outspanned his oxen and they had been watered, he would go home, and sinking into his chair call for one of the maids to bring water and a basin to wash his feet and scrape the earth from between his toes.

Plodding heavily in pairs the oxen walked with the chains between them sagging from yoke to yoke, the hook of the last one cutting a little furrow like the spoor of a snake in the rough track that led up from the lands to the homestead. Tonight they walked back, tomorrow they would walk down again. To work was their life, the purpose for which they had been bred: to work, and finally to be eaten.

But when Hendrik returned to his house he found the children alone and crying. Sannie was gone and Jakalaas and the lion were also absent. There alone remained a Bushman maid from whom he could get no sense, even after he had struck her.

Here was something very strange, not that Sannie had gone walking as was her custom, but that she had not returned to feed and wash her children; here was some mischance. He must go and find her, but to do this he must have a horse. Quieting the children as best he could and putting them to bed, he set off to Martinus' house. Martinus would lend him his horse. As he went out the moon rose from behind the crest of the mountains, first setting its fanged edge alive with a running flame of orange light, then climbing into sight, growing in size and paling as it rose.

Martinus was asleep when he got there but came out pulling on his buckskin trousers.

'Ja,' he said, 'ja, Hendrik, what is it that you come now? But wait, come inside for it must be something great that has happened or you would not be abroad at this hour. Have you been ploughing?' he asked. 'Magtig,' he went on, 'the ploughing was good today, the rain has gone in deep and the soil turned richly like a fat cheese. Now, Oom Hendrik, what is it?' he said as they went in and he lit a candle.

'It is that my horses have been lamed.'

'Lamed! Magtig, who has done that?'

'Who has done it can wait, later I will deal with that matter, but in the meantime I am dismounted.'

'For a Boer to be horseless is as if he had no legs,' Martinus said. 'Ja, this is serious, but what do you want of me?'

'I want the loan of your roan horse, Martinus.'

'My horse, Hendrik, my horse! All else you can have, but my horse, my gun and my wife I never lend. I will come with you willingly, ja, I will come, but Kaffreland I will not lend; no one has ever ridden him but me.'

'Then lend me another. Have you others that are used to a gun?'

'You know very well that I have not; either they are too old, or too young and as yet untrained. With Marietje ill and our baby dead I have not been in the mood to train horses. It is not good to work with beasts when one's heart is bitter, for one vents its anger upon them which is not just.

'But why do you need a horse now? Do you know who it was that lamed your beasts? Shall I come tomorrow and help you catch him?'

'I do not know, and as I told you he can wait.'

'Then what is it? What is it, Hendrik!'

'It is Sannie, my wife, she is missing. Something has happened to her for she has never been as late as this before.'

'Do you mean that she is not back?'

'Ach, ja, that is what I mean. Why are you so foolish to-night, that you cannot understand? Does a man come by the light of the moon to borrow a saddle horse for nothing? Do you think that after a day's work I walk for amusement, like a young man who is in love? My wife, the mother of my children, is missing, and they cry for her, Martinus. Lend me Kaffreland so that as soon as it is light I may follow on her spoor.'

'Ja, now I understand, Hendrik, and if I was slow at first it was that you roused me from my sleep, but my horse you cannot have. Listen,' he went on, 'I will come with you, I will come at once.' He pulled on his jacket and went to the bedroom for his gun. 'I will lend you a young horse, and then we will go and see where we can find a trained one from whose back you can shoot. Let us ride to Anna de Jong's, she has many horses; the one that Jappie had is too old, but she has another that I think will be good for our purpose. Come,' he said, 'let us go at once,' and turning he led the way up the mountainside to the kraal where his horses were kept.

'Have you got another saddle?' Hendrik asked.

'Ja, I have two saddles,' Martinus said.

3

They were met by the old woman who, with her blunder-buss in her hand, and wearing one of her husband's coats over her nightshirt, faced them angrily.

'Halt or I fire,' she cried. 'Who are you who ride to a widow's house by night with guns, and what is it you want?'

'A horse,' Hendrik cried. 'Lend me a horse, Tante Anna.'

'So it is you,' she said. 'And where are your own horses, and what is that that you ride?'

'It is Sannie who is gone,' he said. 'She is lost, and I need a hunting horse to follow her.'

'Lost!' Tante Anna said. 'I do not think she is lost, but you will need wings to follow her, Hendrik.'

'Do you mean she is dead?'

'No, Hendrik van der Berg, I think she is alive. I think you have digged a pit and fallen headlong into it. Ja, you can have any of my horses, all but my driving horses, for those I need tomorrow when I go to a lying-in. Now I would sleep for I must rise early, so take what you want and go, but remember, Hendrik, what it says in the word.'

'Thank you, Anna, for the horse, but what must I remember?'

'That they who sow the wind reap the whirlwind, that those who have ploughed wickedness shall reap iniquity. Surely these words are not new to you who read so much? Why,' she went on, 'it is less than a week since I heard Sannie teach them to the children. It is as if she knew. Is it not as if she knew, Hendrik?' she asked. 'So take my horses and ride, take your friends and your gun, for it is in my heart that you will need all that you have and more than you have to find her, for at last the dumb dog has learnt to bark and the silent bird to sing.'

'You are mad. You talk in parables.'

'I am sane, Hendrik, and think well of my words as you ride, for with each mile they will make more sense till at the end, when you have read their meaning, you yourself will be broken and your pride humbled. You have been weighed in the balance and have been found wanting.'

'Explain,' Hendrik said.

'Ja, I will explain. One more thing will I say, and it is this, a question which you should be well able to answer. Can two walk together unless they be agreed?

'Now go and hunt your wife, spoor her, chase her with dogs, tie her and bring her back, if you can. If you can.' Tante Anna laughed.

'Do you mean that she has left me and her children?' he shouted.

'That is what I mean.'

'And where has she gone? Where could she go?'

'This is a big country, my friend.'

'So big that it is small for a woman on foot, and alone.'

'But is she on foot? And is she alone? Has no one passed by, Oom Hendrik? Is there no young man who, with his people, all mounted on horses swifter than ours, who has passed this way? And now good-night, Hendrik van der Berg. Ride on her spoor, and when you are tired come back and return my horses to me. You are drunken, Hendrik, but not with wine, you are drunken with pride and blind with vanity.' With a last look at her nephew by marriage, Mevrou de Jong went in, banging the door after her.

'You heard what she said?' Hendrik asked.

'Ja, I heard, and I do not like it, for I am no hunter of women, and Zwart Piete knows no law.'

'She is a harlot, and if you will not come I will hunt her alone. And he,' Hendrik said, 'is a seducer and an adulterer. He shall die,' he shouted, 'a thief who steals men's wives is a dog, and shall be shot like a dog.'

'That may be so, but he is over big for me. Remember that I have a wife, and I would as soon pull a lion's tail as hunt Zwart Piete du Plessis. Be warned, Hendrik, and let them go. He is younger than you, stronger, better mounted, and knows the country like the fingers of his hand. Also it is well known how he fights for no reason save that he enjoys it, and if this be so how will he fight when he has such a reason as Sannie? Nie, nie, my friend, this is a domestic affair and one in which I will not meddle.'

'Where have they gone? And do you think Tante Anna is right when she says that she has gone with him?'

'She is right, of that I am sure, and as to where they have gone that we shall soon see when we pick up their spoor.'

'Sannie's spoor will be hard to find.'

'Why seek it? Let us rather follow the horses, for by and by the two will meet.'

'What you say is good,' Hendrik said. 'And you are coming with me, then?'

'Only till we find the two spoors meeting and then I will turn back. Now let us get the horses; you had better take two, also you must have food and ammunition, for I think your hunt will be a long one. And remember, if you come up with him do not wait for him to stand at bay; by this act he has outlawed himself, and it seems to me that when you see him you must shoot. For up there in the north there is no law, no jurisdiction, and who is to know that he went forth and did not return; even his sister's word and that of their Bastard would not be taken against yours who are well known for your integrity.'

At dawn, riding together the two men followed Zwart Piete's spoor. On leaving the settlement they had taken the hunters' road which was used by such as went into northern bush veld, but after following it for some miles, they had branched off, riding east on a wide curve which would in the end bring them back to the vicinity of the horse-shoe berg.

'Ja, Hendrik,' Martinus said, 'old Tante Anna is right, this is a wise young man. Just look at the plan that he has made, first to lame your horses, for certainly it is he who did it or caused it to be done, and then knowing you to be mounted on a strange horse tired by the delay and time spent obtaining it, he leads you on a chase like this. Just look at the spoor; where they could, they have gone fast, and when we pick up Sannie's footmarks at the place where they arranged to meet our horses will be already tired while theirs will be rested. It will be a hard chase. That man is of iron and tireless, and if his horses fail him he will stand and fight. Why not let them go, Hendrik? Either she will return because the life is too hard for her or because of her children, or she will not return, in which case it is as well. She has gone,' he repeated; 'it is as if she had wings, Hendrik, and does one pursue a bird on horseback? Truly, my friend, the desire of a woman gives her the wings of a wild goose, the heart of a lion, and a mind

that is as cold as the water that comes from the melting snows
on the hillsides. It is in my heart, Hendrik, that you face not
only a man, his sister and their servant, all hunters, but also
your wife, she who for so long has been meek to you, but who
will now stand at the side of her man, facing you as though
you were a stranger and an enemy. Believe me, Hendrik,
I do not think that this thing was done without thought and
planning. It is arranged, and when we find their spoor and
see the way that they have gone I will leave you and return,
for though I am reputed bold I am not bold enough for this,
nor is my heart in it.'

To nothing that Martinus said would Hendrik listen, his
mind was made up, he was adamant, and with each stride
of his horse his anger rose, his determination becoming more
fixed and his purpose more clear. Even the strength and
skill of his rival only added to his fury, for his superiority
had been questioned and Hendrik van der Berg, the chosen
of God, was not one to admit a weakness. By this act Zwart
Piete's hand was against every man's and every man's hand
was against him. Few and evil had the years of his life been,
and that life he proposed by the help of God to end with a
bullet when he came up with him, as in time he must, since
the speed of those he pursued was determined by the stamina
of the weakest among them, by the strength of Sannie his
wife. She was the weakest link in the chain of their flight, and
he, in the full power of his maturity and cunning, was strong.
He would drive them till she broke.

'Ach, ja, Martinus,' he said, 'Africa is wide, none of us
know how wide it is, but my anger is wider, it is a net cast
about the world.'

'It must be wide and strong to catch the fish you seek, for
they are wise, slippery and well armed.'

Martinus and Hendrik had no difficulty in following the
spoor of the horses in front of them, no effort had been made
to disguise it. Zwart Piete and his people had ridden unhesitatingly. Some ten miles from the settlement, as they

breasted a tree-clothed rise, Hendrik and Martinus pulled
up in astonishment. There in a small clearing were a number
of Kaffirs, some whose faces they knew, ones that had worked
for them or their neighbours, and some that they did not
know, wild Kaffirs, and with them were some of the dreaded
naked Kaffirs, the sweepings of the Zulus. All were armed
and dressed for war, and as the Boers appeared they rose
from the ground and seized their spears.

'So Piete was right, Hendrik,' Martinus said, 'they are
ready for war.'

'Charge, Jong,' Hendrik said, as with a wild shout he drove
his horse at them.

A knob kerrie whistled past his ear, and a big Kaffir who
had once worked on his farm raised his spear and was shot
by Martinus. Hendrik shot another, and then the natives
broke and scattering, ran in all directions.

Pulling up their horses the Boers fired again, bringing down
two more.

'So,' said Hendrik, 'they run, they are easily dispersed.
A great company of Kaffirs dispersed by two men who are
white.'

'Ja, they are dispersed, but they live. That young man
has something in his kop. He was right and we were wrong,
Oom Hendrik, and to tell you the truth I wish he were with
us, for he's a great fighter.'

'I would rather die than fight in the company of an
adulterer,' Hendrik said. 'Rather let us have our children
killed than that they should owe their safety to such as he.
Nor could he help, for by having him with us the Lord would
abandon us, for he is a jealous God, Martinus.'

'Perhaps you are right, but I am not sure. No, I am not
at all certain of this matter. And what will you do now?'
he asked.

'I shall go on, and you can go back and tell the people
that there is some danger from the Kaffirs, but tell them also
how they ran from us, and publish it among the natives that

we know of their intentions and are ready for them. Johannes van Reenen on whom my authority devolves will see to it. There is little danger now that we are prepared.'

'But had we not been prepared? Had we not met them as we did, what then?'

'It was arranged by God that we should meet them.'

'Then was it arranged by God that Sannie should run off with Zwart Piete so that in pursuing them we should come across this band?'

'It was arranged. It was arranged so that we should know, and so that I, the instrument of God, should destroy Zwart Piete whose ways are evil; and though we walk through the valley of the shadow of death the Lord will be our rod and staff. This is I say to whom the Lord God has spoken in the night watches. Now go back, my friend, while I ride on.'

'Come with me, Hendrik, come back I say and let them go.'

'I will go on. Their spoor is my road until I come to the end of it. Ja, my friend, I am running hot on a blood spoor, and at the end of it there will be death and food for the vultures, so go back and await my return; do not fear for me, Martinus.'

'This is your last word?' Martinus asked.

'It is all that I have to say,' Hendrik said as he turned his horse.

4

The sun was falling through the trees when Hendrik came to the place where Zwart Piete and his sister had camped. With the failing light he cast round for Sannie's spoor, and having found it and followed it to the place where it met Zwart Piete's, he gave up for the day and settled down to make his camp.

Inevitably he thought of the time that he had found her spoor and that of his son intermingled by the great Kaffir boom whose scarlet flowers had flamed so brightly by the drift; and now again he must kill for her, but this time it was an armed man supported by others, this time it was no defenceless boy who walked singing through the trees. This time it was something else, but he was not one to faint in the day of adversity, nor did he fear his adversaries. They had sinned and their punishment was in his hand.

His drifting thoughts turned from Sannie to Louisa whom he desired and took so brutally, hating her as he did it, despising her while he bent over her in lust, staring into the reddish irises of her eyes, which were so constructed that in them he could see a reflection of himself. That was all he could ever see in them, there was no depth in her, no feeling, save a lust that sprung up in answer to his own, and a fine contempt for the men who abased themselves in their need of her. Swift in her coming, swift in her going, both silent and unobtrusive as the gliding of a snake she remained untouched no matter what he did, no matter what she permitted, no matter what he forced upon her. She was a wild thing, untamed and untamable. He thought of her hair which had a scent of its own, a faintly musky scent. Of her lips, of the skin of her body which was so soft to his hands. Turning on his side he tried to sleep but could not, and lay watching the shadows of the trees in the moonlight undoing the intricacies of the patterns they wove, staring upwards at the leaves and latticed branches, listening with open ears to the crying barks of the jackals and the laughter of the hyenas. It was night, but the night in Africa was more alive than the day, more dangerous and more to be feared, for at night death walked without subtlety, naked and undisguised.

5

Day after day, mile after mile, Hendrik's pursuit drove on, his anger growing as he went. Anger against Sannie, against Zwart Piete who had come with such soft words, come courting not maids but wives, for while the words in his mouth had been smoother than butter there had been war in his heart. His words softer than oil yet were they drawn swords. Hendrik's anger flamed also against the horses he rode which were not equal to his own, the dead Jappie having been no judge of horseflesh and having mated his stock carelessly, letting them go as they would, and not caring that his horses took their own dams or that his colts served their sisters. Time and time again he thought of his black horse, and of how with him he would have gained distance where he now lost it.

He soon realised that Piete knew the country and was riding by night, whereas he, who had to follow the spoor must ride in the heat of the day and go less fast, for here and there on hard stony ground he had to seek, casting about like a searching hound for the mark of a hoof or some scattered dung, while all the time the sun lashed at him remorselessly and the dust was scorched into his skin, sweated out of it and burnt in again till every pore of his body cried for water and for rest from this infernal heat that thrust down at him from the brazen sky, only to rise again off the parched, hot ground with such shimmering malignance that it made his eyeballs ache.

Unshaved and unwashed, hungry, for he never paused to hunt, and shot only such beasts as rose in his path, Hendrik van der Berg rode on, less a man than a motive force, conscious only of one thing, the necessity of getting north on the spoor that he followed, of catching and of punishing, beyond this he did not look.

Merciless, relentless and unthinking, he urged his horses forward, changing his saddle from one to the other every hour and grudging them the time that they took to drink or to roll; jealous even of the hours they grazed, he went on, moving through a world devoid of all reality.

Time after time it rained, and time after time he pressed

on through it, never changing his clothes but riding on in them, letting them dry on his body, while he rode. It was due to a great shower that he lost the track of those he followed, and drawing a bow at a venture turned along a river where he thought he saw something that indicated their passing.

The ground fell rapidly here and the going was difficult for the grass was heavy, the bush thick, and the mosquitoes ravenous for blood. They settled on him in swarms and, hardened as he was, bit him till his face was so swollen and his eyelids so inflamed that he could scarcely see. It was here too that he went down with fever, managing to just reach a native kraal as it gripped him, shaking him till his teeth chattered. He was at the end of his endurance, and his anxiety to kill, his lust for revenge was now changed into a desperate desire that he himself should live. Revenge was relegated to a later day; since it could not now be prosecuted, it would have to wait; for vengeance was dependent on the strength of his arm and the sureness of his hand. The Kaffirs gave him food and his constitution, reasserting itself, he at last recovered sufficiently to feel himself capable of achieving the return journey.

That was a thing to which he was not looking forward, for he was beaten. He was returning in defeat where he looked to come back in triumph. But here again his nature bade him go back so that he might think and plan again. Now I must wait, he thought, till I hear where they are settled, for a man with a woman cannot fly for ever. Some day in some place they would have to rest; till that day came he would wait and behind him, in the place whence he had come, was Louisa the coloured woman for whom he yearned.

CHAPTER XXII

I

RIDING at night and resting by day Zwart Piete, Sannie, Sara and de Kok rode north. Often as he looked into Sannie's tired face, or at her small shoulders drooping over the saddle, he thought of halting and standing to fight. Had he done so the end was never in doubt for he, with his skill, could have stalked Hendrik and shot him like a buck at water. Yet because of Sannie he did not wish to kill for it would be murder or, even in open fight without witnesses, would be accounted as such. For himself he did not care, but with a woman on his hands he did not wish to cut himself off forever from his people. Her children were there and one day the call to go back would come to her; one day, he knew, they would return for them.

Running as they were he was certain that they had gained on Hendrik, and having put two hundred miles between themselves and the settlement he called a halt.

Apart from Sannie, who was all but exhausted, the horses were tired, and even he was feeling the strain of riding so hard and watching both by day and by night. Now they would ride by day and sleep at night. Now they would substitute cunning for speed. Adept in his art as a hunter he looked for stony ground, and led his party over crags where they had to hold their horses by their bridles and down water courses, risking the danger of crocodiles, till he was certain that no one, not even a wild bushman, would be able to pick up their spoor.

After this they went more slowly, proceeding normally

and covering only fifteen to twenty miles a day according to the kind of country they traversed; and now at last he and Sannie were one, their union consummated in its entirety, under the bowl of the blue African night with the distant roaring of a lion in their ears; and Sara who had for so many years slept beside her brother now slept apart. It was all as she had pictured it but a thousand times worse than she had imagined possible, for where her thoughts had been whips the actualities were scorpions. Alone, lying awake, under the too bright stars, she waited each night for them to be done.

She who had been one with him was no longer even a comrade, not even a sister, but instead became something quite foreign, something midway between a brother and a servant, and most of the hunting was left to her. Unable to bear the company of de Kok who, though he could not express his feelings, felt an insupportable sympathy for her, she hunted alone.

Able only to half imagine what went on in Piete's mind, feeling rather than knowing because she was his twin, and suffering intensely from the loss which was his gain, she wondered what the end of it all would be. Wondered where and how the end would come, for in this, as in all else, there must be an end.

Piete looked through her now with vacant eyes as if he did not see her, answering her questions absent-mindedly till he remembered, and then recovering himself, became effusive and thoughtful for her, both things so contrary to his nature, that they hurt her more than a blow.

This girl who had, in spite of the Boer tradition of chastity and faithfulness, given herself to him was the hub of her brother's life, the linchpin of his existence. All else but this woman was nebulous, all else a fantasy, and only she was real. The more he tried to palliate, the more he attempted to explain, the more she felt his sympathy for her, the more hurt Sara became. His affection was salt to her wounds, and his thoughts for her, when they came, a rubbing in of the salt. And yet from the beginning she had helped and abetted him. That Sannie was beautiful and desirable she acknowledged freely; it was a fact beyond all argument, but her brother's love for this woman was a curtain between them, something thick and impalpable against which she flung herself in vain. She had not realised that his possession of Sannie would mean that she lost him so completely, nor had she realised that if she had refused to help him it could have been no worse. It was just that Sannie was an obsession, a thing which filled his mind to the exclusion of all else. Still, had she refused to support him in her abduction he would have hated her, thinking that she had betrayed him, whereas now he did not hate but only ignored.

As she lay listening to the horses stirring uneasily, and staring at the sky, she saw a star fall with its trailing tail of fire. Sara thought of the future, trying to pierce it as a spear pierced the skin of a buck, driving deep into its flank. But the future was not vulnerable, the future would not be pierced and all her thoughts led backwards to what had been, to such happiness as she had known. At twenty-three her life lay in the past, it was over unless she were strong enough to make a new plan, to build it up anew, ignoring the old foundations, and stand alone where before she had been one with Piete, foursquare with him and indivisible, two people who were as one.

2

They had almost reached the country of the Masai when Sara, hunting one evening, came upon the spoor of a solitary buffalo bull. Following his heavy hoofmarks through the vlei where the high grass was broken by patches of mud and shallow water she came up to him.

He was big, even bigger than she had thought and almost hairless. Coated with mud he stood with his head up and his curved horns lying over his shoulders; his shining wet black muzzle quivered as he scented her.

If she turned he would charge, if she waited he would charge. Sara had hunted too many buffaloes not to know the danger in which she stood; there was no other course open to her but to fire. She was directly opposite to him, and the only shot she could take was one below his raised head, through the lower jaw into his chest.

The light was failing and she had not got her heavy gun, also she was hemmed in on either side by high dry reeds in which she could not swing her horse but must fire straight over his ears, and this was more than even a trained hunting horse would stand; yet since there was no other course she raised her gun, aiming for the throat; but she had waited too long; as the sights covered her mark the buffalo lowered his head to charge.

Now it must be the spine; she could see its ridge between the massive shoulder blades, and without further hesitation fired, heard the bullet strike the cuirass of his horns and knew that she had failed.

Launching himself like a projectile at her, the bull charged, travelling at an incredible speed; with his hoofs widely spread as they adjusted themselves to the wet ground, he came at her.

Dropping her gun and slipping her feet from the stirrups Sara waited. Here was the end. Here was the solution of her problem, and the future need no longer trouble her. It seemed an age before he came, it seemed an interminable time between the firing of her shot and the shock of his impact.

Using all her strength on the heavy bit, holding her reins close up to the horse's neck and driving her heels into his flanks she held him facing the charging beast, dragging him up into a rear as the buffalo came so that the great cycle horns and iron forehead took his belly. Feeling the lift of the buffalo, and with the squeal of her horse ringing in her ears Sara slipped out of the saddle and ran. There was a thorn-tree near-by, a small one, and to reach it was her only chance.

Clambering up it, despite the tearing of the thorns, fighting her way through their matted hooks into its topmost branches she waited and watched the destruction of her red horse. Saw him tossed like a sack over the shoulders of the buffalo, saw him fall and struggle to rise with the saddle, which had slipped, supporting his entrails. Heard the harsh neigh of an angry stallion, as he tried to fight, turn into the horrible scream of a dying and terrified horse as the buffalo, maddened, charged again, battering him down by the sheer weight and the fierceness of his attack. Trembling, she watched her horse gored, ripped up like material with a sickening tearing sound, scattered and flattened till the stallion that a few moments ago had been so full of life and fire was just something red and dirty spread over the trampled grass. And still the bull did not give up but knelt upon him, rising at intervals with bloody knees and spattered dewlap to roar before he began his work again, going on and on till the horse was no more than a smear. Not only was his life gone, but so also was anything which would have made one believe that this had once been a horse.

So died her horse, a bold horse in war, a cunning one in hunting or in the cutting out of cattle, and his death had saved her. Surely now the buffalo would give up, surely now, his temper exhausted, he would go; but he did not; his rage was unappeased.

Instead, with his head high he sniffed the evening breeze and came to the foot of the tree to which she clung, standing motionless below it so that she could see the fresh grey scar, the gash her deflected bullet had cut in the base of his horns.

As she fired he must have raised his head a fraction; perhaps as preparing for his effort and feeling his hoofs sinking into the mud of the vlei he had done this. It had needed so little, for her mark had been less than three inches in diameter, and for once the luck which had so long been hers and her brother's had deserted her. Had she not been alone, had Piete been with her his bullet would have killed the beast for he never missed and never went out without his heavy gun. But he had not been with her and she had been too tired lately to carry her elephant gun; also she must have been mad to ride so casually after a lone buffalo, she who had been hunting all her life and should have known the risk she took. Or was it that she did not care? That now she sought risks deliberately, courting them, as if in risks she would find at once her opportunity and her release?

Staring at the beast below her she saw the ticks clustered in his ears and on his eyelids, and his small eyes, red and flaming with anger met hers as he stood stamping his feet and casting up dust in clouds at his belly.

After a pause in which he seemed to be thinking, the buffalo began to rattle his horns against the tree, and then setting his forehead against it tried to push it over, straining at it, arching his back in his endeavours till the spring of his loins took the root of his tail from her view as he butted against it. Finding this unavailing, for the tree stood on a slight rise and the ground round it was hard and dry, he drew back and charged it repeatedly, trying by this manoeuvre to shake Sara, like a fruit, from the branches to which she clung. The shock of his charges were such that she only just succeeded in holding on as the tree bent and swayed beneath them.

Knowing what she did of these beasts Sara was certain now that the buffalo would go on till he dislodged her, or till she fell, unable from hunger and exhaustion to hold on. Far the most dangerous and rancorous of all wild beasts these animals never gave up. Either she would die beneath his horns or he would fall to the bullets of those who in the morning would come to seek her, for a buffalo would remain below a tree for days, lying down beneath it while he waited, and leaving it only to drink or to graze in the vicinity, hoping that by doing this his victim would be tempted down.

All she could do was to wait and in order to wait with any security she must tie herself into the tree, else if she dozed off or lost strength, a sudden onslaught might easily send her to the ground; so taking off her belt she strapped herself to a branch and waited for the dawn that was eight hours away. With the dawn her brother and de Kok would come to find her, of this she was sure. In the distance she could hear the sound of the shots they were firing at regular intervals. Shots that, had she been lost, would have guided her back. She pictured him sitting with Sannie and de Kok awaiting her return. They would be talking about her and wondering where she was. They would have built a big fire so that she would be able to see it from a great way off, and the light of the flames would be reddening Sannie's golden hair. Perhaps Piete would put out his hand to touch it. He often touched her hair.

But the buffalo was not defeated; he now tried, by plunging upwards, to hook her down, and finding this of no avail raised his head, bending his neck till the back of it and his face were in one straight line, he extended his long tongue and reached for her bare legs. Sara could get them up no higher; now she knew she had reached the end. These things were known among the hunters. Retief, a friend of her father's, had died in this manner. A shiver of horror went through her as she realised that long before the dawn came the buffalo would have stripped her feet and ankles of all meat, filing at them with his tongue as if it were a rasp, rubbing the flesh away and enjoying the salty taste of her blood. Before the dawn she would be as empty of blood as a leaking bag of water. That was what they would find when they came, a woman scarcely alive, bloodless and already dead, or dying.

Reaching for her knife she bent down and stabbed savagely at the tongue that had already begun its work, trying to pin it to the trunk of the tree but failing, and almost falling in her effort. Once again she tried, and this time the branch to which she had tied herself cracked. If it broke she was finished. Her legs she could get up no higher, as it was her knees were pressed into her breasts. One thing remained that could be done, and taking a thong from her belt she tied her knife to her foot and succeeded in stabbing the black nose which she saw shining moistly below her. With a bellow of rage, and faster than she had imagined possible, the buffalo with a sudden sideways sweep of his horns caught her leg, tearing it open before she could withdraw it, dragging off her shoe and the knife with it.

3

Reaching the vlei as the sun rose Zwart Piete and de Kok cast about for Sara's spoor and soon found it. She had been riding slowly, at a walk, drifting idly this way and that apparently without purpose. They found a place where her horse had floundered in the mud, sticky black turf. They followed her across it and their own horses went in up to their girths so that they had to dismount and drag them out. They went on, through some high reeds whose feathery tops brushed their hats. A sacca bula, gorgeous in his black spring feathers, his wings blotched with red, flew past them followed by his wives that were grey and dull in colouring as partridges. The tail of the male was long and his flight dipping like that of a swimming fish. As he flew, just skimming the tops of the reeds, he looked like the head and neck of a snake the undulations of whose body were hidden.

Following his flight the eyes of the two men were drawn to the solitary haak doorn on their left.

'Look,' de Kok said, 'she is there. She is in the tree and hangs like one who is dead.'

Dismounting they left their horses with the reins trailing from their bridles, and advanced, their guns held ready.

Zwart Piete hardly looked at his sister as she hung limp as a rag from the tree.

Since she was treed something had done it. Not a lion, because a lion could have reached her. Not an elephant, because it could have pulled her down or uprooted the tree in which she had sought safety. It must therefore be a rhinoceros or a buffalo, a vlei like this was likely to harbour either.

As they approached they saw the beast. The buffalo was lying down a few yards from the tree, his jaws moving rhythmically as he chewed the cud. He was drenched with blood, his horns, face and chest were covered with it and blood still dripped from his torn nostril. As he chewed his head was raised and his eyes never left the girl. Near him was the thing which had been her horse.

With a feeling of nausea Piete realised what had happened, and stepping forward faced the buffalo which rose to its knees as it saw them. Its eyes glinting savagely the buffalo prepared to charge, but before it was up the two men fired, Zwart Piete's bullet taking it in the chest and de Kok's breaking its back. For a moment the beast swayed and, as the men reloaded, collapsed, rolling heavily onto its side. The buffalo was dead. With a final glance at it Piete and de Kok ran forward.

'Sara!' Piete called. 'Sara!'

His sister did not answer. She opened her eyes, looked at him for an instant and closed them, her head falling on her breast.

They had come. She had known they would come, but they had come too late.

While Piete climbed into the tree to get her down, de Kok picked up her bloodstained knife and held out his arms to ease her. Even de Kok who was not squeamish felt his stomach turn as he looked at his mistress's legs. One lacerated by a slash of the buffalo's horn had the calf all but detached from it, while the flesh of both her feet was gone and the slender bones leading from her toes to her ankles were exposed, white, in a mass of bloodless sinew.

The ground beneath the tree was muddy with blood and the tree trunk stained with it. Already there were flies on it and the ants worked up and down, running, in closely formed columns over the rough bark.

Carrying Sara to the waiting horses Zwart Piete put her onto his own, and while de Kok held her in front of his saddle, mounted. Slowly, riding with infinite precaution they returned, and as they rode Zwart Piete considered what they should do.

As he held her he could feel her heart beating faintly. She was not dead, but he wondered if she would ever walk again. Perhaps his sister who was a hunter, who was almost his equal in strength, would be a cripple, unable to move or to stand alone, and if it was so, if this came about, it was his fault. He had only himself to blame.

It might have been better if she had died, if she had been flattened and blotted out as her horse had been. Such a death could not hurt much, it was too sudden, too savage. It was even one that he had foreseen for himself, a man's death and Sara had so nearly been a man. He looked down at her pockmarked face, pitted and scarred, comparing it with Sannie's, and suddenly saw her tragedy. Before God he had been blind in his own happiness. The form he held was that of a woman, and in her mind there must have been the thoughts of a woman. In this matter de Kok the Griqua was right, and her death was due to him and to his neglect of her. In order to forget her misery she had hunted, piling risk onto risk, uncaring, till at last they ceased to be risks and became the certainty of death. Because he had been happy with the cup of his life full to overflowing his sister had died, paying the price demanded of the careless hunter without regret.

At the camp Sara came to and looked at them, first one and then the other, with a smile.

'It is finished, Piete,' she said. 'It is done.'

'Before God it is not done,' Zwart Piete said. 'We will deal with your hurts as best we may, and then we will ride to Sibas Kraal. In three days we shall be among friends and will send for Rinkals who will cure you.'

'And how can I ride?' she asked. 'Let us wait here till it is over. De Kok can hunt and you can stay with Sannie whom you love, and then when I am dead you will bury me on the veld with stones piled over me to mark the place where I died. Just another hunter who has died of her hunting, and that done, you can go your ways. But think of me sometimes, Piete, for I have been a good comrade to you, putting you always before myself.'

'How will you ride?' Piete said. 'You will ride as you rode here in front of my horse, with my arms about you.'

'I am too heavy for your horse,' she said. 'I am as heavy as a man.'

'You are not too heavy, and my horse will do all that I ask of him.'

'Did you see my horse?' Sara asked. 'My red horse. I think it is a pity that I was not with him, for even if I live I shall be useless and a charge upon you. That was a good horse, Piete, and of great courage. It was poor Herman's horse, and it seems that those who ride him have no luck.'

That night Sara died.

CHAPTER XXIII

I

WHEN Hendrik had gone Jakalaas came down from the mountain where he had lain hidden with the lion. The master had gone, and without doubt he would be away some time. Zwart Piete was not one to go slowly, and it would be a hard long chase, one in which, given good fortune, his master might easily be killed.

Jakalaas hated Hendrik with a deep and bitter hatred, for not only was he a hard and cruel master, but an unjust one, who beat his servants without cause, and he was not Hendrik's servant, but Sannie's, and he had only been held by his love for his mistress to a place he loathed, and was now held there by his love for the children she had left. One day she would come back and ask him of his stewardship. One day she would return and say:

'What of my children, Jakalaas, that I left in your charge?'

That she had gone, abandoning them, he understood, for without doubt she would have plenty more by the man she had gone with and to whom she now belonged, and though the difference between one child and another was great, it was not so great as some thought; provided they were numerous, a woman always considered the last one to the exclusion of the others, the helpless one that was so near her and that had so recently quitted the recesses of her body. This was natural and a fact beyond contention, and now that the way was clear he must take the children to Tante Anna de Jong and their grandfather. Then he would return because of the lion which the old woman could not tolerate and which he was not certain of, under surroundings other than those to which it was accustomed. Besides, with Hendrik away he was content to stay. His hut was comfortable and with no one to order him about he would be able to sit in the sun and dream. To sit thinking of the past, of his mistress who was gone and of the others whom he had known that were dead, finding a curious comfort in these thoughts, and comfort was all that Jakalaas could now ask of life. He was feeling old, much older in the last few days, as if time, which had merely passed before, was now hurrying him, bidding him make haste to enjoy those things which were his: the sun, the air, the humming of the insects and the passing of the cattle, which was so beautiful to watch as with swinging heavy bodies and long sweeping horns they went to and fro from their kraals.

Ai, much had he seen, but the pageant of passing cattle never palled. Cattle were the first thing he had seen as a child, little oxen fashioned of sun-baked mud had been his toys, cattle would be his last thought when he died, and perhaps, if he was lucky, he would be buried in a kraal and lie at peace under the feet of the cattle, hidden warmly by their piled-up dung.

He sat for hours thinking of the beasts, of the cows, the oxen and the heifers he had known. Of small calves that, almost while you waited, had grown into great bulls which led the herds till they themselves grew too old and were replaced by their sons. He had no sons of his own, or at least his sons were grown up and had gone. He wondered how many sons he had; it was either three or four, and there had been another who had died. He wondered about their mothers, certain only that they had had mothers, but unable to remember their names or anything that distinguished them from other women. 'Ja,' he thought, 'if they came now I should not know them; but all the cattle that I have ever handled I should know.' There was no mistaking cattle; each one was different, each had its own ways that were not the ways of its fellows. Even their expressions differed and the sound of their voices. Day followed day, and night followed night, the cows calved and everything went as it should go. Weeks became months and still nothing happened.

2

For the first time in his life, Hendrik van der Berg knew defeat, knew what it was to set out to accomplish something and not to achieve it. God seemed to have abandoned him, and he wondered, puzzling his brain, as to what he had done to anger the God whose servant he was. Again and again as he tramped his way back he weighed himself in the balance and found nothing wanting. All that a most jealous God could have demanded he had done — aye, even to the sacrifice of his son — and for this the light of his eyes had been taken from him: Sannie, who now that he had lost her, he knew to be the world to him, without her everything was dark. What, he wondered, was the answer to this? Where was it to be found? Was not his little finger thicker than the loins of the others? Was it possible that God had made an error and underestimated his true worth?

Everywhere as he marched he sought for these answers, looking into the tree-tops for them, watching the flight of the birds and the drinking of the wild animals at water, certain that somewhere the Lord God would give him a sign and acknowledge his supplications. But the Lord God only answered him with another bout of fever of which he nearly died, and, nearly dead, his mind clouded by hallucinations, his body racked, sweating and shivering in turns with ague, he staggered on. Whatever else was impaired, his will remained indomitable, strong enough to string his body to its purpose. So, hunting a little, taking easy shots with his gun rested, and living partly on meat and partly on such herbs, roots and berries as he had learnt of from the Kaffirs, he continued south. On, ever voorvarts, caught without option in the web of lives other than his own, a thick thread in a complex pattern of varying human motives, he was forced back, and as he got nearer so did he think more of Louisa and of her charms. He thought of her with anger, but with the anger was desire which, like a rat, gnawed at his vitals.

When he was rested and grew stronger desire would grow till it was like a tiger inside him, racking him and demanding appeasement. This he knew would happen and looked forward to it, for its gratification would free him from this intolerable feeling of failure, and for awhile, at any rate, he would know success: facile, sensual, but still success, a thing from which he could go on. And for what he had endured others should pay: all those who had made him suffer the manifold indignities of the last three months, the agony, the despair and finally the breaking of his health. Since the sinners had, for the time being, gone, he would wreak his vengeance on those who remained. On Frikkie, Sannie's bastard by his son; he now faced this fact, accepting it, where before he had slurred it over by pretending to himself that his son's son was his own, by a subtle prolongation of his potency into another generation, but now all pretence was stripped from him: the boy was of his blood, no more than that, and he hated him because he had been begotten joyously and sired in affection. Sannie had given his son freely a few times what he had taken so often in hatred. Jakalaas, her servant, should also pay, and the lion should pay with his life for the caresses she had lavished upon him. Before God all these, one and severally, should pay, because they had loved her and she had loved them.

Approaching his home through the trees, slipping carefully from behind one trunk to another, he advanced. Never had he moved more cautiously than now, and even in distress, his hunter's instinct alert, he worked upwind.

No smoke came from his chimney, and the pot plants on the stoep were dead. The few chickens scratching round the house only added to its air of desolation. Had the house been occupied, the poultry would have been less bold.

As he waited, watching, a red cock flew on to the low rail of the stoep and clapping his golden wings to his sides crowed loudly with his neck stretched upwards. He crowed twice and then flew down to drag his wing in the dust beside a hen. First she ran and then, acknowledging her weakness, crouched beneath him as he flung himself upon her.

Hendrik's knees were weak under him as he leant against the tree. How often had he seen Sannie standing at the double door which was now so firmly closed, or leaning over the rail from which the triumphant cock had flown. How often had he come in from the lands or from hunting and taken her? One after another these questions whipped him, stinging his memory with thoughts that were now best forgotten.

And for all this what had he obtained? What had he achieved? Only one sickly daughter, another added to those that he already had. Was it, that like some bulls, he could only get heifers, and those sparsely? He had possessed such a bull once, one who missed often, and when he got calves had six heifers to one bull. After two years of this he had cut him and worked him in the plough. It was curious how a bull, castrated adult, never lost his shape, and except for that which had been removed remained a bull so that all must look at him twice to know him for an ox.

But surely the answer to all this must be a greater effort on his part, and a further endeavour. His firstborn had been a son, and out of Louisa he would get others. He would take Louisa in his wagon and they would go hunting, for having got here he knew he could not stay to be tormented by his memories and his thwarted hopes. 'Ja, I must get out on to the veld again,' he thought.

Like a wounded beast he had returned to his lair, only to find it untenable and peopled by the ghosts of those who had been there, filled with the shadowy remembrances of the things which had happened inside those walls, and still more by the thoughts of the things which had not happened. By his failure to master Sannie while he had her.

Now angry, to gain release he must kill. He must get out alone with his woman into the wilderness and abide there hunting till he had built up his strength and regained his pride. It was no use farming this year, apart from being unequal to it physically; the season was too far advanced, and his lands would be filled with weeds too high to turn in with a plough. Nor had he the heart to work here now. He would go and not return till his vengeance was accomplished. But before he could continue with his vengeance he must go back, as a beast did when about to make a leap. He must put all this from his mind, cut it off till he was well and could once more plan and act decisively. A man was lost without a plan, and just now planning was beyond him. His power of coherent thought was gone, lost in a mist of anger, clouded by the humiliation of defeat.

As he watched, Jakalaas and the lion passed across the open space in front of the house. The old Kaffir was smoking contentedly, and the lion, looking larger than ever, was at his heels.

Stepping back from the tree, Hendrik raised his gun, resting it against the trunk. By a supreme effort of will he controlled the wavering muzzle and brought the sights to bear on the beast. It was a fine opportunity, for the lion, less than forty paces distant, offered himself broadside on, suspecting nothing, and stood motionless staring at the house as if he expected to see his mistress come out of it.

Aiming for behind the shoulder, Hendrik fired. The lion sprang into the air, and with a loud roar fell back, twitching spasmodically, his hind legs reaching up towards his shoulders as if he was galloping. A second later he dragged himself up onto his forelegs, sat for an instant with the blood pouring from his mouth; then he fell onto his side. His muscles quivered, rippling under his tawny skin, his claws went out and were retracted, and with a final gasp that ended with a rush of blood from his mouth and nostrils he lay still. Sannie's lion was dead.

Coming out from his cover as he reloaded, Hendrik raised his gun again. But Jakalaas was too quick for him. Dropping the kaross that he was wearing against the chill of the morning air, the old man ran, and Hendrik's bullet — he had been slow in his loading — missed him as he dodged into the bush.

Running swiftly, the old Kaffir made for Tante Anna de Jong's. Here he would be safe. His lion was dead, and only by chance was he himself alive.

His master must be very sick to have missed such a shot as he had offered standing beside the dead lion. It had all been so sudden that his mind, dulled with the good living and idleness of the past months, had been unable for an instant to grasp what had occurred. He had remained planted beside the twitching beast, staring in amazement at Hendrik van der Berg, astonished at the change in him.

His master was on foot, which was odd for a man returning from a chase, and because he was thinner, with his torn clothes hanging raggedly about him, he seemed taller, and his eyes, always large, now appeared larger and sunk deeply into their sockets, had blazed madly. His veldschoen were worn out and roughly patched with the hides of the animals he had shot. Like an apparition from another world he had come, gun in hand, out of the silent bush.

3

Tante Anna de Jong was drinking coffee when Jakalaas arrived.

'He has come back, mevrou,' he said. 'And he has killed our lion.'

'So he has come,' Tante Anna echoed. 'Ja, I always thought he would come back. And he has come alone?' she went on. 'He has not caught them? Is that not so?' she asked.

'He came alone,' Jakalaas said. 'He is sick and on foot.'

'Ach so, then my horses are lost. They were good horses,' she added. 'It is indeed as I said. I told him that to pursue Zwart Piete wings and not horses were necessary, but still they were good horses, and he will have to replace them.'

'When he had shot the lion, he tried to shoot me, mevrou,' Jakalaas said, 'so I ran. Ja,' he said, 'today I have run like a young man.'

'You were wise to run and he foolish to try to shoot you. Also, he must be very sick and weak to have missed you, for he is a fine shot. But, all the same, it is an evil thing to try to shoot a man — even a Kaffir — except in war. But I am glad the lion is dead, for I did not like it.'

'Yet that lion was like a little brother to me, mevrou,' Jakalaas said, 'and a great comfort to my old age. Truly, mevrou, my heart is sore for my lion. Can I stay here, mevrou?' he asked, 'for he will follow me.'

'You can stay. Go now to the other Kaffirs and remain among them while I await his coming.'

As he left her Jakalaas heard her call Louisa.

'Keep the coffee hot,' she said, 'and bring another cup, for Hendrik van der Berg will soon be here. Also bring me my knitting.'

'Has he sent you a message?' Louisa asked.

'Ja, he sent Jakalaas running to tell me of his return,' Tante Anna de Jong said, laughing softly.

'So Mynheer van der Berg is back,' Louisa said.

'If he were not back he could not come, fool, also he has shot that lion, which is a good thing and a great comfort to me, for I was frightened of it, and it is not good for me to be frightened; it makes my heart flutter like a fink in my bosom and my bowels to turn over in my belly. I am too fat to be frightened, Louisa. All that I ask of life now is peace and quiet, and yet no sooner do I sit down than something happens to disturb me.'

When Hendrik came Tante Anna was ready for him, and,

knitting placidly, her needles clicking against each other as she worked, she watched him ride up on his black horse. This man was, for the time being at any rate, beaten. Later he might recover, or he might not: it would depend on many things.

Smiling, she watched him dismount and saw that his legs would scarcely carry him. She watched him come towards her and saw him endeavouring to recapture his old arrogance of manner as he addressed her.

Without greeting he said: 'Is Jakalaas here, Anna de Jong? For if so I would take him back.'

'Take him back?' Tante Anna said. 'Why would you take him back? If he was here, that is.' She looked round. 'But I do not see him, Hendrik,' she said.

'I wish to beat him. After that,' he went on, 'if he still lives you can have him.'

'But he is not your servant, Hendrik: he is the servant of Johannes van Reenen and of his daughter Sannie.'

'Sannie is my wife, and what was hers is mine, so I will beat him till he cannot stand. It is my right.'

'That, Hendrik van der Berg, is an idle boast. The time has come when you can no longer do as you will. The time has come when you merely assert and assert in order to reassure yourself of what you hope to do. Did you think of my last words as you hunted your wife, those words in which I reminded you that he who sows the wind reaps the whirlwind. Ja, as you have sown, so will you reap, and the time of your harvest is near. It is the dead flies that cause the ointment of the apothecary to send forth a stinking savour and your pot is broken. Ja, Hendrik, the silver cord is loosed, and the golden bowl is broken. The pitcher broken at the fountain and the wheel broken at the cistern. And does it not say in the Book that the strong shall be as tow, and the maker of it as a spark, and that they shall both burn together, and none shall quench them? Ja, all this is so and all this will come to pass. But where are my horses that I lent

you, Hendrik?' she asked, changing her tone. 'The bay
hunting horse with black points and the red horse with a
drooping ear?'

'Your horses are dead.'

'Ja, they are dead, and you are sick and your wife is gone.
How are the mighty fallen, Hendrik van der Berg. And is
it not said that mighty men shall be mightily tormented, and
that mighty men shall be searched out mightily? Do you
think that you are the only man who reads the word and can
find therein that with which to serve his turn, distorting
God's Word to his purpose? Truly the ways of the Lord God
are remarkable. There is a pattern to this existence, and it
seems to me that the string of your life will soon be ended,
cut off like a piece of wool in woven carpet that is no more
wanted, one whose usefulness is done. It seems to me that
where you have waxed you will now wane, and I am glad of
it, for you are a hard, proud man who set yourself up too
high.'

'That I have fallen is due to Sannie, who is an adulteress.'

'And did you not first commit adultery? And did you not
slay your son? And does it not say, let him who is without
sin among you cast the first stone?'

'That comes from the New Testament, mevrou.'

'Ja, but can you deny that it is the word of God and found
in His Book? Sannie loved Herman, your son, whom you
shot when he was alone and without arms. He was a beautiful
young man, clean and strong, and now he lies in the wilderness beside my Jappie, whom you persuaded to trek against
his will and mine. Nie, nie, Hendrik, Jakalaas is here and remains here with me and Johannes. From another you might
be able to take him, but from me never.'

'And my children,' Hendrik asked. 'You have them,
too?'

'Ja, I have them.'

'Where are they?'

'That I do not know. When they heard you coming they

ran away, for they are afraid of you. If you can catch them, do so, for they are yours, all but Frikkie, who remains.'

'He shall not remain. By what right do you hold my children?'

'No right when they are your children, but very well do you know whose son Frikkie is. He is Herman's son, the fruit of Sannie's and Herman's love. It would be wise to let him remain, Hendrik, without argument, for I am stronger than you. Only in success did you obtain obedience because you were feared, while now, in your weakness, you will get no help. You have no following, whereas I am of some importance. My gold is gold, while yours is dross. A few may cling to you, but they will not be many, nor will they be the best among us, and it will be better to leave things alone, much better, for I do not like to be roused up.'

'I shall go and hunt,' Hendrik said. 'I shall inspan my wagon and go away till I have regained my strength, and then you shall pay for this.'

'Ja, Hendrik, that is wise. Go out and kill till your senses are returned. Certainly it is good council that if it is in your heart to kill, it is better to slay wild beasts, though they also are of God's creation, and to keep your hands from men. But before you go send me horses to replace those that are dead.'

'I will send them,' Hendrik said as he mounted.

4

Towards evening the two horses were sent over, and not long afterwards before the sun set, when Anna de Jong called for Louisa she got no answer. Louisa had gone, taking her child with her. Next day when Anna de Jong sent a Kaffir over to Hendrik van der Berg's to spy out the land she learnt that he had gone. His wagon was no longer there, and the spoor of its wheels led north. He had taken some saddle-horses with him, and the balance of his livestock he had confided to Martinus, giving him a share of the increase for the trouble of looking after it. It appeared that he did not know how long he would be away. It may be a year or it may be more, he had said.

5

In this manner did Hendrik begin his chase again, but this time he would go more slowly, hunting northwards, so that each outspan would bring him ever nearer to Sannie and Zwart Piete. Working in wide circles, he would seek information, searching till he got it.

The old hound was not as fast as the young, but he was very certain. Tireless and remorseless, he would prosecute his search, going on till he wore them down.

6

Had Frikkie and Hendrik's children not been with her Tante Anna would have missed Louisa's yellow child. She had grown very fond of it, and recognised many of her husband's traits in the infant. However, as it was she was well content, for provided there were children near her she was happy. She liked children about, she liked to feed them, to kiss them, to slap them, to watch them at play and to hear their laughter. Even their tears gave her some pleasure, for then she could comfort them, taking them to her wide bosom, where, feeling safe in its amplitude, they soon calmed down, their cries fading to whimpers as they fell asleep in her arms. Ja, the Lord gave, and the Lord God took away. He had taken Jappie and had left her his bastard. He had taken the child and had given her others to replace it. And perhaps when she died, God having taken her life would give her a new one where once more she would be reunited to Jappie, her poor weak Jappie, who, while he still loved her, had deceived her, stealing her servant because, like a child wanting a sweetmeat, he had seen her and was unable to resist. Ach, ja, Louisa's cream-coloured flesh was sweet to men, very sweet with its hot, yielding softness, but afterwards it left a bitter taste in their mouths; for, having once tasted of her, they would take and take till they could take no more, till at last their tired bodies turned against their imaginings, striving against them; till set one against the other, their minds contrary to their flesh, their carnal lusts forced by their thoughts to burn upwards long after natural desire was done, her lovers were consumed.

What things had happened since they trekked. What a lifetime of events had been compressed into so small a compass. As she looked back she saw how one thing fitting into another had made a third. Event had followed event, and if one thought of it seriously it was impossible not to see the inevitability of every happening. In life there was no way out; one must go on to the end, be that what it might. Each effect was the result of a cause, and each effect became a cause itself, being followed by a new event. There was no such thing as accident. Nothing was fortuitous.

Anna de Jong sighed and folded her hands on her lap. She was tired of thinking and planning. Also for the moment there was no more to be done. As water ran down the side of a hill, so were the lives of those with whom she was intimately concerned, moving in a given direction. Sannie was happy with the man she loved, Frikkie was safe and well, Hendrik, weakened by disease, was on the way to madness, and when once it was known that he had taken Louisa with him openly, his power would be completely broken, for such things were not tolerated. Also, since the native rising had been discovered there was no immediate danger, though doubtless it might re-occur, perhaps when the meilies were high and when, having used up their stores of grain, the Kaffirs became hungry for the riches of the Boers. That might be so, but it would be later, and did it not say in the Bible, 'Take no thought for the morrow, for the morrow shall take thought for the things of itself, and sufficient unto the day is the evil thereof.'

Also sufficient for the day was the thought thereof.

Things were going well, and Tante Anna became practical, weighing the merits of Baboti against those of Sasaties for supper.

CHAPTER XXIV

I

RINKALS was more than contented while he waited among the Masai for the coming of his master, for here he was both feared and respected. More than this no man could ask, for by it were many benefits obtained. True that at first there had been some unpleasantness when he had returned with the mothers of the king's wives, but this had to a great extent been mitigated by the fact that the king had taken many new and younger wives and no longer cared much for those whose mothers had come with Rinkals. These women had lost significance; and since their daughters were no longer favourites, they had no following.

Also the magic he had made had been good, and the river since his going had run very freely, never failing even in the driest winter, and the girl who had helped him in his task had given birth to a fine child, a boy that was held in great reverence as the son of the water gods.

In consequence of all this there was meat and beer in plenty for Rinkals, and his life ran very smoothly, as sleekly as the hair lying along an otter's back. Men brought him gifts and came from afar to ask his advice as he sat in council behind the king.

Also he knew that Zwart Piete, his master, would be pleased with his work, for he had found that these people had much ivory hidden away which the king was willing to trade. He even knew where it was hidden and the number of tusks. This information he had obtained by his magic and some subtly prosecuted inquiries among the women, the wives of those who had buried it. Women were always curious about the future, which was an open book to him, and were relieved to pay him with words rather than in kind, for words were not missed like cattle, and the spoken words of a wife away from her husband could not be counted, being numberless and easily denied.

Their method of hiding the ivory was simple. They dug a great pit in a known place and buried it, flattening the ground above the hole. Then they set the veld alight so that a great area was burnt, and as soon as the young grass sprang up, all was hidden, so that only those who knew the landmarks could find it again.

Ai, when his master returned he would be glad. They would discuss the matter with the chief and make a trade, and then they would go to the fort of the Portuguese and return with slaves to carry away the tusks. One to each slave for those of small dimensions, and two for the large ones, which could be carried lashed to a long pole that went from the shoulder of one onto the shoulder of the other.

In the meantime he was content to wait, having built up an honourable condition for himself and greatly increased his reputation both by his magic and his judgments in the legal discussions at which he had assisted.

It was therefore with some surprise that he heard the rumour of Zwart Piete's return, for he had not expected him so soon, and listened with consternation to the news that followed. Sara was dead, killed by a buffalo, her feet having been licked till the flesh was sucked from the bones, and Zwart Piete had a second woman with him, a new one, and behind him, many days away, there was a man who pursued them.

The warrior who had brought these last tidings was all but foundered when he came, for he had run fast.

Here was much food for thought. This was what occurred when he did not accompany Zwart Piete. Truly the young could not safely be left alone. Had he been there this would not have happened; he would have seen a way out, for his mind was beautiful, like a thin spear that found the crevice in each and every situation.

For an hour the old man sat still and then made his way to the chief's hut, pushing aside those who tried to stay him.

'Give me three men,' he said, 'young strong men to help me on my way, to protect me from wild beasts and to carry my mouti, for I must go to my master.'

'I will give them to you,' the chief said. 'But what of your white ox and your women?'

'They must stay here for a while in your charge, oh elephant that shakes the world with his trumpeting.'

'Must the mothers of my wives also remain,' the chief asked, 'for I find them tedious.'

'They must remain,' Rinkals said, and then seeing the king's face fall added: 'But they can follow me slowly with the maid whom the gods love and my white riding ox. I am going fast, oh chief. The spirits of the dead ones will bind wings to my feet.'

'It shall be as you say,' the king answered. 'You will go fast with the young men that I shall give you, and the others will follow more slowly.'

'Then farewell, chief, till we meet again, for we shall meet. Our paths cross often — this I have seen when I looked into the beyond — therefore tend my cows well and look to their increase. When I return my master will trade with you for your ivory, which is no good to you lying buried in the veld. We will give you beads and anklets for your women, also blankets of red and yellow, knives and axes.'

'I will trade,' the chief said, 'and your cows will be looked to; they shall run with my own on the best pastures.'

'Then let them only run, oh chief,' Rinkals said. 'Let there be no confusion between those calves which are mine and those which are yours. On the justice of this matter rests the strength of the stream which runs through your land, for what I have made I can unmake.'

With that, accompanied by the men he had asked for, Rinkals left the chief's kraal to go to his master.

2

When Rinkals came to Zwart Piete's camp he found him much distressed. The tale of Sara's death was soon told and Sannie's presence explained.

With the warriors standing beside him as he squatted on the ground, Rinkals listened till Zwart Piete and de Kok were done, and then his eyes fixed on the fire he spoke.

'Lord, much of this which has occurred I had foreseen, and some of it I could have staved off; and yet,' he went on, 'it came to me that by doing so I might be returning evil for good. Certainly much of this I foresaw, but the manner of its happening I did not see. Your sister saved my life, by coming when I called to her, and raising me up when I had fallen, but when you, the twin branch of her life, took this woman,' he looked at Sannie, 'you sowed the seed of your sister's death by taking the joy out of her and replacing it with a burden too great for her to bear, one beneath which she sank into despair as is the manner of women, who without intelligence, cling to that which they have always known and fear the mysteries of the future. Had I saved her, lord, when she was without the desire to live, she would have cursed me.

'And now, lord,' he said, 'let me sit, for I would think and consult the spirits, who are my familiars; also I must make mouti. Already,' he continued, 'this place is full of the departed; they close round us in readiness. I can see them,' he went on, his voice pitched high, 'grey spirits who stand in numbers about us. They are angry that I have come, for they know my power and fear me. Ai, the coming of this woman, the one with the yellow hair, I foresaw long ago, and with her come great complications; the wings of death are upon us all. Also somewhere in this, with her hand in it, is a fat woman, very wise and shaped like a kopje that is sunk in on itself. The owner of your woman, lord, approaches with death in his heart, that I can see, but I fear him not, for he will be destroyed by his own anger and eaten up by his pride. Still it were well to send watchers back, that they may spy on him and tell us of his movements, for of an enemy enough is never known.'

'I fear no man,' Piete said, 'and what I hold, I hold. Still, let us do as you say, Rinkals, for your council is always good.'

3

What Rinkals had said confirming de Kok's words made Zwart Piete wonder how it was that this, which seemed so apparent to them, had been unnoticed by him. Even now it seemed incredible that Sara should be dead. He could not believe it, and when the horses came in from grazing he still looked for her red horse, and when they ate he still turned to the place at his side where for so many years she had sat sharing everything with him.

She was dead, she would never ride out with him; she would never smile at him; he would never hear the sound of her deep, husky voice in his ears again.

The shape of his life had changed; it was taking a new direction. He had Sannie, and Sara's death was part of the price he had had to pay for his possession of her. Seeing this clearly now, he put all thought of Sara from him and spoke no more of her, but there were new lines in his face and a still greater determination to go on in his mind. If Sannie must be paid for, he would pay. If Sara had lost her life because of her, he was also ready to lose his own. The spear of his action was flung. It was out of his hand.

CHAPTER XXV

I

WITH bitterness in his heart Hendrik van der Berg went north with Louisa and her child in his wagon and his servants about him. Once he got away, when he was well beyond the ordinary range of his folk, he began to hunt, changing his camp at intervals as he picked up news of the fugitives.

Putting away all thought of the future and of his revenge, which would be doubly sweet, since it had been delayed from him, he set about curing himself and began to rebuild the tower of his strength. Stone by stone he did it, the base of his structure being his continuous and uninterrupted possession of the coloured maid.

Following the path he had taken alone, he went on, and where he had lost the trail at the river he crossed it and drove towards the country of the Masai, hunting all the time and obtaining news as he hunted. Zwart Piete was well known and his passing an event to the Kaffirs who had seen him.

Several times he found the old ashes of his fires and the scattered bones of the beasts he had eaten.

At last in a place where game was more than usually plentiful, and wishing to make a final pause in which to recover completely before he attacked, Hendrik halted and made a semi-permanent encampment.

His powers were returning; in a month he would be well and ready to fight. God was with him, and as a sign that this was so, Louisa had declared herself to be with child.

2

Hendrik van der Berg pulled up his horse under a spreading vaal-bos and stared about him. His hair and beard were almost white, but he had put on flesh, and his bearing was once again that of a man who was successful; he had regained control of himself.

Sitting motionless, his eyes searched the bush for movement. Inevitably, if one waited long enough, watched long enough and in the right place, something moved. There would be a glint of sunlight on a dark horn, an ear would flicker or a tail twitch. He could see nothing; everything in that world of grass was still, and then suddenly, high up among the thorn trees not forty yards away, he saw what he searched for.

Trusting to its colour, to the broken discs of its pale chestnut hide divided by lines of white, a giraffe stood motionless. Even Hendrik, trained as he was by years of hunting, would have passed it by had it not been for the Rhenoster birds that ran in and out of its ears and over its face, searching its lips and eyelids for the parasites which clung there.

A kameel, a lone bull. Touching his horse's neck with the rein, Hendrik swung him sideways.

Already, as he raised his gun, he was calculating how many whips he could make from the skin. He liked making whips, and whips of giraffe hide were the best. But he had calculated too soon, for before his gun had reached his shoulder the giraffe was off. Breaking suddenly into a lumbering canter, it left the clump of bush where it had been standing, crossed a small open leegte and made for the tree-dotted plain beyond it.

Ramming his heels into his horse's flanks, Hendrik galloped after it, trying to cut it off and get in a crippling shot. He shot well from a horse, and his black knew its work. With the single rein hanging loose, the horse dodged through the bush, changing feet as he swung round the thorny trees, jumping the low scrub, galloping hard with his eyes fixed on his quarry.

At first it looked as if the horse was holding its own, and then the giraffe disappeared. From being a hundred yards ahead he suddenly melted away and was gone.

Cursing himself for his slowness, Hendrik pulled up, hesitated for a moment and with a glance at the sun turned towards his camp.

Such things did not happen often, but when they did, magtig, how his blood boiled. To think that a kameel, a great, stupid spotted thing like that, had eluded him. Still, tomorrow he would try again; a lone bull would not travel far, and he would get him. Ja, tomorrow he would get him, or the next day, and he thought of the whips he would make from his skin. There was a demand for his whips; they were well known; and so cunningly were they brewed, so neatly trimmed with a waisted belly on them that he always boasted that he could recognise the clap of one of them when it was cracked. Hundreds of oxen must have felt them on their flanks; been cut by them, for he had made them since he was a boy, and a properly made whip of kameel hide drew blood.

As he smoothed his gun with his big brown hand the metal felt sleek and warm to his touch. What a gun it was. It was like a child to him. No, it was more than a child, for children were easily begotten — he thought proudly of Louisa and his returning strength. No, a gun was more like a father to a man, standing between him and death from wild beasts. And was it not the gun that provided? Was not a gun, in a way, the instrument of God, killing men and animals for his benefit, killing them so that he might eat and live? And was it not right that it should be so? Where not the Boers God's chosen race? And was he not one of the foremost among them, for where was there a man more feared, more fecund or more upright than himself?

The cattle were being driven in from grazing when he

reached his camp. The great kraal of trees dragged with their trunks pointing inwards and their branches interlaced made an impenetrable hedge round the wagon which was his home. It was stood under a big hartekoal, a dying giant of a tree that dominated the surrounding bush.

Louisa was preparing the evening meal and her child sat on a sheepskin with her dark eyes fixed on her mother.

Some distance away the Kaffirs grouped round their fire looked very black against the glowing flames and the pale-blue smoke that rose in vertical columns, to meet the evening sky.

A boy came to take his horse, a yellow mongrel bitch, one of the few that had survived and was now salted to red-water, came towards him fawning, followed by her pups.

Hendrik was glad to be back, and as the smell of the meat cooking on the embers came to him he realised that he was both tired and hungry. It was many hours since he had eaten. Also, he was angry that he had killed nothing, that he had not even fired a shot. Of course not, for with him to fire was to kill.

'Give him water,' he shouted to the boy who had taken the horse, as he sat down heavily.

Louisa looked up at him inquiringly as he glowered at the fire. Knowing what was in her mind, he did not wait to be questioned, but said:

'I have not shot anything today, but I have seen a giraffe.'

'Geseen?' she echoed in surprise.

'Ja, geseen,' he repeated. 'But I did not shoot.' Did the woman think he had missed? Was he going to explain that he had been too slow? Well, tomorrow she would see. To-morrow he would hunt that giraffe. One did not argue with women. One did not even talk with them.

'Give me food,' he said.

When he had eaten he got out his Bible and read to the coloured girl aloud from it, but all the time as he read he saw the giraffe. The printed page was patterned like its skin. Tomorrow, he said as he put the Book away, but it was not tomorrow, nor was it even the day after.

3

Sometimes as he hunted he got a glimpse of the giraffe moving through the bush, but was never near enough to hazard a shot.

His first hot anger against the beast had changed into a cold rage: at all costs now he must get it. At all costs. He was not going to be defeated by a stupid beast that could not even make a sound when it was distressed, that was unable to bellow or to low, and whose horns were not horns, but just fur-covered knobs. Ja, soon he would get him as he had got others of his kind. It was only a matter of patience — and did he not know patience, he who had lived by hunting all his life? But somehow patience eluded him.

Day after day he continued to hunt, on horseback, on foot; alone, with Kaffirs; but always without success. Neglecting everything else, ignoring even Louisa, till this animal was dealt with, he hunted on. The giraffe had become an obsession, and in his success in this matter his success in all else seemed to be bound up.

Once he got near enough to chase it, tearing his shirt and scratching his face in a mad gallop through the heavy thorn scrub. That day he came home livid with rage and covered in blood; that day he cursed Louisa and kicked the fawning bitch as she lay on her back in front of him.

In the week that this hunt had lasted he had grown thin again, losing much of the flesh he had put on. Never, even as a young man, had he hunted harder and, always taciturn, he now hardly spoke at all. Each day before dawn he would be off, watching water-holes, spooring, following or waiting hidden, hunting remorselessly, going without food except for the Boer rusks and biltong that he carried in a bag tied to his saddle.

At night he dreamed of the giraffe, saw its skin being cut up into strips, saw it being breyed. Saw the sharp knives of his Kaffirs shear through its spots. Instead of being as big as plates they became thin, yellowish-brown strips divided by small white lines. But before it could be breyed it would have to be soaked in water to soften it and to loosen the hair. He saw it floating, weighted down with stones; it would still be belly upwards, and when it was ready they would cut it into long riems, which would be joined together till they formed a wet slippery raw-hide rope which would be thrown over the branch of a tree, loop after loop of it. Over the branch and through the handle of a great stone, made by fastening a piece of curved wood to it so that it looked like an enormous flat iron. The stone would rest on a block while this was being done. Then the support would be pushed away and the strips of hide would take up the weight, stretching as it dragged at them. A Kaffir would insert a long stick into the handle of the stone and walk round and round till the stone was high up in the air and the water wrung from the riems would run down the stick onto his hands and arms, and loosened hair and water would fall onto the ground at his feet. With a swift movement the boy would withdraw the stick, and the stone, released, would come twisting down, turning faster as it came with a rustling sound that would end with a rattle as all the strips of hide which went over the bough and through the handle of the stone quivered against each other. All day the boy would do this for three or four days. Round and round, tramping a circle under the tree till the veld was bare of grass. Stopping only to rub fat into the throngs as they grew dry. Fat from round the giraffe's own kidneys into its hide. This was his dream. It never went beyond the breying. It never reached the making of the whips.

On the tenth day when he was riding through a leegte a few miles from his camp he got his chance. The black turf soil was covered with a carpet of dry, sweet grass. It was almost white and crackled softly under his horse's hoofs. All about, were trees scattered in ones and twos, or in groups, as symmetrically as if they had been planted.

He passed some ostriches. With their heads turned they stared at him, following his movements till he came near them, and then trotted away with their feathers fluffed and their legs lifted high, while Hendrik, a hard smile on his lips and his gun half raised, watched them go. Ach, ja, they were safe; everything was safe now but the kameel. No shot would he fire till this animal was dead. Its pursuit had become symbolic; it was part of his chase of Sannie and her lover. Never since the beginning, when he had first seen the giraffe and it had escaped him, had he stopped thinking of his wife, of her supple acquiescent beauty. Everywhere he looked he saw her, she came between him and all he did. The giraffe, Zwart Piete and Sannie were tied together in his mind. All three had escaped him, and when he got the one the getting of the others would follow. This was the test that the Almighty had put upon him. A trial of his skill and his endurance.

'If only I could see him now,' he thought, 'where there is room to ride and one can see to shoot.' And as if in answer to his prayers he saw it. Standing by a group of haak doorns. Quite motionless it stood there, with its spotted skin blending into the strong light and shadows of the trees.

This time, there was no hesitation. The horse must have seen him as soon as his master, for he pulled up, and stood, his ears pointing towards the group of trees, his tail lashing spasmodically at the flies that clustered on his belly and, crawling up his legs, bit his tender skin.

Raising his gun, Hendrik fired. There was a pause before he heard the smack of the bullet and saw the giraffe stagger as the lead found flesh and bone. Automatically, hardly looking down, he reloaded. The giraffe swayed like a felled tree, his long neck weaving about among the branches, his legs sagging. Hendrik watched the giraffe's mouth open and close in a soundless bleat, watched his long legs give way beneath him, saw him stagger and come to his knees.

'He is bigger than I thought,' he said, as he cantered towards him.

The giraffe looked round, its lips were frothed with blood, and, summoning up all the reserves of his big body, lurched to his feet and, swaying drunkenly from side to side at first, soon settled down to a steady gallop.

The next shot missed him; he was a small mark from behind. Still thinking of Sannie, Hendrik reloaded again and galloped on, furious that his impatience had overcome him. Wondering why he had not put at least one more bullet into the wounded beast before going up to him, or better still, why, since it was hard hit, he had not just waited, leaving him to lie and bleed, waiting for the blood to coagulate and the wound to stiffen? And yet as he wondered he knew why he had not done so: he had waited so long and hunted so bitterly that this had ceased to be an ordinary hunt. It was a revenge on an animal that had thwarted him and which must pay in fear and agony for what it had done, for its failure to recognise its master.

He was galloping fast with his eyes fixed on the giraffe when his horse fell. Putting its foot into an ant-hole, the horse recovered, but fell as its other foot went into a second hole beside the first. Hendrik, with a wild clutch at his horse's mane, went over its head. His finger had been on the trigger, and as he fell the gun went off, the bullet wounding him in the foot.

The report checked the giraffe, which stood still as if unable to go. Oblivious of his wound, Hendrik reloaded and, lying on his belly, put bullet after bullet into the great spotted shape in front of him. Each made it reel, the first bringing it down to its knees, its hocks collapsed with the second, and then like a foundering ship the giraffe reeled over, its long legs kicking at the red dusty soil.

It was done. The kameel was dead. He had mastered it.

Pulling off his shirt, Hendrik cut a strip to bandage his wound. His shoe, as he took it off, was filled with blood that ran out of its shot-off end. A great puddle, where he had lain, was soaking into the ground. Ach, blood, and he was emptying of it like a vessel which is cracked, like a pierced water-bag. Lashing up his foot firmly, drawing the linen strip as tight as it would go, he paused to think.

Here was a nice business, to find himself wounded and some way from camp. He looked for his horse and found it grazing near him, its rein was broken and hung dragging from the bit, but he seemed unhurt. From the horse he looked at the giraffe. Magtig, it was dead at last. He had conquered, and nothing else mattered. The first stage was over: the Lord God had given him a sign.

He stared at the cloven hoofs — they were as big as dishes — and at the white belly streaked with blood. Unable to resist the impulse, he crept nearer to the beast and, leaning with his back against it, considered the situation. There was only one thing to do: he must get on to his horse and go back. It was his right foot: he would therefore be able to stand on his left one and cling on to the horse's mane as he mounted. It was indeed lucky that the horse was steady and would allow himself to be caught without difficulty.

4

Louisa could not understand Hendrik. To her a giraffe meant nothing; they were common and of no great value; even his talk of whips was nonsense, for to make whips was a long and tedious business, an occupation for an idle hour, no more than this, and that a man should hunt a kameel so madly was more than odd.

Why, if it had been an elephant with tusks of solid gold he could have done no more, and it was not her fault that he could not kill it. Yet from the way he behaved one would have imagined that she was to blame for his ill-success.

She wished now that she had not come. There was no one to talk to here, no one to boast to about her dominion over Hendrik, no coloured men to pass her time with, no white men to look back at over her shoulder. Ach, this bushveld was boring; there was nothing to do and nothing to think of.

She was used to women about her and to the rivalry of women. She was used to Tante Anna de Jong's biting tongue, her gossip and her occasional blows. The life she had led in Canaan seemed gay now, and carefree, by comparison, and she wished she was back: more particularly did she wish it since she was going to have a child. She must get back before her time came. Still, she supposed something would happen soon — either Hendrik would kill the kameel or he would not kill it — and then they would move on in this mad hunt for Zwart Piete and Sannie. Why did he worry about Sannie, who was like skim milk and without richness, when he had her? Why did he risk his life against Zwart Piete du Plessis the hunter? Unquestionably, as Anna de Jong had often said, all men were mad; only women understood the true worth of things and were able to compute and weigh the practicalities of existence. She began to think of von Rhule, the German. Perhaps it would have been better to have taken him. She had thought of it; but at the time Hendrik had loomed so much larger than he. Walking discontentedly about the camp, very much at a loss and unable to explain to herself how she came to be in this situation, Louisa waited for her man's return. This time it was she who was angry; she had done enough. Whatever she said he could do no more than beat her, and that he did anyway, whether she angered him or not.

She was standing by a tree staring with vacant eyes into the bush when she saw Hendrik come in. He was covered with blood, and she was glad. He must have killed the giraffe, and they would be at peace; he would talk to her now and make love to her again. But his face seemed white and the lines about his mouth were grim.

'You have killed it,' she said as she went towards him.

'Ja, I have killed it. The kameel is dead.'

It was only as he dismounted, staggered and nearly fell that she saw he was hurt and realised that the blood which plastered him was not only that of the giraffe.

'You are wounded,' she said, staring at him. His face was a sickly white beneath its tan. It was inconceivable that this man should be susceptible to hurts like other men. It had never occurred to her that anything could happen to Hendrik van der Berg, the leader. Always, till now, he had come out of everything unscathed.

'It is nothing, Louisa,' he said, 'nothing at all. My horse fell and the bullet went through my foot. Bring turpentine, bring all that we have, for it is still bleeding, and turpentine will burn up the veins. Ja,' he went on, 'I can feel it bleeding. First it runs hot and then it grows cold. It must be stopped, for I can afford to lose no more. Bring turpentine,' he said to the girl. 'And inspan the oxen at once, Jan,' he shouted, 'for we are going back to the kameel that I have shot. Tonight we camp beside it.'

5

With his wound only partially dressed, Hendrik lay waiting for the dawn when they would skin the beast that he had killed. They had thrown thorn branches over it and built fires round it to keep the night prowlers from the body. In the morning Hendrik watched them flay it, watched his Kaffirs pulling the great skin, like a carpet from the flesh it covered, cutting with their knives the adhesions of tissue which bound the skin to the body and then, when it was done, and the skin loaded, he sat on it, where it lay folded, oozing pinkish moisture that ran over the bed of the wagon and dripped between the planks. It was now time to attend to his wound properly. His work, that of killing and skinning the giraffe was done and he had time at his disposal — unlimited time — for while his wound healed he must sit.

Ach, God, how his boot hurt him now. It throbbed, for with the giraffe skinned, the pain which had been subordinated to the excitement of his revenge was striking at him, dealing him blow after blow, causing him to flinch each time the wagon rocked. As they made their way back his mind dealt with the question of the future. His foot, the skin, its breying and the making of the whips while his foot healed. After that — Zwart Piete and Sannie.

The delay caused by this accident was an annoyance, no more than that, and it might in the end prove to be an advantage, lulling Zwart Piete into a sense of false security. That his injury would heal he had no doubt, for he had in his life suffered many wounds and all had healed well; his flesh was good and healthy, and soon, when he had dealt with it, the wound would close as the others had, closing up till he was whole once more. And what, after all, was it to lose a toe? It hurt, certainly, and he had lost much blood, but it might have been worse: before God, it might have been much worse.

As soon as they reached the camp he soaked off the blood-stained bandages and examined his injury. It was not a clean wound: the nail and top joint were gone, and there were fragments of bone which must be removed and the ragged flesh that lay across the middle of the ball of the toe would have to be trimmed down. Telling Jan, his most trusted Kaffir, to bring him a block of wood, he settled down to sharpen his knife, rubbing it up and down on a stone. Louisa was told to bring the turpentine again and to cut more linen for bandages.

'What are you going to do?' she asked.

'I am going to make this wound right,' he said. 'I am going to take away the splintered bone and cut off the loose flesh round it so that it will be clean. Look,' he said, 'it is now foul, blackened by powder and dirty with even fragments of the leather from my shoe driven into it. It cannot remain like that.'

'And you will do it yourself?' she asked.

'Who else is there to do it? And what must be done for me, I am capable of doing.'

As Louisa stared, unable to take her eyes from the wound, the Kaffir returned with a wooden block on which Hendrik set his foot.

'Bring me a new voorslach now, Jan,' he said, 'and a small stick.' When these were brought he tied the thin leather lash below the wound and, inserting the stick, twisted it till it bit deeply wrinkling into the flesh, then, running his thumb over the blade of his knife, he bent over the block.

6

But the wound did not heal as it should have done; black marks appeared on his leg and a lump grew at his groin; but still, though he was in great pain, he feared nothing. The swelling would go down, he said, and the sickness pass. It was just that he was still weak from fever, and the operation had tired him. Ach, God, he sweated still as he thought of what he had done to himself, and of how he had tried while he did it to pretend that he was doing it to another; tried by sheer will-power to consider his foot as if it was something apart and detached from himself while he cut at it. And twice since then he had to scrape away the dead flesh from the wound, using more turpentine and sprinkling the raw surface with finely powdered sugar. It was astonishing how much blood could come from so small an extremity when the great veins had been severed and the muscles exposed; but most had been lost as he rode back; his horse's off-elbow had been so drenched with blood that it had run down the inside of his leg till it reached the hoof. Hendrik kept thinking over the last fortnight, considering it in detail from the first time he had seen the giraffe up to his accident and its death, to the dressing of his wound and of how, when they had gone to fetch the giraffe, one of the Kaffirs had found the top of his toe lying on the ground by the ant-hole where his horse had fallen.

All day now he sat propped up against the high back wheel of his wagon with his Bible open on his knees, watching the Kaffir who was breying the skin.

It was just as he had dreamed it would be. There it was in strips, hanging over the limb of the hartekoal. Round and round the Kaffir went, leaning against the long stick, pressing against it as he circled till the heavy stone was high above his head. Then as the stick was withdrawn the stone came uncurling down, untwisting slowly at first, gaining speed till it spun so fast that he could hardly see it turn, then hanging poised for a moment before going back on itself in the opposite direction till it came to rest and the thongs which were now nearly dry rattled against each other.

To try to reduce the inflammation in his foot Hendrik sent out a Kaffir to get a buck and bring it back alive. This was done, and the still warm stomach taken out and placed over his foot, which eased his pain, but did no more than alleviate it, for the warm stomach of a buck was in no way equal to that of a goat, especially one that had been grazing on the speckboom bushes, which was what the Boers always used in these cases. Yet it was something to gain relief even for an hour or two, and to this end his Kaffirs hunted, bringing back wounded buck tied and struggling on their horses so that their master, his foot hidden in the steaming paunch, could rest in comparative comfort.

And still the breying went on, for with whips everything depended on this, and good was not good enough — for Hendrik these riems must be perfect — but at last it was done and the native, undoing a couple of riems, brought them over to him for his inspection.

'Is it good, baas?' he asked.

Hendrik fingered the riems. The leather was white-grained, and supple, a few hairs still clung to the riems, but they felt greasy and good to his accustomed fingers as he kneaded them.

'Ja, it is good,' he said, as he continued to hold them, running them through his palm and bending them this way and that. 'Make loose,' he said. 'They are well breyed, and will make good whips.'

The long rope of hide was undone into its component parts which were tied into bundles of a dozen each, by a strip of thong being threaded through the holes that had joined them to each other.

Hendrik examined each one, throwing them aside as he finished, till he appeared to be surrounded by a heap of slim white snakes.

'Hang them up,' he said, when he had done.

'The baas is pleased? The baas thinks I have breyed them well?' the Kaffir asked.

'Ja, you have done well. They are the best riems you have ever breyed, but that is because I have sat here watching you.

'Tomorrow, Louisa,' he said, 'I will begin. It will be work for my hands while I lie sick, and I think I shall make them a little thicker than is my custom, so that their bite will be deeper. I will sleep now,' he said, 'for I am tired,' and, easing himself, he lay down to rest.

That night he raved, frightening Louisa and the Kaffirs with his words. Sannie, Zwart Piete and the kameel were all one in his mind. The two hunts were confused as the pictures of the one were superimposed on pictures of the other. Louisa and her coming child he cursed as the cause of his undoing, and then towards dawn, before it, when the night was at its coldest, he died.

Next day they buried Hendrik van der Berg. There was no sorrow in the hearts of those who stood about his grave, no regret. He had been like a mountain about which they had clustered, awed by its magnitude, and they missed him as a mountain would be missed by those who had dwelt under its shadow. No one had loved Hendrik van der Berg; he had been too strong, too overbearing to be loved.

They dug a deep hole by the hartekoal; it was a landmark that could be seen for miles. So like his son Herman, and his friend Jappie de Jong, Hendrik lay under one of these giants, a tree that was perhaps five hundred or more years old.

They buried him by that tree because it seemed the obvious place for the grave, and one which could be easily found again. And the place they chose for the hole was the centre of the circle of grass which was surrounded by the path tramped bare by the Kaffir who had breyed the riems.

The short grass was covered with flies that, crawling over the fragments of fat and hair which had fallen from the skin, rose and buzzed about the men who dug. Having made the grave, they lowered Hendrik into it with the riems he was to have made into whips, the strips of kameel hide, because they were hanging from a branch of the tree and were ready to hand.

CHAPTER XXVI

I

WHEN the men sent by Rinkals to watch Hendrik returned to say that he had lost the spoor and was lying sick in a native kraal, the old man laughed. 'Ai, I have smitten him, baas,' he said, 'his teeth are drawn. Far indeed can I spit my venom and very precise are my expectorations. Yet,' seeing Sannie's face, he went on, 'do not fear, inkoose. You are safe with me. Rest content in the bosom of your Little Cloud; for where I have spat as a gentle warning I can strike, and I will send these fools back to their place.'

Turning to the warriors, he said, 'Dogs, when your hounds run on a blood spoor do they return till the buck is down? Beware,' he said, 'lest I turn you into jackals and put jackal pups into the wombs of your expectant wives. Nor would this surprise them, for the sons of jackals are jackals. Return,' he screamed, 'follow him back. Ai, follow him to the very kraal where he lives, and when it is over come to me.'

Picking up their spears the men left and Rinkals continued to search the seams of his kaross for vermin while his women served him beer.

Sannie put her hand on Zwart Piete's arm. 'Let us go on,' she said. 'Let us flee on.'

'Nie, mie Sannie, we have fled far enough. I am at bay. Before God, it is not my nature to stand pursuit. So far have I run and no farther will I go till this thing be done. I will wait for your husband here.'

Looking up from the kaross Rinkals said, 'He will not come, baas. He is sick and has gone home.'

'He will return,' Zwart Piete said.

'Ai, the trap is baited with meat.' Rinkals shot a quick glance at Sannie and laughed till he choked. 'But much lies between the old lion and his kill. Fear not, Lord, but wait. We live in comfort here and your hunting is good. Leave events to me who am capable of managing them and enjoy the fruit of your courage; for there is a wall of spears about you and the milk of my intelligence is warm for you and your woman.'

2

When the watchers sent by Rinkals at last saw the end of Hendrik they were pleased, for now their work was done. Trotting without haste northwards, along the game paths and native tracks, they pondered on what they had seen.

The man they had been sent to spy upon was dead: of this they were certain, for they had watched him buried and seen his wagon, inspanned, go back on its tracks.

Ai, the old wizard would be pleased, and perhaps reward them. Often, as they had stood hidden, observing Hendrik van der Berg, they had wondered why they had not been allowed to kill him; it would have been so easy. Not once, but a hundred times, they could have done this as he hunted alone, but their instructions had been specific: he was to be watched only, and on no account was he to be harmed.

Once again the doctor's reputation rose as they realised that he must have foreseen this end; in their minds there was no doubt that the death of this man was due to a spell which had been put upon him, and they were certain that while they had watched the old wizard had been working for his destruction.

Ai, without doubt the white man's gun had been be-witched, and while they waited, hidden in the trees, the old wizard, squatting by his fire, had made strong medicine and sent the lost ones to do this thing.

So they ran on rejoicing, they were young men with wives, soon they would be home, soon they would see their herds on the hills and be back among their friends. This watching had been a dull business, and one unsuited to those who were warriors. What they liked was to hunt and to fight. To kill swiftly and not to hang, furtive as jackals, skulking round the camp of an enemy.

3

When Rinkals received their news he smiled, baring his toothless gums and nodding his head till his rat tails of clay-smeared hair swung to and fro.

'So you see,' he said, 'my mouti is stronger than your spears, for sitting here alone, without moving, I have turned the white man's gun against him, and he who has killed so many by it is dead of it himself. Truly,' he went on, 'in all this land there is no one who for either power or wisdom can compare with me. I am indeed like an elephant among spring hares.'

To Sannie and Zwart Piete the news was more than welcome, for they both had feared that which might so easily have come upon them. For Hendrik was a strong man, and it was his right to try to kill the man who had stolen his wife. Thus they had been caught in the cleft stick of their own act and able only to run or fight. And now came the news that he was dead of an accident, that he had been struck down before he could harm them further; and the ghost of Sannie's unhappiness was laid. It could rise no more and she would no longer lie in Zwart Piete's arms, trembling at her fears; for ever since she had come with him this had been her over-mastering emotion, swamping even the love she bore him; this terror of being taken back and again possessed by the man who was in law her owner and her husband. Day after day, when she had least expected it, the thought of this possibility had come to her, striking her a sudden blow, making her feel sick, turning her bowels to water, so that she had to lean bent over for support till she had conquered her terror.

And it was over; the man who had used and abused her was dead, and gaiety that she had not known since her girlhood came, like a bird, back into her life.

'Then we can go back, Piete,' she said.

'Ja, we will go back, for you must have your children, and this I promise you, mie Sannie, that your children by Herman and Hendrik van der Berg shall be as my own, as much to me as those of mine that you will bear. Are you coming with us when we return, Rinkals?' he asked.

'I will come, baas,' Rinkals said. 'Our paths are one, twisted together like a plaited whip. You, the yellow bastard, the woman you have brought with you and I are tied by inseverable bonds and yoked by strong powers. But listen well to my counsel before you start. Where you go I will follow, but here, where you stand now, is a forking of the ways, and I say stay here and trade and go later for those children that are not sprung from your loins. Yet as I speak I can read it in your face that you will not stay, that because you love this woman you will go back. Then we will go, lord; but profit well by your time; love much and long, for the days of your loving may be few. Look at the sun as it rises, watch the moon riding on her back through the night sky, for I see death and war. Ai, the cast bones tell me of death though whose I do not know, nor how many will die. And yet,' he went on, 'what is death? — It is a change, the passing from one state into another — no more than that — and it is foolish to fear it. Also it may be better to die young, having known the love of a woman and the madness of war, than to sink struggling like beasts caught in the mud of age. War and love, these two are the greatest things, and having known them you can know no more, nor can they be repeated in all their glory. Ai, baas, as you grow old so do you forget. Let us go on, then, lord, boldly and without fear, boldly as elephants, for what must be will come to pass, and though by my magic I can do much to avert disaster, there are some things which are beyond me; this, being very old and wise, I acknowledge freely to such as I can trust.'

4

It was not long after Hendrik had left Canaan with Louisa and his servants that news came in of a predicant who was on his way to Lemansdorp, where he had relations. He would be the first of his kind to come north, and, as Tante Anna said, would collect a fine harvest of souls for the Lord and many payments in cash and kind for himself as a reward for his long and tedious journey. Tante Anna could well have gone longer without taking communion, but among the devout people of her race she stood apart in this, isolated by her philosophy and the strength of her character. Her scepticism, the natural outcome of her experiences, had resulted in a wide tolerance that took exception at nothing but the bigoted cruelties inflicted in the name of religion and the hypocrisy of some of its ministers. Black crows that demanded tithes, who stood watching disaster, rubbing their hands softly together. Ach, ja, a predicant was neither a man nor a woman, but something between the two and inferior to either. Their fingers were always soft and often moist with sweat, their faces beardless and their tongues smoother than polished brass.

Still a nachtmaal was a nachtmaal, and people would go to it from all round; from Canaan, from Paul Pieter's place, from Tricharts, and from other places still more distant. There would be a great reunion, where the men would talk and trade and women show each other the children they had borne since their last meeting. The young people would dance and make merry, despite the disapproval of their elders, and out of their meeting would come weddings and more children. Ja, there would be merrymaking and talk and trading on the Friday, and on the Saturday they would all prepare for Sunday, getting out their best clothes, and then on Monday they would inspan and turn homewards, going, like the spokes of a wheel, outwards, each towards the place whence they had come.

She wondered how many children there would be for baptism: certainly a great number, and many of them three or more years old. Some would even profit by this event to get married under the auspices of the church instead of by the landroost of the district. All this would be most interesting to watch, and something to remember when it was over. It would be a fine spectacle to see so many wagons assembled, and a veritable town of tents go up. There would be hundreds of wagons there, all drawn up, lying side by side; the whole might of the Boers in the north would be congregated together, and by performing her duty towards the children in her charge, by taking them to the baptism, she would be able to see her grandson and the widow Coetzee that he had married. If she went to Lemansdorp she could not help seeing them, nor could she, under such conditions, be accused of a curiosity, which, as all who knew her would agree, was entirely foreign to her nature. This charge which had been levelled against her at various times enraged Anna de Jong. Not only for its obvious injustice, but at the stupidity of those who made it, being unable to differentiate between an idle curiosity and a permissible interest in the affairs of one's neighbours. As if a woman of her social standing could be curious.

Still it would be pleasant to see Gert and Martha and, having met them, they could hardly help asking her to visit them. It would be very good to see Gert again, watch him being set in his place, for a cross-eyed man who married a rich woman was a fool and as helpless as a buck gripped in the coils of a python. Certainly a wife richer than her husband was a bruised reed on which to lean, one which would go into his hand and pierce it if he were not careful. Life was certainly most interesting, and the immediate pattern of it nearing some completion. Of this she became more and more certain as she sat thinking of Hendrik van der Berg, of Sannie who had been his wife, and of Zwart Piete du Plessis who had taken her.

Ach, ja, something would come of all this, and what came she would be there to see.

For the nachtmaal she would wear the new white linen kappie that she had made for just such an occasion. Never before had she made so fine a one, one which had so many tucks, gathers and pleats. And she would travel in her own wagon, with her own span, as befitted a widow of her position. She only wished that its paint had been fresh. It had been so beautiful when they set out, with a sky-blue body and orange-scarlet wheels, and of all that colour little remained intact except some that clung to the back of the spokes and such other places as were protected, and even there it was peeling.

Poor Jappie had painted the wagon so happily, whistling as he worked. They had set out so gaily. And now he was dead and the paintwork scorched and blistered.

Still the wagons of the others would be in the same condition, and certainly her oxen were more beautifully matched, not only in colour, but even to the shape of their horns, all curving upwards in a wide sweep from their foreheads. A full span of sixteen she would take, and if the wagon was paintless the tent at least would be clean; it was already prepared, washed and rewashed till it was as white as a linen sheet. From where she sat she could see it glistening as her servants stretched it over the wooden hoops of its frame.

In ten days now they would be off, and she hoped that they would arrive on the Thursday before it was dark, so that she would be able to choose a good place to outspan, one well

in the centre where she would be able to see and to hear all
that went on. Nor would she hurry her beasts; they must
arrive fat and sleek, for not in all that vast concourse would
there be any oxen better than her own and few to equal them.

As Johannes van Reenen came in she called to him and
asked who he was leaving behind to look after the place in
their absence.

'No one, Anna,' he said. 'All are going.'

'Then who will see to the cattle and horses?' she asked.

'The servants and Kaffirs who remain. We shall not be
long away.'

'And is this wise when we know that we are threatened?'

'We threatened?' Johannes echoed. 'Surely you do not
think that we are still in danger? Surely you do not still
believe that Zwart Piete, who stole my daughter from Hendrik van der Berg, is to be trusted? What confidence can be
placed in a man who runs off with another's wife?'

'And if you took this running off so hard, Johannes, why
did you not join in the pursuit?' Tante Anna asked.

'Though she did wrong, she is still my daughter, and I
stand by my blood. But if she hated Hendrik as you say,
why did she not come to me, instead of running away with
a landless man?'

'This is a profitless discussion, one that we have dealt with
not once but many times,' Tante Anna said. 'But apart from
Zwart Piete's warning, the fact remains that Hendrik and
Martinus saw armed Kaffirs.'

'Ja, they saw them, but it was long ago, and they put
them to flight. That action finished it. Before that there
might have been some danger, but now there is none. Besides,' he went on, 'if I told some to remain I should not be
obeyed. I should be laughed at, and they would say, "Oom
Johannes, you are getting old, or is it that you think we are
children to be frightened by spooks?"'

'And yet I am not sure. It is in my heart that all should
not go.'

'Well, Anna, who do you think would remain? Can you think of any who would miss this gathering? And if they will not remain, they will not. This talk of yours is woman's talk and foolishness.'

'Ja, it is woman's talk, and it seems to me that sometimes women talk to some purpose, and that where men see only the distant mountains it is the women who see the small night-adder curled up in the path at their feet.'

5

That night Louisa returned to Canaan with the tale of Hendrik's death and the manner of his passing. Her shoulders sore from the beating her mistress had given her, she related everything down to the smallest detail.

'Can I stay, mevrou?' she pleaded. 'From now on I am changed.'

'Ja, you can stay. You have been beaten but I think it is time that you married, Louisa, and when I have some leisure I will find someone that will marry you.' She paused and went on: 'Do you know why I say you can stay, Louisa?'

The coloured girl did not answer.

'You can stay because we are soon going to the nachtmaal, and there is no one who can iron out my kappies as you do. No, not even I can do it so well. Now leave me, for I must think.'

So Hendrik was dead; everything which had been his now belonged to his children and to Sannie. For awhile she sat perfectly still. Sannie could now return and Zwart Piete could go in peace. They would all be reunited again, and happiness, which a few hours ago had seemed so distant, was now in view.

One thing she must do at once, and that was, taking Jakalaas with her, go to Hendrik's house and collect his papers, his Bible and his devotional books. These his children should take with them so that their baptism could be entered on the fly leaf of the Holy Word with all formality. This they would be proud of one day, for it would be something to have been baptised at the first nachtmaal in the north.

6

Driving round to the back of the house because Jakalaas said that this door was the easiest to force, Anna de Jong got down from her cart and waited for him to open it. It was strange to be here alone, with Hendrik dead and Sannie gone, strange to see the house so much the same, with even the dirty crockery left lying as it had been put down, and the clothes still hanging from wooden pegs driven into the interstices of the mud-plastered walls. There were the beds they had slept in, there were the meilie cobs hanging from the rafters among riems, broken saddlery and strips of biltong. Tobacco in leaf and some in roll hung there also, and the half carcass of a sheep which had long since gone rotten and been eaten away by maggots.

Going to the window, she opened the shutters, lifting the heavy bars that held them and dropping them on the floor.

The books she sought were stuck in a corner where the angles of the rafters joined the heavy tiebeams which ran across the house from wall to wall.

With a last look at the room she went out, glad to be free of a house that was so filled with painful memories. She thought of the meals she had eaten there with Sannie silent, while Hendrik boasted loudly and a Kaffir maid wielded a fly whisk, made from the tail of a wildebeeste, to prevent the swarming flies from settling on the food they ate.

With the hymn books and papers under her arm, she went out into the bright sunlight and bent down to brush away the fleas which, having bred in the empty house, swarmed hungrily up her dress and legs.

The Bible she knew would be in the wagon that lay outspanned a few yards away. It looked very desolate with its tent torn and the trek gear lying stretched out awry. Suddenly she wished that she was home. There was a menace about this house below the berg; it was as if the stones alone knew what had happened here and were trying to speak. Hurrying away, she caught her foot in a chain that was sunk in the grass and fell, her ankle twisting under her.

'What a fool I am,' she thought, as she rose to her knees, 'not to have remembered the lion's chain.'

'You are hurt, mevrou,' Jakalaas said, running towards her.

'Ja, I am hurt. I cannot walk,' she said as she felt her leg.

'What shall I do?' the old Kaffir asked.

'First you will get the big Bible from Baas Hendrik's wagon-box. Then you will fetch water from the fontein, and while I attend to my hurt you will seek help. Go to Baas Martinus and bring back enough Kaffirs to raise me into my cart. And listen, you skelm, all this is due to your verdamnat lion. Had there been no lion, there would have been no chain, and I should not have fallen. I wish now that I had let Baas Hendrik beat you. Thus it always happens that by doing good one harvests evil. Go, fool, get the book and the water, and then the help. It will take four strong men to raise me, and I would be back before it is dark.'

CHAPTER XXVII

I

TANTE ANNA'S accident did not prevent her going to Lemansdorp, for, as she said, she could rest on the bed in her wagon as comfortably as in her bed at home; and apart from being safe from the Kaffirs, who, in her opinion, would come marauding as soon as they knew that the Boers were gone, she would have the changing scenery to look at as they travelled. Besides which, was she, one of the foremost of the voortrekkers, to be defeated by so small a thing as a wrenched ankle? So with Louisa to attend her personally and accompanied by her servants she left with the others, her wagon following that of her brother-in-law as it climbed the mountain road and swung west towards Lemansdorp, a unit in one of the many long lines of wagons that were approaching that place from all sides; wagons whose occupants went their way rejoicing at the change, at the prospect of seeing old friends, of making new ones, and at being able at last to have their children baptised. With much singing, laughing and clapping of whips the men drove their spans or rode beside the high turning wheels which carried all that they held dear.

Gaily, the young men made their horses dance about the white-tented wagons that had borne them so far and staunchly, firing their guns in pleasure at any encounter, while the girls bandied jokes with them and debated among themselves on what finery they would wear, arguing with each other about the respective merits of the frocks at their disposal, getting out their small parasols, and borrowing combs of tortoiseshell and ribbons with which to dress their hair.

So they advanced over the rough mountainous roads, the wagons riding lightly, for they were unloaded, the people happy and the oxen fat and fresh. At night, they sat or stood singing by their fires to the accompaniment of such instruments as they had, many clustering round the one who played. It was a holiday and a festival. Its spirit was abroad, communicating itself even to the beasts and to the Kaffirs that tended them.

2

Tante Anna had been right about the numbers of the people who were gathered at Lemansdorp. Already when they of Canaan arrived there were two hundred wagons outspanned, and each hour more arrived.

Whips and guns cracked, oxen bellowed and fought, children strayed, got lost and were found again, and the smoke from a hundred cooking fires sweetened the air with the scent of burning wood and dung.

Many there were whom Tante Anna knew, and many that she did not know. Also there were many whom she had known and after whom she inquired who had, since she had last seen them, died of one thing or another.

There were even doppers at Lemansdorp, who, though they did not hold with the new and reformed church, had still come, drawn by the desire to be among so great a concourse of people and to hear such news as there was. These men were easily recognisable, for they clung to the old ways, not only in theology, but also in their dress; and, scorning belts or braces, held up their trousers, which were of the klapbrook kind with a flap in front, by means of draw-strings; and as they wore their jackets shorter than other men and their trousers always sagged, they invariably showed an expanse of white shirt between the bottom of the one and the top of the other, so that from behind they looked like the white-rumped springbok of the plains.

One in particular, Andries Beyers by name, pleased Tante Anna very much, so much that she kept watching for his passing, for he was a very big young man who wore a very short coat of blue-and-red striped nankeen and breyed leather trousers that only reached half-way down his calf. He was the Samson of the doppers, and was said to be able to lift a big Kaffir in each hand and to deal with sacks of grain, loading them onto a wagon as if they were parcels.

Never anywhere had such a variety of clothes been seen, for many had been made of anything that was available, irrespective of its suitability to the purpose, and these made a curious contrast with the garments of others which were as neat as if their wearers were still in the colony.

White, black and coloured folk seethed about the tents and wagons greeting each other, and asking tidings of their friends. Inevitably there was much talk of hunting, cattle and crops, but always, no matter how the conversation went, it turned in the end to the Kaffirs and the English. Men told of how the English had come to Natal, annexing it; of how Mapela and Makapaan had raided and murdered. Not once, but many times, were Potgieter, who had been flayed alive in the presence of his groom, and Piet Retief, whom the Zulus had killed as he and his men stood unarmed in the king's great kraal, spoken of and mourned. But of all that was said the story of those women and children, murdered and eaten in the Zoutpansberg, came nearest to them, for they had known many of them, and the Zoutpansberg was not far off — less than two hundred miles away. The commando which had ridden out to avenge them had found some of their blood-stained clothes and portions of their bodies, shoulders and arms which had been roasted on the spit. When this tale was told the men looked longingly at their loaded guns that leant against their wagons.

It was into this vast company that Zwart Piete and Sannie rode one day. Accompanied by de Kok, in charge of their pack-horses and loose ones, he rode confident that his reputation for daring would be enough to stay any insult that might be put upon his woman.

With the butt of his long gun resting on his thigh he rode his grey horse among them, moving aside for no one, but pulling up his beast and waiting till they drew away from his angry eyes.

'Zwart Piete du Plessis the hunter is here,' they said, and the men who did not know him stared, surprised that he should be so young, while the women pulled aside the curtains of their tents and envied Sannie.

To everyone he asked only one thing:

'Where is Mevrou de Jong's wagon? She is here from Canaan.'

And when they told him he rode on till he found her.

'Hearing of Hendrik's death, we have come for Sannie's children, Tante Anna,' he said. 'It seems that they are with you.'

'They are with me, Zwart Piete.'

'And you will take Sannie?'

'I will take her. But where are you going? Have you not come far enough? Paul Pieters, your uncle, and all your friends are here.'

'Have I friends, Anna de Jong?' Zwart Piete asked bitterly. 'That we shall see when I ride among them. I came not to pass the time of day with doubtful friends, but to seek the children for whom Sannie pines, and to ride with them into the east, which is now my country, and where an adulterer, if he can ride and shoot, is still a man.'

'You are hard, Piete.'

'I have been hunted like a dog, Tante Anna. I am angry, and now I have returned to find the whole world mad. Take Sannie,' he said, 'for I must have words with Johannes van Reenen.'

'With Johannes?' Tante Anna said. 'But why? For now that Hendrik is dead he will be at peace with you.'

'I did not come to discuss my affairs with van Reenen. Those can wait,' he said. 'And for what I have done I alone am answerable. No, Tante Anna, I wish to see him that I may assure myself of his sanity, to be certain that he is not mad.'

'Mad, Piete?'

'Ja, mad to have left Canaan as he has with all your houses, your beasts and flocks open to the Kaffirs. Mad to have left some of his folk without protection. Marietje was there with her husband when I came. Where is Johannes?' he repeated. 'Now that I have left Sannie with you I must find him. He must return, or give me men to take back.'

'You think there is danger, Piete?'

'I do not think, I know: I can smell it in the air. Where are the Kaffirs that were walking when I was last there? The place is empty of life, Tante Anna; there is no movement, save that of the herders, who will run at the first spear. Marietje, I think, is safe, for I have sent her with Martinus and my Kaffir, Rinkals, who is very wise, into the hills, where they will hide till our return. But what of the homes and the beasts? Did you work in order to throw away what you have done? Would you leave your breeding herds to be meat for Kaffirs?' he asked. 'As I rode through Canaan,' he went on, 'a calm like a pall was spread widely over it. Before all things I am a hunter, and I know the menace that is hidden. Where is Johannes van Reenen, I say? Almost do I wish Hendrik van der Berg alive, for he, obstinate as he was, would not have been such a fool as this.'

'Oom Johannes is over there,' Tante Anna said. 'He is with the other leaders talking to the predicant.'

Wheeling his grey, his gun still on his hip, Zwart Piete rode towards the group she had pointed out.

'Johannes van Reenen,' he said, 'I would speak with you.'

'You would speak with me?' van Reenen said. 'And how can you ride in like this and demand audience, you who should come humbly?'

'This is the adulterer of whom we have heard,' the leader of the doppers said. 'This is Zwart Piete, the son of Satan. Are we to be polluted by listening to such as he?'

'Ja, I am Zwart Piete du Plessis, whom men call the hunter, and I have come to warn the folk of Canaan; and if I am the son of Satan, you are the sons of fools. Listen, van Reenen' — he turned to Sannie's father. 'If you value your homes and your cattle, send some men back; let them draw lots if they do not wish to go.'

'There is no danger. Had there been danger, would we have left Martinus and his wife, who is sick? And did they believe in danger when you told them of it? It is in my mind that they only laughed at you, told you that you were mad and dreaming. The Kaffirs round Canaan are tame; they are not like those of the Zoutpansberg or Natal.'

'So mad did Martinus and Marietje think me, mynheer, that they followed me into the mountains, where I have hidden them.'

'They have gone?' van Reenen said. 'Then there are no white people there to watch over our farms?'

'There are none, but there remain your riches in livestock and furniture. If you value these go back, or give me men and I will lead them.'

'Do you think men will follow you?' the dopper asked.

'If there is danger they will follow me,' Zwart Piete said, 'for I am well known as a Kaffir fighter.'

'I will do nothing,' van Reenen said. 'Nor will I discuss the matter with you. We are gathered here together that we may worship, and God will protect those things which are ours in our absence.'

'Then your ruin is upon your own head,' Piete said, 'for it is in my heart that the Philistines will be upon you, and like sheep without a shepherd your flocks will be taken and your possessions scattered.' Raising his voice, he went on: 'Once again, I tell you, once again I caution you publicly. More than this I cannot do.'

'More you can do,' the dopper said. 'You can leave our company and go back to the wilds, where you belong. I also can warn,' he continued, 'and if you remain you will be hunted out.'

'Hunt, then,' Zwart Piete said. 'When you are ready you will find me off-saddled over there.' He pointed with the muzzle of his gun to a small tree which stood apart from the outspan. 'Those who seek Zwart Piete will find him easily,' he said. 'Tot seins, mynheeren. When you want me, I shall be there; and I think before long you will come begging with your hats in your hands for my assistance.'

For a moment he sat looking at them, staring into the eyes of those around him till they lowered them, and then without a word he left them, and they saw him off-saddle his horse and watched his servant take the gear from the backs of his pack-horses and stack it. His words and bearing had made them uneasy. This young man was no liar; he had nothing to gain by lying.

3

As Tante Anna had anticipated, it was not long before her grandson came her way. Gert Kleinhouse was more than ready to make peace with his grandmother, whom he feared greatly. In addition to this she was old — and was he not her nearest relation?

If it was only a matter of pigs he would give her some, for he now had many, having obtained them from a neighbouring settlement; and if she insisted he would also give her a cow, not perhaps quite as good a one as that which he had driven over the mountains as a present to Martha Coetzee, not as beautiful or as tame as Bloometjie, but nevertheless a good cow. Surely this would satisfy her; and then when she died, which might be soon, he would get back the pigs and the cow with their progeny. It was in a sense no more than a loan — and people as stout as Anna de Jong could not go on forever.

When he found her confined to her bed, his heart was very sad. Poor woman, no doubt this was the beginning of the end.

'I am sorry, ouma,' he said, 'to find you like this.'

'Like what?' she said.

'So sick, ouma.'

'I am not sick; it is merely that I fell and twisted my foot.'

'Ach, ja,' he said, 'no doubt it was due to a rush of blood to the head. You have too much blood, ouma. I have always said that you had too much blood,' he went on.

'It seems to me, Gert, that it is for me to say whether I have too much blood or not.'

'Ja, natuurlik, it is for you to say, but anyone can see that it is true.'

'And since when have you become a doctor of medicine, Gert?'

'I am no doctor, but what I see I see; and now before we go further I wish to say that I am sorry for what has passed. I am very alone in the world, and I am of your blood.' He paused. 'I wish therefore to make amends. If it is a matter of pigs, you shall have them, two small sows and a young boar.'

'And what about my cow Bloometjie. Are my cows to lose quarters for nothing? Are they to be driven at a speed over the hills without recompense?'

'How many quarters did she lose?' Gert asked.

'Two quarters.'

'Then for those two quarters I will give you a cow. It is too much, I know. There is no justice in it, but you are my grandmother, and I would be on terms with you again.'

'How old is this cow that you would give me?' Tante Anna asked.

'She is six.'

'Then what is the matter with her?'

'Nothing is the matter. She is a beautiful cow, one that gives much milk.'

'Marriage has certainly changed you, Gert, for where you were mean you are now generous, and where you were small you are now big. Truly your offer melts my heart — three young pigs and a cow. And yet it is said that the leopard cannot change his spots, nor the Ethiopian the colour of his skin. It says this in the twenty-third verse of the thirteenth chapter of the Book of Lamentations. Remember also, Gert, that I knew your father and your uncle. They were slim men and full of guile.'

'My heart is clean,' Gert said, 'and to prove it I would ask you to come and rest with us when the nachtmaal is over. Stay with us till you are well,' he said, 'and let Martha, my wife, nurse you.'

'I thank you, Gert. It is in my heart that I have misjudged you, and I will accept your offer in the spirit in which it is made. On Monday, therefore, I will come to you, bringing my maid, my servants and the children of Sannie van Reenen, who will stay with me till her affairs are settled.' Gert stood still staring at his feet.

'I said we would come Monday, Gert,' Tante Anna repeated.

'It was you I asked and not Sannie, the adulteress. Think of my wife. Ja,' Gert said. 'Martha is pure.'

'If it gives you pleasure, Gert, I will think of your wife, an ugly woman; and, since she married you, a foolish one. It is in my heart that she has not been greatly tempted to sin. For in adultery the man must be willing, he cannot be dragged to bed on a riem. Shall I go on thinking, Gert,' she asked, 'or may I now consider my cattle and my properties in the Colony? And Gert,' she added, 'did you think that Sannie would leave Zwart Piete to stay with you? Nie, nie, jong, she will stay with her man; that is her place. Only Frikkie and Jacoba come with me.'

4

When the nachtmaal was over the people dispersed and van Reenen led back his folk to Canaan. They were less gay now than when they had set out, for Zwart Piete's words had gone far; and many thought now, that it might be too late, that they should not have come, that some, at any rate, should have remained to watch over the property of the others.

Behind them, riding apart, came the outcasts, the adulterers, with their servant and the two coloured men that Piete had borrowed from his uncle Paul Pieters who, partially convinced by Piete's statements, saw in this, if he were right, a way of reinstating his nephew. 'Call on me if you need me,' he had said, 'for though openly I am against you, my heart is yours whatever you have done or may yet do.'

But long before they reached Canaan Johannes van Reenen saw a small figure coming towards him. It was that of an old Kaffir, one who was a stranger to him. As the wagons approached he stood in the middle of the road and halted them with upraised hands.

'Greetings, white man,' he said. 'Is my master with you? For I have tidings for him.'

'Who is your master?' van Reenen asked. 'And who are you?'

'My master is called Zwart Piete the hunter, and I am known by many names, Little Cloud That Comes Before the Storm being one of them, Little Flower another.'

'And what do you want?'

'I want nothing; I am too old and too wise for worldly wants. Words do I deal in, and spells and magic, but this I would say, white man: call upon your men and let them go in front. Call also on my master and let him lead them, for much evil has befallen under the berg. The houses are burnt, the servants are dead, and the cattle driven off. All this I saw from my hiding place, where I remained with the sick white woman and her husband. Also while I was there I cured her by my magic, and she is now whole, though still weak.'

'We have been raided, you say? So he was right after all.'

'Who was right, lord?'

'Your master, Zwart Piete.'

'Ja, he was right if he warned you. That young man has much wisdom. In a short space of time he has learnt much from me.' As Rinkals spoke Zwart Piete, Sannie, de Kok and the coloured men rode up; they had recognised him.

'So, Rinkals, it has come?' Zwart Piete said.

'It has come, master.'

'If you want me, I am ready,' Zwart Piete cried. 'I will swallow the words which have been said, for I know that I did wrong, and what I have bought I will pay for.'

'That is well spoken, Piete,' van Reenen said, holding out his hand, 'for in war there is no man I would sooner have beside me.'

'I will not be beside you, van Reenen. If I am with you in this, it must be I who am in command.'

'You are over young to command.'

'Do you count the days of a commander? In war, Oom Johannes, I am old,' he said bitterly, 'for all my life I have known little else. Come, call up your people and ask them if they will follow me. Sound your horn and let them come. Bid them span out while we make a plan. Let them all come,' he added, 'not only the men, but the women also, for this is a matter for everyone, since not a single head of stock remains in Canaan.'

Drawing a cow's horn from his belt, van Reenen sent his call wailing over the mountains, and the people assembled quickly while the servants, their dark faces grey with fear, spanned out and stood herding their respective spans.

5

For a moment Zwart Piete sat his horse, looking at the bearded faces of those who stood about him, the older men grimly ill at ease fingering their guns, the young men and boys staring at him in wonder. Even to those who knew him well this man was different now, a thing of steel and flame whose nervous energy flowed through him and was communicated to the restive horse he gripped between his thighs. This was Zwart Piete the hunter, the man whose name was a power in the north. They saw to what he owed his achievements and, forgetful of his crime, were grateful for his company in this crisis.

The neigh of Zwart Piete's grey, confronted by so many strange stallions, broke the silence and, quieting him, his master began to speak.

'People of Canaan, you know me,' he said. 'You know what I have done. I took this woman' — he pointed to Sannie — 'from Hendrik van der Berg. I have her and will hold her; also, lest you think I am ashamed, I will tell you now that what I did I would do again. But this is war, and it is for you to choose if you would be led by me or if, because you are in doubt as to the ways of my life, you would prefer another. It is your choice. I have led too long to serve, and if you do not want me to lead you I will turn aside and leave you. Think well before you speak and ask your women, for this is no light matter; all your beasts are dead or gone, and your houses are burnt. My plan,' he went on, 'is this: that I take the young men with me and recover the stock while van Reenen and the others go into laager, for it may well be that the whole country is up and that right through the north men and women lie murdered on the veld and the smoke of their homes rises high into the skies.

'If you do not want me,' he said, 'there are others who will. There are many who in such times will welcome Zwart Piete the hunter, and those that he has with him.'

As he finished speaking the Boers burst into argument, some being for and some against him.

Dismounting, Zwart Piete stood leaning against his saddle with his rein looped over his arm talking to van Reenen and Rinkals, while Sannie and de Kok prepared food and Paul Pieters' men looked to their weapons, firing their guns and reloading them with slugs.

As Zwart Piete had known, it was the women who were for him and who convinced the men that he was right. Whatever he had done, he was a man, a leader, decisive and energetic, and surely one bold enough to carry off a woman from Hendrik van der Berg would be able to get back their stolen beasts.

Their houses could be rebuilt, but their herds were their very lives and irreplaceable.

At the end of an hour the men came forward.

'We will ride with you,' they said. 'Pick those that you want.'

Slowly, weighing each according to what he knew of him — his age, his appearance, and the quality of his mount — Zwart Piete chose twenty men. They were young men, who, unless he were wrong, would fight and follow without argument.

'Are you ready?' he asked.

'We are ready,' they said.

'Then we will ride. Sannie,' he said, 'you will remain with your father. And Rinkals' — he turned to the old Kaffir — 'guard her with your wisdom, for she is my life; and if I do not return, you will collect that which is owing to me and pay it to her.'

'Lord,' Rinkals said, 'your words are my law. What you say is already done.'

Wheeling his horse, Zwart Piete rode down the steep hillside with his men strung out behind him. They moved off silently, and only the noise of their horses' hoofs on the loose stones was heard.

The women watched them go anxiously, for each of these men was loved by a wife or a mother, and on their success depended the livelihood of all.

CHAPTER XXVIII

I

THE settlement presented a spectacle that made the Boers look at each other in angry dismay. It seemed incredible that in the few days they had been away such a change could have taken place. Only Zwart Piete, riding at their head, smiled grimly, for this was what he had foreseen.

Not a homestead was left standing; all had been fired, and the thatch, falling inwards, had consumed everything that was in the houses, so that only the blackened walls, cracked by the heat of the flames, remained. Buildings were destroyed, trees, felled and uprooted, while their servants, such as they had left in charge of their homes and who had remained faithful to them, lay ridiculously dead, fallen without dignity, grasping with already putrid hands at the spears which pierced them.

The cattle, horses, sheep, goats and donkeys were gone. Dogs, cats and poultry were dead, farming implements broken, and the work of the years they had spent in Canaan was made as nothing and less than nothing, for they were left without even the wherewithal to begin again. There was no living thing in Canaan, and save for the vultures perched on the trees which rose heavily as they came, and the pigeons that wheeled about above their broken cotes, there was no life, no movement. Some buildings still smouldered, and the scent of the acrid smoke mixed with that of the rotting dead was sickly sweet in their nostrils.

Homestead after homestead they passed, and each was

the same, a ruin that still smouldered or was burnt out; in this lay the only difference between one house and another.

The lands, too, were devastated. Here was wanton anger let loose. Here was the result of taking land from the natives and thinking that those who came down from their mountain fastness to stare and to trade, or even to work, were tame.

It was not hard to see what had happened. The Kaffirs had come in three parties, one from each side of the mountain, following its horse-shoe bend, while the third and strongest had come out of the bush. Working inwards towards the centre of the settlement, driving the stolen beasts in front of them, the Kaffirs had met and, merging the cattle into a single herd, had driven them off. Their spoor was like a road; the grass that had been under their feet was crushed and pulverised, and the thorn scrub hung with hairs torn from their tails. Ja, to follow them was easy enough, and it should not be difficult to get them back. But what then? What would happen next? This problem occupied Zwart Piete, for, encouraged by this facile victory, the Kaffirs would undoubtedly return; and the question of ammunition was uppermost in his mind as he rode towards the hills, for save that which the Boers had with them on their persons or in their wagons there was none. The reserves which had been left barrelled in their homes were gone, exploded by the fires, while their pigs of lead were melted down and lost in the wastage of the houses.

2

Riding ahead of his men with three scouts extended on either side of him, Zwart Piete followed along the spoor.

To the main body of young Boers his progress seemed incredibly slow, for he never advanced till his scouts were in possession of every strategical point, and one scout never went forward till he was covered by the guns of the others.

Ach, God, to think that Zwart Piete is as young as we, they said, and yet his movements are as slow and cautious as those of an old man. They were hot, angry and inexperienced, while Piete du Plessis was none of these things. He had come to destroy those who had destroyed, and like an angel of vengeance his spirit soared on slow, strong wings.

As he rode he did not look young, but old; his face was unmoved, like stone, his dark eyes expressionless and pre-occupied, his hands did not tremble, and his movements were deliberate and controlled. Without joy or hope or fear he went forward, and, thinking of nothing but the business that he had on hand, he led his men cautiously through the hills, controlling them with a word or by a gesture when they wished to press on. Beside him rode his servant de Kok and the two that his uncle Paul Pieters had lent him.

On the success of this venture rested Sannie's safety, for within a given space of time blows must be struck, and either the Boers or the Kaffirs must conquer. He thought of what old Jakalaas had said of the naked Kaffirs, for it was these that he feared. They were real men, warriors bred to war, men with nothing to lose and all to gain. How many of them were there? Who was their leader and how were they organised?

Still thinking of the renegade Zulus he went on. Alert for signs of danger, he continued to think of the powder and the lead, of Sannie and the numbers and the qualities of his enemies. Kaffirs he did not fear, Zulus he knew enough of to dread. Their fighting was well organised, they were full of stratagems, and their courage and physique were unsurpassed. Well disciplined and utterly careless of their lives, conscious only of the thirst of their spears, these men were irresistible; unintimidated by the deaths of their comrades, encouraged even by their deaths, the survivors would leap their writhing bodies and plunge into the encounter with their terrible war cry. Bulala! Bulala! was their cry — kill, kill. To kill was their pride — it was the one thing they knew, and with a shortage of ammunition the success of the Boers depended on the ratio between the numbers of the Zulus and the amount of lead and powder at their disposal.

All this, however, was a matter to be considered later; and though he toyed with it in his mind as a problem that would have to be faced, Zwart Piete concentrated on the matter in hand: the recapture of the stolen herds.

3

It was late evening when Jan Schoeman galloped in from the extreme right flank with the news that high up on the berg he had discovered the native stronghold.

'Were you seen?' Zwart Piete asked.

'I was not seen,' he said. 'I left my horse hidden and crawled like a snake on my belly till I was near them. They are ours, Piete,' he said, 'for they feast and suspect nothing.'

'Ja, they are ours if what you say be true.'

'Do you think I lie?' the young man asked.

'No, I do not think that you lie, but it is possible that you deceive yourself.' Piete hesitated for a moment with his eyes fixed on the flat-topped hill that Schoeman had pointed out, and then he said:

'How far is it, Jan?'

'Four or five miles.'

'Then we can do it in an hour.'

'Easily we can do it,' the boy answered.

'Come, we will go,' Piete said, turning his horse. 'We will go and reconnoitre.'

'What, are we going alone?'

'Yes,' Zwart Piete said. 'If they are not prepared we are in no danger.'

It was midnight when Zwart Piete and Jan returned to the waiting Boers.

'What is the news?' they asked. 'Is it good?'

'Ja, it is good. Were it not, you had not seen us, and the credit belongs to Jan.'

'You saw the cattle?'

'We saw some of them, not all, but a big clompie of a thousand head or more; but it was very dark, and at night it is hard to see how many beasts there are in a herd.'

'Ja, it is hard,' they agreed.

'Now, my friends,' Zwart Piete said, 'this is my plan: that we leave our horses at the foot of the berg with four men to watch them, while we climb the mountain, going slowly, with our veldschoen slung about our necks by their laces, arranging to get there before the dawn breaks. We will then attack and wipe these Kaffirs out. I have been right round the mountain top, and on the far side there is a krantz. That is the only place we will leave open, for,' he went on, 'it is only a fool who surrounds an enemy. They will run towards this place, not realising their danger, and will stand to fight there, not with their backs towards a wall, which is good, but with their backs to a void which every now and then they will turn to look at as we press them. Their fear from the rear will become as great or greater than their fear from the front, and thus caught between the two, the fire of our guns and the emptiness of the precipice, their resistance will crumble. Some will run towards us valiantly, trying to fight their way out, while others will endeavour to escape down the steep mountain-side. Are you agreed that this plan is good?' he asked.

'We are agreed,' they said; and, mounting, they followed him into the darkness of the hills to the place he had selected for the horses to wait.

At first the going was easy, but later, as the slopes steepened, they had to fight for their breath to keep up with their leader. Black kloofs were penetrated, moonlit krantzes passed, and still they climbed. The stronghold had been well chosen and, had the Kaffirs been ready for them, was well-nigh impregnable. But they were not ready, and Zwart Piete was a fine and resourceful leader.

Nevertheless, it was jumpy work for those unaccustomed

to war, for they could easily have been ambushed by Kaffirs hidden behind the rocks that were scattered so profusely about the mountain-side or in one of the deep sluits that ran down almost vertically from the narrow terraces that were interspaced among the ridges. Not daring even to whisper, the men climbed with the sweat running from their foreheads into their eyes.

All went well till they reached the top, and then a dog barked, waking the warriors, who should have been on watch, but who, lulled into security by the beer they had drunk and the meat they had eaten, slept by the dying fires. Brandishing their spears, they rushed forward, only to turn back as they saw the Boers, silhouetted against the paling sky, emerge from the blackness of the mountain-side. Not even waiting to throw their weapons, they ran shouting the alarm.

'Put on your shoes,' Zwart Piete cried, 'and charge before they can form up.'

Cursing and shouting as they ran, the Boers closed in, and to the surprised Kaffirs seemed much more numerous than they really were.

As the newly awakened warriors ran from their huts the Boers shot them down and, surrounding the village, fired the huts and forced them back towards the krantz. The Kaffirs fought as Zwart Piete had said they would, spasmodically, rushing forward, then losing courage and turning back, and each time after each stand they made, they were nearer to the cliff. As they were driven they kept looking over their shoulders and, fighting more desperately, tried to break through; but the Boers, who at first had been bent over a wide arc, many paces apart, were now standing almost shoulder to shoulder, and fired consistently into the crowd of Kaffirs in front of them, pouring volley after volley into them.

There were not only men: women and children had also run out, and these hampered the men; and it was they who in the end led the panic by leaping from the top of the precipice.

'Drive them now,' Zwart Piete shouted. 'Close in and drive them.' Firing a last volley, the Boers clubbed their guns and charged, forcing the few Kaffirs who remained firm by the sheer force of attack and the weight of their anger to leap.

So ended the fight on the flat mountaintop, a victory in which more Kaffirs died by leaping down the krantz than from the Boer bullets.

And in the morning, when they looked down, the trees below the mountain were festooned with bodies, many of which still moved, while others lay broken on the rocks of the valley.

Setting light to the rest of the huts, the Boers collected their cattle, some nine hundred and fifty head, only a third of what they had lost, but a third was a great deal to people who had lost all, and turned homewards.

4

Driving the cattle in front of them, the Boers rode towards Canaan. Led by the bulls, the herd surged over the veld in an ever-changing formation, sometimes as solid as a carpet, at others straggling into a woof of isolated threads that broke away to snatch hungrily at the grass they passed. So they advanced, fanning out in the open country or closing in as they defiled through the narrow kloofs of the echoing hills, strung out in an endless necklace of long black-tipped horns and parti-coloured hides. A necklace that writhed back on itself, twisting like a hurt thing as the maddened beasts strove to readjust themselves under the herding of their masters who pressed them on.

Calves and older beasts lagged and were abandoned, for there was no time to waste, and the speed of the herd was no longer the normal one; it was no longer regulated to the speed of the weakest and the slowest beasts. This was no drifting of cattle: it was a wild and bitter herding.

'Why so fast, Piete?' Jan Schoeman asked. 'We are foundering them.' The questioner looked at a young cow that was calving on the road behind them: she was in some difficulty, and his farmer's instinct was to help her.

'She is mine,' he said, 'and it is her first calf.'

Pulling up his sweating horse and facing him, Zwart Piete answered angrily:

'Before God, with you it is always why? Are you a woman, that you must question? For years now I have led men who followed me without asking. When I fail you it will be time enough to ask; such of you who live can then ask what you will,' he concluded bitterly. 'But I will tell you why I am hurrying. Our guns are needed at the laager. And where do you think we are going to put the beasts when we get them back? Can a thousand odd head go into the laager? Can they be ringed about by the wagons. Will you tell me that?' he asked. 'Tell me,' he insisted, 'or are you so foolish that you have never thought of this?'

'I do not know where we will put them, Piete,' Jan said.

'You do not know, because there is nowhere, and all we can do is to make them run, and by the time I get them back they will be so tired and footsore that they cannot be driven off again. So ride, fool, and drive them hard. If we lose the half, we will still have some, and those that are left will be the best and the strongest. This is war,' he said. 'It is not a children's game, and had you listened instead of laughing at me when I warned you of this danger, it would never have come about.'

Leaving the astonished man, Zwart Piete drove his horse into the tail of the herd, using his sjambok on the flanks and quarters of those that were moving too slowly, forcing them up among their companions, so that they plunged, rearing up into the backs of those in front of them in their effort to escape his blows.

Zwart Piete was only aware of the urgency of speed. At all cost the herd must be hurried; and with the thunder of hoofs in his ears he rode on, at times only able to see his horse's ears above the dust of the moving cattle. This work with cattle was new to the grey arab, and he did not take to it kindly; he was restive and angry under Zwart Piete's hand.

It was at this moment that a group of young men who should have been on the flanks of the herd rode up.

'We have seen more beasts,' they said, 'another clompie over there, and we are going after them.'

'You are mad,' Zwart Piete said. 'First we must get these back, and when we have broken the Kaffirs we will collect our herds and theirs as well.'

'We are going,' they said.

'Ja, we are going; I saw the beasts.' It was Beyers who spoke. 'Do you think we will leave our cattle when we have seen them?' he asked. 'Hundreds of them in a kloof, and all moving slowly towards the hills.'

'I am in command,' Zwart Piete said, 'and it is my word that you remain.'

'You were in command for the attack,' they said. 'Ja, and very well you conducted it. But these are our beasts.'

'Then go, fools. But how many will stay with me?' he asked, looking round. 'How many are there who are not mad?'

'Ten of us are going, and the rest say they will remain to take on the herd we have.'

'I have done what I can,' Piete said, 'and I can do no more. You asked me to lead, and now you are divided against me. By God, you are fools and the sons of fools to think that you can teach me my business; you are like children who play at being men.' And, wheeling his horse, he left them, galloping after the herd, which had gone on.

5

In Canaan, Johannes van Reenen was organising his defence. Roused at last out of his lethargy by the necessity of the moment, he drove his people into laager, and once again, for the first time since the trek had ended, the wagons were lashed together in a great circle, once again the patient oxen spent the night tied to their trek tows, a wall of living flesh about the wagons.

The ring of wagons was set against one of the arms of the river, so that there would be no difficulty in getting water, and as an added protection from attack on that side. Every gun was loaded and the powder and ball distributed so that all had ammunition. The old iron cannon was cleaned up and lashed down with rawhide strips to the bed of a wagon. Von Rhule the soldier had made this his special charge.

Then came a period of waiting and speculation. When would they be attacked? Where was Zwart Piete with the young men? And where were their beasts?

The time was passed in the reading of the Bible and in the cleansing of their weapons by the men, while the women, assuming a false courage, knitted with trembling fingers to pass the dragging time.

At van Reenen's instructions such lead as there was they melted down into slugs, which they set in cylinders of hard fat or wrapped in little bags of oiled rawhide which would slip easily down the barrels of their smooth-bore guns. At close quarters these cartridges did great execution, and half the pockets of the wide leather bandoliers the Boers wore were filled with them.

The shining tin plates of the women that were among their most treasured possessions were sacrificed and melted to mix with the lead to give it hardness, one part tin to two parts lead being the best proportion. Hunting knives were sharpened till their blades were like razors, and such Kaffirs as were faithful stropped their spears, rubbing them continuously against soft greased stones, or fitting new shafts to old discarded heads, tried their balance in their hands; for in the winning of this battle was their safety dependent, and, lacking the Boer faith in God, they trusted to the guns of their masters and to the sharpness of their own spears.

All was prepared and the laager good when Zwart Piete and his depleted force rode in with the exhausted beasts. Two hundred had fallen by the way, and those that he drove before him were scarcely recognisable by their masters when they rode out among them.

'What have you done to our beasts, Zwart Piete?' they asked. 'Certainly you may be a good captain in war, but you are no farmer to over-drive our cattle thus,' they said. And again Zwart Piete had to explain.

Leaving the Boers staring disappointedly at their stock, he rode round the laager, seeking a way into it as though he were an enemy. He tested the lashings of the wagons, dragged at the bush that had been pulled fast beneath their beds and found himself satisfied in all but one particular.

'The wheels are not safe, Johannes,' he said. 'We have here forty wagons, that is eighty wheels on the outside of the ring, and I want eighty oxen killed so that their hides may be spread over the wheels and harden there before we are attacked.'

'You want eighty head of cattle killed?' Johannes said. 'Before God, Zwart Piete, they will never do this thing.'

'You are right, Johannes, they will never do it, so I must. Sannie is here, and their wives and children are here, yet they still will hesitate; always they talk and wait, hoping for miracles and looking to the sky as if the angels of God, the cohorts of the Almighty, would come springing to their assistance.

'Call them,' he continued. 'I am the leader, and I will take the responsibility. Before God, if they insist on it, I will repay them with my own beasts, those that my uncle has in his keeping, if they live to demand repayment.'

And so to the astonishment of the Boers, to their anger, which they dared only express in mutterings when faced by Zwart Piete's scorn, they watched their beasts being slaughtered by his men. De Kok and the two he had with him killed them while he sat on his grey horse supervising the butchery, and the Kaffir servants flayed them.

The dripping skins were spread over the wheels, and were soon as hard as drums and all but impenetrable to spears, so tightly did they contract as they dried in the hot evening sun.

6

Beyers, when he left Zwart Piete, led his party through the foothills to where he had seen the beasts.

'Ja,' he said, 'they are still there, and are drifting upwards towards the mountains.'

From where they sat on their horses, the Boers looked and, shading their eyes with their hands, stared at the cattle moving above them.

'There are not very many,' they said, as with practised eyes they estimated their numbers.

'There are more than that,' Beyers said. 'Look farther among the trees,' and following his gesture, they saw a large herd. They could not tell how many there were, but they could see them clearly enough — red, black and particoloured — as they grazed their way along. Two hundred, anyway, perhaps three hundred or more; and, following their leader's signal, the Boers rode on.

The cattle they were following behaved curiously, for instead of choosing the best grazing, they seemed to go consistently towards the worst, making for a dry plateau, where the stunted bush was thick and the grass looked scarce, thin and harsh. Still, no matter where they went, they would follow; they would show Zwart Piete that he was not the only one who could recapture stolen cattle, and that they, the farmers on whom he had poured his contemptuous anger, were as capable as he.

They heard them now, heard the bellow of a bull and the low call of cows to their calves.

Following Beyers' plan, they spread out to cast a net about them, to surround them and turn them back; but they went warily, for no doubt there would be some Kaffirs with these beasts; but, elated by their previous victory, the Boers were not afraid. Even when they found themselves in bush so broken that they could scarcely see each other as they rode and their direction was hard to keep, they did not lose confidence. In this kind of country they were no longer a firm body of mounted men: instead, they were a collection of isolated units which picked their way among the thorn scrub as they followed the spotted hides of the beasts that moved in front of them. The animals seemed to be slowing up: certainly they were gaining on them.

At the sound of a shot they charged forward, intending to ride through the beasts and turn them, driving them in front of them as they fought their way back. But as they galloped up to the herd its shape changed, the long spotted forms that they had seen through the bush became vertical, and the naked Kaffirs who had led them into this ambush by hiding behind their oxhide shields, pretending to be cattle, sprang up and turned upon them. There were a few cattle in the herd, some thirty head at most, and the rest that they had seen were men, savages who had led them on into a country where they were helpless, and where the dismounted men, armed with spears and kerries, had the advantage over them. From all sides the Zulus ran in upon the Boers, not giving them time to reload. Beating their shields, they came from all sides, shouting wildly for blood. Dragging the white men from their horses as they ran beside them, leaping up behind their saddles, the naked Kaffirs butchered the Boers, who were as helpless as calves in their hands, and of whom not one remained alive.

CHAPTER XXIX

I

IN THE laager day followed day, and still the young Boers did not return, for which Zwart Piete, since he had been in charge of the expedition, was blamed by their parents and their friends, as if his authority had been enough to stay them.

Very well he knew what had happened. Simple farmers greedy for the recapture of their stock, they had thought that native warriors under organised chiefs could be dealt with in the same offhand manner as a party of thieving Kaffirs, who, hungry for meat, stole a straying cow.

The more he thought of it the more Zwart Piete saw the seriousness of the situation. For though as yet no natives had been seen, there were many signs of them. The smoke of their cooking fires rose in thin straggling columns on the hillsides, and flocks of birds that should have rested in the heat of the day flew screaming up from the surrounding bush.

It was war, war such as even he had never seen, and this defensive fighting was contrary to his nature, fighting in which no chances must be taken because of the women and children with him, and in which because he had only old men, or men who if they were not actually old were past their prime, and boys to help him, he could not use to take the offensive, but must wait, allowing to the enemy the initiative which he had hitherto considered his prerogative. He thought longingly of his men in Mozambique, of his Arabs, his bastards and his N'coussie. Before God, with these he would not have been tied down to a wagon circle. With these he would have taught the Zulus a lesson.

The loss of ten guns, ten mounted Boers whom he could have used to sally out and counter-attack was a great blow to his plans, all but wrecking them, and the period of waiting for action affected him more than it did the others, for his was not a nature that was accustomed to delay, and day by day the weight of his responsibility bore more heavily upon him.

What fools these men about him were. Why had they not taken his advice earlier? Why had they not hunted the naked Kaffirs out of their land and broken them? But they had not, and now he must pay for their folly, and Sannie must pay. The thought of Sannie's danger made him, who had known many fears, afraid in a way that he had never been before, twisting his mind till it became a blank of horror.

Like a dog Sannie followed him about, and was herself followed by Jakalaas. Her fears for Piete were as great as his fears for her, or greater, for she knew that, whatever happened, he would be to the fore, the first to face the flying spears, and the last to turn from them.

It was arranged between the three of them that if the end came they would kill her, either he or her servant, with one swift stab; and they were not the only ones in the laager who had come to this arrangement, and many men looked at the breasts of their wives wonderingly, their fear being that there might not be time, or that the women who promised so freely now, would blench.

But at last their anxiety ended, and it was almost with relief that they heard the natives calling to one another in the mountains, throwing their voices from peak to peak through the still morning air.

'They are coming,' they said as they tightened their belts. The period of waiting was over, the issue was at hand. As the sun rose in the sky, band after band appeared, the natives from nearby looking like pigmies beside the plumed and naked Zulus, who, holding themselves in groups, stood proudly apart. Keeping out of range, the Kaffirs circled about the laager, shouting defiance as they drove off the cattle for a second time.

Calling on six of the best mounted Boers to follow him, Zwart Piete rode out to try and tempt the Kaffirs nearer; but he failed in this, for the natives would not approach, and answered his taunts by their own, telling him of how they had eaten up his young men in the mountains. Boasting of how they had once again recaptured the cattle and threatening the white women and children, they exulted over their future possession of them.

'Ai,' they shouted, 'your women shall be the mothers of our bastards; they shall be slaves and you will be food for vultures and jackals, and your bones will be widely spread, for we are like lions, fearless and hungry for flesh. Our spears are thirsty, their points eager to bite, their blades anxious to shear.'

'We must wait,' Zwart Piete said. 'The initiative is in their hands, and they are well led.' Soon there would be a battle, and his blood sang as he thought of its magnitude; win who might, the dead would be piled high about the wagons when it was over.

'They will not attack today,' he said, 'for they still raise men. They have sent out messengers, dragging the bleeding tails of tigers and of lions, calling all their people to war, for this time it is in my mind that they mean to make an end of the white man's dominion in their land.'

And as they watched they saw more and more men come in. Some in great companies of shouting, vainglorious warriors, others in small detachments, while some, who had been delayed by their affairs, came in alone, trotting over the veld, their spears rattling against their shields as they ran. The numbers of the Kaffirs seemed endless, and the stout hearts of the Boers sank as they thought of the scarcity of their powder. So far in all their wars no laager had been taken while the ammunition held. But if it did not hold — what then?

A swift estimate of the forces opposed to them, as their strength increased, soon convinced Zwart Piete that the fight would be bitterly contested, and the chances of victory no more than even.

There remained the possibility of obtaining assistance from Lemansdorp if that place was not also being besieged, and if they could hold out till it came. But how to get it? Who to send? And would help come in time? At least if they died they would be well avenged, Zwart Piete thought, seeking comfort in this. His uncle would see to it; he would not rest until payment in full was made. Before God, there would be much death in the land when Paul Pieters came and the warm air would be sweet with the scent of Kaffir bodies. But revenge was for others, for their friends and relations, for those who would see to it that, once and for all, that there was no recurrence of such an event as this.

While he sat on a wagon-box thinking, Rinkals came up to him. The old man's eyes were bright with excitement.

'Lord,' he said, 'I have seen visions.'

'Ja, Rinkals, I also have seen visions,' Zwart Piete said, jerking his thumb over his shoulder towards the Kaffirs. 'More than I want to see,' he added.

'The baas remembers that before we started I counselled him not to come and that, as I looked into the future, I saw death,' Rinkals said.

'You old aasvogel, you always see death,' de Kok said; 'but it is others who die, while you live — you, who should long since have died still drink beer and go with women.'

'Ai, I have seen visions,' Rinkals repeated; ignoring de Kok, he screamed, 'The dead were piled like pumpkins on a rich soil about the laager.'

'Must one be skilled in witchcraft to know all this?' de Kok asked scornfully. 'Even I, who am a Griqua Bastard, know of it.'

'You know nothing,' Rinkals said, 'your mother's milk being scarcely dry upon your lips. Ai,' he continued, 'what can you know compared to me, who have made nations and unmade them, who can cause water to flow and barren women to give birth? Wide is my fame, and so strong my medicine that did I wish it I could make myself invisible and walk out through the hosts that oppose us.'

'Could you go to Lemansdorp?' Zwart Piete asked suddenly.

'I could go anywhere, lord, and because you are in haste I will go there in the guise of a bird, flying straightly over the high mountains about your business. Give me letters,' he said. 'Prepare them while I make the mouti which turns me into a bird of the air, and as soon as darkness falls I will go, and none shall know that I have passed. For who counts the nightjars or the owls that wing their way by night?'

'Then get ready and prepare while I write,' Zwart Piete said.

2

And still the natives did not attack. Secure in the knowledge that the Boers were birds in their hands, the counsel of the chiefs was to wait, letting the white men tire themselves with watching and exhaust their ammunition with long and futile shots. Time, since they had meat in plenty, being to the Kaffirs less than nothing, and each hour more men arrived to assist in the eating up of the Boers, and greedy for the loot of the wagons.

More and more men came till their numbers rose to a thousand, and their shouting was a never-ceasing noise. Under the guns of the Boers and covered by the old iron cannon, the horses and oxen were watered, but they got no grazing, and stout horses trembled under the weight of riders, whose eyes were red with sleepless watching and whose faces were drawn with fear.

Husbands avoided looking at their wives, and women were sharp with their children or too tender.

As darkness fell the Boers tied lanterns to the tops of their long wagon whips and rested, waiting for the attack that did not come.

The letter ready, Zwart sent de Kok for Rinkals.

After some delay the coloured man returned.

'He comes, baas,' he said. 'He comes, but the night bird is very drunk; his mouti has been dop which he has stolen.' As he spoke Rinkals appeared, naked, except for a loincloth of breyed hide, every bone of his skinny body was outlined with phosphorescent paint. Even his face was painted as a skull, and on his shoulder, tied to the left side of his neck, was the woman's skull from which he was never parted. This also was painted, so that he appeared to be the moving and luminous skeleton of a two-headed man.

A woman screamed as she saw him, and Rinkals, reeling towards her, laughed.

'Ai, ai, lord,' he said to Zwart Piete. 'If I frighten the white people, will not the Kaffirs flee from me? Is this not better than being a bird? For thus I shall strike terror into the hearts of our enemies, and then later, when I have done this, I will set on my wings and fly with quick beats to Lemansdorp. Ai,' he went on, as he leant against a wagon wheel for support, 'nowhere in these regions is there one to compare with me either for intelligence or perspicacity. I can make the waters to flow or to stop flowing, give birth to Zulu impis and attend to the making and unmaking of great kings.'

'And did you make these Zulus, you skelm?' de Kok asked. 'By God, he is very drunk, baas,' he said.

'Why have you been drinking?' Zwart Piete asked as he gave him the letter and watched him tuck it into his loincloth.

'Why did I drink?' Rinkals repeated. 'Ai, now the baas has asked me a question. I think because I like to drink, and because I found the dop easy to steal and ready to my hand. Also,' he continued, 'it warms my belly, which is cold, puts courage into my heart and dreams into my head.

Are these reasons enough?' he asked. 'If not I can think of further reasons if the baas will give me time.' Straightening himself, he said, 'Listen, lord, I am not so drunk as I appear to be, but I was very frightened, for this is no small thing that I do.'

'It is no small thing,' Zwart Piete said.

'Will the baas take my hand before I go?' the old man asked.

'I will take it. You have been a good friend and servant to me.'

'Ja, baas, that is true, and I have brought you much good fortune, gold and ivory and the woman with the honey-coloured hair that has sent you mad. And you have been a good master to me, save on the one occasion when you allowed that lioness to play with me as a cat plays with a mouse, withholding your hand for a great space of time before you killed her; but even this I have forgiven, returning good for evil, as is my custom, since after mature thought I have reached the conclusion that it was the act of a young and mischievous man and done without ill-feeling. Now, baas, I go. Farewell. My spirit is above you, and should we not meet here again I will serve you in the land of the lost ones, where I have many friends and familiars, and where the women will no longer trouble us as they do down here.'

'Help me, yellow dog,' he said to de Kok. 'Help me over the wagons and past the sleeping oxen.'

'Wait,' Zwart Piete said. 'I will get some men, and we will follow you, for it is in my heart that thinking you a spook we can strike death into them as, confused by your appearance, they break and flee.'

Collecting some fifteen men, Zwart Piete followed his servant towards the native fires.

Keeping well behind him and rather to his flank, they advanced. The eyes of all the Kaffirs would be focussed on Rinkals, and any movement away from him was unlikely to be perceived.

When he reached the open ground old Rinkals began to

dance, running forwards and then backwards, waving his arms and contorting his body, presenting a truly terrible and frightening spectacle to the Kaffirs, who, springing up from their fires, stood hesitating in groups. As he came nearer, moving ever more slowly and with a certain dignity which his condition rendered more impressive, since a drunken ghost was inconceivable, the vaguely swaying and tentative advance he made impressed the Kaffirs as being that which a skeleton, long dead and weak, would make as it strove to regain those powers it had known in the flesh.

With a wild yell the Kaffirs broke and ran before him, and as they ran the Boers fired, killing and wounding several.

One man who, badly hit, had fallen into a fire screamed terribly in his pain and, unable to extricate himself, was left by those who had run, to burn.

Lying down so as to render themselves invisible, and to get the Kaffirs against the bright light of their fires as they trotted hither and thither in their alarm, the Boers fired again and again till certain that Rinkals was past their lines and running free in the bush beyond them, they retired as silently and as swiftly as they had come.

It was a good omen for the future, they thought, to have inflicted many casualties and suffered none themselves, and all were much encouraged by it. Part of the debt was paid: some black lives were set against the ten young white ones that had been taken in the mountains.

3

All night the Boers watched, but nothing happened. Looking out from their wagons, they could see the Kaffirs squatting very near to their fires, could see the firelight glinting on their shining bodies as they leant towards each other talking excitedly.

Above them, unmoved by all that passed beneath it, the big moon moved slowly through the sky. Night birds in search of the moths that fluttered in clustering circles round the high lanterns, dived into the lighted area and out of it, profiting by this unforeseen opportunity to eat plentifully and without trouble.

Tireless, Zwart Piete walked round the wagons encouraging and comforting those who were in despair. Coldly angry, knowing himself cornered, he still considered the situation as a problem, as something apart, and not as an experience through which he was living.

Certainly they owed a lot to old Rinkals, whose ruse had saved them from a night attack. The old witch-doctor would escape — he might be the only one of their company who did — but there was no question of his courage, even if it were flavoured by discretion. If he got through, and if the rising was not general, they would be relieved.

In his mind Zwart Piete saw the rising of his people, saw the Boers call for their horses, strap on their bandoliers, clap a bag of rusks and biltong, a flask of water onto their saddles as they mounted and, taking their women into their arms for a moment, wheel, clattering off to their meeting place, the long tails of their horses flowing in the dust raised by their hoofs. A commando, when the call came, was quickly formed in an hour — in two at most; the Boers were there and ready to move. By the day after tomorrow the people of Lemansdorp would be riding towards them. But would they come in time?

For himself he did not care, or at least cared not greatly: he had not been born to die in bed like a woman. It was only when he thought of Sannie that his courage waned, Sannie, who was so beautiful and who was his, for whom, since he had known her, his love had grown till now it was his life. Drifting from group to group, he kept coming back to her and, leaning on the long barrel of his gun, he watched her sleep. Her fair hair was hanging over the bed, her white throat was bare, she lay with one of her breasts exposed and her arm folded over the other.

Feeling his hand on her, she stirred and, without waking, moved towards it, while his eyes searched her. There, just below the left breast, was where he would strike; between her ribs, into the soft white skin he would drive the knife his father had given him till the guard of the hilt sank into her flesh.

Old Jakalaas squatted beside his mistress, with his spears held in his folded hands, their butts between his feet, their points in the air. Their eyes met and the old native nodded his head.

'I shall be there, baas,' he said, 'when they come.'

As if he were patting a dog, Zwart Piete put out his hand, touching the curled grey twists of hair.

'It may not be so, Jakalaas,' he said. 'Before God they may yet come in time.'

'Time, baas. Ja, it is a matter of time, but I have thought well on this matter, and if the wizard takes two days to reach Lemansdorp and they take but two days to come, or even one day, it is still too long — for those Kaffirs will not wait. There are great fighting chiefs among them, lord, men from the south who are well skilled in war. It is in my heart that this is the end of us all, and that like winnowed chaff we shall be driven before the wind of their coming. Can we not ride out, lord,' he asked, 'and fight our way through? It has been done, baas, and it could be done again.'

'There are too many women and children here,' Zwart Piete said, 'and some are sick. Nie, old one, we must stand and fight. Like a lion caught in a high-walled kloof we must turn; and if we die, there will at least be many dead about us.'

'It is of her that I think,' the old Kaffir said, pointing with his spear at the sleeping girl.

'Then watch her, old one,' Zwart Piete said as he turned away. 'Watch her well.'

4

The Kaffirs did not attack until the late morning, and then it was not the Zulus but the others, who formed up under their captains, came forward, while the naked Zulus stood like black statues watching them contemptuously.

To them, real fighters, the posturing antics and the manœuvres of these men were a joke, a laughing-stock.

Ai, these Kaffirs were herders of cattle and workers in the fields, and their leaders, for all their leopard skins, were but small men. So, leaning on their spears with their big oxhide shields beside them, they watched, smiling grimly. Let these monkeys play at war, and later, when they had had enough, and the white men were tired, they would sweep in and finish it. Like a herd of bulls their coming was irresistible; the thunder of their feet would shake the wagons on their axles, and their ostrich plumes foaming, like water falling from a high place, the ornaments of their legs wetted with blood, they would kill.

Spread out in a long line the Kaffirs attacked, slowly at first, and then as the Boers' guns began to take effect, in short rushes, advancing after their own fashion, flinging themselves sideways, falling down and stepping first this way and then that in a futile endeavour to evade the bullets that the Boers poured into their ranks. Already the laager was hardly visible for the blue smoke of the guns.

Time after time Zwart Piete and de Kok fired. They were lying on the bed of Johannes van Reenen's wagon with Sannie beside them, loading for them both. Coolly, as if they were firing at a mark, the two men shot, and each time they fired a Kaffir fell, some throwing up their arms as they spun round, while others crumpled up, collapsing as if their feet had been cut from beneath them.

As the Kaffirs came nearer the width of their attack narrowed, and they closed in, concentrating on the point that they deemed weakest. At fifty paces they began to throw their assegais. They threw them high, so that the curve of their flight dropped them like rain from the air into the laager, where many stood embedded in the ground, their thin shafts trembling.

Out of the corner of his eye Zwart Piete saw von Rhule, with two sweating bushmen servants to help him, swing the muzzle of his cannon, levelling it at the largest group of Kaffirs.

Letting them approach, the German waited till they were almost up to the muzzle, and then set the flaming stick he held in his hand to the touch-hole. There was a roar that shook the gun, making it leap back on its mountings, and as the smoke cleared Zwart Piete saw the Kaffirs hesitate and, appalled at the carnage, turn back.

The attack was broken, and the dead and wounded lay piled in a half-circle about the wagons.

After firing twice more at the running Kaffirs and bringing down a man each time, Zwart Piete got up and went round the laager. No one was killed or wounded, but three horses and some cattle had been struck.

Ja, it was something to have beaten them off, but it was not these Kaffirs but the Zulus who were feared by Zwart Piete. There were some hundreds of them, and they were untouched and confident, trained by Dingaan and officered by men who, bold enough to acknowledge failure, had refused to return to their homes, where, having failed, they would have had to pay the price of failure in the place of death, leaping over the high krantz to make a meal for the royal vultures, and had chosen to stay in the north. Servants of their spears, the Zulus served them well, and when they came the fighting would be bitter. It would end at the wagon wheels, for they would not be turned back. A regiment of Zulus was like a stout hound unleashed: once loose, it was beyond recall — they attained their objective or they died there.

In the laager the servants were collecting the assegais for

those unarmed with guns to use, and the Boers were washing the grime and sweat of battle from their bodies.

For the moment it was over, but the contest had been joined and the strain of waiting past. After a hasty survey Zwart Piete returned to his post and began to count the dead and watched the wounded crawl off, dragging themselves away, creeping like broken toys along the ground. They would not fight again, and ammunition was too short to waste on such as they. Smiling grimly, he watched their efforts, and then, tiring of this, he lay down to sleep, his loaded gun beside him and his head on a pile of skins. Rest must be stolen in odd snatched hours, for without sleep one's hands trembled and one's eyes betrayed one. De Kok lay on his belly, with his head pillowed on his folded arms, beside his master. He had been told to sleep, and he slept.

They were woken by Sannie.

'They come,' she said. 'They are getting prepared.'

Springing up Zwart Piete shaded his eyes against the glare and looked towards the native encampment.

Sannie was right: the Zulus were moving about: they were forming up.

From where he stood he could hear their laughter and see them adjust their shields to their arms.

This was going to be a different kind of action; these men were going to fight, and would not be deterred by a few killed and the roaring of a cannon. All round him the Boers were waiting, their eyes fixed on the naked Zulus who moved about so freely, just out of range, in front of them.

At a signal from their chief they advanced behind their shields, shouting, rattling their spears and beating their heavy kerries against them.

At first they came slowly, in close formation, halting to stamp their feet and raise their assegais as they chanted their song of death. The song of their thirsty spears, of how they were bulls and lions, of how they were elephants and unbeatable.

Still not in range, they halted and called to the Boers, throwing their voices, high-pitched, across the space between them, challenging them to come out, bidding them to come out and fight, for only in this way could the women and children be saved.

Zwart Piete answered them, his tones loud and clear.

'Dogs and renegades,' he said, 'failures, who feared to return to your master, your words are lies, and you halt because you fear us. Ai, for all the plumes on your heads and the ornaments of hair below your knees, you fear. Even the mountain Kaffirs, who are dogs and less than dogs, are braver than you, for they attacked without hesitation, flinging themselves to die upon the muzzles of our guns. Ai,' he went on, 'Chaka was a great king, Dingaan was great, even Panda was great, but the Zulus are changed when the men talk like women, when they fear like children, when instead of fighting they stand to parley.'

Lowering his voice, he said to Sannie, 'Give me my gun when I pass my hand back; they are coming nearer as I mock them. Zulus,' he went on, 'I do not think you are Zulus. You are Fingos, Basutos; even the Swazis are greater than you, who are but the excrement of your people, what they left behind them to stink in these parts when the royal impis swept this way.'

The cries of the warriors drowned his voice as their anger rose.

'Bulala!' they cried, stamping their feet and tossing their spears. 'Bulala! Already you are carrion, white men; already your children are spitted on our spears that are thirsty and cry for blood.'

With his eyes on the chief, who alone wore a kilted belt of leopard tails, Zwart Piete's hand went back and closed round the small of his gun.

Stepping forward, he raised it and fired. It was a long shot, but it told. The induna, struck in the chest, fell, and his men with a roar of rage jumped forward with raised spears.

Withholding their fire, the Boers again waited till they were almost upon them before they pulled the triggers of their guns, then from all round the laager the guns spat smoke and fire as they drove their heavy bullets into the seething mass of black bodies that ran like a solid wall upon them. Men, women and children all fought, loading and firing frenziedly. To miss at this range was impossible.

Stripped to the waist, Otto von Rhule fired his cannon, sponged it out and reloaded from the heap of scrap iron, the legs of broken pots and round stones at his side.

Still the Zulus came on, some throwing assegais wrapped with flaming grass at the wagons, hoping to explode the powder stored in them, or at any rate to set the tents alight.

Right up to the wagons the remnants of the force came surging, and with their hands on the side rails sought to climb them. Their shouts rising louder and louder, their plumes bloodstained and awry, they tore at the thorn scrub fastened under the beds of the wagons or tried to cut with their stabbing assegais the hard stretched ox skins that were spread over the wheels. They were fighting among and on top of the plunging oxen that were tied to the outside of the wagon ring, and their bellows of pain as they were stabbed, or smashing the riems that held them, ran screaming away, were hardly audible in the noise of the battle.

To each Boer the fight was something intensely individual, the bed of his wagon, like the deck of a ship, being all that he could see, and the rest of the fight no more than something which was happening all round him, but to which he had no real relation. All, but the one small space in front of him that he defended, where out of the smoke, black faces kept rising, hideous faces with bloodshot eyes and writhing lips, was nothing. Faces, plumes, spears and kerries, dark menacing hands were all they saw, firing their guns into the bodies that rose in front of them, or clubbing them, struck, while their servants fighting beside them used their assegais, thrusting them down savagely. For a moment that seemed an hour the outcome hung in a balance, the fight swayed up and down, neither side gaining mastery; black men and white were locked together in a struggle that became terrible in its silence, for now nothing was heard. There was no firing, since there was no time to load, and no shouting, for neither the Zulus nor the Boers had the breath to shout, but all fought bitterly with set mouths, and only the screams of the wounded and the rattle of steel against steel was to be heard.

Had the mountain Kaffirs reinforced them at that moment it would have been over. Had the rest of the Zulus — for they were apparently of two factions, and jealous of each other — flung themselves into the combat, it would have been more than over. But neither of these things happened. The mountain Kaffirs had suffered enough in their attack to make them hesitate before they launched another and, like wounded dogs, rested to lick their wounds, while the rest of the Zulus — and they were the greater party — stood leaning on their spears watching the battle, which to them was no more than a show. Had the leader of the attackers, he of the leopard tails, that Zwart Piete had shot, lived, it might have been different, for then they would have fought on. Instead they slacked and suddenly, as if at a given signal, drew back to meet the jeers and laughter of their comrades. But this time the Boers had suffered. Three men were killed and six were wounded, among whom was one woman and a child. Also much ammunition had been used, and several guns were broken. There were also deaths among the coloured servants and tame Kaffirs, and more horses had been struck down.

It was apparent to them all now that, though they were inflicting heavy casualties on the enemy they were being worn down. A second attack they might stand — a third they could not.

With his eyes on the piled-up dead and wounded, Zwart Piete issued his instructions. These men were not ordinary Kaffirs, and many who were down were not dead; there might even be some who were quite unhurt and would attempt to crawl up, moving slowly an inch at a time, till they were near enough to attempt an entrance by subterfuge.

'Shoot the wounded,' he said, 'but be careful not to waste a lead on those who are already dead.'

'That is good counsel, Piete,' the Boers said, 'for these Zulus are like mambas. But how are we to know the quick from the dead?'

'Look carefully,' Piete said. 'Watch and you will see some of them sweating. It is hot,' he went on; 'and dead men cannot sweat.'

'Look there,' he said, pointing to a big Zulu who lay on his back, his arms outspread less than thirty yards away. As they watched they saw a ripple pass over him as he levered himself along the ground. 'Let him come nearer,' Piete said, 'and you will see.'

'Nearer,' the Boers said. 'But he may get up and fling his spear.'

'He will not get up while I am here, for before he is on one knee he will be dead, but I wish to make what I say clear, so that you may watch for others.' And as they looked they saw that Zwart Piete was right, for where the true dead lay, with their skins a dull black, this man shone as the sweat ran in thin streams over his oiled chest and in runnels from his armpits.

'Take him, Piete,' they said.

'Nie, why shoot when he is so near? Throw your spear, Jakalaas, throw well.'

Balanced on the balls of his feet, the old Kaffir drew back his hand, his body poised; he paused and then swung forward with his throw. The assegai struck the Zulu where the neck joined his body, passed through him and pinned him to the ground, where he lay writhing and grasping at its shaft with both hands as he strove to pull it out.

'Shall I finish him, baas?' Jakalaas asked.

'Why finish?' Piete said. 'He can do no more, and it will

teach the others that we are ready. But watch well,' he said, 'and remember no Zulu is dead while the water runs from his body.'

5

As it grew dark the Boers waited with an ever-increasing anxiety for a further attack, but the Kaffirs had settled down to feast, and no longer did they remain isolated in their clans and factions, but mixed together and appeared to have a perfect accord with each other, and their drums both big and small beat unceasingly. Very well did the Boers know the effect of these drums which, never ceasing, whipped up the blood of the warriors into a frenzy before which nothing alive would escape their spears. Smeared with grease and red and yellow ochre, with the white feathers on their heads and the hair ornaments they wore on their arms and legs red in the firelight, they danced and shouted.

The fires they made were big, with high, leaping flames and the throb of their frenzied music shook the leaves on the trees and sent the birds that slept there screaming up into the air.

Cattle were brought up and slaughtered, and some were not slaughtered, but had meat cut from them while they still lived and fought, bellowing madly, with the men who held them. The air was filled with the scent of smoke and of the meat they grilled on their spears.

Their nerves strained by the waiting which they had to endure, the Boers stared and listened with their guns in their hands or held over the crook of their arms.

They had given praise to God for their double victory, and had prayed that Leman and his men would come soon. It must be soon or it would be too late. It must be soon or this place would know them no more and the land of Canaan be as the valley of the shadow of death and the furnace of affliction. It was as they stood thus talking in groups that Martinus came up to Zwart Piete, Sannie and her father.

'Marietje is sick,' he said. 'I think she is going to die.'
He paused and went on, speaking so softly that they could
hardly hear his words. 'Marietje has asked me to sing the
old songs,' he said, 'that my great voice may drown the
sound of the Kaffirs and give her peace. It is fitting,' he said,
'that I should sing to my wife as she goes, for it was by singing that she came to me.'

Resting his gun against the wagon, he turned to tune his
little harp, turning the pegs till the strings were taut, plucking at them one after the other, playing notes and chords
till, satisfied, he drew breath and raised his voice. Deep and
strong, it soared over the camp, rising and falling, tragic in
its pathetic and simulated gaiety.

First he sang the song he had sung at the dance three
years ago, the one of his own composition that dealt with the
trek they had made, and others.

His voice now low, now loud and as clear as the call of a
trumpet, song after song he sang for an hour or more, till
even the wild Kaffirs were stilled and many Boers wept; and
all the time amid the gathering of the people who had closed
round him, Martinus was alone and, singing with his eyes
half closed, saw only his wife who lay dying on the riempie
bed of his wagon, and the children who were dead, his, hers,
and the one that they had shared.

6

It came at dawn. Massed in serried ranks, the natives
ringed them below the mountain. The Kaffirs were on the
flanks, and the Zulus in the centre. Their minds misted by
the blood in their brains, their wide nostrils dilated by the
smell of battle, they were eager and impatient as horses,
stamping their feet. Soon their spear tips would bite into
flesh, soon they would feel their edges grind against bone.

In front of them was their captain and the lesser captains
under him, and as they watched the Boers saw this man

throw down all his spears but one, and this one, bending the shaft over his knee, he snapped. With a wild shout his men did likewise. This was death, this time they would throw no assegais; they would leave that to the mountain Kaffirs: for they were Zulus, and would charge with their shortened spears, stabbing and ripping.

Still they did not attack, but stood out of range of the guns gloating, savouring the pleasure of the battle in anticipation, dancing and swaying their plumes, beating their shields with their kerries and shouting boasts, challenges and insults as they stamped, their feet moving faster and faster as the pulse of their blood rose.

A hundred and fifty yards of open ground separated them from the Boers, and on it lay the many dead who were already grotesquely swollen, the residue of the tide of war, and the outcome of the actions on the previous day. Bold as they were, the even distribution of these bodies was a deterrent to the impetuosity of the warriors: before they could get in with their spears they must cross this ground, cross it and face the withering fire that destroyed men as a fire on a high wind destroyed grass.

As they waited, wondering at the delay, the Boers saw a party of Kaffirs break away from the others and trot off into the veld. When they had left, the warriors sat down squatting on their heels, or lay down to rest. They were laughing.

'What devilry is this?' the Boers asked of each other, and it was not long before they knew, for soon they saw a great cloud of dust as the cattle which had been stolen from them were driven back. As they arrived the natives opened up to make a way for them and then, closing behind them, goading them forward with their spears, charged down upon the laager, running amid the maddened beasts.

Shooting was all but impossible, for the Zulus were clouded by dust and hidden by the bodies of the cattle. Horns, headdresses and spear tips were all that could be seen, the shields of oxhide blending with the live beasts as the crouching warriors ran beside them and, abandoning them as they reached the wagons, leapt out as the herd, breaking into two, ran sideways round the laager.

Like a black wave crested with white plumes the Zulus leapt upwards and were met by bullets fired so close that the explosion of the guns burnt their chests. Falling back, the attackers were replaced by a second wave and a third. The weight of the attack was such that it rocked the wagons, and the dead were piled higher than the hubs of the wheels.

As he fought Zwart Piete saw Sannie fall with an assegai through her breast and, unable to reach another, turned, his gun in his hand, and brought the butt crashing down onto the head of the Zulu nearest to him. All round the shouts of battle were deafening, and the cries of the wounded a refrain that sounded above it. More and more Zulus poured into the laager.

Here and there, standing back to back, men and women still fought, with their dead children at their feet, fought and were overwhelmed.

For an hour or more the Kaffirs ravaged the wagons, looting and killing the wounded, pursuing the horses and spearing the dogs. Then there was silence.

It was over in Canaan, and the Kaffirs bending to wipe their spears on the tussocky grass drew off to rest. They carried guns and knives and axes in their hands. They had eaten up these white people, defeated those whom by repute were invincible. They had captured great herds of cattle, horses, sheep and goats, and the song they sang was that of victory.

They were elephants that trampled those who opposed them. They were lions who ripped up and destroyed. They were Zulus: their glory was undenied.

CHAPTER XXX

I

IT WAS early morning when Rinkals reached Lemansdorp. He had come fast for so old a man, and was wellnigh exhausted when he found Gert Kleinhouse in his cattle kraal, supervising the milking of his cows.

'Who are you? And what do you want?' Gert asked.

'I am Rinkals, the snake who spits venom, and where is the white woman Mevrou de Jong, baas, for I bring a letter to her from my master who says that she is here with you. Baas,' he said, leaning against the milking post to which a cow was tied. 'Send for your horse. It is war. The country they call Canaan is besieged, and the naked Kaffirs and those of the mountains are like locusts and ants about it. I have come over the hills with wings on my feet. Ja, over the mountains and the krantzes I have come more swiftly than is possible for mortal man. For two more days they may hold out, for they are short of food for their guns in Canaan, but for no longer — perhaps not even for so long. Therefore you must ride, master, and call up the others before all is lost.'

'Give me the letter,' Gert said.

He read it slowly. 'So what you say is true. This is from Zwart Piete, and he cries for help.'

'Zwart Piete the hunter is my lord,' the old Kaffir said.

'Lucas, Kleinboi,' Gert shouted, 'leave the cows. Leave them, I say, and get my horse. Tell Frantz that I want him to ride with me. Come to my house now,' he said to Rinkals, 'for you must have food and rest.'

A few moments later, having bidden his wife and grandmother good-bye, Gert left Rinkals to them, and rode off to raise the people. Christian Leman, to whom he went first, heard his tale, read Zwart Piete's letter and sent out his call. In two hours the commando was assembled and ready to move off, and hardly had they gone when the first of the wagons lumbered up into the outspan, for here, according to Leman's orders, they were to laager.

Mounted and armed coloured guards were flung out beyond the cattle and horses which had, as soon as danger threatened, been drafted into one great herd.

Lemansdorp was ready if the Kaffirs came, and messengers were speeding over the veld to warn the other settlements that the black people were up, and that Canaan was besieged.

Soon every village would be in laager, and commandos from each would be steering their way towards Canaan, to rescue or revenge.

2

In the laager on the outspan Tante Anna questioned Rinkals. Till now there had been no time, what with the hurried preparation of food for the men who were going, and the packing of the wagons for those who remained. Nor had Rinkals been in a condition to speak, faint with weariness, he had gorged himself and slept.

But now there was time. Ach, God, how much time there was, time which must be spent waiting and wondering.

'Now, tell me, Rinkals,' said Tante Anna, whose foot had recovered miraculously at the first sign of danger, 'what do you know of all this? Tell me who you are and of your life.'

'Shall I tell you all?' Rinkals asked.

'Ja, tell me all.'

He looked at the tree beside them and pointed up into its branches. 'Were I to tell you all, mevrou,' he said, 'we should have to wait for that tree to bloom again, and for new beans to be hanging where those are now, and still we should be here and still I would be talking. Nie, mevrou, beautiful as you are,' he looked at her vast bulk in admiration, 'I could not tell you all, nor would it be seemly. Besides, I am a silent man, strong and taciturn and not one given to boasting; yet, were I to tell you the truth it would sound as though I boasted, for I have done things that are unbelievable; and were I not to tell you the truth it would be lies, and that I should speak lies is distasteful to me. A lie, mevrou, scorches my tongue and burns up the water in my mouth. Therefore, I prefer to hold my peace, for there is wisdom in silence. Silence being held against no man nor can what he has not said be quoted against him.'

'God give me patience,' Anna de Jong said. 'Were you an ordinary Kaffir I should have you beaten.'

'Ja, mevrou, that is so, but I am not an ordinary Kaffir. I am Rinkals the wizard, whom some call The Little Cloud Which Comes Before the Storm, and others Mamba. Also, have I been called Little Flower; for though I am small of stature, in my youth I was a beautiful young man and much beloved by women.'

'That was a long time ago,' Tante Anna said.

'Ja, mevrou, that was many hundreds of years ago when the world was young. But this I will tell you, mevrou, that the doom of Canaan is upon your head; this I have seen clearly when I have looked into the other world, for in everything that has happened I have seen your hand. Aye, many stones have you thrown at the hornet's nest, and now it is fallen and they buzz about our ears. Ja,' he went on, 'you have stirred the pot, but you knew not what you cooked; and as I cast my spirit into the beyond I saw that which makes my heart sore. For those who ride to Canaan ride too late to save, mevrou; all they can do now is to avenge the dead. Canaan is no more, mevrou. I saw Canaan as wheels whose spokes have fallen from the nave and lie scattered in an emptiness of grass.'

For days they talked, these two, the old Kaffir and the

old white woman, for in both there was much wisdom, and each could see into the mind of the other and admire its dexterity.

Louisa was lost in admiration for the witch-doctor, who, to pass the time, taught her some of his magic. Such small things as might be useful to a woman; the casting of the evil eye, the making of simple love potions and one or two subtle poisons which would defy detection, tricks suitable to one who already had some gifts in this direction, but whose knowledge was intuitive and hereditary rather than the result of continuous study under a professional adept at wizardry.

To Rinkals, Anna de Jong soon talked openly of Sannie and her lover Herman, whom she had admired.

And Rinkals spoke to her of Sara who had saved his life, of the Griqua whom he hated and of Zwart Piete whom above all other men he loved. He told her what a fine hunter he was, he told her how he had allowed a lioness to play with him, and how he once got into difficulty by lying when he was drunk to a Portuguese, and of how he, Rinkals, had saved his face by his ever-ready wit.

'Ja, mevrou, Baas Piete was very drunk that day,' he said, 'and boasted of having shot an eland through the head and the hind foot with one shot.'

'That could not be done,' Tante Anna said.

'Of course it could not be done, but he turned to me for confirmation of his tale, and I confirmed it. Ja, ja,' he said, 'my wit is as ready and as strong as a river flowing through the rich land of my knowledge.'

'Ja, it was a good lie,' Tante Anna said, 'and you were most cunning to tell it.'

'But I have not told you what I said,' Rinkals protested.

'Oh, did you not tell me? I thought you had or it may be that I grow confused, for in these last days you have said sc much.'

'Since I came I have hardly spoken,' Rinkals said; 'my

heart is too full of sorrow for me to speak and my tongue a dead thing in my mouth. But since you desire to hear this story, you shall have it, for I would not let my private sorrow impinge on my duties as the mevrou's guest. It was done in this fashion,' he continued. 'As we mounted the lower steps of the Lembobombo hills, my master saw a great eland bull and determined to slay it, but not wishing to spoil the meat, he shot it through the head.'

'Ja, he could well do that,' Anna de Jong said; 'but what of the foot, since he shot it in the head how could he also shoot it in the foot with one ball?'

'That is the point, mevrou, he did not do it, nor could he have explained it away without my aid. When he asked me to corroborate this tale I was for the moment perplexed, and so I said "Ja, lord, of course you shot the eland through the head and the hind foot with one shot." And to give myself time, I began to laugh holding my belly, and as I laughed a great thought came to me. It was done this way, I said. As my lord fired so did the eland scratch his ear with his hind foot. But such things as these should not be held against him, mevrou, for he is young and there was a time when even I had no skill in such matters. Nie, mevrou, the art of conversation is not learnt in a day, neither is it learnt in a year. But my master is a great man, and I fear that he is dead.'

3

For a month nothing happened in Lemansdorp and they heard no news. Another week passed and then those in the laager saw the dust of a vast herd of cattle coming towards them, and an hour later the commando rode in. These were the recaptured beasts of Canaan which were now ownerless till the heirs of those who had died were traced, and with them were the Kaffir cattle that they had taken.

Their story did not take long to tell, and Leman in a few words told it.

'When we got there,' he said, 'it was already finished. Riding hard as we did, we were still too late. All were dead, their bodies stuck as full with spears as porcupines with quills. Aye,' he said, 'nothing was left, and the wagons were burnt, broken and tipped sideways. Their wheels had collapsed beneath them, the Kaffirs had stripped off the iron tyres for the forging of spear-heads.

'But there had been a great fight. Those folk had fought to the last and the dead were about them so thick that our horses had to pick their way over them, ja, they lay like a parapet heaped up to the very beds of the wagons. Nothing is left,' he said. 'Nothing. Canaan is no more. Today it is a place of weeping that hunters will pass by, and Kaffirs, even by day no longer approach.

'There was no work left for us save to bury our dead, which we did, and to ride out for our revenge and we have taken it.

'Kraal after kraal we have destroyed, and here are the cattle we have captured, those that were stolen and many more besides. We have also prisoners, young boys and girls that we have taken as apprentices, and we have lost but one man, Jan Schoeman, who was killed in our first battle and only four men are wounded.'

Sitting with her arms folded, Tante Anna looked at Frikkie playing on the stoep beside her.

4

So this was what was left of their effort. This was what remained of those who had ridden out of the Cape. Death had touched them with cold-fingered hands. Babylon was fallen and the folk of Canaan were as dust and scattered. Of that company which had followed Hendrik van der Berg, none were left but herself, Gert Kleinhouse, Frikkie, Jacoba and Louisa. Hendrik's seed was sown on stony soil. All that was left of it was his son's son, a small branch of a great tree, and the girl Jacoba. His other children had gone back with Sannie and were dead.

Much had been destroyed, but something remained. If he lived, the boy would rebuild the race of van der Berg. Sannie's beauty was gone the way of Herman's youth and Hendrik's strength, but their seed went on, the blood of these three was now concentrated in one small body; if it was not lost, one day it would become active and potent, but she would never see that day. She was old and felt the weight of her years. What she wanted now was comfort, a place to grow her vegetables and where she could keep pigs. It might even be that she would stay here with her grandson and his wife. Blood was thicker than water, and if they wished to profit by her death, they would, until it occurred, treat her with that consideration to which a rich and aged relative was entitled. Ach, ja, they would keep her for many years in great comfort, and should their kindness wane she had other relatives, a mention of whom would be enough to ensure the peaceful life that she desired.

THE END

GLOSSARY OF SOUTH AFRICAN WORDS

Aasvogel, vulture
Assegai, native spear

Baie Dankie, Thank you very much
Bang vir die spoke, afraid of ghosts
Biltong, sun-dried meat
Brey, tan

Disselboom, pole of wagon or cart

Ek weet nie, I do not know

Goed genoeg, good enough

Hammel, wether
Hartekoal, hardwood tree

Jong, young man

Kaross, rug of skins sewn together
Kloof, a valley or crack in the hills
Knob kerrie, a wooden club with
    round top
Krantz, a cliff
Kyk daar, look there

Laager, defensive camp of wagons
    arranged in a circle
Leegte, a clear, flat piece of land
Lekker lewe, good or free life

Maak gou, jou skelm, ek is haastig,
    baie haastig, Be quick, you ras-
    cal, I am in a hurry, a great hurry
Mak, tame
Meilies, maize or corn
Mis, dry cattle dung

Mooi meisie, pretty girl

Natuurlik, naturally
Niks maak, do nothing

Outspan, to unyoke, or resting-
    place where animals are unyoked

Pad, road or path
Pas op, look out
Poort, a break in the mountains

Rankie, small, long hillock
Riem, rawhide thong
Roinek, Englishman; from the way
    his neck burns red in the sun

Skelm, rascal
Skey, peg through ox-yoke
Spruit, a small river
Strop, leather loop joining skey to
    skey
Suikerbos, hardwood tree

Tiger, leopard
Tolly, young ox

Vaal, yellow
Veldschoen, rawhide, home-made
    shoes
Verneuk, swindle
Versie, heifer
Vlei, a marsh
Voorloper, one who leads oxen
Voorslaag, lash of whip

Wach 'n bietje, Wait a bit